Batty Langley

The builder's complete assistant, or, A library of arts and sciences

Absolutely necessary to be understood by builders and workmen in general.

Fourth Edition

Batty Langley

The builder's complete assistant, or, A library of arts and sciences
*Absolutely necessary to be understood by builders and workmen in general. Fourth
Edition*

ISBN/EAN: 9783741176234

Manufactured in Europe, USA, Canada, Australia, Japa

Cover: Foto ©Andreas Hilbeck / pixelio.de

Manufactured and distributed by brebook publishing software
(www.brebook.com)

Batty Langley

The builder's complete assistant, or, A library of arts and sciences

THE

Builder's Complete Affiftant;

OR, A

LIBRARY

OF

ARTS AND SCIENCES,

Abfolutely Neceffary to be underftood by

BUILDERS and WORKMEN in general.

VIZ.

I. ARITHMETICK, Vulgar and Decimal, in whole Numbers and Fractions.	IV. MENSURATION.
II. GEOMETRY, Lineal, Superficial, and Solid.	V. PLAIN TRIGONOMETRY.
	VI. SURVEYING of Land, &c.
	VII. MECHANICK POWERS.
III. ARCHITECTURE, Univerfal.	VIII. HYDROSTATICKS.

ILLUSTRATED by above Thirteen Hundred Examples of *Lines, Superficies, Solids, Mouldings, Pedeftals, Columns, Pilafters, Entablatures, Pediments, Impofts, Block Cornices, Ruftick Quoins, Frontifpieces, Arcades, Porticos,* &c.

Proportioned by MODULES and MINUTES, according to *Andrea Palladio;* and by EQUAL PARTS.

LIKEWISE

Great Varieties of *Truffed Roofs, Timber Bridges, Centerings, Arches, Groins, Twifted Rails, Compartments, Obelifks, Vafes, Pedeftals* for *Buftos, Sun-Dials, Fonts,* &c. and Methods for raifing heavy Bodies by the Force of *Levers, Pulleys, Axes in Peritrochia, Screws,* and *Wedges;* as alfo *Water,* by the common *Pump, Crane,* &c.

Wherein the Properties, and Preffure of the Air on Water, &c. are explained.

The whole exemplified by 77 large Quarto Copper-plates.

By *BATTY LANGLEY.*

The FOURTH EDITION.

LONDON:

Printed for I. and J. TAYLOR, at the ARCHITECTURAL LIBRARY, No. 56, HOLBORN.

A
T A B L E
OF THE
P L A T E S,
A N D
Pages wherein they are explained.

A 2

A TABLE

OF THE

CONTENTS.

THE
BUILDER's Complete ASSISTANT;

OR, A

Library of Arts and Sciences, &c.

PART I. *Of* ARITHMETICK.

S E C T. 1. Of the feveral Parts of Arithmetick, and the Notation or Art of expreffing Numbers by Characters, and to read their Values.

P. *What is Arithmetick?*
M. Arithmetick is a *Greek* Word, and imports an Art or Science, that teaches the Ufe and Properties of Figures, or right Art of numbering.

P. *What doth right numbering confift of?*
M. To denote any given Quantity with proper Characters, and to exprefs them by Words, which is called Notation.

P. *How many are the Kinds of Notation?*
M. There are many Kinds of Notation by which Quantity is expreffed, but the moft ufual are *Literal* and *Figural.*

P. *What is Literal Notation?*
M. The expreffing Numbers by Letters, and is therefore called *Literal,* and which was anciently made ufe of by the *Hebrews* or *Jews, Chaldæans, Syrians, Arabians, Perfians,* and others of the Eaftern Nations. The *Greeks* alfo expreffed Numbers by divers of their alphabetical Letters, and initial Capital Letters of fome of their numeral Words, as, Π Πέδτε, Five; Δ Δέκα, Ten; E Εκαδὸν, an Hundred; Χ Χίλιοι, a Thoufand; Μ Μύριοι, Ten Thoufand.

P. *Pray what Kind of Letters are ufed now for Notation?*
M. Divers of the *Roman* Capitals; which Method, 'tis very reafonable to believe, the *Latins* firft took from the *Greeks,* as is very evident from the initial Letters of feveral of their numeral Words, as follows, *viz.* The Capital C, which is the initial Letter of *Centum,* the *Latin* Word for an Hundred, is now ufed of itfelf to fignify an Hundred.

P. *But pray how is half an Hundred expreffed?*
M. By the Capital L.

P. *Pray, why is half an Hundred expreffed by an* L?
M. You muft underftand, that the ancient Form of the Capital C was thus written Ⅼ; and as it then fignified an Hundred, therefore the Ancients fignified half a Hundred by one half Part of it, as thus Ⅼ; which being like unto the Capital L, therefore Printers take the Liberty to denote half a Hundred by that Letter.

P. I thank you, Sir; pray proceed.

M. I will. The Capital Letter D, which is the initial Letter of *Decem* (the *Latin* for Ten), was anciently used by the *Latins* to denote Ten; and one Half thereof, as thus Ɒ, did also denote Five. Now as this half Letter hath more of the Likeness of the Capital V, than of any other Capital, therefore Printers and others have used the V (instead of the half Letter Ɒ) for Five; and to denote Ten, instead of using the Capital D, as the Ancients did, they joined together two Vs at their narrow Ends, the one upright, the other downright, in Manner of the Capital Letter X, which now is used to denote Ten.

Again, as *Mille* is *Latin* for a Thousand, therefore the Ancients used the Capital M to denote a Thousand, as it is now used at this Day; and as the old Character of the Capital M was this ⅭⅠↃ, whose right-hand Side being like unto the Capital D, therefore Printers, &c. denote five Hundred by the Capital D. You are also to note, That, as this ancient M ⅭⅠↃ had some Resemblance of the Letter I, placed between two Cs, of which one is turned the wrong Way, as thus CIↃ, therefore those Letters are now used by some to denote a Thousand, instead of the Letter M; and IↃ to denote five Hundred, instead of the Letter D.

P. Pray by what Character did the Ancients use to denote One?

M. Both *Greeks* and *Latins* denoted *One* by one single Stroke, as being the natural and most simple Character of one single Thing; and therefore *One* is represented by the Letter I. Now from these several Characters the following Numbers are expressed by the *Romans* or *Latins, viz.* I One, II Two, III Three, IV or IIII Four, V Five, VI Six, VII Seven, VIII Eight, IX Nine, X Ten, XI Eleven, XII Twelve, XV Fifteen, XX Twenty, XXX Thirty, XL Forty, L Fifty, LX Sixty, LXX Seventy, LXXX Eighty, XC Ninety, C a Hundred, CC two Hundred, CCC three Hundred, CCCC four Hundred, D or IↃ or IↃ five Hundred, DC six Hundred, DCC seven Hundred, M or CIↃ or cIↃ a Thousand, IↃↃ five Thousand, CCIↃↃ ten Thousand, IↃↃↃ fifty Thousand, CCCIↃↃↃ an Hundred Thousand, IↃↃↃↃ five Hundred Thousand, CCCCIↃↃↃↃ a Million; and so MDCCXXXVIII, or CIↃDCCXXXVIII, denotes the Date of this Year, One Thousand Seven Hundred and Thirty-eight.

P. But pray, Sir, why are Nine and Eleven denoted by the same Letters?

M. As the I, being set after the X, thus XI, adds One to it, and makes it Eleven; so on the contrary, when the I is set before the X, thus IX, it lessens its Value One, and therefore signifies but Nine. For the same Reason the I, placed before the V Five, lessens its Value One, and signifies but Four. The same is also to be observed of Forty and Ninety, where the X, being set before the L Fifty, lessens its Value Ten, and signifies but Forty; and being placed before the C, a Hundred, lessens its Value Ten, and signifies but Ninety. And it is further to be observed that some use IIX to denote Eight, and XXC to denote LXXX, as being more concise. The V and L are never repeated, nor are any of the other Characters repeated more than four Times; the I repeated four Times, thus IIII, signifies Four; but the V is Five, not IIIII. So likewise 4 Cs, thus CCCC, signify four Hundred; but five Hundred is denoted by D, or IↃ, as aforesaid, and not by CCCC. Now as by this Method the Notation of Numbers by Letters is very tedious, the Figural Notation was invented, as being more expedite.

P. What is Figural Notation?

M. The Manner of expressing Quantities by the Ten *Arabick* Characters, *viz.* 1 2 3 4 5 6 7 8 9 0, which signify as follows, *viz.* 1 one, 2 two, 3 three, 4 four, 5 five, 6 six, 7 seven, 8 eight, 9 nine, o nought, Cypher, or nothing.

P. Pray how long may these Characters have been used in England?

M. Dr. *Wallis* in his Treatise of Algebra, Page 12, says they were introduced about the Year One Thousand One Hundred and Thirty, which is six Hundred and eight Years since.

P. How many distinct Parts is Arithmetick divided into?

M. Three; two of which are properly called Natural, and the third Artificial.

P. What are those which you call Natural?

M. The

M. The firſt Part is that Kind of Arithmetick which is called *Vulgar*, and which is the Doctrine of whole Numbers ; and the moſt plain and eaſy, becauſe every Unit or One (which is called Integer) repreſents or ſignifies one entire Thing, or Quantity of ſome Kind of Species, as a Nail, Lath, Brick, &c. The ſecond Part is the Doctrine of broken Quantities, or Parts of Units, or Integers, which is called Vulgar Fractions, and wherein the Unit or Integer is divided into a certain Number of even or uneven Parts : as, for Example, if a Foot be the given or propoſed Unit or Integer, and be divided into twelve Inches, then one Inch becomes a Fraction or twelfth Part thereof, two Inches one ſixth Part, three Inches one fourth Part, four Inches one third Part thereof, &c. This Part of Arithmetick may be conſidered either as pure, conſiſting of fractional Parts only, each leſs than a Unit, as Quarters, Halves, &c. ; or of Integers and Fractional Parts intermixt, as one and a half, two and one third Part of one, &c. The third Part, which I call artificial, is alſo called Decimal Arithmetick, which is an artificial Method of working Fractions or broken Numbers in a much eaſier Manner than that of Vulgar Fractions, and which differs very little from Vulgar Arithmetick.

P. Pray why is this Artificial Kind of Arithmetick called Decimal Arithmetick?

M. From the *Latin Decem,* Ten, into which every Integer is ſuppoſed to be ſubdivided ; and indeed, in many Caſes, every Subdiviſion is ſubdivided again into 10 leſſer Parts, &c. Suppoſe one Foot in Length be an Integer or Unit given, and let it be divided into 10 equal Parts, then we ſay the Foot is decimally divided ; and if every tenth Part be decimally divided again, in the like Manner, then the Foot will be divided into one Hundred Parts, and is then ſaid to be Centeſimally divided.

P. I underſtand you, Sir ; and deſire to know, in the next Place, what Uſe is the Cypher of, ſince that of itſelf it ſignifies Nothing ?

M. To augment or increaſe other Figures ; thus, if next after the Figure 1 I place a 0, as thus 10, they together ſignify Ten, and 20 ſignifies Twenty, 30 Thirty, 40 Forty, &c. whereby the Value of every Figure is increaſed ten Times. So alſo if to 10 you add another Cypher, as thus 100, it will increaſe the 10 ten Times, and together ſignify one Hundred. So in like Manner 200 ſignifies two Hundred, 300 three Hundred, 400 four Hundred, &c. And if to 100 you add another Cypher, as 1000, it will increaſe the 100 ten Times, and make it one Thouſand.

So, in like Manner, 2000 ſignifies two Thouſand, 3000 three Thouſand, 4000 four Thouſand, &c. Again, if to 1000 you add another Cypher, as thus 10000, the 1000 will be made ten Thouſand ; and in like Manner if a Cypher be added to 2000, as thus 20000, they will ſignify twenty Thouſand, and 30000 thirty Thouſand, &c.

P. Very well, Sir ; and ſuppoſe that to 10000 I add one, two, or more Cyphers, will they always increaſe the Value of the former ten Times ?

M. Yes; for if to 10000 you add another Cypher, as thus 100000, the Value is increaſed from ten Thouſand to one Hundred Thouſand ; and ſo in like Manner the Addition of another Cypher to 100000, as thus 1000000, will increaſe them unto ten Hundred Thouſand, which is called a Million.

Now if you conſider the Increaſe that has been made by the Addition of the Cyphers, it will be very eaſy to read or expreſs the true Value of any Number of Cyphers, when written, or to write down any given Number propoſed. But, to make this more plain, I will give you a Table of the Increaſe of Unity, by the Addition of Cyphers, unto one Thouſand Millions, as follows.

1, Unit
10, Ten
100, one Hundred, or ten times Ten
1000, one Thousand, or ten times one Hundred
10000, ten Thousand
100,000, one Hundred Thousand, or ten times ten Thousand
1,000,000, one Million, or ten times one Hundred Thousand
10,000,000, ten Million
100,000,000, one Hundred Million, or ten times ten Million
1000,000,000, one Thousand Million, or ten times one Hundred Millions.

P. I perfectly understand the Increase that is made by adding of a Cypher or Cyphers to any of the nine Figures; but how are Numbers to be understood when divers of them are placed together, either with or without Cyphers, as 12, or 123, or 1234, &c.?

M. This I will make very easy to you. They increase each other's Value just in the very same Manner as is done by the Addition of Cyphers: as, for Example, if to 1, I place 2, as thus 12, they together signify Twelve, which is no more than the Value of the 2, placed in the Cypher's Place, added to 10; and so in like Manner 13 signifies Thirteen, 14 Fourteen, 15 Fifteen, &c. so likewise 23 signifies Twenty-three, 25 Twenty-five, &c. So 'tis plain that the first Figures to the Right signify so many Units, and the other so many Times Ten as their Characters express; and therefore the first Place is called the Place of Units, and the second the Place of Tens. And as the Figures in the second Place are Tens, and signify ten Times their Number of Units; so the Figures in the third Place are Hundreds, and signify ten Times their Number of Tens; as 123, wherein the 1 signifies one Hundred, the 2 Twenty, and the 3 Three, and the whole one Hundred Twenty and Three.

To make this plain, observe the following Range of Figures, where every one signifies ten Times the Figures it precedes, and where their Places are not only expressed in Words at Length, but are also divided into the several distinct Columns or Periods by which they are to be numbered or expressed.

Period of Quadrillions.	Period of Trillions.	Period of Billions.	Period of Millions.	Period of Units.
Thds. Units.	Thds. Units.	Thds. Units.	Thds. Units.	Thds. Units.
353, 333,	777, 777,	444, 444,	444, 444,	371, 524.
HTU, HTU,	HTU, HTU,	HTU, HTU,	HTU, HTU,	HTU, HTU
Thds. Qua-	Thds. Tril-	Thds. Billions	Thds. Mill.	Thou- Hun-
of drill.	of lions.	of	of	sands dreds
Qua- **I.**	Tril- **G.**	Bil- **E.**	Mill. **C.**	**B** **A.**
drill.	lions	lions.	**D.**	
K.	**H.**	**F.**		

Now it is to be observed, First, that the Places of Numbers are always first reckoned or numbered from the right Hand to the left, and then read or expressed in Words from the left to the right. So in the first Column A, to reckon the Number 524, I begin at the 4, calling that Units; then proceed to the 2, calling that Tens; and lastly to the 5, calling that Hundreds; saying, Units, Tens, Hundreds: which I then read from the left to the right; saying, Five Hundred twenty and four Units. Again, if to the Column of Units I join 371, the Column of Thousands, I begin to numerate them as before; saying, Units at 4, Tens at 2, Hundreds at 5, Thousands at 1, Tens of Thousands at 7, and Hundreds of Thousands

fands at 3; which I exprefs or read, Three Hundred Seventy and one Thoufand
five Hundred twenty and four, and fo in like manner any other Number.

Secondly, by the Capital Letters H T U, placed under the Figures of every
Column, you are to underftand the repeating of the Denominations of Units, Tens
and Hundreds of the Units and Thoufands of each Period.

P. *Pray, what do you mean by a Period?*

M. A Period is a Quantity expreffed by fix Figures, and are Units, Millions,
Billions, Trillions, Quadrillions, Quintillions, Sextillions, &c. So here, the
Period of Units is the Columns A B, which are three Hundred feventy and
one Thoufand, five Hundred twenty and four Units. The Period of Millions is
the Columns C D, which are four Hundred forty and two Thoufand, four Hundred forty and four Millions. The Period of Billions is the Columns E F,
which are four Hundred forty and four Thoufand, four Hundred and forty four
Billions, and fo the like of Trillions, Quadrillions.

P. *Pray, what do you mean by a Billion, Trillion, &c. ?*

M. A Billion is a Million of Millions, a Trillion is a Million of Millions of
Millions, &c. and therefore as you fee that every Column confifts but of three
places of Figures, *viz.* of Units, Tens, and Hundreds, which in general begin
with Hundreds, altho' the Units may be Units, as in Column A, or Thoufands
as in Column B, or Millions as in Column C, &c. and as every Period contains two Columns, or fix Figures, 'tis very eafy to read any range of Figures
that can be propofed, as is evident from the aforefaid, which are thus expreffed in
Words, *viz.* three Hundred thirty and three Thoufand, three Hundred and
thirty three Quadrillions; feven Hundred feventy and feven Thoufand, feven
Hundred feventy and feven Trillions; four Hundred forty and four Thoufand,
four Hundred forty and four Billions; four Hundred forty and two Thoufand,
four Hundred forty and four Millions, three Hundred feventy and one Thoufand,
five Hundred twenty and four.

But that you may perfectly underftand how to reckon or numerate any Range
of Figures propofed, and to truly underftand the value of their refpective Places,
I will therefore give you the following Table.

TABLE of N U M E R A T I O N.

Trillions.	Hundreds of Thoufands of Billions.	Tens of Thoufands of Billions.	Thoufands of Billions.	Hundreds of Billions.	Tens of Billions.	Billions.	Hundreds of Thoufands of Millions.	Tens of Thoufands of Millions.	Thoufands of Millions.	Hundreds of Millions.	Tens of Millions.	Millions.	Hundreds of Thoufands.	Tens of Thoufands.	Thoufands.	Hundreds.	Tens.	Units.
																1	2	3
															1	2	3	4
														1	2	3	4	5
													1	2	3	4	5	6
												1	2	3	4	5	6	7
											1	2	3	4	5	6	7	8
										1	2	3	4	5	6	7	8	9
									1	2	3	4	5	6	7	8	9	8
								1	2	3	4	5	6	7	8	9	8	7
							1	2	3	4	5	6	7	8	9	8	7	6
						1	2	3	4	5	6	7	8	9	8	7	6	5
					1	2	3	4	5	6	7	8	9	8	7	6	5	4
				1	2	3	4	5	6	7	8	9	8	7	6	5	4	3
			1	2	3	4	5	6	7	8	9	8	7	6	5	4	3	2
		1	2	3	4	5	6	7	8	9	8	7	6	5	4	3	2	1
	1	2	3	4	5	6	7	8	9	8	7	6	5	4	3	2	1	2
1,	2	3	4,	5	6	7,	8	9	8,	7	6	5,	4	3	2,	1	2	3

B   Ia

In this Table, you fee a Demonftration of all that I have been informing you, with regard to the places of Figures, exceeding each other ten times.

P. *'Tis very true, Sir ; pray is there any thing further to be known, relating to the Numeration and Expreſſion of Figures?*

M. Yes ; 'tis neceſſary, and indeed a very ready way, in long Numbers, to place a Comma before every third Figure, thereby diſtinguiſhing the Units, Tens, and Hundreds in every Column as aforefaid, and the Millions, Billions, Trillions, &c. by one, two, three, &c. Dots or Points placed under them, as is done under the lowermoſt Line of the preceding Table.

LECT. II. Of ADDITION.

P. *What is to be underſtood by Addition?*

M. To colleƈt, or gather into one Sum or Total, all fuch Sums or Quantities, as may be given or propoſed, which is performed by the two following Rules.

RULE I.

Place all the Numbers given, to be added together, fo as that each Figure may ſtand direƈtly under thoſe Figures of the fame Value, *viz.* Units under
7012 Units ; Tens under Tens ; Hundreds under Hundreds, &c. Which be-
540 ing done, (always) draw a Line under the lowermoſt Number, to feparate
12 their Sum when found. As for Example Suppoſe the Numbers 7012,
90 540, 12, and 90, were to be added together, they muſt be placed as in
——— the Margin.

RULE II.

Always begin to add the given Quantities together, at the place of Units; adding together all the Figures that ſtand in that Column ; and if their Sum be lefs than Ten, fet it down underneath the faid Column; and if their Sum be more than Ten, fet down only the Overplus, or odd Figure more than Ten or Tens; and as many Tens as are contained in the Column of Units, fo many Ones you muſt carry and add unto the fecond Column of Tens ; adding them, and all the Figures that ſtand in the Column of Tens together, in the fame manner as thoſe of the Column of Units were added : and fo in like manner proceed to the Column of Hundreds, Thouſands, &c. until every Column is done ; and placing the whole Amount of the laſt Column underneath the fame, the Sum ariſing from thoſe Additions will be the total Amount required.

EXAMPLE I.

To 7543 add 2345, which place as in the Margin.

Praƈtice. Begin at the Place of Units, and fay, 5 and 3 is 8,
7543 which being lefs than Ten, fet it underneath that Column. Then
2345 proceed to the fecond Column of Tens, and fay, 4 and 4 is 8,
——— which being lefs than ten, place it alfo underneath that Column.
Sum 9888 Again, in the third Column of Hundreds fay, 3 and 5 is 8,
which being alfo lefs than ten, place it alfo underneath that Column. Laſtly, in the Column of Thouſands, fay 2 and 7 make 9, which place underneath that Column ; then will the Produƈt be equal to 9888, the true Sum required.

EXAMPLE II.

To 9999999, add 8888, which place as in the Margin.

Praƈtice. Beginning at the Column of Units, fay, 8 and 9
9999999 is 17; now, as 17 is 7 more than 10, therefore fet the 7
8888 underneath, and carry the ten unto the fecond Column or
——— place of Tens, calling it one, and then faying, one that I car-
Sum 10008887 ry and 8 is 9, and 9 is 18 ; then place the 8 under the place of Tens, and carry the ten unto the next Column of Hundreds,

dreds, (becaufe 10 times 10 is one Hundred) faying, one that I carry and 8 is 9, and 9 is 18 ; place the 8 under the Column of Hundreds, and carry one for the ten, to the next Column of Thoufands (becaufe 10 Hundred is equal to one Thoufand). Proceed in like manner to the Column of tens of Thoufands, &c. and the true Sum required will be 10008887.

EXAMPLE III.

It is required to find the true Sum of 1430, more 234, more 456, more 789, more 91, which place as in the Margin.

Begin as before, at the Column of Units, faying, 1 and 9 is 10, and 6 is 16, and 4 is 20. Now as 20 contains ten twice, and none remains, therefore under the Column of Units place a Cypher o, and carry the two tens to the Column of Tens, faying, 2 that I carry, and 9 is 11, and 8 is 19, and 5 is 24, and 3 is 27, and 3 is 30. Now as 30 contains ten three times, and nothing remains, therefore under the Column of Tens place an o, and carry 3 to the place of Hundreds, faying, three that I carry, and 7 is 10, and 4 is 14, and 2 is 16, and 4 is 20. Now as 20 contains 10 twice, and nothing remains, therefore place o under the Column of Hundreds ; and carrying the two Tens to the place of Thoufands, fay, two that I carry and 1 make 3, which being placed under the place of Thoufands, the true Sum will be 3000, as required.

$$\begin{array}{r} 1430 \\ 234 \\ 456 \\ 789 \\ 91 \\ \hline \text{Sum } 3000 \end{array}$$

P. I underftand your Method of cafting up every Column by itfelf, and to carry the Tens forward when they happen, and can perform any Sum required. But before you proceed any further, pray demonftrate the Reafon thereof.

M. I will with the laft Example, as following.

Add together each fingle Column of Figures by itfelf, as if there were no other Columns of Figures to be added, and underneath each Column place the Product.

Thus the Product of the firft Column of Units, is 20 ; the Product of the Column of Tens, is 28 ; the Product of the Column of Hundreds, is 17 ; and the Product of the Column of Thoufands, is 1.

Now thefe four feveral Products being added together, in like manner, their Product will be 3000, as following.

1	4	3	0
2	3	4	
4	5	6	
7	8	9	
	9	1	

	2	0
2	8	
1	7	
1		

| 3 | 0 | 0 | 0 |

By this continual Addition of the Products, they at length terminate in the Total, which was to be demonftrated.

	2	0
1	7	
1		

} The particular Products of the above four Columns.

	1	0	0
2	9		

} Their Sums added as above, a fecond time.

1	0	0	0
2			

} Their Sums added as above, a third time.

| 3 | 0 | 0 | 0 | The Total or Product, as above.

P. I thank you, Sir, for this Demonftration, which has well informed me of the reafon of carrying on the Tens, as they arife, to the next Column. Pray, Sir, be

pleafed,

pleafed, in the next place, to proceed to other Examples, for 'tis a pleafure to work, *when I know the reafon of my Operations.*

M. I am glad to find that you are fo pleafed with *Demonftrations*, which very few Youths care to trouble themfelves with.

P. *Such there are, there's no doubt of* ; but *did they know the Sweetnefs of Demonftration, they would ftrictly purfue it* ; *for by this fingle Demonftration only it is* proved, *That the whole is equal to all its Parts taken together* ; that is, *I am taught to know that the Numbers which are propofed to be added together, are the feveral Parts, and their total Sum found by Addition to be the whole.*

M. 'Tis true, you rightly conceive it, and you will as eafily conceive the reafon of the Proof of Addition.

P. *Pray, how do you prove the truth of Addition ?*

M. By parting or feparating the given Quantities or Numbers into two (or more) Parcels, according to the largenefs of the feveral Numbers contained therein ; and then adding up each Parcel by itfelf, their particular Sums being added together, the Sum total thereof will be equal to the other Sum total firft found, if the Work be truly performed ; if otherwife, 'tis falfe, and care muft be taken to difcover and correct the Error, by going over the whole again.

EXAMPLE.

$$
A\begin{array}{r}123456\\214365\\241356\\423165\\432615\\\hline\end{array}
\qquad
B\begin{array}{r}123456\\214365\\241356\\\hline 579177\end{array}
\qquad
C\begin{array}{r}423165\\432615\\\hline 855780\end{array}
$$

1434957

(1) In this Example, the given Quantities are 123456, more 214365, more 241356, more 423165, more 432615, whofe Sum total is equal to 1434957.

(2) Dividing thefe five given Quantities into two parts, as the firft three by themfelves, as B, and the laft two by themfelves, as C ; their two Sums or Totals, added together, will be equal to the Total of the whole five Numbers taken together at A.

The Sum Total of B, is 579177
The Sum Total of C, is 855780.

The grand Total is - - 1434957, which is equal to the Total of the five given Numbers at A, as required. And fo in like manner any other Sum or Quantities given, may be proved.

P. *I underftand you perfectly well, and can now* prove *the truth of any Total required. Pray proceed to my further Information in other things neceffary to my purpofe.*

M. I will : and firft, with refpect to Meafures of Length.

P. *What Meafures of Length are moft generally ufed in Bufinefs ?*

M. The Foot, the Yard, and the Pole or Perch.

P. *How is the Foot commonly divided ?*

M. Generally into twelve equal parts, called Inches, and every of thofe Inches into eight, and fometimes ten equal parts, which laft is called a Decimal Divifion of the Inch, and then the whole Foot is divided into 120 equal parts.

P. *Is the Foot divided into any other forts of Parts or Divifions ?*

M. Yes, 'tis fometimes divided into one hundred parts ; which is called, the centefimal Divifion of the Foot, as has been already obferved ; by which the Dimenfions of Glafs, Marble, &c. are taken.

P. *Pray give me fome Examples in thefe kinds of Feet Meafure ?*

M. I will ; and firft, of the Foot divided into 12 Inches, and each Inch into eight parts.

II. *Addition of Feet, Inches, and 8ths.*

EXAMPLE I.

Feet. Inch. 8th Parts.

Collect into one Sum these several Lengths, *viz.*

Feet	Inch.	8th Parts.
27	11	7
13	7	5
7	10	3
23	4	4
14	7	5
18	4	2
9	10	1

Rule.

For every 8th Parts, carry 1 to the Inches; for every 12 Inches, carry 1 to the Feet, which add as Integers.

Answer 115 .8 3

Take the following Examples for Practice.

EXAMPLE II.

Feet. Inch. 8ths.

27	2	5
4	10	2
5	11	7
18	2	1
9	11	7

Sum 66 2 6

EXAMPLE III.

Feet. Inch. 8ths.

123	11	7
33	7	4
5	9	5
172	11	4
75	10	0

Sum 411 2 4

I will now proceed to Examples of Foot Measures, centefimally divided; that is, the Foot divided into 100 equal Parts.

III. *Addition of Feet and Parts.*

Feet. Hund. Parts.

Collect into one Sum these several Lengths, *viz.*

Feet.	Hund. Parts.
123	,09
456	,75
789	,99
101	,82
071	,29
172	,25
222	,50

Sum total 1937 ,69

Now, as the Foot is here fuppofed to be divided into 100 equal parts, which is a Centefimal Divifion; therefore the manner of adding thefe fums together, is the very fame as in whole Numbers; the Tens of every Column being carried on to the next, and the Remainders placed underneath : this is fo very plain, needs no further Examples hereof. But obferve, that as the Foot contains 100 parts, 75 parts thereof is equal to ¾ of a Foot; 50 parts thereof is equal to ½ a Foot; and 25 parts thereof is equal to ¼ of a Foot.

P. *I thank you, Sir; thefe Examples are both eafy and pleafant, and I am much delighted therewith. Pray now proceed to the other Meafures you before mentioned; which, if I remember right, you faid, were the Yard, and the Pole or Perch.*

IV. *Addition of Yards, Quarters, and Nails.*

M. The Yard is a Meafure of Length, containing three Feet precifely; of which other Meafures of Length are compofed, as the Pole or Perch, Furlongs, Miles and Leagues.

P. *In what manner is the Yard ufually divided ?*

M. Into four equal Parts or Quarters, each (containing nine Inches) fubdivided into four equal parts, called Nails; therefore the Divifions of a Yard, are Nails and Quarters, and the Manner of their Addition is performed by this Rule.

EXAMPLE.

EXAMPLE.

The following Lengths are to be added into one Sum.

Yds. Quar. Nails.

123	3	3	For every 4 Nails, carry
456	1	2	1 to the Quarters; for e-
789	2	1	very 4 Quarters carry 1 to
987	0	3	the Yards, which add as
966	3	2	Integers.

Sum total required 3323   3   3

Take the following Examples for Practice.

Yds.	Qu.	Nails.		Yds.	Qu.	Nails.
765	3	2		1456	3	3
834	2	1		325	1	3
799	1	0		444	2	3
888	2	2				

Total 2227   0   1

Total 3288   1   1

You muſt alſo underſtand, that there are three other ſmall Meaſures of Length proceeding from the Yard, namely, the *Flemiſh* and *Engliſh* Ells, and the Fathom. The *Flemiſh* Ell is equal to three quarters of a Yard; the *Engliſh* Ell is equal to one Yard and quarter; and the Fathom is equal to two Yards, or ſix Feet.

P. Thank you, Sir; I ſhall remember their Quantities: pray proceed unto the larger Meaſures, as Poles, Furlongs, &c.

M. I will; but firſt, 'tis neceſſary that you ſhould have, at leaſt, one Example in each of the preceding Meaſures: for always remember, that the practice of one ſingle Example ingrafts a ſtronger Impreſſion on the Mind, than the bare hearing or reading of twenty.

V. *Addition of Cloth-Meaſure, Flemiſh.*

Fl. Ells. Inch.

Collect into one Sum theſe ſeveral Quantities, *viz.*

213	26	Rule.
271	17	For every 27 Inches carry
123	11	1 to the Ells, which add as
721	20	Integers.
222	15	

Sum total 1553   8

VI. *Addition of Cloth-Meaſure, Engliſh.*

El. 4ths Yd. Na. of Yd.

Collect into one Sum theſe ſeveral Quantities, *viz.*

12	4	3	Rule.
123	3	2	For every 4 Nails carry 1
71	4	2	to the Quarters; for every
72	4	1	5 Quarters carry 1 to the
			Ells, which add as Integers.

Sum total 281   2   0

VII. *Addition of Fathoms.*

Fath. Feet.

Collect into one Sum theſe ſeveral Lengths, *viz.*

123	2	Rule.
173	1	For every 6 Feet carry 1
275	5	to the Fathoms, and add
222	4	them as Integers.
999	5	

Sum total 1794   5

Now I will proceed to Poles, Furlongs, *&c.*

P. Pray, what number of Feet are equal to one Pole or Perch ?

M. There are three different Poles or Perches, by which Lands are meafured. The firft is called the *Statute Pole*, containing 16 Feet and ⅓. The fecond, the Woodland Pole, containing 18 Feet ; and the third, the Foreft Pole or Perch, containing 21 Feet.

The Statute Pole is ufually ufed in the Menfuration of meadow, arable, and pafture Lands, and Brick-works, &c. the Woodland Pole in the Menfuration of copious Woods, &c. and the Foreft Pole in the Menfuration of large Chaces, Forefts, &c.

VIII. *Addition of Statute Poles.*

Poles. Feet.

Collect into one Sum thefe feveral Lengths, *viz.*

Poles	Feet	
999	13	*Rule.*
127	15	For every 16 Feet and ⅓
729	11	carry 1, or for every 33
888	2	Feet carry 2 to the Poles,
777	4	and add them as Integers.

Sum 3522   12

IX. *Addition of Woodland Poles.*

Poles. Feet.

Collect into one Sum thefe feveral Lengths, *viz.*

Poles	Feet	
796	17	*Rule.*
127	15	For 18 Feet carry 1 to the
493	11	Poles, which add as Inte-
101	16	gers.
222	9	

Sum 1742   14

X. *Addition of Foreft Poles.*

'Tis required to collect into one Sum, the following Lengths.

Poles. Feet.

Collect into one Sum thefe feveral Lengths, *viz.*

Poles	Feet	
9999	20	*Rule.*
777	19	For every 21 Feet carry
888	15	1 to the Poles, which add
201	20	as Integers.
555	9	

Sum 12423   20

Thefe are the various kinds of Poles, of which the Statute Pole is the moft in ufe, and it is by the Statute Pole that Chains, Furlongs, Miles, and Leagues, are compofed.

P. Pray what Meafure is a Chain ?

M. A Chain is a Meafure of Length, containing four Statute Poles, precifely equal to 66 Feet, and is divided into 100 equal Parts, called Links : it is by this Meafure, that Land is ufually meafured ; and was firft invented by that late eminent Mathematician, Mr. *Edmund Gunter* ; and as the whole Length is divided into 100 Links, and contains 4 Poles, therefore 25 Links is equal to one Pole ; 50 Links equal to two Poles ; and 75 Links equal to 3 Poles.

XI. *Addition of Chains and Links.*

Cha. Links.

Collect into one Sum thefe Quantities, *viz.*

Cha.	Links	
10	75	*Rule.*
5	95	For every 100 Links carry
2	99	1 to the Chains, which add
27	21	as Integers.
28	96	
00	18	

Sum 76   04

XII.

XII. *Addition of Furlongs, Chains, and Poles.*

P. *Pray, what is a Furlong?*

M. A Furlong is a Length, containing 10 Chains, or 40 Statute Poles or Perches, and is one eighth part of a Mile. It is also called, an Acre's length; and one Chain's length is called an Acre's breadth; because a piece of Land, whose Length is 10 Chains, and Breadth one Chain, is equal to 160 square Poles, the Quantity of one Statute Acre.

The Addition of these Measures, is made by this Rule:

For every 4 Poles, carry 1 to the Chains, for every 10 Chains, carry 1 to the Furlongs, which add as Integers.

E X A M P L E.

	Fur.	Ch.	Po.
Collect into one Sum these several Lengths, *viz.*	212	3	3
	122	9	2
	777	5	2
	222	3	1
	000	7	0
Sum	1335	9	0

P. *Sir, I now understand these Additions very well, and therefore desire you to proceed unto Miles, Leagues, &c. Pray, how many Furlongs are equal to one Mile?*

XIII. *Addition of Degrees, Leagues, Miles, and Furlongs.*

M. Eight Furlongs are equal to one Mile, and three Miles are equal to one League.

P. *And is a League the greatest Measure of Length?*

M. No; a Degree is the greatest Measure of Length.

P. *What is a Degree?*

M. A Degree is stated at 60 Miles, of which, 360 is said to be the Circumference of the Earth.

P. *Pray give me an Example hereof.*

M. I will.

E X A M P L E.

Collect into one Sum the following Measures.

Rule. For every 8 Furlongs carry 1 to the Miles, for every 3 Miles, carry 1 to the Leagues, for every 20 Leagues, carry 1 to the Degrees, and add them as Integers.

Degr.	Lea.	Mi.	Fur.
70	18	2	7
25	15	1	6
18	18	2	5
25	04	0	2
Sum 140	17	1	4

These are the several Measures of Length used in *England,* whose Proportions to each other are exhibited in the following Table.

A Table

A Table of English *Measures of Length.*

Barley-corns, taken out of the Middle of an Ear of Barley.

3	Inch											
36	12	Foot										
81	27	$2\frac{1}{4}$	Flemish Ell									
108	36	3	$1\frac{1}{3}$	Yard								
135	45	$3\frac{3}{4}$	$1\frac{2}{3}$	$1\frac{1}{4}$	English Ell							
216	72	6	$2\frac{2}{3}$	2	$1\frac{3}{5}$	Fathom						
594	198	$16\frac{1}{2}$	$7\frac{1}{3}$	$5\frac{1}{2}$	$4\frac{2}{5}$	$2\frac{1}{2}\frac{1}{4}$	Statute Pole					
648	216	18	8	6	$4\frac{1}{5}\frac{3}{5}$	3	$1\frac{1}{11}$	Woodland Pole				
756	252	21	$9\frac{1}{3}$	7	$6\frac{6}{13}$	$3\frac{1}{2}$	$1\frac{3}{11}$	$1\frac{1}{6}$	Forest Pole			
2376	792	66	$29\frac{1}{3}$	22	$17\frac{1}{5}\frac{2}{5}$	10	4	$3\frac{2}{3}$	$3\frac{1}{7}$	Chain		
23760	7920	660	$993\frac{1}{3}$	220	176	110	40	$36\frac{2}{3}$	$31\frac{3}{7}$	10	Furlongs	
190080	63360	5280	$7946\frac{2}{3}$	1760	1408	880	320	$293\frac{1}{3}$	$251\frac{3}{7}$	80	8	Miles
1	2	3	4	5	6	7	8	9	10	11	12	

P. *Pray explain unto me the Nature and Use of this Table.*

M. I will. You see that it contains 12 Columns, as numbered, 1, 2, 3, 4, 5, 6, 7, 8, 9, 10, 11, 12, each representing the number of Times that they are contained in the next greater Measure. Thus in a Mile, there is contained 190080 Barley-corns Length, or 63360 Inches; or 5280 Feet; or 7946⅔ *Flemish* Ells; or 1760 Yards; or 1408 *English* Ells; or 880 Fathom; or 320 Statute Poles; or 293⅓ Woodland Poles; or 251$\frac{3}{7}$ Forest Poles; or 80 Chain; or 8 Furlongs; as exhibited in the lowermost Line of the Table. Again, admit it was required to know what Number of Inches is in a Furlong, &c. proceed as follows.

First, find out the word Furlong on the right hand Side of the Table, and bringing your Eye level therefrom, until you come under the Title (or Column of) Inch, in the second Column, there stands 7920, the Number of Inches contained in one Furlong, as required. Likewise under the Title *Foot*, stands 660, the Number of Feet in a Furlong; and so in like manner, any other Measure, or its Parts of which 'tis composed, may most readily be found by Inspection.

P. *Sir, I am very much obliged to you for your painful Information of Long Measures, pray be pleased to instruct me in like manner, of such Square Measures as are used in Business.*

M. I will. The square Measures by which Works, &c. are performed and sold, are, the Yard, the Foot, the Square, and the Rod, or Pole.

P. *What do you mean by the Foot? You have already informed me, that a Foot is a Length containing 12 Inches, which I already know.*

M. 'Tis very true a Foot in Length is 12 Inches as you say, but a square Foot is a square Space, each Side thereof equal to 12 Inches; that is, as well in Length as in Breadth, and contains 144 square Inches.

P. Pray explain this to me in such a manner as I may rightly understand it ; for at present I cannot comprehend your Meaning.

M. I will, 'tis very easily understood : Suppose that the Square A B C D, *fig.* IX. *Pl.* LVII. have each of its Sides equal to one Foot in Length. And each Side divided into 12 equal Parts ; that is, the Inches in a Foot. Then I say that if from the several Divisions of the Inches at the Points 1, 2, 3, 4, 5, 6, 7, 8, 9, 10, 11, and 12, in the Sides A B and A C, right Lines be drawn from Side to Side, respectively opposite, they will form 144 little Squares or square Inches : For every one thereof will be an Inch square precisely. Hence it is, that a square Foot contains 144 square Inches.

P. Sir, I understand you perfectly well, and upon the same Principle I suppose that a square Yard contains 9 square Feet.

M. 'Tis true. For if each of the Sides of the Square A B C D, *fig.* I. *Pl.* LVII. contain one Yard, divided into 3 equal Parts or Feet, as at the Points 1, 2, 3, 4, &c. and the Lines 3, 7 ; 4, 8 ; and 1, 5 ; 2, 6 ; be drawn, they will divide the square Yard into nine little Squares, each containing one square Foot. Therefore 'tis evident, that one square Yard contains 9 square Feet, as you have before observed.

P. I see plainly that it doth, but what do you mean by the Measure which you call a Square ?

M. A Square of Work is a Space containing 100 square Feet, or it is a square Figure whose Sides are each equal to 10 Feet, divided into Feet, as the Square A B C D, *fig.* II. *Pl.* LVII.

P. I understand you, Sir, and see that if from the several respective Divisions of Feet, there be right Lines drawn, in the same Manner as before in the square Foot and Yard, they will generate 100 little Squares, each equal to one square Foot. Pray wherein is this kind of Measure used ?

M. In the Mensuration of Flooring, Tyling, Slating, &c. which you'll be acquainted with, when you come to learn Mensuration.

P. Thank you, Sir, pray be pleased to proceed.

M. I will. The next square Measure is a Rod or Pole, and is a Space containing 272 ¼ square Feet.

P. Pray shew me its Figure.

M. I will. Suppose each Side of the Square A B C D, *fig.* III. *Pl.* LVII. to contain 16 Feet ½, divided into 16 Feet and ½ as at the Numbers 1, 2, 3, &c. in the Sides A B and A C. Then I say, that if the right Lines 1 *a*, 2 *b*, 3 *c*, 4 *d*, 5 *e*, &c. be drawn, as before in the preceding square Figures, they will generate 256 complete little Squares, each containing one square Foot, as in the Scheme.

P. Very well, Sir, but I thought that you said, that a square Rod contained 272 ¼ square Feet, and herein you produce but 256.

M. Within the Square of 16 Feet ½ A B C D, there are 32 little long Squares, or Oblongs, marked with Dots ; now as each of these Oblongs is 6 Inches in Breadth, and one Foot in Length, therefore one of them is equal to but ½ of one of the whole square Feet. And consequently the 32 being taken together, are equal to but 16 whole Feet.

Now if unto 256
You add   16 .

The Sum is 272 The Number of Feet in one Rod. And lastly the little Square *r*, at the corner D, having each of its Sides equal to but ½ a Foot or six Inches, therefore it contains but ¼ of a Foot ; that is, 36 Inches, which is but ¼ of 144, the Number of square Inches (as before proved) in one square Foot.

Therefore the Sum of the whole Square is equal to 272 ¼ Feet. Having thus defined unto you these several square Measures, I will in the next place proceed to some Examples of the Addition of such Quantities.

XIV. *Addition of square Feet.*

Note, That as the square Foot is divided into Quarters, therefore one Quarter contains 36 square Inches.

Sq. Feet. Qrs. Sq. In.

Collect into one Sum these several Quantities, *viz.*

Sq. Feet.	Qrs.	Sq. In.	Rule.
123	3	31	For every 36 Inches carry
729	2	29	1 to the Quarters; for every
80	1	25	4 Quarters carry 1 to the sq.
71	0	35	Feet, which add as Integers.

Sum 1005   1   14

I must also inform you, that the square Foot is by some divided into 12 equal Parts, each being 12 Inches long, and one Inch in breadth, as *a b c d e f g b i k l m*, in *fig*. VIII. *Pl*. LVII. Which Parts are called long Inches, of which you'll see more at large in cross Multiplication hereafter. By this manner of dividing the square Foot, its Parts are most readily added together, as following.

EXAMPLE.

Sq. Feet. Inches.

Collect into one Sum these Quantities, *viz.*

Sq. Feet.	Inches.	Rule.
999	11.	For every 12 Inches, carry
10	10.	1 to the Feet, and add them
7	6.	as Integers.
2	3	
99	8	

Sum 1120   2

XV. *Addition of square Yard Measure.*
EXAMPLE.

Yds. Feet.

Collect into one Sum these Quantities, *viz.*

Yds.	Feet.	Rule.
27	8	For every 9 Feet carry 1
12	7	to the Yards, and add them
9	4	as Integers.
5	8	
6	2	

Sum 62   2

XVI. *Addition of square Measure, as Flooring*, &c.

Sq. Feet.

Collect into one Sum these several Quantities of Flooring, *viz.*

Sq.	Feet.	Rule.
10	.95	
123	.75.	Add up the Feet as Integers,
70	.83	and for every 100 carry 1 to
70	.96.	the Squares.
10	25	
100	50.	
9	3	

Sum 396   27

XVII. *Addition of square Pole Measure.*

Note, That in Business the fractional Part or one Quarter of a Foot is generally omitted, and then,

The Rod is taken at   272 Feet.
The 3 Quarters   204
The Half   136
The Quarter   68

C 2

	Rod.	Qr.	Ft.
To add thefe Quantities together, this is the *Rule*. For every 68	27	3.	30
Feet carry one to the Quarters, and for every 4 Quarters carry 1	29	1	38
to the Rods.	16	3.	2
The Quantities in the Margin, are given to be added into one	8	1	9
Sum.			
Sum	82	1	11

XVIII. *Addition of Land Meafure.*

Note, That an Acre of Land contains 160 Poles or 4 Roods, and each Rood 40 fquare Poles or Perches.

<table>
<tr><td></td><td>Acr.</td><td>Rd.</td><td>P.</td><td></td></tr>
<tr><td></td><td>27</td><td>3.</td><td>39.</td><td>*Rule.*</td></tr>
<tr><td>Collect thefe feveral Quan-</td><td>26</td><td>2</td><td>21.</td><td>For every 40 Poles carry</td></tr>
<tr><td>tities into one **Sum**, *viz.*</td><td>18</td><td>1</td><td>35.</td><td>1 to the Roods, for every 4</td></tr>
<tr><td></td><td>20</td><td>3.</td><td>38.</td><td>Roods carry 1 to the Acres,</td></tr>
<tr><td></td><td>21</td><td>1.</td><td>30</td><td>which add as Integers.</td></tr>
</table>

Total   115   2   03

A Table of fquare Meafures.

Sq. Inches					
144	Feet				
1296	9	Yards			
14400	100	11⅑	Squares		
39204	272¼	30⅜	2¹¹⁄₁₇	Statute Poles	
1568160	10890	1210	108⁷⁄₁₀	40	Roods
6272640	43560	4840	435⁶⁄₁₀	160	4	Acre

Thus have I delivered unto you all the ufeful fquare Meafures, by which all manner of fuperficial Works are meafured. I fhall now exhibit them together in this Table, which by Infpection will fhew their refpective Quantities, in any of the leffer Meafures.

P. *Pray fhew me the Ufe of this Table.*

M. I will. Suppofe it was required to know how many fquare Feet were contained in one Acre of Land, *Statute Meafure*; looking in the fecond Column, under the Title *Feet*, and againft the word *Acre*, ftands 43560, the Number of fquare Feet in an Acre of Land, as required; and fo in like manner any other Meafure in the Table.

P. *I thank you, Sir, I underftand it, and fo in like manner an Acre of Land is equal to 6272640 fquare Inches, or 4840 fquare Yards, or 435⁶⁄₁₀ Squares of 100 Feet; or 160 fquare Statute Poles; or 4 Roods. And a Rood is equal to 1568160 fquare Inches, or to 10890 fquare Feet, or to 1210 fquare Yards; or to 108⁷⁄₁₀ Squares of 100 Feet; or to 40 Statute Poles.*

M. 'Tis very well, I find you have a right Underftanding of its Ufe. I fhall in the next place proceed to inform you of the feveral Weights ufed in this Kingdom, from which the feveral Meafures of Capacity were taken.

P. *I thank you, Sir, but if there were any folid Meafures neceffary to follow the fuperficial or fquare ones now taught me, I fhould gladly know them.*

M. There are folid Meafures which you are to be informed of, as the folid Foot, which contains 1728 folid or cubick Inches; and the folid Yard, which contains 27 folid Feet, a Tun of Timber 40 folid Feet, and a Load 50 folid Feet.
But

But before I can inform you thereof regularly, I must teach you Multiplication, or otherwise you cannot so readily, or so well understand them.

P. I ask pardon for my Forwardness. Pray proceed to the account of the Weights you was mentioning.

M. I will. The original of all Weights used in this Kingdom was a Grain of Wheat, taken out of the middle of a well-grown Ear, and being well dried, 32 of them were called and made a *Penny Weight*, 20 Penny Weights one Ounce, and 12 *Ounces* one Pound. *See* the Statutes of 51 *Hen.* 3. 31 *Ed.* 1. 12 *Hen.* 7. But the Moderns since the making of these Statutes, have divided the aforesaid Penny Weight into 24 equal Parts, which are called *Grains*, and is the least Weight now in common use.

P. What do you call this original Weight?

M. It is called *Troy* Weight, because 'tis supposed to be the same that was used by the *Trojans*. By this Weight *Osbright*, a *Saxon* King of *England*, 200 Years before the Conquest, caused an Ounce Troy of Silver to be divided into twenty pieces, which at that time were called Pence, and at that time an Ounce of Silver was worth but 20 Pence.

This value of Silver continued unto the Reign of *Hen.* VI. who to prevent the enhancing of Money in foreign Parts, valued the Ounce at thirty Pence, and accordingly divided the same into thirty pieces, each being then a Penny. And the old Pennys made in *Osbright*'s time went then for Three-pence half-penny each, and which continued unto the time of *Ed.* IV. who valued the Ounce of Silver at 40 Pence, and divided it into 40 pieces each a Penny, and then the old Penny of *Osbright*'s went for Two-pence.

This continued until the Reign of *Hen.* VIII. who valued the Ounce of Silver at 45 Pence, which was not altered until the Reign of Queen *Eliz.* who valued the old Penny of *Osbright* at Three-pence; so that at that time, all Three-pences coined by Queen *Eliz.* weighed but one Penny Weight, every Six-pence two Penny Weight, and the like proportion in Shillings and other pieces then coined.

This last Alteration was the cause of the Ounce *Troy* of Silver to be valued at 60 Pence, or five Shillings, as it now is at this Time.

By this Weight Jewels, Gold, Silver, Corn, Bread, and all Liquids are weighed.

XIX. *Addition of Troy Weights.*

These Weights are added together by the following *Rule.*

For every 24 Grains carry 1 to the Penny Weights, for every 20 Penny Weights carry 1 to the Ounces, and for every 12 Ounces carry 1 to the Pounds.

EXAMPLE.

lb.	Oz.	Pw.	Gr.
22	11	19	20
16	9	11	17
20	8	3	4
16	11	7	8
Sum 77	5	2	11

But besides these common Divisions of the Troy Pound, I find in the Present State of *England*, for the Year 1699, that the Grain is subdivided as following, *viz.* 1 Grain is divided into 20 Mites, 1 Mite into 24 Droites, 1 Droite into 20 Periots, and 1 Periot into 24 Blanks, from which the following Table of Troy Weight is made.

Blanks

Blanks

24	Periot						
480	20	Droite					
11520	480	24	Mite				
230400	9600	480	20	Grain			
5529600	230400	11520	480	24	Penny Weight		
102892000	4608000	230400	9600	480	20	Ounce	
1,234,704,000	55,296,000	2764800	115200	5760	240	12	Pound

These Weights are added together by the following *Rule*.

For every 24 Blanks carry one to the Periots, for every 20 Periots carry 1 to the Droites, for every 24 Droites carry one to the Mites, for every 20 Mites carry 1 to the Grains, for every 24 Grains carry one to the Penny Weights, for every 20 Penny Weights carry one to the Ounces, and for every 12 Ounces carry 1 to the Pounds.

E X A M P L E.

	12 Pounds	20 Oun.	24 Pwts.	20 Gr.	24 Mites	20 Droit.	24 Per.	Blanks
To	16	7	9	18	15	17	19	23
Add { 20	5	7	13	16	14	18	16	
02	11	19	19	18	16	15	11	
Total	40	0	17	4	11	1	14	2

Now seeing that by this Table a Grain contains two Hundred and thirty Thousand, four Hundred Parts, or Blanks, surely the Commodities that have been sold by these Weights must have been of great Value, as that they themselves must be real Atoms, or at least as small as one particle of the finest kind of Sand. But this Example I give you more for Curiosity than real Use.

By Avoirdupoife Weight all kind of heavy Commodities are sold, as Iron, Lead, Brafs, Copper, Grocery Wares, &c. whose smallest part is called a Dram, of which 16 make one Ounce, 16 Ounces one Pound, and 112 Pounds one Hundred Weight, 56 Pounds half a Hundred, and 28 a quarter of a Hundred.

P. *Pray is the Pound Troy, and Pound Avoirdupoife equal to each other?*

M. No. The Pound Avoirdupoife is equal to one Pound two Ounces and 12 Penny Weights, of Troy Weight, and the Pound Troy, is but nearly 13 Ounces 2 Drams and a half of Avoirdupoife; so that the Pound Avoirdupoife is about two Ounces 13 Drams and a half Avoirdupoife, greater than the Troy Pound, which is very near a sixth part of a Pound Avoirdupoife, less than a Pound Avoirdupoife. And therefore six Pound of Bread, which is sold by Troy Weight, is very little heavier than five Pound of Butter or Cheese, which is sold by Avoirdupoife Weight. So that those who believe the Pound Troy and Pound Avoirdupoife to be equal, are much mistaken; but, however, though the Pound Troy is less than the Pound Avoirdupoife, yet the Ounce Troy is heavier than the Ounce Avoirdupoife, for 292 which are the number of Penny Weights in 14 Ounces 12 Penny Weights, which are equal to one Pound Avoirdupoife, being divided into 16 equal Parts, each Part will be found to be but 18, and five sixteenths, which are the Number of Penny Weights in one Ounce Avoirdupoife, of which the Ounce Troy contains 20.

N. B.

N. B. The Hundred Weight Troy, is 100 lb. the half Hundred 50 lb. and quarter of a Hundred 25 lb.

The following is a Table of Avoirdupoife Weights.

Drams					
16	Ounce				
256	16	Pound			
7168	448	28	Quarter of a Hundred		
14336	896	56	2	Half a Hundred	
28672	1792	112	4	2	A Hundred
573440	35840	2240	80	40	20 A Ton Weight

XX. *Addition of Avoirdupoife Weight.*

Thefe Weights are added together by the following *Rule.*

For every 16 Drams carry 1 to the Ounces; for every 16 Ounces carry 1 to the Pounds; for every 28 Pounds carry 1 to the Quarters; for every 4 Quarters carry 1 to the Hundreds; and for every 20 Hundred carry 1 to the Tons.

EXAMPLE.

A Smith made five parcels of Iron-works;

	To.	H.	Q.	P.	Oz.	Dr.	
The firft weighed	7	15	3	27	13	14	
The Second	2	11	2	14	10	11	I demand the to-
The Third	9	19	1	9	7	15	tal Weight of the
The Fourth	27	15	2	25	12	9	whole.
The Fifth	18	17	1	11	15	15	
Anfwer	67	0	0	5	13	00	

P. Pray why is this kind of Weight called Avoirdupoife?

M. From the *French, Have your Weight*; that is, you fhall have *full Weight*, and therefore the 12 Pounds over and above 100 are added.

P. Pray is the Troy Pound divided in any other manner than the preceding?

M. No: but the Troy Ounce is, by Apothecaries, as follows, *viz.* Firft into 8 Parts, called Drams, a Dram into 3, called Scruples, and a Scruple into 20, called Grains; therefore

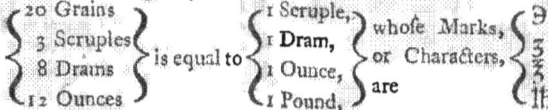

Note, That by thefe Weights, Medicines are compounded, but Drugs are bought and fold by Avoirdupoife Weight.

From the Pound Troy, all the Meafures of Capacity were taken; a Pound of Wheat filling that which was called a Pint: but in regard to the Difference that was found in Wheats, which were fome of more material Subftance and Space than others, and thereby filled more or lefs Space, as fome but 286, and others 288 folid Inches; it was therefore ftated by Parliament, that 282 folid Inches, fhould be equal to one Gallon of Beer Meafure; and 231 folid Inches, to one Gallon of Wine Meafure; and from hence it follows, firft in Beer Meafure, that 2 Pints make 1 Quart; 2 Quarts one Pottle; 2 Pottles 1 Gallon; 8 Gallons 1 Bufhel;

1 Bufhel ; 9 Gallons 1 Firkin ; 2 Firkins 1 Kilderkin ; 2 Kilderkins 1 Barrel ; 63 Gallons 1 Hogfhead ; and 2 Hogfheads one Pipe or Butt ; and therefore

Pint		35 and 1 quarter
Quart		70 and 1 half
Pottle		141
Gallon		282
One { Bufhel	contains	2156 } folid Inches.
Firkin		2438
Kilderkin		4876
Barrel		9752
Hogfhead		17762
Butt		35532

II. In Wine Meafure, that 18 Gallons and half make 1 Runlet of Wine ; 42 Gallons 1 Tierce, or third part of a Pipe , 84 Gallons 1 Tertian, or third part of a Tun ; 63 Gallons one Hogfhead ; 2 Hogfheads 1 Pipe ; 2 Pipes one Tun ; and therefore

Pint		28 and 7 Eighths
Quart		57 and 3 Quarters
Gallon		231
One { Runlet	contains	4273 and half } folid Inches.
Tierce		9702
Tertian		19404
Hogfhead		14553
Pipe		29106
Tun		58212

Example I.

XXI. *Addition of Beer Meafure.*

Bn. K. F. G.

Four Veffels contain thefe feveral Quantities, I demand the total Sum of the whole.

$$\left\{ \begin{array}{cccc} 3 & 1 & 3 & 8 \\ 2 & 0 & 3 & 7 \\ 4 & 1 & 2 & 6 \\ 5 & 0 & 2 & 7 \end{array} \right.$$

Total 16　0　1-1

Rule. For every 9 Gallons carry 1 to the Firkins ; for every 2 Firkins carry 1 to the Kilderkins ; for every 2 Kilderkins carry 1 to the Barrels, which add as Integers.

Note, That altho' 4 Firkins of 9 Gallons each, which are equal to 36 Gallons, make 1 Barrel of Beer ; yet a Barrel of Ale contains but 32 Gallons.

Example II.

B. Hhs. Gal.

Four Veffels contain thefe feveral Quantities, I demand the Total.

$$\left\{ \begin{array}{ccc} 3 & 1 & 53 \\ 7 & 0 & 61 \\ 5 & 1 & 27 \\ 9 & 1 & 39 \end{array} \right.$$

Total 26　1　54

Rule. For every 63 Gallons carry 1 to the Hogfheads ; for every 2 Hogfheads carry 1 to the Butts, and add the Butts as Integers.

XXII. *Addition of Wine Meafure.*

Tu.	Pip.	Ter.	Tier.	Run.	Gal.	Qu.
5	1	1	1	1	37	3
7	0	1	1	0	40	2
7	1	0	0	1	41	3
2	1	1	1	0	39	2
Total 24	1	0	0	0	33	2

Four Veffels contain thefe Quantities, I demand the Total.

Rule. For every 4 Qu. carry 1 to the Gallons ; for every 42 Gallons carry 1 to the Runlets ; for every 2 Runlets carry 1 to the Tierces ; for every 2 Tierces carry 1 to the Tertians,

Tertians, for every 1 and half Tertian, carry 1 to the Pipes ; for every 2 Pipes, carry 1 to the Tons, and add the Tons as Integers.

XXIII. *Addition of Dry Measure.*

Note, That 4 Bushels make one Sack or Comb ; 2 Combs 1 Quarter ; 4 Quarters one Chaldron of Corn ; 5 Quarters 1 Wey ; 2 Weys 1 Last.

E X A M P L E I.

Chal. Quar. Comb. Bush. Gall.

	Chal.	Quar.	Comb.	Bush.	Gall.	
Collect these several Quantities into one Sum, *viz.*	9	1	1	3	7	*Rule.*
	5	0	0	2	6	For every 8 Gallons carry 1 to the Bushels ;
	7	3	1	3	5	for every 4 Bushels carry 1 to the Combs ;
	2	2	1	3	7	for every 2 Combs
Total	25	1	0	2	1	

carry 1 to the Quarters ; for every 4 Quarters carry 1 to the Chaldrons, and add them as Integers.

E X A M P L E II.

Lasts. Weys. Quar. Bush. Gall.

	Lasts.	Weys.	Quar.	Bush.	Gall.	
Collect these several Quantities into one Sum, *viz.*	7	1	4	7	7	*Rule.*
	5	1	3	6	5	For every 8 Gallons carry 1 to the Bushels ;
	2	0	4	7	7	for every 8 Bushels carry 1 to the Quar-
	7	1	3	5	6	ters ; for every 5
Total	23	1	2	4	1	

Quarters carry 1 to the Weys ; for every 2 Weys carry 1 to the Lasts, and add the Lasts as Integers.

Note, A Chaldron of Coals is 36 Bushels, and one Hundred of *Scotch* Coals, 112 Pound, Avoirdupoise.

XXIV. *Addition of Decimals.*

Note here, the Integer is divided into ten equal Parts.

Integ. 10ths.

	Integ.	10ths.	
Collect these several Quantities together, *viz.*	271	9	
	541	7	*Rule.*
	32	9	For every 10 in the 10ths carry
	11	8	1 to the Integers, which add as
	6	4	before taught.
	7	9	
Total	872	6	

Note, Decimals are usually expressed by having Fractional Parts separated from the Integers by a Comma, which is called a Separatrix, as in the Margin ; where the aforesaid Example is expressed in that manner.

271,9
511,7
32,9
11,8
6,4
7,9

872,6

XXV. *Addition of Duodecimals.*

Note, As in Decimals, the Integer is divided into 10 equal Parts ; so here in Duodecimals the Integer is divided into twelve equal Parts (as the Inches in a Foot, or Pence in a Shilling). It is also to be noted, that in many Cases not only the 12ths are divided again into 12 Parts called Primes, but each Prime into 12 again, called Seconds, and every Second, in like manner, into 12, which are called Thirds, &c. which are denoted by Dashes over them, according to their Place or Value As for Example, 10 Primes are expressed thus, 10' ; 10 Seconds, thus, 10'' ; 10 Thirds, thus, 10''', &c.

D

Collect

′ ″ ‴

Collect into one Sum the following Quantities, *viz*. {	10	10	10	11
	9	11	7	10
	5	9	4	7
	2	7	11	11

Rule.

For every 12 Thirds carry 1 to the Seconds; and the same from the Seconds to the Primes; and from the Primes to the Integers, which add as before taught.

Total 29 3 11 3

XXVI. *Addition of Degrees and Minutes.*

Note, A Degree is divided into 60 equal Parts, called Minutes.

Deg. Min.

Collect into one Sum these several Degrees and Minutes, *viz*. {	27	59
	2	47
	7	59
	9	42
	8	55

Rule.

For every 60 Minutes carry 1 to the Degrees, and add them as Integers.

Total 57 22

XXVII. *Addition of Time.*

Note, A Year is supposed to be divided into 12 equal Months; a Month into 4 equal Weeks; a Week into 7 Days, of 24 Hours each; an Hour into 60 Minutes, and a Minute into 60 Seconds.

	Years.	Mon.	Weeks.	Days.	Hours.	Min.	Sec.
Collect into one Sum these several Quantities of Time, *viz*. {	17	11	3	6	17	57	50
	15	10	2	5	23	55	59
	20	9	3	4	22	40	30

Total 54 7 3 3 16 34 19

XXVIII. *Addition of Sand and Lime.*
Example I. *Of Sand.*

Note, A Load of Sand is 18 heaped Bushels.

Loads. Bush.

Collect into one Sum these several Quantities of Sand, *viz*. {	27	11
	18	17
	15	13
	16	16
	12	9

Rule.

For every 18 Bushels carry 1 to the Loads, and add them as Integers.

Total 91 12

Example II. *Of Lime.*

Note, 25 Bags, which ought to be one Bushel, is accounted one Hundred of Lime; and in many Countries, 30 Bushels is called a Load.

Hund. Bags.

Collect into one Sum these several Quantities of Lime, *viz*. {	2	21
	3	17
	4	24
	5	22

Rule.

For every 25 Bags carry 1 to the Hundreds, which add as Integers.

Total 17 09

Loads. Bush.

Again, collect into one Sum these several Quantities of Lime, *viz*. {	2	17
	3	29
	4	26
	2	18

Rule.

For every 30 Bushels carry 1 to the place of Loads, and add them as Integers.

Total 14 10

XXIX.

XXIX. *Addition of Bricks.*

Note, 500 Bricks make 1 Load.

Loads. Bricks.

Collect thefe four Quantities of Bricks into one Sum,
viz.

2	480
3	472
2	137
5	498

Rule.

For every 500 Bricks carry 1
to the Loads, and add them
as Integers.

Total 15 087

XXX. *Addition of Timber and Planks.*

Note, That 50 folid Feet make 1 Load.

Loads. Feet.

Collect into one Sum thefe
feveral Quantities of Timber,
viz.

2	45
3	42
2	28
1	37
2	49

Rule.

For every 50 Feet carry 1
to the Loads, and add them
as Integers.

Total 14 01

Note, That in the Addition of Planks, 1 Inch in thicknefs, every 600 Feet
is 1 Load; of 1 Inch and half thicknefs, 400 Feet; of 2 Inches thicknefs,
300 Feet; of 3 Inches thicknefs, 200 Feet; and of 4 Inches thicknefs,
150 Feet.

XXXI. *Addition of folid Yards*

Note, That in 1 folid Yard there are 27 folid Feet.

Yards. Feet.

Collect into one Sum thefe
feveral Quantities, *viz.*

3	26
2	17
4	25
5	26

Rule.

For every 27 Feet carry 1 to
the Yards, and add the Yards
as Integers.

Total 17 13

XXXII. *Addition of Money.*

Note, That *l.* ftands for Pounds; *s.* for Shillings; *d.* for Pence; and *qr.* for
Farthings; with refpect to *Libra,* which fignifies a Pound; *Solidus,* a Shilling; *Denarius,* a Penny; and *Quadrans,* a Farthing.

	l.	*s.*	*d.*	*qr.*	*Rule.*
	12	17	11	3	For every 4 Farthings car-
Collect into one Sum thefe	10	15	9	2	ry 1 to the Pence; for
feveral Sums, *viz.*	12	7	8	3	every 12 Pence carry 1 to
	15	19	11	2	the Shillings; for every
	123	16	7	3	20 Shillings carry 1 to the

Pounds, which add as In-

Total 175 18 1 1 tegers.

As I have thus gone through the Addition of all that is neceffary, I fhall therefore conclude this Lecture with obferving.

1. That a Load of Earth is one folid Yard.
2. A Hundred Weight of Nails, Iron, Brafs, *&c.* is 112 Pound.
3. A Hundred of Deals or Nails, fix Score, or 120.
4. A Bundle of 5 Feet Laths, 100; and 4 Feet in Length, 120, which fhould
be 1 Inch and half in Breadth, and half an Inch in thicknefs.
5. A Fodder of Lead, is 19 Hundred and a half, or 2184 Pounds Avoirdupoife.
6. A Bale of Paper is ten Reams; a perfect Ream, 20 Quires, or 500 Sheets;
1 perfect Quire, 25 Sheets.

	lb.	10ths.
7. A folid or Cubick Foot of fine Gold, weighs ——	1352	4
Ditto of Standard Gold——————————	1180	4
Ditto of Quickfilver —————————	874	9
Ditto of Lead ————————————	707	7
Ditto of fine Silver —————————	693	1
Ditto of Standard Silver ———————	658	3
Ditto of Copper —————————————	562	4
Ditto of Brafs —————————————	521	8
Ditto of Caft Brafs ————————————	500	0
Ditto of Steel —————————————	490	7
Ditto of Iron —————————————	477	5
Ditto of Tin —————————————	457	4
Ditto of Marble —————————————	196	3
Ditto of Glafs —————————————	161	2
Ditto of Alabafter————————————	117	0
Ditto of Ivory —————————————	113	9
Ditto of Clay moderately moift ———————	112	0
Ditto of fandy Gravel of common Moifture ——	96	0
Ditto of Sea Water ————————————	64	1
Ditto of River Water ————————————	62	3
Ditto of Dry Oak ————————————	57	8

8. A circular Foot contains 113 fquare Inches, and one feventh of an Inch; that is, there are fo many fquare Inches in a Circle of one Foot Diameter, which I call a circular Foot, for the fame reafon as a fquare Foot, which makes a fquare Figure, is called a fquare Foot.

9. A folid or Cube Foot, is 1728 folid Inches, that is, 12 Times 144, the fquare Inches in a fquare Foot.

10. A Cylindrical Foot is 1573 folid Inches, and two fevenths of an Inch; that is, 12 times 113 and one feventh, the fquare Inches in a circular Foot.

11. A Cylindrical Foot of Sea Water, is about 50 Pound and a half, and of frefh Water, about 49 Pound and one tenth.

LECT. III. *Of* SUBTRACTION.

M. Subtraction is a Rule for finding the Difference of any two Numbers, by taking or drawing the leffer from the greater, whereby the Difference or excefs (which is called the Remainder) will appear.

P. *Pray what is particularly to be obferved herein?*

M. To take care that you always place the leffer Number under the greater, and that the Units, Tens, &c. of the fubtrahend, be placed under the Units, Tens, Hundreds, &c. of the given Number.

P. *Pray which of the two Numbers are the Subtrahend, and which the given Number?*

M. The greateft is the given Number, and the leffer the Subtrahend, as this Example makes plain.

I. *Subtraction of Integers.*

EXAMPLE I.

Place your Numbers as in the Margin, and beginning at the right hand, fay, 1 from 7, there remains 6, and 2 from 8, remains 6.

Note, if in Subtracting, any want fhould happen, then borrow 10 from the next Place, and for every 10 fo borrowed, carry 1 to the next Place.

From 87 the given Number,
take 21 the Subtrahend,

rem. 66 the Difference or Excefs.

Operation

Operation. First, 3 from 4 remain 1; secondly, 4 from 2 I cannot, but 4 from 12 (for borrowing 10, makes the 2, 12) and there remains 8; thirdly, 1 I borrowed, and 6 is 7, from 5 I cannot, but (borrowing 10 as before) 7 from 15, rest 8. Lastly, 1 that I borrowed, and 5 is 6, from 7, rest 1, so the remains is 1881.

EXAMPLE II.
I bought 7524 Bricks, and have sold 5643, what are remaining?

Answer 1881 remain.

P. *Pray how shall I know when Subtraction is truly performed?*

M. All kinds of Subtraction are proved, by adding the Subtrahend and Remains together, which will be equal to the given Number, if the Subtraction be truly performed. As for example, if 5643, be added to 1881, the remains, their Sum will be 7524, as in the Margin, which being equal to the given Number, the Subtraction is therefore truly performed.

7524 given Number,
5643 Subtrahend.

1881 remains.

7524 Sum of given N° and **Subtrahend.**

Other Examples for Practice.

From 547213
take 439197

remains 108016

Proof 547213

From 772543279
take 619987654

remains 152555625

Proof 772543279

II. *Subtraction of Money.*

EXAMPLE I.

	s.	d.	q.
From	19	11	3
take	17	9	2
rem.	2	2	1
Proof	19	11	3

EXAMPLE II.

	l.	s.	d.
From	272	19	10
take	229	15	9
rem.	43	4	1
Proof	272	19	10

EXAMPLE III.

	l.	s.	d.	q.
From	275	5	1.	2
take	199	19	3	3
rem.	75	5	9	3
Proof	275	5	1	2

EXAMPLE IV.

	l.	s.	d	q.
From	927	5	7	1
take	832	19	8	3
rem.	94	5	10	2
Proof	927	5	7	1

In these last two Examples, at the Farthings you borrow 4, and carry 1 to the Pence, because 4 Farthings make one Penny; at the Pence you borrow 12 and carry 1 to the Shillings, because 12 Pence make 1 Shilling; and at the Shillings you borrow 20 from the Pounds and carry 1 to the Pounds, because 20 Shillings make 1 Pound. The Pounds you subtract as Integers.

III. *Subtraction of Inches and 10ths.*

EXAMPLE I.

Inch.	10ths.
From 372	09
take 245	09
rem. 127	00
Proof 372	09

EXAMPLE II.

Inch.	10ths.
From 342	5
take 213	9
rem. 128	6
Proof 342	5

EXAMPLE III.

Inch.	10ths.
From 971	2
take 725	9
rem. 245	3
Proof 971	2

Here,

Here, at the 10ths, you borrow 10 from the Inches, and carry 1 to the Inches, because 10 Parts make 1 Inch.

IV. *Subtraction of Feet and Inches.*

EXAMPLE I.	EXAMPLE II.	EXAMPLE III.
Feet. Inch.	Feet. Inch.	Feet. Inch.
From 279 5	From 972 3	From 999 8
take 217 11	take 165 7	take 777 11
rem. 61 6	rem. 806 8	rem. 221 9
Proof 279 5	Proof 972 3	Proof 999 8

Here, at the Inches, you borrow 12 Inches, or 1 Foot, from the Feet, and carry 1 to the Feet, because 12 Inches make 1 Foot.

V. *Subtraction of Decimals.*

EXAMPLE I.	EXAMPLE II.	EXAMPLE III.
From 217,9	From 2754,8	From 729,02
take 206,5	take 1234,9	take 561,97
rem. 011,4	rem. 1519,9	rem. 167,05
Proof 217,9	Proof 2754,8	Proof 729,02

Here you subtract the whole as Integers.

VI. *Subtraction of Duodecimals.*

P. *Pray what are Duodecimals?*

M. Duodecimals signify twelfths, and as these Examples are of Feet, Inches, and Parts, you are to observe, that the Inches are each divided into 12 Parts, the same as the Feet are divided into 12 Inches.

EXAMPLE I.			EXAMPLE II.			EXAMPLE III.		
Feet.	Inch.	Parts.	Feet.	Inch.	Parts.	Feet.	Inch.	Parts.
From 12	7	3	From 92	9	9	From 67	2	9
take 07	11	11	take 73	11	11	take 27	10	10
rem. 4	7	4	rem. 18	9	10	rem. 39	3	11
Proof 12	7	3	Proof 92	9	9	Proof 67	2	9

Here, at the Parts and the Inches, you borrow 12, and carry 1 to the Inches, and to the Feet, because 12 Parts make 1 Inch, and 12 Inches 1 Foot.

VII. *Subtraction of Yards, Feet and Inches.*

EXAMPLE I.			EXAMPLE II.			EXAMPLE III.		
Yds.	Feet.	Inch.	Yds.	Feet.	Inch.	Yds.	Feet.	Inch.
From 127	2	7	From 72	1	3	From 172	0	5
take 97	2	11	take 43	2	9	take 99	2	10
rem. 29	2	8	rem. 28	1	6	rem. 72	0	7
Proof 127	2	7	Proof 72	1	3	Proof 172	0	5

Here, you borrow 12 at the Inches, and carry 1 to the Feet; and borrow 3 at the Feet, and carry 1 to the Yards; because 12 inches make 1 Foot, and 3 Feet 1 Yard.

VIII.

VIII. *Subtraction of Cloth Measure.*

EXAMPLE I.			EXAMPLE II.			EXAMPLE III.		
Yds.	Qurs.	Nails.	Yds.	Qurs.	Nails.	Yds.	Qurs.	Nails.
From 527	1	2	From 270	2	1	From 127	3	2
take 399	3	3	take 211	3	2	take 96	3	3
rem. 127	1	3	rem. 58	2	3	rem. 30	3	3
Proof 527	1	2	Proof 270	2	1	Proof 127	3	2

Here, at the Nails, and at the Quarters, you borrow 4, and carry 1 to the Quarters and to the Yards, becaufe 4 Nails make 1 Quarter, and 4 Quarters 1 Yd.

IX. *Subtraction of Flemifh Meafure.*

EXAMPLE I.		EXAMPLE II.		EXAMPLE III.	
Ells.	Inch.	Ells.	Inch.	Ells.	Inch.
From 2794	22	From 37255	18	From 32594	22
take 1372	26	take 27532	20	take 12345	23
rem. 1421	23	rem. 09722	25	rem. 20248	26
Proof 2794	22	Proof 37255	18	Proof 32594	22

Here, at the Inches, you borrow 27 and carry 1 to the Ells, becaufe 27 Inches make one *Flemifh* Ell.

X. *Subtraction of* English *Ells.*

EXAMPLE I.			EXAMPLE II.			EXAMPLE III.		
Ells.	Qurs.	Nails.	Ells.	Qurs.	Nails.	Ells.	Qurs.	Nails.
From 772	2	1	From 987	2	3	From 888	3	2
take 666	4	3	take 912	4	4	take 699	4	3
rem. 105	2	2	rem. 074	2	3	rem. 188	3	3
Proof 772	2	1	Proof 987	2	3	Proof 888	3	2

Here, at the Nails, you borrow 4 and carry 1 to the Quarters, becaufe 4 Nails make 1 Yard. At the Quarters you borrow 5, and carry 1 to the Ells, becaufe 5 Quarters make one *Englifh* Ell.

XI. *Subtraction of Fathoms and Feet.*

EXAMPLE I.		EXAMPLE II.		EXAMPLE III.	
Fath.	Feet.	Fath.	Feet.	Fath.	Feet.
From 729	4	From 999	3	From 3279	4
take 499	5	take 777	4	take 1999	5
rem. 229	5	rem. 221	5	rem. 1279	5
Proof 729	4	Proof 999	3	Proof 3279	4

Here, at the Feet, you borrow 6, and carry 1 to the Fathoms, becaufe 6 Feet make 1 Fathom.

XII. *Subtraction of Statute Poles.*

EXAMPLE I.		EXAMPLE II.		EXAMPLE III.	
Poles.	Feet.	Poles.	Feet.	Poles.	Feet.
From 729	14	From 987	13	From 3729	12
take 666	15	take 599	16	take 1999	15
rem. 062	15½	rem. 387	13½	rem. 1729	13½
Proof 729	14	Proof 987	13	Proof 3729	12

Here you borrow 16 Feet and ½ from the Poles, and carry 1, becaufe 16 Feet and ½ make 1 Statute Pole.

XIII.

XIII. *Subtraction of Woodland Poles.*

EXAMPLE I.	EXAMPLE II.	EXAMPLE III.
Poles. Feet.	Poles. Feet.	Poles. Feet.
From 972 10	From 275 11	From 299 13
take 699 17	take 196 15	take 199 16
rem. 272 11	rem. 78 14	rem. 099 15
Proof 972 10	Proof 275 11	Proof 299 13

Here you borrow 18 from the Poles, and carry 1, becaufe 18 Feet make 1 Woodland Pole.

XIV. *Subtraction of Forest Poles.*

EXAMPLE I.	EXAMPLE II.	EXAMPLE III.
Poles. Feet.	Poles. Feet.	Poles. Feet.
From 1234 15	From 222 19	From 777 13
take 788 20	take 211 20	take 237 19
rem. 445 16	rem. 010 20	rem. 539 15
Proof 1234 15	Proof 222 19	Proof 777 13

Here you borrow 21, and carry 1; becaufe 21 Feet make 1 Foreft Pole.

XV. *Subtraction of Chains and Links.*

EXAMPLE I.	EXAMPLE II.	EXAMPLE III.
Chains. Links.	Chains. Links.	Chains. Links.
From 72 65	From 27 85	From 279 88
take 37 98	take 19 99	take 176 94
rem. 34 67	rem. 07 86	rem. 102 94
Proof 72 65	Proof 27 85	Proof 279 88

Here you borrow 10, and carry 1, as in Integers, becaufe 130 Links make 1 Chain.

XVI. *Subtraction of Miles, Furlongs, Chains and Poles.*

EXAMPLE I.				EXAMPLE II.				EXAMPLE III.			
Mi.	Fur.	Ch.	Po.	Mi.	Fur.	Ch.	Po.	Mi.	Fur.	Ch.	Po.
From 7	2	5	2	From 29	4	7	1	From 127	6	5	2
take 5	7	9	3	take 12	7	8	3	take 99	7	9	3
rem. 1	2	5	3	rem. 16	4	8	2	rem. 27	6	5	3
Proof 7	2	5	2	Proof 29	4	7	1	Proof 127	6	5	2

Here at the Poles, you borrow 4, at the Chains you borrow 10, at the Furlongs you borrow 8, becaufe 4 Poles is 1 Chain, 10 Chains is 1 Furlong, and 8 Furlongs is 1 Mile.

XVII. *Subtraction of Degrees, Leagues, Miles, and Furlongs.*

EXAMPLE I.				EXAMPLE II.				EXAMPLE III.			
Deg.	Lea.	Mi.	Fur.	Deg.	Leg.	Mi.	Fur.	Deg.	Lea.	Mi.	Fur.
From 27	15	1	4	From 127	12	1	5	From 29	15	2	5
take 14	19	2	7	take 99	18	2	6	take 21	19	2	7
rem. 12	15	1	5	rem. 27	13	1	7	rem. 07	15	2	6
Proof 27	15	1	4	Proof 127	12	1	5	Proof 29	15	2	5

Here you borrow 8 at the Furlongs, 3 at the Miles, and 20 at the Leagues, becaufe 8 Furlongs make 1 Mile, 3 Miles 1 League, and 20 Leagues 1 Degree.

XVIII.

XVIII. *Subtraction of Degrees, Minutes, and Seconds.*

EXAMPLE I.			EXAMPLE II.			EXAMPLE III.		
Deg.	Min.	Sec.	Deg.	Min.	Sec.	Deg.	M.	Sec.
From 102	40	49	From 221	47	23	From 28	47	49
take 97	57	54	take 127	55	47	take 19	49	53
rem. 4	42	55	rem. 93	51	36	rem. 08	57	56
Proof 102	40	49	Proof 221	47	23	Proof 28	47	49

Here at the Seconds, and at the Minutes you borrow 60, and carry one to the Minutes and Degrees, becaufe 60 Seconds make 1 Minute, and 60 Minutes 1 Hour.

XIX. *Subtraction of fquare Feet and fquare Inches.*

EXAMPLE I.		EXAMPLE II.		EXAMPLE III.	
Feet.	Inch.	Feet.	Inch.	Feet.	Inch.
From 729	19	From 927	075	From 555	139
take 672	141	take 526	135	take 274	141
rem. 56	22	rem. 400	084	rem. 280	142
Proof 729	19	Proof 927	75	Proof 555	139

Here at the Inches you borrow 144, and carry 1 to the Feet, becaufe that 144 fquare Inches make 1 fquare Foot.

XX. *Subtraction of fquare Feet and long Inches.*

EXAMPLE I.		EXAMPLE II.		EXAMPLE III.	
Feet.	Inch.	Feet.	Inch.	Feet.	Inch.
From 127	7	From 271	05	From 555	04
take 93	11	take 136	10	take 449	10
rem. 33	8	rem. 134	7	rem. 105	6
Proof 127	7	Proof 271	5	Proof 555	04

Here at the Inches you borrow 12 and carry 1, becaufe 12 long Inches (which are each 12 Inches long and 1 wide) make 1 fquare Foot.

XXI. *Subtraction of fquare Yard Meafure.*

EXAMPLE I.		EXAMPLE II.		EXAMPLE III.	
Yds.	Feet.	Yds.	Feet.	Yds.	Feet.
From 73	7	From 92	3	From 27	5
take 51	8	take 57	7	take 18	8
rem. 21	8	rem. 34	4	rem. 08	6
Proof 73	7	Proof 92	3	Proof 27	5

Here at the Feet you borrow 9 and carry 1, becaufe 9 fquare Feet make 1 fquare Yard.

XXII. *Subtraction of folid Yards.*

EXAMPLE I.		EXAMPLE II.		EXAMPLE III.	
From 45	21	From 72	20	From 97	19
take 36	26	take 49	25	take 96	24
rem. 08	22	rem. 22	22	rem. 00	22
Proof 45	21	Proof 72	20	Proof 97	19

Here at the Feet you borrow 27 and carry 1, becaufe 27 folid Feet make 1 folid Yard.

E

XXIII.

XXIII. *Subtraction of Squares, as of Flooring, &c.*

EXAMPLE I.	EXAMPLE II.	EXAMPLE III.
Squ. Feet.	Squ. Feet.	Squ. Feet.
From 25 98	From 29 11	From 127 86
take 15 99	take 21 75	take 97 99
rem. 09 99	rem. 07 36	rem. 29 87
Proof 25 98	Proof 29 11	Proof 127 86

Here at the Feet you borrow 100 and carry 1, because 100 square Feet make 1 Square of Work, as of Flooring, Roofing, Tyling &c.

XXIV. *Subtraction of Land Measures.* I. *Of square Statute Poles.*

EXAMPLE I.	EXAMPLE II.	EXAMPLE III.
Poles. Feet.	Poles. Feet.	Poles. Feet.
From 192 120	From 275 51	From 123 270
take 72 152	take 223 127	take 99 271
rem. 119 240	rem. 51 196	rem. 23 271
Proof 192 120	Proof 275 51	Proof 123 270

Note, That although a Statute square Pole contains 272 square Feet, and one Quarter, yet in these Examples the Quarter of a Foot is rejected, as it usually is in Business, and the square Rod or Pole is allowed at 272 square Feet only; therefore at the Feet, borrow 272 and carry 1.

II. *Of Woodland Poles.*

EXAMPLE I.	EXAMPLE II.	EXAMPLE III.
Poles. Feet.	Poles. Feet.	Poles. Feet.
From 76 311	From 217 199	From 279 138
take 36 320	take 120 220	take 172 219
rem. 39 315	rem. 96 303	rem. 106 243
Proof 76 311	Proof 217 199	Proof 279 138

Here at the Poles you borrow 324 and carry 1, because 324 square Feet make 1 Woodland Pole.

III. *Of Forest Poles.*

EXAMPLE I.	EXAMPLE II.	EXAMPLE III.
Poles. Feet.	Poles. Feet.	Poles. Feet.
From 82 399	From 594 322	From 123 138
take 71 439	take 437 440	take 75 375
rem. 10 401	rem. 156 323	rem. 47 204
Proof 82 399	Proof 594 322	Proof 123 138

Here you borrow 441 and carry 1, because 441 square Feet make 1 square Forest Pole.

XXV. *Subtraction of Acres, Roods and Poles.*

EXAMPLE I.			EXAMPLE II.			EXAMPLE III.		
Acres.	Rds.	Poles.	Acres.	Rds.	Poles.	Acres.	Rds.	Poles.
From 127	2	31	From 27	1	27	From 120	1	19
take 93	3	39	take 18	3	38	take 11	3	35
rem. 33	2	32	rem. 08	1	29	rem. 108	1	24
Proof 127	2	31	Proof 27	1	27	Proof 120	1	19

Here at the Poles you borrow 40 and carry 1, and at the Roods borrow 4 and
carry

carry 1 to the Acres, which subtract as Integers, because 40 Poles make 1 Rood, and 4 Roods 1 Acre.

XXVI. *Subtraction of Troy Weights.*

EXAMPLE I.				EXAMPLE II.				EXAMPLE III.			
lb.	Oun.	Pwt.	Gr.	lb.	Oun.	Pwt.	Gr.	lb.	Oun.	Pwt.	Gr.
From 25	9	14	17	From 21	8	17	12	From 127	5	5	5
take 17	11	19	18	take 17	10	19	14	take 83	10	17	12
rem. 07	9	14	23	rem. 03	9	18	22	rem. 43	6	7	17
Proof 25	9	14	17	Proof 21	8	17	12	Proof 127	5	5	5

Here at the Grains you borrow 24, at the Penny Weights 20, and 12 at the Ounces, because 24 Grains make 1 Penny Weight, and 20 Penny Weights 1 Ounce, and 12 Ounces 1 Pound.

XXVII. *Subtraction of Apothecaries Weights.*

EXAMPLE I.					EXAMPLE II.				
lb.	Oun.	Dr.	Scr.	Gr.	lb.	Oun.	Dr.	Scr.	Gr.
From 12	9	4	1	15	From 127	5	3	1	17
take 9	11	7	2	19	take 99	10	7	2	18
rem. 2	9	4	1	16	rem. 27	6	3	1	19
Proof 12	9	4	1	15	Proof 127	5	3	1	17

Here at the Grains you borrow 20, at the Scruples 3, at the Drams 8, and 12 at the Ounces, because 20 Grains make 1 Scruple, 3 Scruples 1 Dram, 8 Drams 1 Ounce, and 12 Ounces 1 Pound.

XXVIII. *Subtraction of Avoirdupoise Weights.*

EXAMPLE I.					EXAMPLE II.				
Hun.	Qurs.	lb.	Oun.	Dr.	Hun.	Qurs.	lb.	Oun.	Dr.
From 27	2	21	13	10	From 25	1	18	7	11
take 21	3	27	15	15	take 17	3	24	14	12
rem. 05	2	21	13	11	rem. 07	1	21	8	15
Proof 27	2	21	13	10	Proof 25	1	18	7	11

Here, at the Drams and at the Ounces you borrow 16, at the Pounds 28, and 4 at the Quarters, because 16 Drams make 1 Ounce, 16 Ounces 1 Pound, 28 Pounds 1 Quarter of a Hundred, and 4 Quarters 1 Hundred.

XXIX. *Subtraction of Beer Measure.*

EXAMPLE I.					EXAMPLE II.	
Bar.	Kilder.	Fir.	Gall.	Quarts	Hog.	Gall.
From 27	0	0	2	1	From 22	57
take 18	1	1	3	3	take 18	62
rem. 08	0	0	7	2	rem. 03	58
Proof 27	0	0	2	1	Proof 22	57

In Example I. borrow 4 at the Quarts, 9 at the Gallons, 2 at the Firkins and at the Kilderkins, because 4 Quarts make 1 Gallon, 9 Gallons 1 Firkin, 2 Firkins 1 Kilderkin, and 2 Kilderkins 1 Barrel.

In Example II. at the Gallons borrow 63, because 63 Gallons make 1 Hogshead.

E 2

XXX. *Subtraction of Wine Measures.*

EXAMPLE I.					EXAMPLE II.			
	Tuns	Pipes	Tier.	Gall.		Tuns	Pipes	Tier.	Gall.
From	57	0	1	35	From	20	0	1	27
take	52	1	2	40	take	15	1	1	41
rem.	4	0	1	37	rem.	4	0	2	28
Proof	57	0	1	35	Proof	20	0	1	27

Here at the Gallons you borrow 42, at the Tierces 3, and 2 at the Pipes, becaufe 42 Gallons make 1 Tierce, 3 Tierces 1 Pipe, 2 Pipes 1 Ton.

XXXI. *Subtraction of Dry Measure.*

EXAMPLE.

	Quarters	Sacks	Bufh.	Pecks	Gall.	Quarts.
From	50	0	2	2	0	2
take	39	1	3	3	1	3
rem.	10	0	2	2	0	3
Proof	50	0	2	2	0	2

Here you borrow 4 at the Quarts, 2 at the Gallons, 4 at the Pecks and Bufhels, and 2 at the Sacks; becaufe 4 Quarts make 1 Gallon, 2 Gallons 1 Peck, 4 Pecks 1 Bufhel, 4 Bufhels 1 Sack, and 2 Sacks 1 Quarter.

XXXII. *Subtraction of Timber.*

EXAMPLE I.		EXAMPLE II.		EXAMPLE III.	
Loads	Feet	Loads	Feet	Loads	Feet
From 123	44	From 57	38	From 75	38
take 117	49	take 26	39	take 25	47
rem. 005	45	rem. 30	49	rem. 49	41
Proof 123	44	Proof 57	38	Proof 75	38

Here at the Feet you borrow 50, becaufe 1 Load of Timber contains 50 folid Feet.

XXXIII. *Subtraction of Plank 1 Inch thick.*

Note, 600 Square Feet at one Inch thick, make 1 Load.

EXAMPLE I.		EXAMPLE II.		EXAMPLE III.	
Loads	Feet	Loads	Feet	Loads	Feet
From 127	425	From 372	472	From 725	500
take 38	599	take 263	525	take 632	584
rem. 88	426	rem. 108	547	rem. 092	516
Proof 127	425	Proof 372	472	Proof 725	500

Here at the Feet you borrow 600, becaufe 600 Feet make 1 Load, as aforefaid.

Note, If the Thicknefs of Plank be 1 Inch and half thick, then borrow 400; if two Inches thick, borrow 300; if three Inches thick, borrow 200; and laftly if four Inches borrow 150, becaufe

$$\left.\begin{matrix}400\\300\\200\\150\end{matrix}\right\} \text{Feet at} \left\{\begin{matrix}1\text{ Inch and }\frac{1}{2}\\2\text{ Inches}\\3\text{ Inches}\\4\text{ Inches}\end{matrix}\right\} \left.\begin{matrix}\text{thicknefs}\\\text{make one}\\\text{Load of}\\\text{Plank.}\end{matrix}\right.$$

XXXIV.

XXXIV. *Subtraction of Bricks.*
Note, 500 make 1 Load.

EXAMPLE I. Loads Bricks	EXAMPLE II. Loads Bricks	EXAMPLE III. Loads Bricks
From 27 491	From 14 057	From 23 372
take 13 499	take 21 451	take 14 428
rem. 13 492	rem. 01 106	rem. 08 444
Proof 27 491	Proof 14 057	Proof 23 372

Here at the Place of Bricks you borrow 500, and carry 1, becaufe 500 **Bricks** make 1 Load.

XXXV. *Subtraction of Lime.*

EXAMPLE I. Hund. Bags	EXAMPLE II. Hund. Bags	EXAMPLE III. Hund. Bags
From 27 19	From 22 19	From 18 15
take 14 24	take 17 21	take 11 21
rem. 12 20	rem. 04 23	rem. 06 19
Proof 27 19	Proof 22 19	Proof 18 15

Here at the Bags you borrow 25 and carry 1, becaufe 25 Bags (which ought to be a Bufhel each) make a Load of Lime.

XXXVI. *Subtraction of Sand.*

EXAMPLE I. Loads Bufh.	EXAMPLE II. Loads Bufh.	EXAMPLE III. Loads Bufh.
From 18 16	From 21 11	From 29 12
take 15 17	take 20 16	take 25 15
rem. 02 17	rem. 00 13	rem. 03 15
Proof 18 16	Proof 21 11	Proof 29 12

XXXVII. *Subtraction of Time.*
EXAMPLE.

	Months	Weeks	Days	Hours	Min.	Seconds
From	11	2	20	20	41	53
take	10	3	26	23	59	59
rem.	00	2	21	20	41	54
Proof	11	2	20	20	41	53

M. As I have now given you a fufficient Number of Examples of all the various Kinds of Bufinefs in general, and which I think are much more copious than has been yet taught by all the Mafters that have wrote on Arithmetic, I fhall now proceed to Multiplication.

LECT. *Of* MULTIPLICATION.

P. *What is Multiplication?*

M. By Multiplication is meant an Increafe, and therefore to multiply is to increafe from a fmall Number to a greater; and which being confidered, is no more than the adding of divers Numbers together.

For

7
7
7
—
21
—

For if 3 times 7 be added together the Sum is 21, as in the Margin: And if 3 be multiplied into 7, the Product is 21 also. Hence 'tis plain that Multiplication is nothing more than a compendious Manner of adding Numbers together, and therefore may be called short Addition.

P. *Pray, what is principally to be observed herein ?*

M. Three Numbers or Members, which are called the Multiplicand, the Multiplicator or Multiplier, and the Product.

P. *Pray, what is the Multiplicand, Multiplier, and Product ?*

M. In every Multiplication, there are always two Numbers given to be multiplied into each other, which are called the Multiplicand and the Multiplier, or Multiplicator, either of which being placed uppermost is called the Multiplicand, and the lower the Multiplier ; as for Example, if 8 be multiplied into 9, as at A, then 8 is the Multiplicand and 9 the Multiplier ; or if 9 be multiplied into 8, as at B, then 9 is the Multiplicand, and 8 the Multiplier, and the Number 2, arising by 9 times 8, and by 8 times 9, is called the Product. But however as it is best to make the greatest Number of the two the Multiplicand, therefore it is most usually done, observing to place the Units, Tens, &c. of the Multiplier, under the Units, Tens, &c. of the Multiplicand.

'A 8 Multiplicand
   9 Multiplier
   —
  72 Product

B 9 Multiplicand
   8 Multiplier
   —
  72 Product

I. *Multiplication of Integers.*

P. *How is Multiplication performed ?*

M. The Multiplication of Integers is performed by the following Rules.

Rule I.

Write down the Multiplicand and Multiplier under each other as aforesaid, and draw a Line under the Multiplier to separate it from the Product, that arises from its first Figure.

Rule II.

Multiply every Figure of the Multiplier into the Multiplicand, observing as you proceed to carry one for every Ten, to the next Place, and set the Remains under it, and the Products arising from the several Figures of the Multiplier being added together, their Sum is the general Product of the whole Multiplication.

Rule III.

When the Multiplier consists of many Figures, as in the following Example, the Product arising from each Figure is to be placed by itself in such manner that the first or right hand Figure thereof may stand under that Figure of the Multiplicator from which the said Product arises.

These will be made familiar by the following Example.

EXAMPLE. *Multiply 7254, by 7349, which place as in the Margin.*

7254
7349

65286 A
29016 B
21762 C
50778 D
———
53,309,646

Begin with 9 the first Figure of the Multiplier, and thereby multiply all the Figures in the Multiplicand as follows. First say 9 times 4 is 36, set down 6 and carry 3, for the three Tens ; then say 9 times 5 is 45, and 3 I carry is 48, set down 8 and carry 4 ; then 9 times 2 is 18, and 4 I carry is 22, set down 2 and carry 2 ; then 9 times 7 is 63, and 2 I carry is 65, which being the last in the Multiplication therefore set down 65, and that Product will be 65286, as at A. Proceed in the same manner to multiply the remaining three Figures of the Multiplier, 4, 3, and 7, into the Multiplicand, and their Products will be as at B, C and D, and which with that of A, being added together, will be 53,309,646, the Product required.

Rule IV.

When Numbers given have one or more Cyphers at the right Hand, the Multiplication may be performed, without Regard being had to the Cyphers, until the Product of the other Figures be found, to which they are then to be annexed.

I

———As

——As for Example, multiply 17 by 60, as at A; 2790 by 500, as at B; 237000 by 25, as at C; which being placed as in the Margin, and Multiplication of the fignificant Figures being made, without any Regard being had to the Cyphers; unto the Sum of their Products, annex or add thereto as many Cyphers, as belong to both Multiplicand and Multiplier: fo to 102, in Example A, you add one Cypher, making the Product 1020: and in Example B, to 1395, the Produce of 279, multiplied by 5, you add 3 Cyphers, which makes the whole 1395000; and fo in like manner 5925; in Example C, by the Addition of 3 Cyphers, belonging to the Multiplicand, the Product is made 5925000.

```
17  A          273|000
6|0             25|  C
               ————
102|0          1185
               474
279|0  B       ————
  5|co         5925|000
————
1395|000
```

RULE V.

When Multiplication has any Cyphers intermixt with its other Figures, the Cyphers need not be regarded; as for Inftance, the Product 1856476665, is produced by the Products at A, B, C, which arifes by the 7, 1, and 2 of the Multiplier, multiplied into the Multiplicand, without regard being had to the Cyphers in the Multiplier.

```
      92745
      20017

A  649215
B   92745
C  185490
  ——————
  1856476665
```

In Multiplication it is of very great ufe to know readily the Product of any two of the nine Digits or Figures; for which Purpose this Table muft be learnt perfectly by Heart.

MULTIPLICATION TABLE.

The Ufe of this Table is eafy. Suppofe the Product of 8 is required; look for 8 on the Side and 9 on the Top, and againft thofe Numbers in the Angle of Meeting is 72, the Product required. So 7 times 9 is 63, and 5 times 12 is 60, as in the Angles of Meeting you will find, and fo of all other Numbers.

1	2	3	4	5	6	7	8	9	12
2	4	6	8	10	12	14	16	18	24
3	6	9	12	15	18	21	24	27	36
4	8	12	16	20	24	28	32	36	48
5	10	15	20	25	30	35	40	45	60
6	12	18	24	30	36	42	48	54	72
7	14	21	28	35	42	49	56	63	84
8	16	24	32	40	48	56	64	72	96
9	18	27	36	45	54	63	72	81	108
12	24	36	48	60	72	84	96	108	144

E x a m p l e s *for Practice.*

EXAMPLE I.	EXAMPLE II.	EXAMPLE III.
Mult. 27960	Mult. 972403	Mult. 7235
By 200	By 30007	By 1000
5592,000 Prod.	6806821	7235000 Prod.
	2917209	
	2917889682 1 Prod.	

In the firſt Example I contracted my Work, by placing the 2 of the Multiplier under the Units of the Multiplicand, which ſhould always be done, when the other Figures of the Multiplier to the right Hand are all Cyphers. In the ſecond Example I contracted my Work, by omitting the Cyphers in the Multiplier, and multiplying only by the 7 and the 3. In the third Example, I add three Cyphers to the Multiplicand, becauſe one neither multiplies or divides.

Multiplication of Integers may be performed without giving any Trouble to the Mind, in carrying on the Tens, according to the Rule I. as follows.

E X A M P L E I.

Multiply 8342 by 7, as in the Margin.

8342
7
———
52214
618
———
58394

Operation. Firſt, 7 times 2 is 14, which ſet down; then 7 times 4 is 28, which ſet down, 2 before the 1, and 8 under the 1; then 7 times 3 is 21, ſet 2 before the 2, and 1 under; then 7 times 8 is 56, ſet 5 before the laſt 2, and 6 under; laſtly, add the two Numbers 52214, and 618 together, as they ſtand, their Sum will be the true Product required.

E x a m p l e II. Multiply 98254, by 3729, as in the Margin.

98254
3729

871436 } Product of the 9.
1285   }
110108 } Product of the 2.
8640   }
651328 } Product of the 7.
3645   }
220112 } Product of the 3.
7465   }

366389166 Product of the whole.

98254 A
3729

884286 Product of the 9.
196508 Product of the 2.
687778 Product of the 7.
294762 Product of the 3.

366389166 Product of the whole as before.

The Operation of this Example is the ſame as the laſt, only it is 4 times repeated; and when the Product of any Figure is leſs than 10, place a Cypher in the Place, where if it had made 10, or more than 10, the Figure for 10, or above 10, muſt have ſtood, as you will ſee in the Product that ariſes by 2, the ſecond Figure of the Multiplier.

For a Proof of this manner of working, I have ſubjoined the ſame Example, worked after the common Method, as at A.

As I have thus explained the Multiplication of Integers, you are to obſerve, that therein is this *Analogy, viz.* As an Unit is to the Multiplier, ſo is the Multiplicand to the Product.

P. *Pray*

P. *Pray explain this, for at present I don't conceive what you mean.*

M. I will: by this Example. Suppoting one Load of Timber coft 50 Shillings, how much will 12 Loads coft?

If 12 Loads be multiplied by 50 Shillings, as in the Margin, the Product, 600 Shillings, is the Anfwer: and therefore one Load being confidered as an Unit, bears the fame Proportion to 50 Shillings, the Multiplier, as 12 Loads, the Multiplicand, do to 600 Shillings the Product.

```
        12
        50
       ---
       600
```

P. *'Tis very true, Sir; pray proceed, for you make Multiplication a Pleafure to me.*

M. The next in order is to fhew you, how in many Cafes you may contract your Multiplications as follows.

CONTRACTION I. *To multiply any given Number (fuppofe 547) by 11.*

Rule. Set down the Multiplicand twice, the lower one being removed one place, either towards the right or left Hand, as at A and B, where at A 'tis placed one place towards the left Hand, and at B, one place towards the right Hand.

```
    A 547      547 B
      547      547
      ----     ----
     6017      6017
```

CONTRACTION II. *To multiply any given Number (fuppofe 7925) by 12, 13, 14, &c.*

Rule. Multiply the Figures in the Multiplicand, by the Units in the Multiplier, obferving, as you proceed, to add that Figure of the Multiplicand, which ftands next on the right Hand, to the Product of the Figure you multiply by. As for Example, multiply 7925, by 14, as in the Margin.

Firft, 4 times 5 is 20, fet down 0, and carry 2; then 4 times 2 is 8, and 2 I carry is 10; and 5 at *a*, being the next Figure on the right Hand of 2, which you are then multiplying, make 15, fet down 5 and carry 1; then 4 times 9 is 36, and 1 I carry is 37; and 2, the next Figure on the Right at *b*, is 39, fet down 9 and carry 3; then 4 times 7 is 28, and 3 I carry is 31; and 9 the next Figure to the Right at *c*, is 40, fet down 0 and carry 4. Now, as there are no more Figures in the Multiplicand, to add the 4 carried unto, therefore adding the 7 to the laft Figure 7 at *d*, makes 11, which fet down, and the Product is 110950, as required.

```
    dcba
    7925
      14
   ------
  110950
```

CONTRACTION III. *To multiply any given Number (fuppofe 99725) by 111, 112, 113, 114, 115, &c.*

Rule. Multiply the Figures in the Multiplicand by the Units in the Multiplier, and as you proceed, add the *two Figures* of the Multiplicand, which ftand next on the right Hand, to the Product of the Figure you multiply by: as for Example, multiply 99725, by 115, as in the Margin.

Firft, 5 times 5 is 25, fet down 5 and carry 2; then 5 times 2 is 10, and 2 I carry is 12, and 5 at *a* is 17, fet down 7 and carry 1; then 5 times 7 is 35, and 1 I carry is 36, and 2 at *b* is 38, and 5 at *a* is 43; fet down 3 and carry 4; then 5 times 9 is 45, and 4 I carry is 49, and 7 at *c* is 56, and 2 at *b* is 58, fet down 8 and carry 5; then 5 times 9 is 45, and 5 I carry is 50, and 9 at *d* is 59, and 7 at *e* is 66, fet down 6 and carry 6; then 6 I carry, and 9 at *e* is 15, and 9 at *d* is 24, fet down 4 and carry 2, which being added to 9 at *c*, makes 11, which fet down, and which makes the Product 11468375, as required.

```
     edcba
     99725
       115
  --------
  11468375
```

CONTRACTION IV. *To multiply any given Number (fuppofe 725432) by 101, 102, 103, 104, &c.*

Rule. Multiply the Figures in the Multiplicand by the Units of the Multiplier, and as you proceed, add that Figure of your Multiplicand that ftands next the right Hand, except one, unto the Product of that Figure you multiply by: as for Example, multiply 725432 by 109, as in the Margin.

F

f e d c b a First, 9 times 2 is 18, set down 8 and carry 1 ; then 9 times 3 is
725432 27, and 1 I carry is 28, set down 8 and carry 2 ; then 9 times 4 is
109 36, and 2 I carry is 38, and 2 at *a* is 40, set down 0 and carry 4 ;
——— then 9 times 5 is 45, and 4 I carry is 49, and 3 at *b* is 52, set down 2
79072088 and carry 5 ; then 9 times 2 is 18, and 5 I carry is 23, and 4 at *c* is
——— 27, set down 7 and carry 2 ; then 9 times 7 is 63, and 2 I carry is
65, and 5 at *d* is 70, set down 0 and carry 7 ; now 7 I carry, and 2 at *e* is 9, set
down 9 ; and because you have nothing to carry to the 7 at *f*, therefore set down
'7, and the Product will be 79072088, the Product required.

II. *Multiplication of Decimals.*

M. Multiplication of Decimals, both in placing the Multiplicand and Multiplier, is the same as the Multiplication of Integers, only when your Work is
completed, you must observe, that with the dash of your Pen you cut off as many
places of Decimals in your Product, as there are places of Decimals both in your
Multiplicand and Multiplier, and in case of want in your Product, prefix Cyphers
to the left Hand.

It is also to be observed, First, that it will be convenient to make that Num-
ber the Multiplicand, which contains the most Places, though sometimes it may
be less in Quantity. Secondly, that if the Multiplicand and Multiplier be both
Decimals, that is, both Parts of Integers, the Product will be a Decimal.
Thirdly, if Multiplicand and Multiplier be mixed, that is, Integers and Decimal
Parts of Integers, the Product will be mixed. Lastly, if the Multiplicand and
Multiplier be mixed, and the other a Decimal, the Product will be sometimes
mixed, and sometimes a Decimal.

EXAMPLE I.	EXAMPLE II.	EXAMPLE III.
Of Decimals alone.	Of Integ. and Decimals.	Where the Multiplicand is mixed, and Multiplier a Decimal.
,7432	7,2345	72,4072
,713	1,25	,357
22296	361725	
7432	144690	5068494
52024	72345	3640350
		2172216
Facit 5299016	Facit 9|042125	
		25	8693594

In Example I. of Decimals alone, the Product is, 5299016, that is, it is
5299016 Parts of an Integer, or 1, divided into 10,000,000 Parts, because the
Denominator of every Decimal consists of as many Places of Cyphers annexed
to 1, as there are Places in the Decimal.

In Example II. there being 7 Places of Decimals in the Multiplicand, I therefore have cut off 7 Places of Figures from the Product, and the Product is 9 Integers, and ,042125 Parts of an Integer, divided into 10,000,000 Parts.

In Example III. I have also cut off 7 Places of Decimals, because there are
4 Places in the Multiplicand, and 3 in the Multiplier, and the Product is 25 Integers, and ,8693594 Parts of an Integer, divided into 10,000,000 Parts.

III. *Multiplication of Duodecimals, vulgarly called Cross Multiplication.*

As in Decimal Multiplication, the Integer is divided into 10 ; so here it is divided into 12 Parts, as a Shilling into 12 Pence, or a Foot into 12 Inches.———
In the following Examples I suppose the Integers to be Feet ; and the Duodecimals Inches. As this kind of Multiplication may be performed, as well by taking
the aliquot or even Parts of 12, out of the Multiplicand, as will be immediately
shewn, as by multiplying the Multiplier into the Multiplicand ; before I proceed
any farther, you are to observe, that the aliquot (which are the even) Parts of a
Foot, are as follow, *viz.* In 12 there is twice 6, three times 4, four times 3, six
times

times 2, eight times 1 and ¼, and 12 times 1 ; and therefore, 6 is a half, 4 is one third, 3 is one quarter, 2 is one sixth, 1 and half one eight, and 1 one twelfth.———
In this kind of Multiplication there is a great Variety, as follows.

I. *To multiply Feet, Inches, and Parts, into Inches, by aliquot Parts.*

Rule. Place under the Multiplicand, the Number of Times that the aliquot Multiplier can be had, in the Feet, Inches and Parts, observing to begin at the left Hand, and for every one that remains at the Feet, more than the Times that the aliquot Multiplier can be had in them, to add 12 to the Inches, and so the like to the Parts, &c.

In Example I. 6 being contained twice in 12, I therefore say the two's in 20 is 10, the two's in 8 is 4, and the two's in 6 is 3 ; so that the Product is 10 Feet, 4 Inches, 3 Parts.

In Example II. 4 being contained 3 times in 12, therefore I say the three's, in 16 is 5 times, and 1 remains, set down 5 under the 16 ; then the 1 remaining being a Foot, equal to 12 Inches, I add it to the 8 Inches which makes 20, and then say, the three's in 20 is 6 times, set down 6 under the Inches, and carry the 2 Inches remaining to the Parts, which 2 being equal to 24 Seconds, and added to the 7, makes 31 Seconds, wherein I find three 10 times, and 1 remains, therefore I set down 10 under the Seconds, and the 1 being one third of 3, the aliquot Part, is equal to 4 Seconds, and the Product to 5 Feet, 6 Inches, 10 Parts, 4 Seconds.

In Example III. 3 Inches being contained 4 Times in 12, I therefore say the fours in 27 is six times, set 6 under 27, and 3 remains, equal to 36, and 11 is 47, which contains 4

EXAMPLE I.

Feet.	Inch.	Parts.
Multiply 20	8	6
By oo	6 Inches	
Product 10	4	3

EXAMPLE II.

Feet.	Inch.	Parts.
Multiply 16	8	7
By	4 Inches	
Product 5	6	10	4

EXAMPLE III.

Feet.	Inch.	Parts.
Multiply 27	11	9
By	3 Inches	
Product 6	11	11	3

11 times, set 11 under Inches, and remain 3, equal to 36, and 9 is 45, which contains 4 11 times ; set 11 under Parts, and the remaining 1, being one Quarter of 4, the aliquot Part is equal to 3 Seconds, and the Product to 6 Feet, 11 Inches, 11 Parts, 3 Seconds.

II. *To multiply Feet, Inches, and Parts, into Inches, by multiplying the Multiplier into the Multiplicand.*

Rule. First, Place a Cypher instead of an Integer, under the Parts of the Multiplicand, and the Inches of the Multiplier, one place farther to the right Hand. Secondly, multiply the Inches of the Multiplier, into the Parts, Inches, and Feet, of the Multiplicand, as if they were Integers or whole Numbers, carrying 1 for every 12, and setting down the first remains, when any, under the Figure you multiply by, &c.

To illustrate the preceding Rule by aliquot Parts, I have here made use of the following Examples.

EXAMPLE I. Feet. Inch. Parts.	EXAMPLE II. Feet. Inch. Parts.	EXAMPLE III. Feet. Inch. Parts.
20 8 6	16 8 7	27 11 9
o 6	o 4	o 3
10 4 3 o	5 6 10 4	6 11 11 3

In Example I. 6 times 6 is 36, set down o, and carry 3, then 6 times 8 is 48,

and

and 3 I carry is 51, set down 3 and carry 4; then 6 times 20 is 120, and 4 I carry is 124, wherein there is 10 times 12 and 4 remains, set 4 under the Inches, and 10 under the Feet, and the Product is 10 Feet, 4 Inches, 3 Parts.

By either of these Rules, any Number may be readily multiplied, when the Multiplier is an aliquot Part of a Foot: But when the Multiplier is not an aliquot Part, then the Operation must be done by the last Rule, which indeed is general.

Note, *For the ready finding the Twelves in any Product, 'tis best to make a Table of Twelves, and to get it perfectly by Heart, as follows,*

$$
\left.\begin{matrix}2\\3\\4\\5\end{matrix}\right\}\text{tim. 12 is}\left\{\begin{matrix}24|6\\36|7\\48|8\\60|9\\|10\end{matrix}\right. \text{tim. 12 is}\left\{\begin{matrix}72|11\\84|12\\96|13\\108|14\\120|15\end{matrix}\right. \text{tim. 12 is}\left\{\begin{matrix}132|16\\144|17\\156|18\\168|19\\180|20\end{matrix}\right. \text{tim. 12 is}\left\{\begin{matrix}192\\204\\216\\228\\240\end{matrix}\right.
$$

III. To multiply Feet, Inches, and Parts, by Parts.

Rule. First, Place a Cypher under the last Place of the Multiplicand, instead of an Integer; and also another Cypher in the Place of Inches, and then the Parts next following to the right Hand. Secondly, Multiply the Parts of the Multiplier, in the Multiplicand, carrying 1 for every 12 as before.

EXAMPLE.

F. I. P.
Multiply 25 11 7 by 9 Parts.
          7 0 9
          ‾‾‾‾‾‾‾‾‾
          1 7 5 8 3

Operation. 9 times 7 is 63, set down 3 and carry 5; then 9 times 11 is 99, and 5 I carry is 104, wherein I have 12 8 times, and 8 remains, set down 8 and carry 8; then 9 times 25 is 225, and 8 I carry is 233, wherein I have 12 19 times, and 5 remains, set down 5 and carry 19. Now as the whole Multiplication is ended, and 19 remains, take 12 out of it, and there remains 7, set down under Inches, and 1 for the 12, under the Feet, and the Product will be 1 Foot, 7 Inches, 5 Parts, 8 Seconds, 3 Thirds.

IV. To multiply Feet, Inches, and Parts, by Inches and Parts.

Rule. First, Place a Cypher under the last Place of the Multiplicand, instead of an Integer, and the Inches and Parts in their Places, towards the right Hand. 2dly, Multiply the Inches in the Parts, Inches, and Feet, carrying 1 for every 12. 3dly, Multiply the Parts into the Parts, Inches, and Feet, in the same manner, and the two Products added together is the Product required.

EXAMPLE.

F. I. P.
Multiply 32 7 9 by 8 Inches, 7 Parts.
          0 8 7
          ‾‾‾‾‾‾‾‾‾‾‾
        21 9 2 0
      1 7 0 6 3
      ‾‾‾‾‾‾‾‾‾‾‾‾‾
      23 4 2 6 3

Operation. First, 8 times 9 is 72, set down 0 and carry 6; then 8 times 7 is 56, and 6 I carry is 62, set down 2 and carry 5; then 8 times 32 is 256, and 5 I carry is 261, wherein I find 12 21 times, and 9 remains, set down 9 and carry 21 to the Place of Feet. 2dly, 7 times 9 is 63, set down 3 and carry 5; then 7 times 7 is 49, and 5 I carry is 54, set down 6 and carry 4; then 7 times 32 is 224, and 4 I carry is 228, wherein I find 12 19 times, and 0 remains, set down 0 and carry 19, out of which taking 12, 7 remains, which set under the Inches, and 1 for the 12 under the Feet.

V. To multiply Feet, Inches and Parts, into Feet, Inches and Parts, when the Feet of the Multiplicand and Multiplier do not exceed 20.

Rule. First, Place the Feet of the Multiplier under the last Place of the Multiplicand, and the Inches and Parts, towards the right Hand in their Places. Secondly, Multiply the Feet, Inches and Parts of the Multiplier, each separately, into the Parts, Inches and Feet of the Multiplicand, as before in the preceding Rules; and their several Products being added, will be the true Product required.

Operation.

Operation. Firſt, 7 times 5 is 35, ſet down 11 and carry 2; then 7 times 6 is 42, and 2 I carry is 44, ſet down 8 and carry 3; then 7 times 11 is 77, and 3 I carry is 80, ſet down 8 and carry 6, which put one Place to the left. Secondly 9 times 5 is 45, ſet down 9 and carry 3; then 9 times 6 is 54, and 3 I carry is 57; ſet down 9 and carry 4; then 9 times 11 is 99, and 4 I carry is 103, ſet down 7 and carry 8. Third-ly, 11 times 5 is 55, ſet down 7 and carry 4; then 11 times 6 is 66, and 4

EXAMPLE.

	F.	I.	P.			F.	I.	P.
Multiply	11	6	5	by		11	9	7
						11	9	7
		6	8	8	11			
		8	7	9	9			
	126	10	7					
	136	1	1	5	11			

is 70, ſet down 10 and carry 5; then 11 times 11 is 121, and 5 I carry is 126, which ſet down, and the Product is 136 Feet, 1 Inch, 1 Part, 5 Seconds, and 11 Thirds.

Note 1. *It matters not whether the Feet, Inches, or Parts, be firſt multiplied, ſo that their reſpective Products are but duly placed.*

V. *To multiply any Number of Feet and Inches into any Number of Feet and Inches.*

Rule. Firſt, multiply the Feet into themſelves as Integers. Secondly, inſtead of multiplying the Feet into the Inches, take the aliquot Parts of a Foot, as often as they can be found in the Feet, that ſtand diagonally againſt them (by Rule I. hereof), and halve them when required. Thirdly, the Inches multiplied into themſelves, every 12 is an Inch, the Remains are Parts.

In Example I. the Feet being firſt multiplied into the Feet, proceed to the Feet into the Inches as following: Firſt, as 3 Inches is the 4th of 12, therefore by Rule I. find the fours in 218, ſaying the 4's in 21 is 5 times, and 1 remains, ſet down 5 as at A; and then ſay, the 4's in 18 is 4 times, and 2 remains, ſet down 4, and the 2 remaining being the half of 4, therefore ſet down half one for it, *viz.* 6 Inches; then will 54 Feet, 6 Inches, which is equal to a quarter Part of 218 Feet, be the Product of 218 Feet, multiplied into 3 Inches. Se-condly, as 6 is contained twice in 12, therefore to mul-tiply 276 Feet into 6 Inches, is no more than to take its half, or ſay, the 2's in 2 is 1, ſet down 1 at B, and ſay, the 2's in 7 is thrice, ſet down 3 next after the 1, and carrying the 1 to the 2, which makes 12, ſay, the 2's in 12 is 6 times, ſet down 6, and then the Product of 272 Feet, into 6 Inches, will be 136 Feet. Thirdly, multiply the 6 Inches into 3 Inches, which is equal to 1 Inch, 6 Parts; and the whole Product is 59486 Feet, 7 Inches and 6 Parts.

EXAMPLE I.

	Feet.	Inch.
Multiply	272	3
By	218	6
	2176	
	272	
	544	
A	54	6
B	136	
		1	6
	59486	7	6

In Example II. Firſt, as 9 Inches is three quarters of 12, therefore to multiply 531 Feet into 9 Inches, firſt take the half of 531, which is 265—6 as at A, and the half of 265—6, which is 132—9 as at B.

Secondly, as 2 is the ſixth of 12, therefore take the 6's in 752, which is 125, as at C. Thirdly, the Inches into themſelves, make 1 Inch 6 Parts, and the Whole being added, as in Example I. is 399835 Feet, 4 Inches, 6 Parts.

EXAMPLE II.

	F.	I.
Multiply	752	9
By	531	2
	752	
	2256	
	3760	
A	265	6
B	132	9
	125	0
		1	6
	399835	4	6

Iɴ

EXAMPLE III.

	F.	I.
Multiply	392	1
	325	11
	1960	
	784	
	1176	
A	27	1
B	196	
C	98	
D	65	4
E	0	11
	127786	5 11

In Example III. First, as 1 Inch is the twelfth Part of 12, therefore to multiply 325 Feet into 1 Inch, take the 12's in 325 which are 27 1, as at A. Secondly, to multiply 392 Feet into 11 Inches, first take the half of 392, which is 196 as at B, whose half is 98 as at C; and which two Products are equal to 392 Feet multiplied into 9. Now as the remains to 11 is 2, which is a sixth Part of 12, therefore by Rule I. take the 6's in 392, which is 65 Feet 4 Inches. Lastly, the Inches multiplied into themselves make 11 Parts, and the several Products added, are 127786 Feet, 5 Inches, and 11 Parts.

EXAMPLE IV.

	F.	I.
Multiply	524	4
	372	5
	1048	
	3668	
	1572	
A	124	
B	131	
C	87	4
		1 8
	195270	5 8

In Example IV First, as 4 Inches is the third of 12, therefore to multiply 372 Feet into 4 Inches take the 3's in 372, which are 124 as at A. Secondly, as in 5 there are two aliquot Parts of 12, *viz.* 3, which is a 4th, and 2 which is a 6th, therefore first take the 4's in 524, which are 131 as at B, and then the 6's in 524, which are 87 4. Thirdly, the Inches into themselves, are 1 Inch 8 Parts, and the whole Product 195270 Feet, 5 Inches, 8 Parts.

EXAMPLE V.

	F.	I.
Multiply	723	7
By	512	8
	1446	
	723	
	3615	
A	256	
B	43	
C	361	6
D	120	6
		4 8
	370957	4 8

In Example V. First, as in 7 Inches there are two aliquot Parts of 12, *viz.* 6 which is a half, and 1 which is a 12th, therefore to multiply 512 Feet into 7 Inches, first take the halves or 2's in 512 Feet, which are 256 as at A, then the 12's that are in 43 as at B. Secondly, as in 8 there are also 2 aliquot Parts of 12, *viz.* 6 and 2, therefore to multiply 723 Feet into 8 Inches, first take the halves or 2's in 723, which are 361 6 as at C, and then the 6's, which are 120 6 as at D. Thirdly, the Inches into themselves, are 56, equal to 4 Inches 8 Parts, and the whole Product 370957 Feet, 4 Inches, 8 Parts.

EXAMPLE VI.

	F.	I.
	259	10
	172	10
	518	
	1813	
	259	
A	86	
B	57	4
C	129	6
D	86	4
		8 4
	44907	10 4

In Example VI. First, as in 10 there are two aliquot Parts of 12, *viz.* 6 which is half, and 4 which is a third; therefore to multiply 172 Feet into 10 Inches, first take the halves or 2's in 172 Feet, which are 86 as at A, and then the 3's, which are 57 4. Secondly, there being the same aliquot Parts in the other 10 Inches, therefore first take the halves or 2's in 259 Feet, which are 129 6, as at C, and then the 3's, which are 86 4, as at D. Thirdly, the Inches 10 into 10 equal to 100, are equal to 8 Inches, 4 Parts, and the whole Product to 44907 Feet, 10 Inches, and 4 Parts.

Thus

Thus have I given you a Number of Examples in all the Variety of odd Inches that can happen, which being well underſtood will make the Menſuration of Superficies and Solids very eaſy and delightful to every Capacity. And, in conſideration that ſome Kinds of Works are performed by Yard Meaſure, I ſhall therefore, before I proceed to Diviſion, ſhew the Multiplication of Yards and Feet.

IV. *Multiplication of Yards and Feet.*

Note, 1ſt, That Yards multiplied into Yards produce Yards. 2dly, That Yards multiplied into Feet every 3 is a Yard, the remains more than 3 are long Feet, a long Foot is one Foot in Breadth, and 3 Feet in Length. 3dly, Feet multiplied into Feet produce Parts, which are ſquare Feet, 3 of which make 1 long Foot aforeſaid.

Operation. Firſt, he Yards being multiplied as Integers, to multiply 251 Yards into 1 Foot, as 1 is the third Part of 3, the Feet in a Yard, therefore take the thirds of 251, which are 83 2, as at A. Secondly, as 2 is two thirds of 3, therefore to multiply 272 Feet into 2 Feet, take the thirds, twice in 273, which are 91, and 91 as at B and C. Thirdly, the Feet multiplied into themſelves are two Parts, and the whole Product is equal to 68788 Yards, 2 Feet, and 2 Parts.

	Feet.
	273 1
	251 2
	273
	1365
	546
A	83 2
B	91
C	91 —
	0 2

The next Thing in Order, to conclude this Lecture, is to ſhew,   68788 2 2

How to prove Multiplication.

Rule. Make that which was your Multiplier your Multiplicand, and then multiplying as uſual, if the Product be the ſame, your Work is true; if not, 'tis falſe.

LECT. V. Of DIVISION.

DIviſion is nothing more than a compendious Subtraction; for as many Times as the Diviſor can be ſubtracted out of the Dividend, ſo many Units is the Quotient. In Diviſion there are four principal Parts to be obſerved; *viz.* 1. The given Number which is to be divided, called the Dividend. 2. The given Number by which the Dividend is to be divided, called the Diviſor. 3. The Number ariſing from the Number of Times that the Diviſor is contained in the Dividend, which is called the Quotient. And laſtly, a Number that ſometimes happens to remain when the Diviſion is ended, leſs than the Diviſor, which is called the Remains.

Diviſion in general is performed by this Analogy, *viz.* As the Diviſor is to 1, ſo is the Dividend to the Quotient; which I ſhall illuſtrate by the following Examples.

EXAMPLE.

'Tis required to divide 9972543 2, by 3725: firſt place the Dividend and Diviſor as at D E, ſeparated by a Crotchet as F. Alſo make another Crotchet as G to ſeparate the Dividend from the Quotient. Secondly, make a Table of Diviſors as in the Margin, thus 1ſt, place 3725 and againſt it ſet 1; 2dly, double 3725, as at A 7450, and

D F E   G
3725)9972543 2(26664 $\frac{3832}{3725}$
  f 7450 : : : : *ab cd e*
  ——— : : : :
  g 2522,5 : : :
  b 2235 0 : : :
  ——— : : :
  i 2475,4 : :
  k 2235 0 : :
  ——— : :
  l 2404,3 :
  m 22350 :
  ———
  n 16932
  p 14900
  ———
  q 2032 remains.

Table of Diviſors.		
H	3725	1
A	7450	2
K	11175	3
C	14900	4
L	18625	5
B	22350	6
M	26075	7
N	29800	8
O	33525	9

against it set 2, signifying that 7450 is the Divisor 2 Times. Thirdly, add 3725 and 7450 together, which make 11175, as at k, against which set 3. Fourthly, to 11175, add 3725, which make 14900, as at c, and against it set 4. Fifthly, to 14900, add 3725, which make 18625, as at l, and against it set 5. Proceed, in like Manner, to add the first and last together, until you have repeated the Operations 9 Times, placing the Number of Times against each. Or otherwise, multiply the Divisor 3725, by 2, 3, 4, 5, 6, 7, 8, 9, and their Products will be as against A, K, C, L, B, M, N, O. This being done, the Work is very easy, and is thus performed. First, as 3725 cannot be had in the first 3 Figures of the Dividend 997, therefore under the fourth Figure 2, make a Point; then say, how often 3725 in 9972: Look in the Table of Divisors for the less nearest Number to 9972, which is 7450, against which stands 2, as at A.

Place 2 in the Quotient as at a, and 7450 under 9972, as at f, and subtract 7450 from 9972, the Remains is 2522, as the first 4 Figures towards the left Hand at g. Secondly, make a Point under 5 in the Dividend, which bring down and place against 2522, as thus, 25225 for a new Dividend. Then say, how often 3725 in 25225; look in the Table of Divisors, for the nearest less Number, which is 22350, against which stands 6; place 6 in the Quotient, as at b, and 22350 under 25225, as at h, and subtract 22350 from 25225, the Remains is 2475, as the first 4 Figures to the left at i. Thirdly, point the next Figure 4, in the Dividend, and bring it down to 2475, as thus, 24754, at i, for a second new Dividend. Then say, how often 3725 in 24754; look in the Table of Divisors, and the nearest less Number is 22350, against which stands 6, as at B; place 6 in the Quotient, as at c, and 22350 under 24754, as at k, and subtract 22350 from 24754, the Remains is 2404, as the first 4 Figures to the left at l. Fourthly, point the next Figure 3, in the Dividend, and bring it down to 2404, as thus, 24043, as at l, for a third new Divisor. Then say, how often 3725 in 24043; look in the Table of Divisors for the nearest less Number, which is 22350 (as before), against which stands 6; place 6 in the Quotient, and 22350, under 24043, and the Remains is 1693, as the first 4 Figures to the left at n. Fifthly, point the next and last Figure 2 of the Dividend, and bring it down to 1693, as thus, 16932, as at p, for a fourth new Divisor. Then say, how often 3725 in 16932; look in the Table of Divisors for the nearest less Number, which is 14900, against which stands 4; place 4 in the Quotient, as at c, and 14900 under 16932, and subtracting 14900 from 16932, the Remains is 2032, and which being the last Remains, is 2032 Parts of 3725; and which together make a Fraction thus, $\frac{2032}{3725}$, which must be set in the Quotient, next after 26664, as in the Margin.

Note, That as many Points as are placed under the Figures of the Dividend, so many Figures will be in the Quotient.

The Value of this Fraction, or any other, in the Parts of the Integer may be found as following. Admit the Integers, in this Example, to be Pounds Sterling.

A 2032
    20

First, multiply 2032, the Remains, by 20, the Shillings in a Pound, as at A, and divide the Product 40640, by 3725, the former Divisor, as at B, and the Quotient 10 are Shillings, and 3390 remains, as at C. Secondly, multiply 3390, the Remains, by 12, the Pence in a Shilling, as at D, and divide the Product 40680, by 3725, the former Divisor as at E, and the Quotient 10 are Pence, and 3430 remains. Thirdly, multiply 3430, the Remains, by 4, the Farthings in one Penny, as at F, and divide the Product 13720, by 3725, as before, and the Quotient 3 are Farthings, and 2545 remains, which are 2545 Parts of 3725 of a Farthing, the Farthing being divided into 3725 Parts. The Man-

B 3725)40640(10 Shillings
       3725

C 3390 rem.
D 12

E 3725)40680(10 Pence
       3725

       3430
       F 4

ner

ner of reducing this and other Fractions, into the   37⅕) 13720 (3 Farth.
leaſt equivalent Parts, is taught in Lecture VIII.   11175
   If this example be well underſtood, it is fully   ————
ſufficient for performing all Varieties of Caſes in   2545 rem.
whole Numbers, that can happen, and more eſpe-
cially when you have alſo learned the following   ————

Contractions in Diviſion.

   I. When the Diviſor is 10, 100, 1000, &c. cut from the Divi- A 10) 732 | 0
dend, the ſame Number of Figures to the right Hand as are B 100) 275 | 43
Cyphers in the Diviſor, and the Figures remaining to the Left C 1000) 72 | 354
are the Quotient required. So 7320, divided by 10, I cut off
the laſt Figure o, and 732 remaining to the Left, is the Quotient required, as at
A. In like manner, 27543, divided by 100, the Quotient is 275$\frac{43}{100}$; and 72354,
divided by 1000, the Quotient is 72$\frac{354}{1000}$, as at B and C, as the Figures cut
off to the right Hand, are ſo many Parts of the Diviſor. And as in every of theſe
Caſes, the Diviſor is decimally divided, therefore theſe Remains are Decimal
Fractions; and though I have here ſet their Denominators under each for Plainneſs
Sake, yet in Practice they are to be omitted, and the Fractions annexed to the
whole Numbers, as following, *viz.* 10,732; not 10$\frac{732}{1000}$, and 275.43, not 275
$\frac{43}{100}$; and 72,354, not 72$\frac{354}{1000}$, of which I have already advertiſed you in the
preceding Lectures.

   II. When your Dividend and Diviſor conſiſt of Cy- 63|000) 7735|000 (122
phers to the right Hand, cut off an equal Number of
Cyphers in both, and then proceed as before taught: So to divide 7735000
by 63000, cut off three Cyphers in each, and divide 7735 by 63, as in the
Margin.

   III. If your Diviſor have Cyphers annexed, and 1200)73¹54|79(6104$\frac{79}{1200}$
your Dividend none, cut off as many Figures in   72 ...
your Dividend, as there are Cyphers in your Divi-   ————
ſor, and then proceed as before. So to divide   12
73²5479 by 1200, cut off 79, the laſt two Figures   054
in the Dividend, and dividing 73254 by 12, the   ————
Quotient will be 6104, and 6 remains as in the   48
Margin. The 6 remaining, is to be placed before   ————
79, cut from the Dividend, making it 679, and   6 rem.
which is the true remains, and the Numerator of   ————
the Fraction $\frac{679}{1200}$, as annexed to the Quotient.

To prove Diviſion.
   Multiply the Quotient by the Diviſor, and to the Product add the Remains,
when any, and if the Work be true, their Sum will be equal to the Dividend.

DIVISION *of* DECIMALS.
   Diviſion of Decimals is performed in every Reſpect as whole Numbers, and
for diſcovering the true Value of the Quotient, this is the general Rule

R U L E.
The Places of Decimal Parts in the Diviſor and Quotient, being accounted together,
muſt always be equal in Number with thoſe in the Dividend; and therefore as many
Figures as are cut off in the Dividend, ſo many muſt be cut off in the Diviſor and
Quotient: or thus; cut off as many Figures in the Quotient, as will make thoſe cut
off in the Diviſor equal to thoſe in the Quotient; always obſerving, that if there be
not ſo many in the Quotient, to add Cyphers to the left Hand. And alſo, that if
your Dividend be an Integer, or have leſs cut off than in the Diviſor, to add Cy-
phers to the Dividend, till they are equal.
   This general Rule admits of four Caſes.

                                               Caſe

EXAMPLE.
25,635) 4672,565 (182
   25,635
  ——— ::
  210906 :
  205080 :
  ———— :
   58265
   51470
  ————

   6995 rem.

Cafe 1. When the Places of Decimal Parts in the Divifor and Dividend are equal in Number, as in this Example in the Margin, where both Divifor and Dividend are mixed Numbers, then the Quotient will be all whole Numbers.

EXAMPLE II.

427) 7254,271 (17,012
  427 · · · ·
  ——— · · · ·
  2984 · · ·
  2989 · · ·
  ——— · ·
   527 ·
   427 ·
  ——— ·
  1001
   854
  ————

  147 rem.

Divide 7254,271, by 427, as in the Margin. Here the Dividend is a mixed Number, and the Divifor is Integers, and as here are three Decimals in the Dividend, and none in the Divifor, therefore cut off 012, the laft 3 Figures in the Quotient, and the Quotient will be 17,012.

EXAMPLE III. Divide 75 by ,0125, as in the Margin.

,0125) 7500 (60
  750
  ———
   00
   —

Here the Dividend is Integers, and the Divifor a Decimal ; and feeing that 75, the Dividend, confifts but of two Places, I therefore add two Cyphers to it, making it 7500, that thereby both Divifor and Dividend may be made Fractions, and by their being both of equal Number of Places, therefore by *Cafe* 1, the Quotient is Integers.

Cafe 2. When there are not fo many Places of Decimal Parts in the Dividend, as there are in the Divifor, then annex Cyphers to the Dividend, to make them equal, and the quotient will be all whole Numbers, as in *Cafe* 1.

A

EXAMPLE IV.

,725) 3425,000 (4724
  2900 · · ·
  ——— · · ·
  5250 · ·
  5057 · ·
  ——— · ·
  1750 ·
  1450 ·
  ——— ·
  3000
  2900
  ————
  100 rem.

,725) 3425,00000 (4724,13
  2900 · · · · ·
  ——— · · · · ·
  5250 · · · ·
  5057 · · · ·
  ——— · · · ·
  1750 · · ·
  1450 · · ·
  ——— · · ·
  3000 · ·
  2900 · ·
  ——— · ·
  1000 ·
   725 ·
  ——— ·
  2750
  2175
  ————
   575 rem.

Divide 3425, by ,725, as in the Margin. Now here the Dividend being Integers, and the Divifor a Decimal, to bring out Integers in the Quotient, I add 3 Cyphers to 3425, the Dividend, and the Quotient is 4724, and 100 remains. But if 'tis required to have the Quotient to a greater Exactnefs, then I add a competent Number of Cyphers more to the Dividend. In the following Example, at A, in the Margin, 'tis required to have two Places of Decimals, after the Integral Part of the Quotient, where the

the Quotient is 4724,13, and 575 remains; for by adding two Cyphers more to the Dividend, than was required before to make the Divisor and Dividend equal; and cutting off the fame Number of Places from the Quotient, leave 13 for the fractional Part required, and 575 remains.

In this Manner, by annexing of a greater Number of Cyphers, you may come nearer to the Truth; but in all Cases like this, where the Divisor is not contained an exact Number of Times in the Dividend, there will always be a Remainder.

Cafe 3. When the Number of Places of Decimal Parts in the Dividend exceed thofe in the Divisor, cut off the Excefs of Decimal Parts in the Quotient. As for Example, divide 71,4038, by 7,54, as in the Margin; where the Number of Decimal Parts in the Dividend is 4, and but 2 in the Divifor; therefore, as the Excefs is 2, cut off 47, the laft two Places in the Quotient.

```
7,54) 71,4038 (9,47
      6786
      ----
      3543
      3016
      ----
       5278
       5278
       ----
        o rem.
```

Cafe 4. If after Divifion is finifhed, there are not fo many Figures in the Quotient, as there ought to be Places of Decimal Parts by the general Rule, then fupply their Defect by prefixing Cyphers before the Figures produced in the Quotient. As for Example, divide 13975 by 43. Now here the Dividend is a Decimal, and the Divifor is Integers, whofe Quotient is 325. But as in the Dividend there are 5 Places, therefore, according to the general Rule, I prefix two Cyphers before the Quotient 325, making it ,00325, which is the true Quotient required.

```
43) ,13975 (,00325
    129
    ---
    107
     86
    ---
    215
    215
    ---
     o rem.
```

Note, When any Decimal Fraction, or mixed Number, is to be divided by an Unit, with any Number of Cyphers annexed, remove the feparatrix as many Places towards the left Hand, as there are Cyphers annexed to the Unit; fo if 57,27, were given to be divided

$$
\text{by} \begin{cases} 10, \\ 100, \\ 1000, \\ 10000, \\ 100000, \end{cases} \text{the Quotient will be} \begin{cases} 5,727 \\ ,5727 \\ ,05727 \\ ,005727 \\ ,0005727 \end{cases}
$$

Now, from the preceding Examples, it may be obferved, firft, That when the Dividend is fuperior to the Divifor, the Quotient is either Integers, or Integers and Decimals: and laftly, That when the Divifor is fuperior to the Dividend, the Quotient is a Decimal, and which in both Cafes holds good in all other Examples.

L E C T. VI. *Of* REDUCTION.

R Eduction is nothing more than Multiplication or Divifion, or both, and its Ufe in whole Numbers is for changing Quantity out of one Denomination into another, as greater into lefs by Multiplication, or lefs into greater by Divifion.

EXAMPLE.

EXAMPLE I. *In 5287 superficial Feet, how many superficial Inches?*

$$\begin{array}{r} 5278 \\ 144 \\ \hline 21112 \\ 21112 \\ 5278 \\ \hline 760032 \end{array}$$

Here, because 1 superficial Foot contains 144 superficial Inches, therefore multiply 5278 by 144, and the Product 760032, as in the Margin, is the Answer required.

EXAMPLE II. *In 760032 superficial Inches, how many superficial Feet?*

144) 760032 (5278
$$\begin{array}{r} 720::: \\ \hline ::: \\ 400:: \\ 288:: \\ \hline :: \\ 1123: \\ 1008: \\ \hline : \\ 1152 \\ 1152 \\ \hline \end{array}$$
o rem.

Here you divide 760032 the Number given by 144, the square Inches in a square Foot, and the Quotient is 5278.

Now these two Examples, which are converse to each other, illustrate all that can be done in Reductions, and therefore I need only add the following Rules, by which Reductions in general may be performed.

Rule 1. To reduce Pounds into Shillings, multiply the Pounds by 20, the Shillings in a Pound, the Product will be Shillings; and to reduce Shillings into Pounds, divide the Shillings by 20, the Quotient will be Pounds.

Rule 2. To reduce Shillings into Pence, multiply the Shillings by 12, the Pence in a Shilling, the Product will be Pence; and to reduce Pence into Shillings, divide the Pence by twelve, the Quotient will be Shillings.

Rule 3. To reduce square Yards into Feet, multiply the Yards by 9, the square Feet in a Yard, and the Product will be Feet; and to reduce square Feet into Yards, divide the Feet by 9, the Quotient will be Yards.

Rule 4. To reduce solid Yards into solid Feet, multiply the Yards by 27, the solid Feet in a solid Yard, and the Product will be solid Feet; and to reduce solid Feet into solid Yards, divide the Feet by 27, and the Quotient will be solid Yards.

Rule 5. To reduce square Statute Rods into square Feet, multiply the Rods by 272¼, the square Feet in a square Rod, and the Product will be square Feet; and to reduce square Feet into square Rods, divide the Feet by 272¼, and the Quotient will be square Rods.

Rule 6. To reduce Squares of Roofing, Tyling, &c. into square Feet, multiply the Squares by 100, the square Feet in a Square of Work, and the Product will be square feet; and to reduce square Feet into square Rods, divide the Feet by 272¼, and the Quotient will be square Rods.

Rule 7. To reduce solid Feet into solid Inches, multiply the Feet by 1728, the Number of solid Inches in one solid Foot, and the Product will be solid Inches; and to reduce solid Inches into solid Feet, divide the solid Inches by 1728, and the Quotient will be solid Feet.

Rule 8. To reduce Loads of Timber to solid Feet, multiply the Loads by 50, the Number of solid Feet in a Load of Timber, and the Product will be solid Feet; and to reduce solid Feet into Loads, divide the solid Feet by 50, and the Quotient will be Loads.

These *Rules*, which are very plain, being understood, will render the Reason of all other Kinds of Reduction easy to the meanest Capacity; and as the Reduction of Decimals will be best understood when Vulgar Fractions have been explained,

explained, I fhall therefore proceed to the Golden Rule, or Rule of Three in whole Numbers.

LECT. VII. The GOLDEN RULE, or RULE of THREE.

THIS Rule for its excellent Ufe is called the *Golden Rule*, and teaches to find a fourth Number, which fhall have the fame Proportion to one of three Numbers given, as they have to one another, 'and therefore is alfo called the *Rule of Proportion*. This Rule is *Direct, Indirect,* and *Compound*.

I. The fingle Rule of Three Direct finds a fourth Number in fuch Proportion to the third, as the fecond is to the firft; or as the fecond is to the firft, fo is the third to the fourth.

EXAMPLE I. *If the Diameter of one Circle be 7, and its Circumference 22, what is the Circumference of another Circle whofe Diameter is 14 Feet ?*

Rule. Firft place your Numbers as in the Margin, fecondly, multiply 14 the third Number by 22 the fecond Number, and divide their Product 308 by 7 the firft Number, the Quotient 44 is the fourth Number and Anfwer required.

D. C.   D. C.
7 : 22 :: 14 : 44
a   *b* 22 *c*

Now you muft obferve that as the firft and third Numbers are always of like Kinds, *viz.* both Diameters, fo likewife are the fecond and fourth Numbers of like Kinds, being both Circumferences, of which the firft is always given, and the laft is the Anfwer required.

28
28
———
7) 308 (44
28:
———

Note, When the fourth Number is thus found, place it next after the third Number, with two Dots of Separation between them as is done at *c*. The fame Kind of Separation muft be alfo always placed between the firft and fecond Numbers, as at *a*. But between the fecond and third, always place four Dots or Points, as at *b*. Thefe Points of Separation, fo placed, fignify the following Words, *viz.* the two Points at *a* thus :, fignify the Words, *is to*, the four Points at *b* thus ::, fignify the Words, *fo is*, and the two Points at *c* thus :, fignify the Word *to*; and therefore the four Numbers, 7 : 22 :: 14 : 44, are thus to be read, *viz.* as 7 *is to* 22, *fo is* 14 *to* 44. And in fo like Manner, all other Numbers having the fame Analogy.

28
28
———
o rem.
———

EXAMPLE II.

If the Circumference of a Circle be 22, whofe Diameter is 7, what is the Diameter of another Circle whofe Cicumference is 44 ?

Here the Nature of the Queftion requires the two firft Numbers to be placed the reverfe to thofe of the foregoing Example; for as there the 4th Number required was the Circumference of a Circle, fo here on the contrary the Diameter of a Circle is required. But the Manner of working by multiplying the third Number by the fecond, and dividing by the firft, is the fame here as before, as is feen in the Margin, where the Quotient 14 is the Diameter required. Now as in both thefe and all other Examples in the Rule of Three Direct, the fourth Number is always equal to, or more than the fecond; fo in the Rule of Three Indirect, the fourth Number is always lefs than the fecond : and as the 4th Number in the Direct Rule is found by multiplying the fecond and third Numbers together, and dividing of their Product by the firft Number; fo on the contrary in the Indirect Rule you multiply the firft and fecond into one another, and divide their Product by the third, as following.

Analogy.
C. D.   C. D.
22 : 7 :: 44 14
7
———
22) 308 (14
22:
———
88
88
———
o rem.
———

II. *The Rule of Three Indirect.*
EXAMPLE.

If 20 Men can perform a certain Quantity of Work in 50 Days, how long a Time will 40 Men be employed to perform the fame ?

Men. Days. Men. Days.
20　　50　　40　　25
　　　20

40) 1000 (25

Rule. Multiply 50 the second Number by 20 the first, and their Product 1000, divide by 40 the third Number, and the Quotient 25 is the Answer required.

III. *The Golden Rule Compound.*

In the Golden Rule Compound, there are five Numbers given to find a sixth in proportion thereto, which Numbers must be so placed, as that the three first may contain a Supposition, and the two last a Demand. And that you may place your Numbers truly, always observe, that the first Number be of the same Denomination with the fourth; the second of the same Denomination with the fifth; and the third with the sixth required.

EXAMPLE I.

If 20 Bricklayers, in 136 Days, perform 680 Rods of Brick-work, how many Rods can 12 Bricklayers perform in 28 Days?

M.　D.　R.　　　M.　D.
20　136　680　　　12　28
　　20　　　　　　　　12
―――――　　　　　―――――
2720　　　　　　　　336

2720　680　336
　　　　　680
　　――――――
　　　26880
　　　2016
　――――――
2720) 228480 (84 A
91760
――――
10880
10880
――――
0 rem.

Rule. First, state your Numbers as in the Margin; secondly, multiply the two first Numbers together, *viz.* 136 into 20, whose Product is 2720, as also the two last, 12 and 28, whose Product is 336. Now the Answer to this Question is found by the Rule of Three Direct, for making 2720 (the Product of the first two Terms) the first Number; the third given Number, 680 Rods, your second, and 336 (the Product of the two last), your third Number; then 228480, the Product of 680, multiplied into 336, the two first Numbers, being divided by 2720, the Quotient is 84, as in the Margin at A, which is the sixth Number, and the Answer required.

To prove the Golden Rule.

As the four Numbers are Proportionals, that is, the 4th is to the 2d, as the 3d is to the 1st; therefore the Square of the two Means (which are the second and third) are always equal to the Square of the two Extremes (which are the first and last): that is to say, if the Product of the first and last Numbers, multiplied into each other, be equal to the Product of the two middle Numbers multiplied together, the Work is right, else not.

336　　　　2720
A 680　　　B 84
――――　　――――
26880　　　12880
2016　　　21760
――――　　――――
228480　　228480

So 228480, the Product of 336, multiplied into 680, which are the two Means of the last Example, as in the Margin at A, is equal to 228480, the Product of 84, multiplied at 2720, the two Extremes of the same Example, as at B. Hence 'tis plain, that when the given Numbers, in the foregoing three Varieties of the Rule of Three are truly stated (and which indeed is the only Difficulty in the whole), the Manner of performing the Operations is very easy.

LECT. VIII. *Of Vulgar and Decimal Fractions.*

I. *Notation of Fractions.*

A Fraction is a broken Number, fignifying one or more Parts, proportionally of any Thing divided, and therefore is always lefs than Unity. It confifts of two Numbers fet one over another, with a Line between them, as $\frac{1}{4}$, which fignifies one fourth, or quarter of an Integer or Unit; and fo in like manner, $\frac{1}{2}$ fignifies one half; $\frac{3}{4}$ three fourths, or three quarters; $\frac{2}{3}$ two thirds; $\frac{1}{3}$ one third; $\frac{3}{8}$ three eighths; $\frac{5}{8}$ five eighths, &c. The upper Number is called the Numerator, and the lower the Denominator. In all Fractions, as the Numerator is to the Denominator, fo is the Fraction itfelf to that Whole, of which it is a Fraction. Hence 'tis plain, that there may be infinite Fractions of the fame Value one with another, for there may be infinite Numbers found, which fhall have the fame Proportion one to another. So $\frac{2}{4}$, $\frac{4}{8}$, $\frac{8}{16}$, are each of the fame Value as $\frac{1}{2}$; and $\frac{2}{4}$, $\frac{4}{8}$, $\frac{8}{16}$, $\frac{16}{32}$, are each of the fame Value with $\frac{1}{2}$. When the Numerator is lefs than the Denominator, the Fraction is lefs than an Unit, and therefore is called a *Proper Fraction*; but when the Numerator is either equal to, or greater than its Denominator, the Fraction is called *Improper*, becaufe 'tis equal to, or greater than an Unit. So $\frac{2}{2}$ is equal to 1, as alfo $\frac{4}{4}$, and $\frac{5}{5}$, &c. and $\frac{6}{4}$ is equal to 1 $\frac{1}{2}$, and $\frac{5}{4}$ to 1 $\frac{1}{4}$. Fractions are fingle or compound: Single Fractions are fuch as have but one Numerator, and one Denominator, as $\frac{2}{3}$ two thirds, $\frac{3}{5}$ three fifths, $\frac{9}{11}$ nine elevenths, $\frac{5}{12}$ five twelfths, &c. Compound Fractions are Fractions of Fractions, and are fuch as confift of more than one Numerator, and one Denominator, as $\frac{1}{4}$ of $\frac{1}{12}$ of $\frac{1}{20}$, that is to fay, one Farthing, which is $\frac{1}{4}$ of a Penny, which is $\frac{1}{12}$ of a Shilling, which is $\frac{1}{20}$ of a Pound Sterling. All Fractions, whofe Numerators and Denominators are proportional to one another, are equal to one another, as before obferved. So $\frac{2}{4}$ is equal to $\frac{1}{2}$, and $\frac{4}{8}$ to $\frac{2}{4}$, &c. When Integers and Fractions are joined together, as 1 $\frac{1}{2}$, or 7 $\frac{3}{11}$, or 15 $\frac{3}{7}$, they are called mixed Numbers. Things commonly expreffed by Fractions, are the Parts of Coin, Weight, Meafure, &c. So Inches are Fractions, in refpect of Feet, and Feet are Fractions in refpect of Yards, Rods, &c. As Addition and Subtraction of Fractions cannot well be performed without the Knowledge of the Reduction, I fhall therefore firft teach you Reduction.

II. *Reduction of Vulgar Fractions.*

By Reduction you are taught, firft, how to bring Fractions into their leaft equivalent Parts, and their various Denominators into common Denominators, or into one Denominator. Secondly, to find the Value of any Fraction in the known Parts of the Integer. And laftly, to reduce whole or mixed Numbers into improper Fractions, and improper Fractions into mixed Numbers.

I. *To bring Fractions into their leaft equivalent Parts.*

Rule. Firft, Divide the Denominator by the Numerator, and the Divifor by the Remainder, if any be: thus continue to divide the laft Divifor, by the laft Remains, till nothing remain, and the laft Divifor is your greateft common Meafure; by which dividing the Numerator and Denominator, and their Quotients being placed in a fractional Manner, will be a new Fraction equal to the given Fraction, and in the leaft Parts.

EXAMPLE. Let $\frac{637}{819}$ be a Fraction given, to be reduced into its leaft Terms.

First, the Denominator 819, divided by 637, the Numerator, the Remains is 182, as at A. Secondly, the Divifor 637, divided by 182, the Remains, as at B, the Remains is 91. Thirdly, the laft Divifor 182, being divided by the laft Remains 91, as at C, and o remains; therefore 91, the laft Divifor, is the greateft common Meafure required. Fourthly, divide 637, the Numerator of the

637) 819 (1
    637

A 182 rem.

182) 637 (3
    546

B 91 rem.

given

C 91)182(2
　　182
　　─────
　　　0

, D 91)637(7 new Numerator.
　　 637
　　─────
　　0 rem.

E 91)819(9 new Denominator.
　　819
　　─────
　　　0 rem.

F ⅞ new Fraction equal to 6 3 7 / 8 1 9.

given Fraction, by 91, as at D, and the Quotient 7 is a new Numerator. Fifthly, divide 819, the Denominator of the given Fraction, by 91, as at E, and the Quotient 9 is a new Denominator. Lastly, the laſt two Quotients, 7 and 9, being placed as at F, will be the new Fraction required; and equal to 6 3 7 / 8 1 9, the given Fraction.

Note, When it happens that your laſt Diviſor is an Unit, the Fraction is in its leaſt Terms already, becauſe 1 neither multiplies nor divides.

It is alſo to be obſerved, that ſome Fractions may be abbreviated, by halving both your Numerator and your Denominator, as often as you can, and which may always be done, when both Numerator and Denominator end with a Cypher.

II. *To reduce ſeveral Fractions, whoſe Denominators are different, into other Fractions having a common Denominator.*

Rule. Firſt, multiply the Denominators into themſelves, and their Product is a new Denominator common to every Fraction. Secondly, multiply every Numerator into each Denominator continually, except its own, which ſhall be new Numerators.

EXAMPLE.　*Let ½, ¾, ⅝, be Fractions given to be reduced into other Fractions, which ſhall have one common Denominator.*

½　¾　⅝
2 4 / 4 8　3 6 / 4 8　4 0 / 4 8
a　b　c

Operation. Firſt, to find the common Denominator, I ſay, the Denominator 2, into the Denominator 4, is 8; and 8 into the Denominator 6, is 48, the new Denominator required, which place under each Fraction, as at *a b c*. Secondly, to find the new Numerators, I ſay, the Numerator 1 into the Denominator 4, is 4; and 4 into the Denominator 6, is 24, which I ſet over 24 at *a*. Then the Numerator 3, into the Denominator 2, is 6, and 6 into the Denominator 6 is 36, which I place over 48 at *b*. Thirdly, the Numerator 5, into the Denominator 2 is 10, and 10 into the Denominator 4 is 40, which I place over 48 at *c*. Then will 2 4 / 4 8, 3 6 / 4 8, and 4 0 / 4 8 which have one common Denominator, be equal to the given Fractions ½, ¾, ⅝, as required.

III. *To find the Value of any vulgar Fraction in the known Parts of the Integer.*

Rule. Multiply the Numerator of the Fraction by the known Parts of the next leſſer Denominator, and that Product being divided by the Denominator, the Quotient is the Parts of that Denominator required.

EXAMPLE. How many Inches are contained in 7 5 / 1 0 0 of a Foot, as the next leſſer denominative Parts of a Foot are Inches? I therefore multiply 75, the Numerator, by 12, the Inches in a Foot, and the Product 900, being divided by 100, the Denominator, the Quotient 9, is the Number of Inches, which are equal to 7 5 / 1 0 0 as required. This may alſo be found by the Rule of Three Direct. For 100 : 12 : : 75 : 9.

　75
　12
─────
100)900(
─────

If the given Fraction $\frac{75}{100}$ be Parts of a Yard, and 'tis required to know how many Feet and Inches are equal thereto, multiply the Numerator 75, by 3, the Feet in a Yard, as at A, and the Product 225 being divided by the Denominator 100, the Quotient is 2 Feet, and 25 remains. Now in all Kind of Cases, when a Remainder happens, multiply the Remainder by the Parts of the next lefs Denomination, and divide by 100 as before. So here, as Inches are the next lefs Denomination,

$$\begin{array}{r} 75 \\ A\ 3 \\ \hline 100)\ 2|25\ (2\ \text{Feet} \\ 25\ \text{rem.} \\ 12\ \text{Inch. in a Foot.} \\ \hline 100)\ 3|00\ (3\ \text{Inches.} \end{array}$$

therefore the Remainder 25 being multiplied by 12, the Inches in a Foot, and the Product 300, divided by 100 as before, the Quotient is 3 Inches. Thefe two Quotients, 2 Feet and 3 Inches, are the Feet and Inches which are equal to $\frac{75}{100}$ of a Yard, as required.

After the fame Manner, the Value of $\frac{111}{480}$ of a Pound Sterling, will be found to be 5 s. 6 d. 2 q. which to find, after having multiplied the Numerator into 20, the Shillings in a Pound, which are the next lefs Denomination, and divided the Product by 480 the Denominator; multiply the Remains by 12, the Pence in a Shilling; and the Remains of that Product, after dividing it by 480, multiply by 4, the Farthings in a Penny, the next lefs Denomination, &c.

IV. *To reduce whole or mixed Numbers into improper Fractions, and improper Fractions into mixed Numbers.*

Firft, If your Number be an Integer, and the given Denominator be 12, it is done by making an Unit the Denominator, and 12 the Numerator, as thus $\frac{12}{12}$. Secondly, if the given Number be mixed, as 1 $\frac{7}{12}$, then making 12 the Denominator, add 7 to 12, equal to 19, is the Numerator, and the Fraction is thus expreffed 1 $\frac{19}{12}$. Thirdly, to reduce an improper Fraction to a proper Fraction, divide the Numerator by the Denominator, the Quotient will be Integers, and the Remains, if any, will be a Numerator to the former Denominator. So $\frac{59}{12}$, is 4 $\frac{11}{12}$, for 59 divided by 12, the Quotient is 4, and 11 remains.

V. *To reduce a compound Fraction into a fingle Fraction.*

Rule. Multiply all the Numerators one into another, for a new Numerator, and the Denominators, one into another, for a new Denominator, which being placed in a Fraction, will be the Fraction required.

So $\frac{11}{12}$ of $\frac{1}{20}$, is $\frac{11}{240}$, that is 11 Pence, which is $\frac{11}{12}$ of a Shilling, which is $\frac{1}{20}$ of a Pound, is $\frac{11}{240}$, that is, it is yet 11 Pence, becaufe the new Denominator 240, is equal to the Pence in a Pound Sterling.

III. ADDITION of FRACTIONS.

Before the Addition of Fractions can be well-performed, you muft firft obferve to reduce every given Fraction to be added, into its leaft Terms, and then the Work is very eafy, as appears by the following Rules.

I. *To add Fractions of the fame Denomination.*

Rule. Add all the Numerators into one Sum, for a new Numerator, keeping the fame Denomination; and when the new Numerator is greater than the Denominator, divide the Numerator by the Denominator, and the Quotient will be the Integers and Parts.

So if $\frac{3}{12}$, $\frac{7}{12}$, $\frac{11}{12}$, $\frac{5}{12}$, $\frac{6}{12}$, be given Fractions to be added, the Sum of the Numerators added together, is equal to 32, and the Fraction is $\frac{32}{12}$; and as the Numerator 32, is greater than 12 the Denominator, therefore divide 32 by 12, and the Quotient is 2 $\frac{8}{12}$, equal to 2 $\frac{2}{3}$, or 2 $\frac{2}{3}$, which is the Sum of the Fractions as required.

II. *To add Fractions of divers Denominations.*

Rule. Firft, reduce the Fractions to be added, into one Denomination. Secondly, add all the Numerators into one Sum. Thirdly, if the Sum of the Numerators be greater than the Denominator, divide the Sum of the Numerators by the Denominators, as before taught, and the Quotient is the Sum required. But

H

when

when the Sum of all the Numerators is lefs than the Denominator, then the Sum of the Fractions is the new Numerator required.

IV. SUBTRACTION *of* FRACTIONS.

Rule. Firſt, reduce the two Fractions into one Denomination. Secondly, ſubtract the leſſer Numerator from the greater, and the Difference is the Remains required.

V. MULTIPLICATION *of* FRACTIONS.

Before Fractions can be multiplied, if there be any mixed Numbers, they muſt be reduced into improper Fractions, and if any are compound Fractions, they muſt be reduced to ſingle Fractions; and then the Fractions being all reduced to the loweſt Terms, this is the Rule.

Firſt, multiply the Numerators into each other, their Product is a new Numerator. Secondly, multiply the Denominators into each other, and their Product is a new Denominator. So ½, multiplied by ⅔, the Product is 2/6, equal to ⅓; and ſo in like manner ⅓, 1/10, ⅛, 1/11, multiplied into each other, their Product is 1/1056; which reduced into the leaſt Terms, is 2/6. Now from hence 'tis plain, that the Multiplication of Fractions is the very ſame thing, as to reduce a compound Fraction into a ſingle Fraction, as was but now taught in the Reduction of Fractions. And ſo in the ſame Manner, ten thouſand Fractions placed before one another in a right Line, may be multiplied into each other.

VI. DIVISION *of* FRACTIONS.

Before any Proceeding can be made in the Diviſion of Fractions, that are mixed or compound, and not in their leaſt Terms, they muſt be prepared as before was taught in Multiplication, and then proceed by the following Rule.

Rule. Multiply the Denominator of the Diviſor, by the Numerator of the Dividend, and their Sum is the Numerator of the Quotient; and the Numerator of the Diviſor being multiplied into the Denominator of the Dividend, the Product is the Denominator of the Quotient.

Suppoſe ¾ be to be divided by ⅗, as in the Margin at A,
then 6 the Denominator of the Diviſor, multiplied into 3, the
A
⅗) ¾ (18/20 or 9/10   Numerator of the Dividend, the Product is 18 for the Numerator of the Quotient, and 5 the Numerator of the Diviſor, multi-
B
⅗) ¾ (18/20 or ⅘   plied into 4 the Denominator of the Dividend, the Product 20 is the Denominator of the Quotient required. So ⅘, divided by 9/10 as at B, the Quotient is 18/20, equal to ⅘.

A general Rule for all Sorts of compound Diviſions.   I. *When there is a Fraction in the Diviſor or Dividend.*

Rule. Multiply the Diviſor and the Dividend by the Denominator of the Fraction, adding the Numerator to that to which it belongs, and their Products being divided as Integers, the Quotient will be the true Quotient required.

So 271, divided by 7⅛, the Diviſor 7 multiplied by 9 the Denominator of the Fraction, whoſe Product is 63, being added to 8 the Numerator of the Fraction, their Sum 71 is a new Diviſor. And then 271, multiplied by the Denominator 9, the Product 2439, is a new Dividend, which being divided by 71, the Quotient is 34 5/71; and ſo in like manner, if 295⅞ be to be divided by 27, then 27 multiplied by 8, the Denominator of the Fraction, the Product 216 is the new Diviſor, and 295 the Integers of the Dividend, multiplied by 8, and the Numerator 7, added to the Product, the Sum 2367 is a new Dividend. Now 2367, divided by 216, the Quotient is 10 207/216, equal to 11/14.

II. *When there are Fractions in both Diviſor and Dividend.*

Rule. Firſt, reduce the two Fractions into one Denomination; ſecondly, multiply the Diviſor and Dividend by the Denominator common to both Fractions, and to their reſpective Products add their Numerators; and then their Sums being divided as Integers, the Quotient will be the Anſwer required. So if 275⅔ be to be divided by 39⅘, the two Fractions reduced into the ſame Denomination, will be 4/8, and 5/8. Now 39, the Integers of the Diviſor being multiplied by 56, and 40 the Numerator of its Fraction added to it, is equal to 2224 which is a new
Diviſor,

Divifor, and 275 the Integers of the Dividend, multiplied into 56, with 21 its new Numerator, added to the Product, is equal to 15421, which being divided by 224, the Quotient is 6$\frac{8 \cdot 8}{2 \cdot 4}$, which Fraction is in its leaft Terms.

VII. REDUCTION, *or rather the changing of* Vulgar *Fractions into Decimal Fractions, and Decimal Fractions into* Vulgar *Fractions*.

Rule. Annex as many Cyphers to the Numerators of the given Fraction, as you would have Places in the Decimal, which being divided by the Denominator, the Quotient will be the Decimal required.

So to reduce $\frac{3}{4}$ into a Decimal of two Places, I add two Cyphers to 3 the Numerator, making it 300, which being divided by 4 the Denominator, the Quotient 75 is the Decimal required. In like manner, if 'twas required to have had the Decimal of 3 Places, then I fhould have added 3 Cyphers to the Numerator 3, making it 3000, which being divided by 4, as before, the Quotient would be 750, which is equal to ,75. For $\frac{75}{100}$ is equal to $\frac{750}{1000}$, becaufe cutting off the laft Cyphers in both Numerator and Denominator, thus $\frac{750}{1000}$ the Remains $\frac{75}{100}$ is then the fame as the other Fraction.

Vulgar Fractions may be changed into Decimal Fractions by this *Analogy, viz.* as the Denominator of the Vulgar Fraction is to its Numerator, fo is the given Denominator of the Decimal Fraction to its Numerator required. So if $\frac{96}{120}$ be a Vulgar Fraction given, to be changed into a Decimal, whofe Denominator is 100 ; then as 120 : 96 : : 100 : 80, fo that 80 is the Decimal required, and on the contrary. Decimal Fractions may be changed into Vulgar Fractions by this Analogy, *viz.* as the Decimal Denominator is to its Numerator, fo is the given Vulgar Denominator, to its Numerator required.

Let $\frac{80}{100}$ be changed into a Vulgar Fraction whofe Denominator is 120 ; then as 100 : 80 : : 120 : 96, fo that $\frac{96}{120}$ is the Vulgar Fraction required.

Note, It will happen in many Cafes, of changing Vulgar Fractions into Decimals, that there will be ftill a Remainder although you fhould annex ten thoufand Cyphers to the Numerator of the given Fraction; and therefore it is to be noted, that if you make the Decimal to confift of five or fix Places, it will be near enough in almoft every Cafe of Bufinefs, and the Remainder may be rejected as of no Value.

Now there only remains to fhew how to find the Value of any given Decimal Parts of a Foot, Pounds Sterling, &c. which is done by this

Rule. Multiply the given Decimal into the Units that are contained in the Integer, (as in Decimal Multiplication) and the Product will be the Value of the Decimal.

EXAMPLE I.

Suppofe ,7852 be a given Decimal, whofe Integer is a Foot.

Here the Decimal ,7852, multiplied by 12, the Inches or Units that are contained in a Foot, which is the Integer, the Product is 9,4124, which is 9 Inches, and ,4124 Parts of an Inch. And if we fuppofe an Inch to be divided into 100 Parts, then multiplying 4124 the Remains by 100, the Product is 41,2400, which is 41 hundred Parts of an Inch, and the Remains 2400, is 2400 Parts of one hundredth Part of an Inch divided into ten thoufand Parts. So that rejecting this laft Remains 2400, the Value of the given Decimal is 9 Inches and 41 hundred Parts of an Inch.

$$\begin{array}{r} ,7852 \\ 12 \\ \hline 9,4124 \\ 100 \\ \hline 41,2400 \end{array}$$

EXAMPLE II.

Suppofe the aforefaid Decimal fignify a Decimal Part of a Pound Sterling.

Thes

,7852

20 the Shillings in 1 *l*.
—————
15,7040

12 the Pence in 1 *s*.
—————
8,4480

4 the Farthings in 1*d*.
—————
1,7920

Then ,7852, multiplied into 20, the Units, or Shillings in the Integer or Pound, the Product 15,7040 is 15 Shillings, and 7070 remains; which being multiplied by 12, the Units in the next less Integer, *viz.* the Pence in a Shilling, the Product 8,4480 is 8 Pence, and 4480 remains; and which being multiplied by 4, the Farthings in a Penny, the Product is 1,7920, which is one Farthing, and 7920 Parts of a Farthing, the Farthing being divided into ten thousand Parts. So the Value of the Decimal, 7852 Part of one Pound Sterling, is 15 Shillings, 8 Pence, and 1 Farthing, rejecting the last Remains 7920. Thus, a due Regard being had to the Number of Units, which are contained in the Denomination of the Integer, to which the Decimal Parts belong, any proposed Number of a Decimal may be reduced or changed into the known Parts of what they represent.

LECT. IX. *The Extraction of the Square and Cube Roots.*

TO extract the square Root, is nothing more than to find the Side of a Geometrical Square, whose Area is equal to a given Number of Units, which are generally called a square Number. A square Number, is that which is produced by any Number multiplied into itself: As for Example, 16 is a square Number, which is produced by 4 multiplied into 4. So in like Manner, 9 is a square Number, produced by 3 multiplied into 3. The Side of a geometrical Square, equal to any given Number, is called its Root.

In the Margin is a Table of square Numbers, whose Roots are the nine Digits, and which being nothing more than a Part of the Multiplication Table, it is supposed you have it already by Heart.

Ro.	Squ.
1	1
2	4
3	9
4	16
5	25
6	36
7	49
8	64
9	81

Let 672 be a Root given to find its square Number.

l 672
m 672
—————
1344
4704
4032
————— *n d e f*
451584 (672
q b c p
36
—————
g t —
12,7) 91,5 first Resolvend,
889
h k —————
134,2) 268,4 second Resolvend.
2684
—————
0 rem.

Rule. Multiply 672 into itself as at *l m*, whose Product is 451584, the square Number required, and whose Root is thus extracted, *viz.* First, place a Point under the first Figure to the right Hand, as at *c*, and at every other Figure towards the Left, as at *b* and *a*; and observe, that as many Points as the square Number contains, so many Places of Figures the Root will consist of. Secondly, make a Crotchet as at *n* and *p* on the right Hand Side of the square Number, as is done in Division; and note, that every two Figures so pointed, are called a Punctation. Thirdly, find in the Table the nearest square Number that is contained in the first Punctation to the left Hand, *viz.* in 45, which is 36, whose Root is 6. Place 36 under 45, and its Root 6 in the Quotient, as at *d*, and subtracting 36 from 45, the Remains is 9, which place under 36. This is your

your firſt Work, and is no more to be repeated. Fourthly, bring down the next Punctation 15, and join it to the Remains 9, making it 915, which is your firſt Reſolvend, and on its left Side make a Crotchet, as is done in Diviſion to ſeparate the Diviſor from the Dividend. Fifthly, double the Root 6, it makes 12, which place on the left of the Reſolvend, as at *g*. Then rejecting the laſt Figure 5 in the Reſolvend (which is always to be done) ſee how often the Diviſor 12 is contained in the remaining Figures 91, which being 7 Times, therefore put 7 in the Quotient at *e*, and alſo on the right Hand of the Diviſor at *i*, and multiply 127, the Diviſor increaſed by 7, whoſe Product is 889, which place under 915, and being ſubtracted from it, the Remains is 26. This being done, bring down the next Punctation 84, and join it to the Remains 26, making it 2684, which is a ſecond Reſolvend, and then proceed as before, as follows, *viz*. Firſt, double 67 the Root ſo far found, makes 134, which place on the left of the ſecond Reſolvend, as at *h*, and ſee how often 134 is contained in the Reſolvend, the laſt Figure excepted, *viz*. in 268, which is two times. Set two in the Quotient at *f*, and on the right Hand of that laſt Diviſor 134, making it 1342, which being multiplied by 2, the laſt Figure in the Quotient, its Product is 2684, which being placed under the ſecond Reſolvend, and ſubtracted from it as before, o remains ; which ſhews that 451584 is a ſquare Number, whoſe ſquare Root is 672, as required.

Note, Firſt, when the ſquare Number contains 4 or more Punctations, as the Remains are produced, the next Punctation is to be brought down, and joined to the Remains for a third, &*c*. Reſolvend ; with which you are to proceed in every Reſpect as before with the firſt and ſecond Reſolvend. Secondly, that if at any time, when you have multiplied the Number ſtanding in the Place of the Diviſor, by the Figure laſt found in the Quotient or Root, the Product be greater than the Reſolvend, then in ſuch a Caſe, you are to put a Figure leſs by one, than the former, in the Quotient, and multiply by it as before : and when the Remainder be greater than the Diviſor, put a Figure greater by one in your Quotient, and multiply it as before. Thirdly, if at any Time the Diviſor cannot be had in the Reſolvend, then place a Cypher in the Quotient, and alſo on the right Hand of the Diviſor, and to the Reſolvend annex the next Punctation for a new Reſolvend, with which proceed as before. When it happens, that, after Extraction is made, there is a Remainder, the Number given to be extracted, is called an irrational or ſurd Number, and its Root cannot be exactly obtained, although by adding Cyphers you may come as near the Truth as is required, but never can come at the Truth itſelf.

As for Example, 'tis required to extract the ſquare Root of 160.

160(12,64911
1
—
22)060 first Resolvend.
    44

x   p —ab
24.6) 1600 second Resolvend.
    1476

z   —c d
252,4) 12400 third Resolvend.
    10096

s   —e f
2528,9) 230400 fourth Resolvend.
    227601

a   —g h
25298,1) 279900 fifth Resolvend.
    252981

x   y —i k
25298?,1) 2691900 sixth Resolvend.
    2529821

162079 rem.

First, The first Punctation being 1, the square of 1 is 1, which place under 1, and subtracting 1 from 1 remains 0; set 1 in the Quotient, and to 0, bring down the next Punctation 60, making the Remains 0,060. Secondly, double the Quotient, 1, makes 2, which place for your Divisor at *l*. Now as 2 is contained 3 Times in 6, if you was to place 3 in the Quotient, and 3 on the right Hand of the Divisor 2, as before taught, to make the Divisor 23, then 23 multiplied by 3, would be equal to 69, which is greater than 60 the first Resolvend, and therefore cannot be subtracted from it: therefore in this Case, as was before noted, place a Figure in the Quotient less by 1 than the 3, *viz.* 2, and the same on the right Hand of the Divisor 2, as at *m*, and then multiplying the Divisor 22, by 2 in the Quotient, the Product is 44, which being placed under the first Resolvend 60, and subtracted from it, the Remains is 16. Thirdly, to the Remains 16, annex two Cyphers, as at *a b*, making it 1600 for a second Resolvend; and then proceeding as before, the next Figure in the Quotient will be 6, and 124 remains, to which annex two Cyphers more, as at *c d*, making the Remains 124,12400, which is your third Resolvend. Proceed in like manner, by continually adding two Cyphers to each Remainder, until you have increased the Figures in the Quotient to as many Places as may be required. In this Example I have increased them to 5 Places, which I apprehend to be near enough for any Business, for if Unity was divided into a hundred thousand Parts, there would not be two Parts wanted; for 12,64911, being multiplied into Itself, its Product is 159,9999837921, which is very near equal to 160, the given number to be extracted, and as the Fraction ,9999837921, is less than the Fraction ,00002, therefore the Root is not two Parts of one hundred thousand Parts of an Unit less than the Truth.

To extract the *Square* Root of a *Vulgar Fraction*, *which is commensurable to its Root*; that is, *a Fraction which, after that Extraction is ended, hath no Remains.*

Rule. Extract the square Root of the Numerator for the Numerator of the Root, and also the square Root of the Denominator, for the Denominator of the said Root.

To extract the Square Root of a *Vulgar Fraction, which is incommensurable to its Root*; that is, *a Fraction which, after that Extraction is ended, hath a Remain.*

Rule. Reduce the given Fraction into a Decimal, and then extract its Root as before taught: or find the integral Part of the Root, to its Quadruple, and then adding Unity for the Denominator of the Fractional Part, the Remainder being doubled, is the Numerator. So the Root of 160 in the foregoing Example, is 12 4/49.

The Extraction of the Cube Root.

A Cube Number, is that Number which is produced by multiplying any Number into itself, and its Product again by the same Number. So 64 is a Cube Number, produced by 4 multiplied in 4, equal to 16, and 16 into 4, equal to 64. A Cube Number, is a supposed Quantity of Matter, put together in the Form of a *Dice*, as Figure Y, Plate II. and the Length or Measure of one Side of such a Body, is called its Root; therefore to extract the Cube Root of any given cubical ed Number, is nothing more than to find the Length of the Side of a Cube which contains a Quantity equal to the Number given.

As in the square Root, a Table of the Squares of the 9 Digits is of use for the ready finding the nearest less Square in a Punctation, so here a Table of the cubick Numbers of the nine Digits is of very great use for the immediate finding the nearest less cubick Number in a Punctation, and is therefore placed in the Margin, and which is thus made.

Ro.	Cu,
1	1
2	8
3	27
4	64
5	125
6	216
7	343
8	512
9	729

Let 8 be a Root given, to find its cubed Number.

Multiply 8 into 8, its product equal to 64 is the cube Number required. This is also called the cubing of a Number, as supposing 8 had been a Number given to be cubed.

To extract the Cube Root.

Let 146363183 be a cubed Number given to find its Root.

First, point the first Figure towards the right Hand, and then every third Figure towards the left, as at *f e d*. Secondly, look in your Table of cubed Numbers, and find the nearest less cube Number to 146, the first Punctation, which is 125, whose Root is 5. Place 5 in the Quotient at *a*, and 125 under 146, and subtracting 125 from 146, the Remains is 21. This is your first Work, and no more to be done. Thirdly, to 21 the Remains, annex 363, the next Punctation, making 21,21363, which is your first Resolvend. Now to find a Divisor, by which you are to divide this Resolvend, its two last Figures excepted, which are always to be rejected, proceed as follows, *viz.* First, square the Quotient 5, makes 25, which Triple makes 75, which is the Divisor required, as at *g*. Then say the 75's in 213 (the Figures remaining in the Resolvend, exclusive of the two last rejected

$$d \quad \text{a} f \; abc$$
$$146363183 \; (527$$
$$125$$

g)
$75)\ 21.3.63.\ \text{first Resolvend.}$
$b\ \ 150$
$i\ \ 60$ } Subducends.
$k\ \ \ 8$

15608. Subtrahend.

$8113)\ 5755,1,83.\ \text{second Resolvend.}$
$m\ 56784$
$n\ \ 7644$ } Subducends,
$p\ \ \ 343$

5755183 Subtrahend.

o rem.

as aforesaid) is 2 times, equal to 150, which place under 213, as at *b*, and set 2 in the Quotient at *b*. Secondly, treble 5, the first Figure of the Root, equal to 15, which multiply by 4, the Square of 2, the last Figure in the Quotient makes 60, which place under 150, one Place forward to the right Hand, as at *i*; also Cube 3, the last Figure of the Quotient equal to 8, which place under 60, one Place more to the right, as at *k*. Then the 3 Subducends, 150, 60, and 8, being added as they stand, their Sum make a Subtrahend 15608, which being subtracted from the first Resolvend, there remains 5755; to which bring down and annex the next Punctation 183, making 5755183, for a second Resolvend, with which you are to proceed, as before; but to make the Performance quite easy, I will explain this Repetition also, as follows.

First, Find a Divisor as follows, *viz.* Square 52, the Quotient already found, makes 2704, which trebled makes 8112 the Divisor required. Then say, how often 8112 in 57551, (for here as before the two last Figures 83, of the Resolvend, are to be rejected) answer 7 times, equal to 56784, which place under 57551, of the Resolvend, and set 7 in the Quotient at *n*. Secondly, treble 52, the first and second Figures of the Root, equal to 156, which multiply by 49 the Square of 7, the last Figure in the Quotient makes 7644, which place under

4

56784, one Place more to the right Hand, as at *n* ; alſo Cube 7, the laſt Figure in the Quotient, equal to 343, which place under 7644, one Place more to the right, as at *p*. Then the three Subducends 56784 at *m*, 7644 at *n*, and 343 at *p*, being added as they ſtand, their Sum make a Subtrahend, 5755183, which being ſubtracted from 5755183, the ſecond Reſolvend, nothing remains ; which ſhews that the given Number 146363183 is a cube Number, whoſe Root is 527, as required.

Note I. *As many Punctations as any given Number contains, except the firſt, ſo many Times is the Work to be repeated.*

II. *That in all Extractions, when a Diviſor cannot be found ſo often as once in its Dividend, or if it can be found, and yet there ſhall ariſe a Subtrahend greater than the Reſolvend, in both theſe Caſes a Cypher muſt be put in the Quotient and annexed to the laſt Diviſor alſo, for a new Diviſor ; and the next Punctation being brought down and added to the laſt Reſolvend, makes a new Reſolvend, with which proceed in every Reſpect as before.*

III. When Numbers remain after the laſt Subtrahend is ſubtracted from the laſt Reſolvend, which very often happen, ſuch are called irrational or ſurd Numbers, becauſe their Roots cannot be exactly diſcovered. But if to ſuch Remainder you annex three Cyphers, continually, as you did two Cyphers in the ſquare Root, you may come very near to the Truth, as was there ſhewn.

To extract the Cube Root of a Vulgar Fraction which is commenſurable to its Root.

Rule. Extract the Cube Root of the Numerator for the Numerator of the Root ; and the Cube Root of the Denominator for the Denominator of the ſaid Root.

To extract the Cube Root nearly, of a Vulgar Fraction remaining, incommenſurable to its Root.

Rule. The Integral Part of your Root being firſt found, as before taught, to the Treble thereof add one, and that Sum added to the Square of the ſaid Root tripled, is a Denominator ; to which the laſt Remainder, after Extraction is finiſhed, is the Numerator.

A Table of the Roots of all ſquare and cubed whole Numbers, from 1 to 50, calculated by THOMAS LANGLEY.

R.	Sq.	Cube	R.	Sq.	Cube	R.	Sq.	Cube	R.	Sq.	Cube
1	1	1	14	196	2744	27	729	19683	40	1600	64000
2	4	8	15	225	3375	28	784	21952	41	1681	68921
3	9	27	16	256	4096	29	841	24389	42	1764	74088
4	16	64	17	289	4913	30	900	27000	43	1849	79507
5	25	125	18	324	5832	31	961	29791	44	1936	85184
6	36	216	19	361	6859	32	1024	32668	45	2025	91125
7	49	343	20	400	8000	33	1089	35937	46	2116	97336
8	64	512	21	441	9261	34	1156	39304	47	2209	103823
9	81	729	22	484	10648	35	1225	42875	48	2304	110592
10	100	1000	23	529	12167	36	1296	46656	49	2401	117649
11	121	1331	24	576	13824	37	1369	50653	50	2500	125000
12	144	1728	25	625	15625	38	1444	54652			
13	169	2197	26	676	17576	39	1521	59319			

Thus

Thus have I given all the useful Rules in Vulgar and Decimal Arithmetic both in whole Numbers and in Fractions, which if well confidered will be, not only very foon and eafily underftood, but vaftly advantageous to every Workman in the Execution of his Employs. And as a perfect Knowledge herein may be foon acquired by employing the leifure Hours of Evenings when the Labour of the Day is over, I humbly conceive that every one who will fo employ himfelf will find, not only a very agreeable Amufement, but very great Helps in the Performance of his feveral Works, exclufive of the Reputation that will attend him alfo. But fuch Perfons who will be fo remifs as to lay by this Work in their Chefts, &c. without taking either Pains or Pleafure herein, cannot expect that Advantage which others will enjoy.

PART II. Of GEOMETRY.

INTRODUCTION.

THE next Science in order after Arithmetic is GEOMETRY, the moft excellent Knowledge in the World, as being the *Bafis* or Foundation of all Trade, on which all Arts depend.

GEOMETRY is fpeculative and practical ; the former demonftrates the Properties of Lines, Angles and Figures ; the latter teaches how to apply them to Practice in *Architecture, Trigonometry, Menfuration, Surveying, Mechanicks, Perfpective, Dialling, Aftronomy, Navigation, Fortification*, &c. This Art was firft invented by JABAL the Son of LAMECH and ADAH, by whom the firft Houfe with Stones and Trees was built.

JABAL was alfo the firft that wrote on this Subject, and which he performed, with his Brethren, JUBAL, TUBAL CAIN, and NAAMAH, who together wrote on two Columns the Arts of *Geometry, Mufick, working in Brafs and Weaving*, which were found (after the Flood of NOAH) by HERMARINES, a Defcendant from Noah, who was afterwards called HERMES, the Father of Wifdom, and who taught thofe Sciences to other Men. So that in a fhort time the Science of *Geometry* became known to many, and even to thofe of the higheft Rank, for the mighty NIMROD, King of *Babylon*, underftood Geometry, and was not only a Mafon himfelf, but caufed others to be taught *Mafonry*, many of whom he fent to build the City of *Nineve* and other Cities in the *Eaft*. ABRAHAM was alfo a Geometer, and when he went into *Egypt*, he taught EUCLID, the then moft worthy Geometrician in the World, the Science of Geometry, to whom the whole World is now largely indebted for its unparalleled Elements of Geometry. HIRAM, the chief Conductor of the Temple of *Solomon*, was alfo an excellent Geometer, as was GRECUS, a curious Mafon who worked at the Temple, and who afterwards taught the Science of Mafonry in *France*.

ENGLAND was entirely unacquainted with this noble Science, until the time of St. ALBAN, when Mafonry was then eftablifhed, and *Geometry* was taught to moft Workmen concerned in Building ; but as foon after this Kingdom was frequently invaded, and nothing but Troubles and Confufion reigned all the Land over, this noble Science was difregarded until ATHELSTAN, a worthy King of *England*, fuppreffed thofe Tumults, and brought the Land into Peace ; when *Geometry* and *Mafonry* were re-eftablifhed, and great Numbers of Abbeys and other ftately Buildings were erected in this Kingdom. EDWIN the Son of ATHELSTAN was alfo a great Lover of Geometry, and ufed to read Lectures thereof to Mafons. He

I · alfo

alſo obtained from his Father a Charter to hold an Aſſembly, where they would, within the Realm, once in every Year, and himſelf held the firſt at *York*, where he made Maſons; ſo from hence it is, that Maſons to this Day have a grand Meeting and Feaſt, once in every Year. Thus much by way of Introduction, to ſhew the Uſe, and how much the Science of Geometry has been eſteemed by ſome of the greateſt Men in the World, and which with regard to the Public Good of my Country, I have here explained, in the moſt plain and eaſy manner that I am able to do, and to which I proceed.

LECTURE I. *Geometrical Definitions. Plate* I.

THE Principles of Geometry are Definitions, Axioms and Poſtulates. *Defini-tions* are the Explication of ſuch Words and Terms which concern a Propo-ſition towards rendering it intelligible and eaſy to the Underſtanding, avoiding in Demonſtration all Difficulties and Objections. *Axioms* are ſuch evident Truths, as are not to be denied, as one and one are two, two and two are four, *&c. Poſtu-lates* are Demands, or Suppoſitions of things practicable, and the manner of doing them ſo eaſy, plain, and evident, that no Man of Senſe and Judgment can deny, or conteſt them, ſuch as to draw a Line by the Side of a Ruler, from one given Point to another.

QUANTITY is conſidered in three different Manners, *viz.* Firſt, Length with-out Breadth, as an Interval or Diſtance between two Points. Secondly, Length with Breadth only, as a Shadow, *&c.* Thirdly, Length with Breadth and Thickneſs, or Depth, as a Brick, *&c.* The Bounds or Limits of *Quantity* are Points, Lines and Superficies.

Def. 1. *Of a Point.*
 A POINT, in the Practice of Geometry, is the ſmalleſt Object of Sight that can be made, and which is ſuppoſed to have no geo-metrical Magnitude, capable of being divided to our Sight, and is made by the Point of a Pin, Pen, Pencil, *&c.* as the Point A, Plate I.

Def. 2. *Of a given Point.*
 THE Varieties of Points, and their particular Denominations, are many; as for Example, if a Point be aſſigned, in any certain Place, as the Point *b*, in the Line *a d*, 'tis called a *given* Point, from whence the Line *b c* proceeds, or to which the Line *b c* is drawn from the End or Point *c*. *Secondly*, when the two Lines cut acroſs each other, as *x c, y y*, or *c b, i f*, the Points *z* and *g*, are called *Points of Interſection*; and when ſuch a Point happens to be in the Middle of a ſuperficial Figure, as *g*, 'tis called its Centre, or *central* Point. *Thirdly*, when two Lines meet together, and ſtop in one Point, as *k m*, and *m l*, in the Point *m*, ſuch a Point is called an angular Point. *Fourthly*, if two Lines touch one another, but do not cut acroſs each other, as at B, the Point of touch B, is called the *Point of Contact*.

Def. 3. *Of a Point of In-terſection.*

Def. 4. *Of an angular Point.*

Def. 5. *Of a Point of Contact.*

 THERE are many other Kinds of Points, in the ſeveral Parts of Mathematicks, which at preſent do not concern us; as for Exam-ple, in Perſpective there are Points of Sight, Points of Diſtance, viſual Points, *&c.* which will be better underſtood hereafter, when I come to explain the Principles and Practice of that Art.

Def. 6. *Of Lines, Super-ficies and So-lids.*
 WHEN Quantities are conſidered as Lengths only, they are called *Lines*; thoſe of Lengths with Breadths only, are called *Su-perficies*; and thoſe of Lengths, Breadths, and Depths, are called *Solids*, or *Bodies*.

Kinds of Line.
 THE Kinds of Lines are three, *viz.* a *right Line*, a *curved Line*, and a *mixed Line*.

I   A RIGHT

A right Line, is a Length without Breadth, as the neareſt Diſtance between two Points; but in Practice, 'tis a ſtraight Line deſcribed by the Motion of a Pen, Pencil, &c. drawn by the ſide of a ſtraight Rule, wherein its viſible Breadth is not conſidered, as *a d*. *Def. 7. Of a right Line.*

A curved Line, is any Line that is not a right Line, and therefore all crooked, arched, or bended Lines, are curved Lines. There are many Kinds of curved Lines, namely a circular or arched Line, as E, *Fig.* II. an elliptical or ovallar Line, as *h l*, or *i m l*, a parabolical Line, as *w z y*, a hyperbolical Line, as 123, a ſerpentine Line, as B, a rampant arched Curve, as F, and an irregular curved Line, as D There are alſo many other Kinds of Curves, as the *Epicycloid, Cycloid, Algebraick Curve, Logarithmetical Curve, Ciſſoid, Catenaria, Evolute Curve, Catacauſtick* and *Diacauſtick Curves, Helicoid Parabola,* or *Parabolick Spiral,* &c. But as they have no relation to the Buſineſs of Builders, for whom this Work is only deſigned, I ſhall forbear to ſay any thing of their Generation and Uſe. *Def. 8. Of curved Lines.*

A circular or arched Line, is that whoſe Curvature or Bending is the ſame in every Part, as *f c e, Fig.* II. *Def. 9. Of a circular or arched Line.*

An ovallar or elliptical Line, is ſo called, as being a Part of the Boundary of an Oval or Ellipſis, as *i h l,* and the Lines *w z y,* and 123, are called parabolical and hyperbolical Lines, as being the Boundaries of a Parabola, and of a Hyperbola. *Def. 10. Of an elliptical, parabolical, and hyperbolical Line.*

A Serpentine Line, as A, is ſo called, from its being like the form of a Snake when 'tis travelling along; and the Spiral Line B, may be alſo called a Serpentine Line, as repreſenting a Snake when coiled up. The *Artinatural Line* C, is ſo called from its being an artificial Repreſentation of the natural Turnings and Windings of Brooks, Rivers, &c. The *rampant Curve* F, is called ſo from its riſing higher on the one Side than on the other. And laſtly, the Curve D, is called irregular, as not having any of its oppoſite Parts equal. The circular Lines uſed in Architecture, are either ſingle or compound, as in *Fig.* III. The Mouldings compoſed of ſingle Curves, are the Ovolo A, the Cavetto B, the Apophyges E, the ſingle Aſtragal G, the double Aſtragal H, the Flute M, the Fillet N, and the Bead I. The compound Curves are the Cima-recta C, the Cima Inverſa D, the Scotia F, and the Volute K. *Reaſons why the Serpentine Spiral, artinatural, rampant, and irregular Lines are ſo calud.*

A mixed Line, is both right and curved, as *f e d c b a, Fig.* IV. being compounded of the right Lines *f e, d e, a b,* and of the two curved Lines *d e* and *b c.* Lines are diſtinguiſhed into finite and infinite, alſo into apparent and occult. *Def. 11. Of a mixed Line.*

A finite Line, is a known Length, bounded by two known Points, as the Line *g h, Fig.* IV. and therefore all Lines of known Lengths, are finite Lines. *Def. 12. Of a finite Line.*

An infinite Line, is that whoſe Length is undetermined, or cannot be known, as the Diameter of the Univerſe, &c. *Def. 13. Of an infinite Line.*

An apparent Line, is a Line deſcribed by the Point of a Pen, Pencil, &c. as *g h, Fig.* IV. *Def. 14. Of an apparent Line.*

An occult Line, is drawn or deſcribed with the Point of a Pair of Compaſſes, and in Practice is always expreſſed by Points as *i k,* and therefore is made generally a dotted or pricked Line. *Def. 15. Of an occult Line.*

Lines have their particular Denominations, according to their different Poſitions and Properties, as following. *Firſt,* If a right Line as *n, Fig.* IV. ſtand on a Line, as on *b o,* ſo as not to incline either to the right Hand or to the Left, it is then called a perpendicular Line, and that the Line *b o* being firſt made, is called a given Line. *Secondly,* If a Line be level with equal Inclination on *Def. 16. Of a perpendicular Line. Def. 17. Of a given Line.*

I 2

both

Def. 18. *Of a horizontal Line.* both Sides, as *p q*, 'tis called a horizontal Line. *Thirdly*, If a right Line be so situated, as to be neither perpendicular nor horizontal, as the Line z z, such a Line is called an oblique Line.

Def. 19. *Of an oblique Line.* And here note, that one Line may be perpendicular to another Line, although it may not be perpendicular to a horizontal Line: So K I is a perpendicular to the oblique Line F E. A Plumb Line is a direct downright Line, as G H, which is always perpendicular to a horizontal Line. *Fourthly*, If two right Lines are at an equal Distance from each other, as *r r* and *s s*, they are called parallel Lines, and which being infinitely continued, would never meet. *Fifthly*, If two circular Lines are at equal Distances from each other, as *t* and *u*, they are called Concentrick Arches, as being both described on the same Center. *Sixthly*, If two circular Lines have two different Centers, as the circular Lines *w x*, they are called excentrick Arches, as being described on different Centers. *Seventhly*, The curved Line that bounds a Circle, Ellipsis, or Oval, is called the Circumference; and by some, the Perimeter, or Periphery, as *b c d g*, *Fig.* V. But the boundary Lines of all right-lined Figures, as of A B C, are called Sides, excepting when at any Time such Figures are placed upright, so as to stand on their Sides, and then the Lower Side of every such Figure is called its Base: therefore that Line on which a Figure stands, is a base Line. *Eighthly*, A right Line drawn through the Center of a Circle, as *b d*, *Fig.* V. is called a Diameter; and one half of such a Diameter, as *b a*, or *a d*, is called the Radius, or Semi-diameter. *Ninthly*, If square Figures, as A or C, *Fig.* V. have right Lines drawn through their Centers, and are parallel to their Sides or Ends, as *k k* in A, and *m m* in C, they are also called the Diameters of those Figures: But all right Lines drawn from one opposite Angle to the other, as *o o* in A, and *n n* in C, are called diagonal Lines. The like is also to be observed in regular Figures, consisting of more Sides than four, as B, where *p p* is the Diameter, and 2 *q* the Diagonal. In all Figures that are not square, as C, the longest Diameter, as *l l*, is called the transverse, and the shortest, as *m m*, the conjugate Diameter; and which is also to be observed in the Diameters of an Oval, and of an Ellipsis, as in D. Every right Line drawn through any Part of a Circle, as *e f*, *Fig.* V. is called a Subtense, Ordinate, or chord Line; as also is a Line which joins the two Extremes of an Arch, as *x x*; and if a right Line be drawn so as to touch a Figure, without cutting into it, be the Point of Contact either at a Side, or at an Angle, as *h i*, in *g*, and 2, 'tis called a tangent Line.

Def. 20. *Of parallel Lines.*

Def. 21. *Of concentrick Arches.*

Def. 22. *Of excentrick Arches.*

Def. 23. *Of the Circumference of Circles and Ellipses.*

Def. 24. *Of the Sides of the right-lined Figures.*

Def. 25. *Of a base Line.*

Def. 26. *Of a Diameter, Radius, and Semi-diameter.*

Def. 27. *Of a diagonal Line.*

Def. 28. *Of transverse and conjugate Diameters.*

Def. 29. *Of a Chord Line.*

Def. 30. *Of a tangent Line.*

Def. 31. *Of the Kinds of Superficies.*

THE second Kind of Quantity, namely Superficies, is a Surface of whatever has Length and Breadth, without Depth or Thickness, (as by Def. 6.) and is of three Kinds, *viz.* First, Exactly flat, as the Surface of a Table. Secondly, Convex, as the Outside of a Ball. Thirdly, Concave, as the Inside of a Bowl.

Def. 32. *Of a Circle.*

SUPERFICIES are bounded by one or more Lines, and from thence it is, that they receive their various Names, by which they are known; as, first, if a Superficies be bounded by one curved Line that is regular in all its Parts as A, *Fig.* VI. 'tis called a Circle.

Def. 33. *Of a Semicircle.*

Def. 34. *Of a Quadrant.*

EVERY half Part of a Circle as D, is called a Semi-circle which is bounded by the Diameter and one half of the Circumference of a whole Circle. A Quadrant as H, is a Figure bounded by two Semi-diameters, (called the Sides) and one quarter Part of the Circumference, called the Limb.

I F

If a Circle be cut into two unequal Parts by a right Line, as *a b, Fig* VI. each part is called a Portion, or Segment, and which are diftinguifhed the one from the other, by greater and leffer ; fo *a c b* is the leffer Segment, and *a d b* the greater ; and

Def. 35. *Of the Segment of a Circle.*

If two Lines as *b k, b i,* in C, are drawn from the Center of any Circle unto its Circumference, and thereby divide the Whole into two unequal Parts, the Part lefs than a Semicircle, as *k i b,* is called a Sector, and the remaining Part, *b k l i,* is called the Complement of the Sector, and by fome the great Sector.

Def. 36. *Of a Sector.*

Now fince, by this Definition, a Sector is a Part of a Circle which is lefs than a Semicircle, therefore a Quadrant is a Sector alfo, as being but half a Semicircle.

The Parts of an Oval, or Ellipfis, are denominated in the fame Manner as the Parts of a Circle. So the Figures B and C, *Fig.* VII. are both Semi-Ellipfes, equal to each other; that of B being on the tranfverfe, and that of C, on the conjugate Diameter. And as every right Line drawn through the Center of a Circle, doth divide the Superficies thereof into two equal Parts, fo likewife every right Line drawn through the Center of an Ellipfis, does the fame. So *c e,* divides the Ellipfis *c m e n* in two equal Parts, as alfo doth either of the Lines *m n,* or *a i.* The Segments of an Ellipfis are either regular as *d c b,* and *k m i,* or rampant as *a k m i;* and the Lines *b d,* or *k i,* are called Ordinates, that of *k i* being an Ordinate on the tranfverfe Diameter, and that of *b d* on the conjugate Diameter. The Sector of an Ellipfis or of an Oval, as in A, *Fig.* VII. is the fame as in the Circle, as likewife is the Complement thereof.

The Parts of an Ellipfis have the fame Denomination as the Parts of a Circle.

Def. 37. *Of the Ordinates of an Ellipfis.*

Sector of an Ellipfis.

Now from hence you fee, that Circles, Ovals and Ellipfes, are the only regular Superficies that are bounded by one Line, and that all regular Superficies bounded by two Lines only, are no other than their Segments, either fingle, as the Segment *a c b,* in B, *Fig.* VI. or compound, as *a b c* and *a d c,* in H, *Fig.* VII. which laft is no more than two Segments, applied together, (the Line *a c* being common to both) and is called an Ox Eye.

Triangles *have their different Denominations, as being of different Forms, viz.* (1) If a Triangle have all its Sides equal as G, *Fig.* VI. 'tis called an equilateral Triangle. (2) If two Sides are equal, and the third unequal, as E, 'tis called an Ifofceles Triangle. (3) If all the Sides are unequal as F, 'tis called a Scalene Triangle. Triangles are alfo diftinguifhed by the Quantity of their Angles ; but this I fhall defer, until I have inftructed you in the Nature and Kinds of Angles.

Def. 38. *Of an Equilateral Ifofceles, and Scalenous Triangle.*

All Triangles, whofe Sides are Arches of Circles, are called fpherical Triangles, as N P Q, *Fig.* VII. And when Triangles are compofed both of right Lines, and circular Lines, as O R S, and V, they are called mixt Triangles, with one or two convex or concave Sides ; as for Example. (1) The Triangle O, hath two Sides that are right Lines, and the third that is a concave Arch. (2) The Triangles R and S, have each but one Side that is a right Line, and the others are Arches of Circles, of which, thofe of the Triangle R are convex, as being fwelling outward, and thofe of S, are concave, as being hollow outward. (3) The Triangle V, hath alfo but one Side that is a right Line, but the other two which are circular are one convex, and the other concave.

Def. 39. *Of a Spherical Triangle.*

Def. 40. *Of mixt Triangles.*

Every Triangle contained under three equal Sides, be they right-lined, circular, or mixt, is called an equilateral Triangle, and fo the like of Ifofceles and fcalenous Triangles ; and to diftinguifh right-lined Triangles from fpherical and mixt Triangles, they are in general called plain Triangles.

Def. 41. *Of plain Triangles.*

SUPERFICIES

I

Four-sided Figures.   SUPERFICIES bounded by four right Lines are the geometrical Square F ; *Fig.* VII. the Parallelogram G, the Rhombus I, the Rhomboides K, the Trapezoid L, and the Trapezium M.

Def. 42. Of a geometrical Square and Parallelogram.   THE GEOMETRICAL SQUARE F, is fo called, becaufe all its Sides are equal and fquare to each other, and the Parallelogram receives its Name from its oppofite Sides and Ends being parallel to each other. The Parallelogram is alfo called a long *Square* or *Oblong*, with regard to its being longer than wide.

Def. 43. Of a Rhombus and Rhomboides.   THE RHOMBUS I, is nothing more than a geometrical Square pufhed out of its natural fquare Form into any other : for fuppofing the Angles *d a e f* of the geometrical Square *d a e f*, in the Rhombus I, have each a moveable Joint at the feveral Angles ; if the Angle *d* be pufhed to *c*, the Angle *a* will be moved to *b*, and the Side *d e* will be removed to *c e*, the Side *a f* to *b f*, and the Side *d a* to *c b*.

The fame is alfo to be underftood of the Rhomboid, which is nothing more than a fquare Parallelogram, whofe Ends are pufhed out of their fquare Pofitions into oblique Pofitions.

Def. 44. Of a Trapezoid.   A TRAPEZOID is a Figure containing four Sides, of which two are parallel, and the other two are not, as Figure L.

Def. 45. Of a Trapezium.   A TRAPEZIUM is a Figure containing four unequal Sides, of which no two of them are parallel.

Def. 46. Of Polygons.   REGULAR Superficies bounded by five or more Sides are called Polygons, or Polygonals, or Multilaterals (that is, many Sides) as 5, 6, 7, 8, 9, 10, 11, 12, &c. and which take their Names from the Number of their Sides,

| So a Plain Figure confifting of | Five
Six
Seven
Eight
Nine
Ten
Eleven
Twelve | Sides, is called a regular | Pentagon
Hexagon
Septagon or Heptagon
Octagon
Nonagon
Decagon
Undecagon
Duodecagon | as are exhibited in Plate II. |

Def. 47. Of an irregular plain Figure.   FIGURES which have the fame Number of Sides and are unequal, are called irregular plain Figures, confifting of 5, 6, 7, 8, &c. Sides, as the irregular Figure under the Octagon in Plate II.

Def. 48. Of an irregular compound Figure.   ALL Figures bounded with right Lines and curved or mixt Lines are called mixtilineal Figures ; which are either irregular or regular ; that is to fay, if an irregular Figure have fome of its Sides curved, and fome that are right Lines unequal, it is called a compound irregular mixtilineal Figure ; but when a Figure is compofed of equal right-lined Sides and of equal arched Sides, they are called compound regular Figures.

Def. 49. Of a regular compound Figure.

Def. 50. Of Imperfect Figures, Concentrick and Excentrick.   WHEN Figures have Voids or Imperfections in their Superficies, they are called imperfect Figures, fuch as, A B, Plate II. wherein the dark or fhaded Parts reprefent the Superficies, and the light Parts the Deficiencies, Voids, or Imperfections thereof, and which are differently diftinguifhed, as thofe of A and B; having their Voids, or defective Parts, bounded by Lines defcribed on the fame Centers, are called concentrick Figures or Superficies ; and that of the Lunula, whofe Void is bounded with Circles defcribed upon different Centers, is called an excentrick Figure or Superficies ; *vide* Definitions XXI. and XXII. The imperfect Figures B and the Square on the Left of the Lunula are alfo to be confidered in the fame Manner, as A and the Lunula, notwithftanding that their Voids are bounded with parallel, right Lines. For as the Center of the Void in B, is the fame as that of the Superficies which bounds it, the whole is therefore a concentrick Figure, for the fame Reafon as is Figure A. And fo in like man-

ner,

ner, as the Center of the Voids, in the Square, is not in the fame Points as the Centers of the fhaded Superficies; that is alfo an excentrick Figure, as the Lunula.

To thefe imperfect Figures I muft add *Fig.* C, which is a Parallelogram divided into four Parallelograms, that meet all together on the Diagonal Line in the Point *n*.

Now if any three of thofe four Parallelograms, as *n d*, *n b*, and *n c*, be taken together, and confidered as one Figure, 'tis called a Gnomon; but if the four Parallelograms are confidered feparately, then the Parallelograms *n b*, and *n c*, are called Parallelograms defcribed about the Diagonal *b c*, and the other two Parallelograms *a n*, and *n d*, are the two Supplements thereof, and which are always equal to one another, as will be hereafter demonftrated. *Def.* 51. *Of a Gnomon.*

As fuperficial Figures are bounded by one or more Lines, fo Solids or Bodies are bounded by one or more Superficies; as for Example, a Brick is a Solid, bounded with fix Surfaces, that are all Parallelograms, *viz.* the upper and the under, the two Sides, and both Ends. *Def.* 52. *Of the Bounds of Solids or Bodies.*

The Number of entire Solids are principally twenty, *viz.* a Sphere, a Spheroid, a Cylinder, a Cone, a Conoid, a Spindle, a Tetrahedron, a Pyramid, a Pyramis, a Pyramidoid, a Conedoid, a Cylindroid, a Prifm, a Hexahedron or Cube, a Parallelopipedon, an Octahedron, a Dodecahedron, an Icofahedron, the twelve and the thirty Rhombufes. *The Number and Names of Solids.*

An entire geometrical Solid is a Body from which no Part has been taken, and therefore the Remains of a Body, when a Part thereof is taken away, is called a Fruftum, as the Fruftum of a Sphere, or of a Cone, &c. *Def.* 53. *Of an entire Solid.*

A Sphere is a round Body, bounded by one convex Superficies, whofe Parts are all at the fame Diftance from the central Point of the Solid; and is commonly called a Ball, as R, Plate II. *Def.* 54. *Of the Fruftum of a Sphere.* *Def.* 55. *Of a Sphere.*

A Spheroid is a round folid Body, bounded by one convex Superficies alfo, but its Curvature is not the fame in every Part over its Center, as the Curvature of the Sphere; becaufe its Length is greater than its greateft Thicknefs, and therefore it is what may be properly called an ovallar Solid, if we confider the Sphere as a circular Solid; as S, Plate II. *Def.* 56. *Of a Spheroid.*

A Cylinder is a long and round Body of equal Thicknefs, as a Garden rolling Stone, or the lowermoft third Part of the Shaft of a Column, as X, Plate II. and is bounded by three Superficies, of which one is convex, and two are plane or flat, and whofe Figures depend upon the manner of the Cylinder being cut at each End; that is to fay, (1) If the Ends of the Cylinder be both cut fquare to its Length, as X, then the Superficies of the two Ends are both Circles (which are equal to each other, becaufe the Cylinder is of equal Thicknefs) and the convex Superficies is no more than a Parallelogram whofe Length is equal to the Length of the Cylinder, and Breadth to its Circumference, being bended about the fame. (2) If a Cylinder as D (on the right-hand Side of the Plate) have its Ends cut obliquely and parallel to each other, the fuperficial Figure of each End will be an Ellipfis, and the convex Superficies will be a double Rhomboides. (3) If a Cylinder, as E, have its Ends cut obliquely, and not parallel to each other, they will be both Ellipfes, but unequal, (as not being parallel, which caufes the tranfverfe Diameter to be longer in the one than in the other) and the convex Superficies will be an irregular Hexagon; a Demonftration of which you will fee in the Menfuration of Solids and their Superficies. *Def.* 57. *Of a Cylinder.* *Def.* 58. *Of the various Kinds of Superficies that bound regular and oblique Cylinders.*

A Cone

Def. 59. Of a Cone. A Cone is a round Solid, which rises either from a Circle or an Ellipsis, with a gradual and equal Diminution until it terminates or ends in a Point, as *Fig.* T, on the left Side of Plate II. and therefore is bounded by two Superficies, of which that of the Outside is convex, and that of its End or Bottom is a circular or elliptical Plane. In every

Def. 60. Of the Vertex and Axis of a Cone. Cone there is an imaginary Line supposed to be drawn from its Top or vertical Point, unto the centrical Point of its Base, which is called the Axis of the Cone, and which is so called because it passes directly through the Middle of the Solid, and on which the Body may be made to revolve or turn about, as that every opposite Part is equidistant therefrom. The same is also to be understood of *a b*, the Axis of the Sphere R, also of *e c*, in the Spheroid S, and of all other regular Solids. Now when a Cone hath its Bottom cut square to its Axis, as T, 'tis called a regular Cone, and its Bottom, which is called its Base, will be a Circle. But if its Bottom be cut obliquely to its Axis, as G, on the right-hand Side of the Plate, it is then called an oblique Cone, and its Base will be an Ellipsis.

Def. 61. Of a Conoid. A Conoid is a Solid, diminishing in its upper Parts nearly the same as a Cone, and takes its Rise from a Circle also; but as the Side of a Cone is straight from its Base to its Vertex, this of a Conoid is either the Semi-curve of a Parabola or of a Hyperbola, or the Segment of a Circle, or an Ellipsis; and therefore terminates at its Vertex either in a Point, as the Cone doth when the outward Curve is of a Circle or an Ellipsis, as B L, or with a curved Top, like unto a Sugar-Loaf, as A, when a Semi-parabola, or Semi-hyperbola.

Def. 62. Of a Parabolick and Hyberbolick Spindle. A Spindle is a Solid, thus to be conceived; suppose *a g* in B, to be the Diameter of a Circle, on which a Semi-spindle is to be raised, whose Axis is *d*; also suppose the Curve *a d* to be the Semi-curve of a Parabola; now if from every Part of the Circumference of a Circle, of which *a g* is the Diameter, a Solid be raised with a Curvature equal to the Semi-parabola *a d*, that Solid will be a Semi-spindle, and therefore two such, being equal and applied together, as B, will form that Solid which is called a Spindle. And as the outward Curve may be either a Hyperbola, or a Parabola, therefore a Spindle may be Hyperbolical or Parabolical.

Def. 63. Of a Tetrahedron. A Tetrahedron is a triangular Solid, which rises from an equilateral triangular Base, with a gradual and equal Diminution, until it terminates in a Point, as a Cone doth, which Point is also called its Vertex. This Solid is terminated by four equilateral Triangles, as B F, on the left-hand Side of the Plate.

Def. 64. Of a Pyramid. A Pyramid is a Solid, which rises from a geometrical Square, with a gradual Diminution, (as the Tetrahedron rises from an equilateral Triangle) and terminates in a vertical Point also. This Solid hath its Height at Pleasure, and is bounded by four Equilaterals or Isosceles Triangles on its Sides, and a geometrical Square at its Base, as *Fig.* V.

Def. 65. Of a Pyramis. A Pyramis is the same Solid as a Pyramid, only with this Difference, that whereas a Pyramid stands on a geometrical Square, and has but four Sides, which are all equilateral, or Isosceles Triangles, a Pyramis has some regular Polygon, as a Pentagon, Hexagon, &c. for its Base, with five, six, &c. Sides which are all Triangles, as in a Pyramid, and meet in a vertical Point also.

Def. 66. Of a Pyramidoid. A Pyramidoid is a pyramental Solid, whose Bottom is a triangle geometrical Square, or some regular Polygon, and Sides are the Curve of a Circle, Ellipsis, Parabola or Hyperbola, as *Fig.* IV.

Def. 67. Of a Cylindroid. A Cylindroid is a Solid, something like B I, the Frustum of a Cone, but with this Difference, that as the Frustum of a Cone is terminated at its Ends either with two Circles, if cut square to its Axis, or with two Ellipses, if cut oblique, or with a Circle and an Ellipsis, if one End be cut fquare, and the other oblique, the Ends of the Cylindroid are both cut fquare to its Axis; but the one is an Ellipfis, and the other a Circle, as *Fig.* C at the Top on the right Hand.

THE next Kind of Solids in order, are Prifms.

A PRISM is a folid Body, of equal Thicknefs as a Cylinder; but as a Cylinder is round, and its Length is thereby bounded by one Superficies only; fo a Prifm is bounded by three, five, fix, or more Parallelograms, and its Ends are either Triangles, geometrical Squares, Trapeziums, or fome Kind of Polygon, as a Pentagon, Hexagon, *&c.* So B C is a triangular Prifm, bounded by two Triangles at its Ends, and three Parallelograms on its Sides. B A is a Trapezium Prifm, bounded by two Trapeziums at its Ends, and four Parallelograms on its Sides. B E is a pentangular Prifm, bounded by two Pentagons at its Ends, and five Parallelograms on its Sides. And laftly, B D is a hexangular Prifm, bounded by two Hexagons at its Ends, and fix Parallelograms on its Sides.

Def. 68. *Of the various Kinds of Prifms.*

IT is alfo to be noted, that if the aforefaid Prifms have their Ends cut oblique to their Sides, then their Sides will be either Trapezoids or Rhomboids, and their Ends will be changed into different Kinds of Triangles, Parallelograms, and unequal-fided Polygons.

A CUBE or Hexahedron, is an exact fquare regular Solid (as a Dice), and is bounded by fix equal geometrical Squares, as *Fig.* Y.

Def. 69. *Of a Hexahedron or Cube.*

A PARALLELOPIPEDON, is alfo called a Long Cube, and by fome a Prifm; but as its Ends, as well as its Sides, are bounded by Parallelograms, which are never more nor lefs than fix in Number, as *Fig.* Z, it is therefore, with refpect to its Surfaces being all Parallelograms, properly a Parallelopipedon.

Def. 70. *Of a Parallelopipedon.*

AN OCTAHEDRON, is a regular Solid, bounded by eight equilateral Triangles, and is compofed of two equal Pyramids, having their Bottoms applied together, fo as to make but one Solid in the whole, as *Fig.* P, Plate II.

Def. 71. *Of an Octahedron.*

A DODECAHEDRON, is a regular Solid, bounded by twelve Pentagons, as *Fig.* O, Plate II.

Def. 72. *Of a Dodecahedron.*

AN ICOSAHEDRON, is a regular Solid alfo, and is bounded by twenty equilateral Triangles, as *Fig.* Q, Plate II.—The twelve Rhombs, and the thirty Rhombs, are Solids, bounded by as many Rhombufes; but though they have a Uniformity in themfelves, yet they are not regular Solids.

Def. 73. *Of an Icosahedron. The* 12 *and* 30 *Rhombs.*

THE regular Bodies are the Tetrahedron, the Hexahedron or Cube, the Octahedron, the Dodecahedron, and the Icofahedron, which being the only Bodies that can be inferibed within a Sphere, are therefore called regular Bodies.

What Solids are ftrictly regular Bodies.

A BODY is faid to be inferibed, when, being inclofed within another Body, every of its folid Angles terminates at the Superficies thereof; and that Body which contains the inferibed Body is called the circumfcribing Body.

The Reafon. Def. 74. *Of inferibed and circumfcribed Figures and Bodies.*

A SOLID Angle, is the meeting together of three or more right-lined Superficies.

A FRUSTUM, as in *Def.* 54, is the Remains of a Body, when a Part is taken away; fo if from the Sphere B G, the Part A be taken away, the Part B G remaining, is the Fruftum of a Sphere; and if from the Spheroid B N, the Part A be taken away, the Part N B is the Fruftum of a Spheroid: and fo the fame of B I, and B K, which are the Fruftums of a Cone, and of a Pyramid, when the top Parts D and A are taken from them. Fruftums of Bodies are cut obliquely, and that not only at their upper, but alfo at their under Parts, as H I K L M, and are then called oblique Fruftums. When a Part is taken from the Bottom of a Pyramid; or of a Cone, as the Parts *a* and *x*, in

Def. 75. *Of a folid Angle. Fruftums of a Sphere, Spheroid, Cone, &c. explained.*

K   F and

F and G, then the remaining upper Parts being confidered feparately, become
entire Bodies with oblique Bafes; but if they are confidered with
Def. 76. Of the Parts *a* and *x*, then they are no more than the greater Seg-
the Segments ments, and the Parts *a* and *x* are the lefler Segments, which to-
of a Cone, gether do but complete the two Solids; and when the upper Parts
Pyramid,&c. are confidered as entire oblique Bodies, and the Parts *a* and *x* are
confidered by themfelves, the Parts *a* and *x* are called Segments
Def. 77. Of of Fruftums, whofe Axis is equal to their perpendicular Height.
the Segment IF all the folid Angles of a Cube be fo taken away, as to make
of a Fruftum. every fquare Face of the Cube an Octagon, then the Remains
The Fruftum will be the Fruftum of a Cube, contained under fourteen Superfi-
of a Cube. cies or Faces, of which eight will be equilateral Triangles, and fix
The Fruftum will be Octagons. If the folid Angles of a Tetrahedron be fo ta-
of a Tetrahe- ken off, as to make each of its equilateral triangular Faces a
dron. Hexagon, the Remains will be the Fruftum of a Tetrahedron,
bounded by eight Superficies; of which four will be equilateral Triangles, and
four will be Hexagons.
I mention thefe Fruftums, only to give a Hint, that by this Method of cutting
off the folid Angles of Bodies, there may be a very great Variety of uncommon
Bodies produced.
The Shaft of THE Body or Shaft of a Column, is compofed of two Kinds of
a Column, is Solids, that is to fay, the lower one third Part of its whole Height,
a Cylinder, up to S B, is a Cylinder, and R, the Remainder, is the Fruftum,
and Fruftum of a Conoid.
of a Conoid. A SECTION of a Solid, is a fuperficial Figure, produced by
Def. 78. Of cutting off a Solid, directly through, in any Part; fo if from a
the Section of Sphere a Segment was to be cut, the flat Surface, or Superficies
a Solid. of that Cut, which is a Circle, is called its Section. And in like
Manner, if any Cone be cut quite through its Axis, from the Top
to its Bottom, the flat Superficies of that Section will be a Triangle.
Def. 79. Of THE Bafe of an upright Line, is a Point.
the Bafe of a THE Bafe of a Circle is a Point alfo, as the Point *g*, of the Cir-
Line. cle E, (*Fig.* V. Plate I.) ftanding on the tangent Line *h i*, which
Def. 80. Of by its Curvature can touch the Line *h i*, but in the Point *g*; for
the Bafe of a as every Point in the Circle's Circumference is at the fame Di-
Circle and ftance from the Center, and as the very next Point to *g*, in the
Ellipfis. Line *h i*, is at a greater Diftance from the Center *a* than the
Point *g*, therefore the Circle cannot touch the tangent Line in two
Points, and confequently the Bafe of the Circle is the Point *g*.
THE fame is to be underftood of the Bafe of an Ellipfis. Right-lined Figures
may have a Point for their Bafe alfo, by being fet on angular Points, as the Hex-
agon B, Plate I. which refts on its Angle 2, on the tangent Line *h i*.
As Points and Lines are the Bafes of Lines and Superficies; fo Points, Lines,
and Superficies, are the Bafes of Solids; as for Example: Firft, The Bafe of a
Sphere is a Point, for the fame Reafon, as it is the Bafe of a Circle; the fame is
alfo to be underftood of the Bafe of a Spheroid. Secondly, If we conceive the
curved Superficies of a Cylinder to be an infinite Number of Circles, like Hoops
fet clofe together, 'tis very eafy to conceive, that the Bafe of a Cylinder lying
down, is a right Line, becaufe every Circle can touch the Plane it lies on, but
in one Point only; and therefore all thofe Points in the feveral Circles of the
Cylinder's Length, will form a right Line.—The fame is alfo to be underftood
of a Cone laid on its Side. Thirdly, If a Cylinder be fet upright, then the
End it ftands on is its Bafe; as, indeed, is every Surface on which any Body
ftands. Fourthly, The Bafe of a Cone, Conoid, Pyramid, Pyramis, Pyramidoid,
&c. is that Superficies which is oppofite to the Vertex, and on which they commonly ftand; but in their Fruftums, the Superficies of both Ends are called Bafes, as the lefler Bafe and the greater Bafe: But though Cuftom has thus diftin-
6   guifhed

guifhed the fmall End from the greater, I muft own, I think it a very improper Manner of Diftinction, becaufe one Body cannot ftand on two oppofite Ends at the fame Time, and therefore cannot be confidered as two Bafes, but as two Ends, as they really are, and which may be diftinguifhed by the Names of Greater and Leffer, by only making ufe of the Word *End*, inftead of the Word *Bafe*; for, ftrictly fpeaking, except the Fruftum of a Cone ftands on one of its Ends, neither of the Ends is a Bafe; for when a Fruftum is laid on its Side, its Bafe is a right Line, contained between the two loweft Points of the Superficies of its Ends.

LECTURE II.
On the Formation, Names, Kinds, and Menfuration of Angles.

THE Angles I am now going to explain, are Angles on Superficies, or rather fuperficial Angles.

A SUPERFICIAL Angle is a Space contained between two Lines, of which one muft be oblique, and which meet each other in the fame Point; as for Example, *Fig.* I. Plate II. If the oblique Line *d e*, be continued forward, fo as to meet the Line *g f*, in the Point *f*; the Space that is contained between them is called an Angle.
Def. 81. Of a fuperficial Angle.

THERE are three Kinds of fuperficial Angles, that is to fay; (1) Right-lined, as *o n p*, *Fig.* II. Plate II. (2) Curvilineal, as *x y z*, and 1 2 3, of which *x y z* is a convex Angle, and 1 2 3 is a concave Angle. (3) Compound, or mixtilineal, as *q r s*, or *t w v*.
Def. 82. Of the Kinds of Angles.

RIGHT-lined Angles have three Denominations, which they receive according as their Openings are greater or leffer, *Right*, *Acute*, and *Obtufe*.
Def. 83. Of the Kinds of Angles.

A RIGHT Angle is that when two right Lines meet, and are fquare to each other, as *h k* and *m k*, *Fig.* II. Plate II. or when a perpendicular Line ftands on a given Line, as *h k* on *m l*; then the Angles on each Side of the Perpendicular *h k*, are both right Angles.
Def. 84. Of a right Angle.

AN Acute Angle is an Angle whofe Opening is lefs than a Right Angle, as the Angle made by the Lines *i k* and *k l*, or by the Lines *i k* and *h k*.
Def. 85. Of an Acute Angle.

AN Obtufe Angle is an Angle whofe Opening is greater than a Right Angle, as the Angle made by the Lines *i k* and *m k*.
Def. 86. Of an obtufe Angle.

AN Angle is meafured by the Arch of a Circle defcribed on its angular Point; and therefore the Meafure of an Angle, is the Quantity of that Arch which is contained between its Sides. The Quantity of an Arch, is the Number of Degrees that are contained therein.
Def. 87. Of the Meafure of an Angle.

A DEGREE is the 360th Part of the Circumference of any Circle, as appears by the following Example. Suppofe the Circle *c*, 90, *b d*, *Fig.* I. Plate II. be divided into four Quadrants, by the two Diameters, *c b*, and 90 *d*, and that the Limb of each Quadrant be divided into 90 equal Parts; then the whole Circumference of the Circle will be divided into 360 equal Parts, which are called Degrees, and confequently any one of them, which is the 360th Part of the whole, is a Degree.
Def. 88. Of a Degree.

AND from hence 'tis very plain, that the Limb of a Quadrant contains 90 Degrees; that the Limb of a Semi-circle contains 180 Degrees; that a right Angle contains 90 Degrees; that an acute Angle contains lefs than 90 Degrees; and that an obtufe Angle contains more than 90 Degrees.
Degrees in the Limb of a Quadrant and Semicircle.

IN every Circle there are 360 Degrees; for if from the Center A, you draw right Lines through every Degree, in the Circle *c* 90, *b d*, unto the Circle *b g f i*, they will divide the Circumference of that Circle into the fame Number of Degrees as the Circle *c* 90,
360 Degrees on every Circle.

b d; and in like Manner, the fame Lines will divide the fmall Circle *m l k a*, for the Arches *q k, p h*, and *o f*, do each contain the fame Number of Degrees.

How to find the Quantity or Meafure of an Angle.

Line of Chords, how made. BEFORE the Quantity of an Angle can be found, a Scale of Chords muft be made, as following, *viz.* Firft, Draw a right Line at pleafure, as *c b, Fig.* III. *Plate* II. and affign a Point therein, as *d*, whereon with any Radius, or Opening of your Compaffes, defcribe a Semi-circle, as *c a b*. Secondly, with any Opening of your Compaffes, greater than *d c*, on the Points *c* and *b*, defcribe the Arches, as *e e*, and *f f*, and from *d*, through the Point of Interfection *h*, draw the Line *d a*. Thirdly, fet the Radius *d c*, from *c* to 60, alfo from *a* to 30, on the Arch *c a*, which will then be divided into three equal Parts, at the Points 30 and 60. Fourthly, divide each third Part of the Arch *a c*, into three equal Parts, and then the whole Arch *a c*, will be divided into 9 Parts. Fifthly, divide each Part into Halves, and each Half into five equal Parts, and then the whole Arch *a c*, will be divided into 90 Degrees.

THIS being done, fet one Foot of your Compaffes on the Point *c*, and the other being opened to 10 Degrees, turn down that Opening, on the Line *b b*, from 10 to 10. In the fame Manner, on the Point *c*, take the Diftances *c* 20, *c* 30, *c* 40, *c* 50, *c* 60, *c* 70, *c* 80, and *c* 90, on the Arch *a c*, and turn them down to the Line *c b*, as before, aand thus you will have transferred every tenth Degree from the Limb *c a*, unto the right Line *c b*. In the fame Manner transfer every intermediate Degree, and then will the Scale, or Line of Chords, be completed and made fit for Ufe.

How to find the Quantity of an Angle. To find the Quantity of an Angle, you muft proceed as follows. Let *d a b, Fig.* II. *Plate* II. be an Angle given, to find its Quantity.

TAKE 60 Degrees in your Compaffes, from the Scale of Chords, and on the angular Point *a* defcribe an Arch, as *e c*; take the Extent of the Arch *e c* in your Compaffes, and apply one Foot to your Line of Chords, at the Beginning *c*, and the other Foot will fall on the Number of Degrees that is contained in the Angle.

Def. 89. Of the Degrees in the Radius of every Circle. THE Reafon why you muft take exactly 60 Degrees in your Compaffes for to defcribe the Arch *e c*, is becaufe that the Radius, or Semi-Diameter of every Circle, is equal to the Chord Line of 60 Degrees of its Circumference. And note, that if, in the meafuring of Angles, it fhould happen that the Sides of an Angle fhould be fhorter than 60 Degrees, the Radius of your Line of Chords, you muft, in fuch a Cafe, continue out the Sides of the Angle unto a fufficient Length.

To lay down any given Angle. To lay down an Angle equal to any Number of Degrees given, is a very eafy Work, and very little different from the laft; as for Example, fuppofe it is required to lay down an Angle equal to 30 Degrees: Firft, draw a right Line, as *b a, Fig.* II. *Plate* II. Secondly, take 60 Degrees in your Compaffes, from your Line of Chords, and on *a*, the End of the Line, defcribe an Arch at pleafure, as *c b*. Thirdly, take 30 Degrees, the Angle given, from your Line of Chords, and fet them on the Arch, from *c* to *c*. Laftly, from *a*, through the Point *c*, draw the Line *a d*; then will the Lines *d a* and *a b* make an Angle equal to 30 Degrees, as required.

Def. 90. Of Minutes in a Degree. As Quantities of Angles are fometimes whole Degrees, and fometimes Degrees and Parts of Degrees, it is therefore to be obferved, that every Degree is fuppofed to be fubdivided into fixty equal Parts, which are called Minutes, and therefore ½ of a Degree is 15 Minutes, ½ a Degree is 30 Minutes, ¾ of a Degree is 45 Minutes, ⅙ is 10 Minutes, ¹⁄₁₂ is 5 Minutes, &c.

DE-

Of GEOMETRY.

3

Degrees and Minutes are thus written or expreſſed, *viz.* ten Degrees, forty Minutes, and twenty-five Seconds, is thus written, 10°, 40′, 25″, and 40 Degrees, 15 Minutes, thus, 40° 15′.

Degrees and Minutes, how written.

Angles are expreſſed by three Letters, of which 'tis to be remembered, that the middle Letter always denotes the angular Point.—As for Example, to write or expreſs the Angle made by the Lines *d a b a, Fig.* II. Plate II. I write thus, the Angle *d a b,* or *b a d;* in both which Caſes you ſee that *a,* which ſtands at the angular Point, is kept in the Middle, and ſo the like of all other Angles.

How an Angle is written and denoted.

The Complement of an Angle is to be conſidered in two different Manners, that is to ſay, when it is to a Quadrant, and when to a Semi-circle. But be it which it will, the Complement of an Arch, or of an Angle, is ſo many Degrees as will make the given Angle, or given Arch, equal to 90, or to 180 Degrees. So 70 Degrees is the Complement of an Angle of 20 Degrees, to a Quadrant, and 160 Degrees is the Complement to a Semi-circle.

Def. 91. Of the Complement of Angles and Arches.

Angles are external, internal, and oppoſite. An external Angle of a Figure is an outward Angle, as the Angle *f* or *g,* in *Fig.* O, Plate IV. whoſe angular Point points outward ; and an internal Angle is an inward Angle that points inward, as the Angle *b,* in *Fig.* P, Plate IV ; but an external Angle, ſingly conſidered, without Reſpect being had to a Figure, is the Complement of an (internal) Angle to a Circle, or 360 Degrees. So the Angle *a x m, Fig.* M, Plate VII. is an internal Angle, whoſe Meaſure is the Arch *i m,* and the external Angle is all the Space that is without the Lines *a x* and *x m,* and whoſe Meaſure is the Arch *i k l m,* which with the Arch *i m,* is a complete Circle, and therefore is the Complement of the Arch *i m,* to 360 Degrees.

Def. 92. Of external and internal Angles.

Opposite Angles are ſuch that are againſt, or oppoſite to, one another ; as for Example, if two right Lines, as *a c* and *b e, Fig.* G, Plate VII. croſs each other, the oppoſite Angles which they make are *b d e,* and *a d e;* that is, the Angle *b d c* is oppoſite to the Angle *a d e.* So likewiſe the Angle *a b d* is oppoſite to the Angle *c d e,* and which are always equal to one another, becauſe the Arches *a b* and *e c,* which are their Meaſures, are equal, and ſo the like of all others.

Def. 93. Of oppoſite Angles.

LECT. III.
Of the Deſcription of Lines.

AS the ſeveral Works of this and the following Lectures are very often dependant on one another (like the Links of a Chain), I ſhall therefore deliver the whole by Way of *Problem,* or *Propoſition.*

A Problem is a Propoſition, for ſomething to be done or made, as following.

Prob. I. *Plate* III. *Fig.* I.
To draw a right Line, from the given Point e, to the given Point X, *and to continue it infinitely from* X *towards f.*

Operation. First, apply the Edge of a ſtraight Ruler to the Points *e* X, and with a Pencil draw the Line required. Secondly, Lay the Edge of a Ruler to the Line *e* X, and applying the Point of a Pencil, *&c.* to the Point X, continue the Line *e* X; from the Point X, towards *f.*

Prob. II. *Fig.* II.
Two Points being given, (as g g*) to find a Point of Interſection, as* i.

Operation. Open your Compaſſes to any Diſtance greater than half the Diſtance of the Points propoſed, and upon the Points *g g* deſcribe Arches, as *g k, g k* ; then will the Point *i* be the Point of Interſection required, the Uſe of which will be preſently ſhewn ; and it is to be obſerved, that 'tis no matter what the Opening of your Compaſſes is, ſo that they are more than half the Diſtance of the given

given Points; and the Reason thereof is, that if the Opening is less than half the Distance, as *g* 4, and *g* 6, the Arches described on that Opening cannot meet to interfect each other, so as to make a Point of Interfection; as is also the Cafe if the Opening be exactly half the Diftance, as *g* 3, as is evident by the Figure. Hence 'tis plain, that unless the Opening be more than half the Diftance of the given Points, there cannot be any Point of Interfection made. The Points *i* and *g*, are both Points of Interfection; that of *i*, being found by an Opening equal to the whole Diftance of the given Points, and that of *g*, by an Opening that is less.

PROB. III. *Fig.* III, IV, V, VI, and VII.

To erect Perpendiculars from given Points, in or near the Middle, and at or near the Ends of given right Lines.

Operation. Firft, in *Fig.* III. let *m* be a given Point, in or near the Middle of the given Line *o n*. Set any equal Diftances on each Side the given Point *m*, as *o* and *n*, whereon, by the laft Problem, find a Point of Interfection, as *q*. From *m* to *q*, draw the Line *m q*, which will be the Perpendicular required: for as *m n*, and *m o*, are at equal Diftances from *m*, therefore (by *Def.* 15.) the Line *m q* is a Perpendicular; becaufe the Diftances *n q* and *o q* are equal.

Secondly, to erect a Perpendicular from the given Point r, Fig. IV. *at the End of the given Line r t.*

Operation. Firft, on the given Point *r*, with any Opening of your Compaffes, defcribe an Arch, as *s x w*, and thereon fet that Opening twice, as from *s* to *x*, and from *x* to *v*. Secondly, on the Points *x* and *v* find a point of Interfection, as *z*: draw the Line *r z*, and 'twill be the Perpendicular required. A Perpendicular may alfo be erected on the End of a given Line, by either of the following Methods. As for Example: Firft, Let 1 2, *Fig.* V. be a given Line, and 1 the given Point.

Operation. Firft, on 1, with any Opening of your Compaffes, defcribe an Arch, as 3, 9, and thereon fet its Radius, from 3 to 4, whereon with the fame Opening defcribe the Arch 3 5 6 8, and thereon fet up its Radius three Times, at the Points 5 6 8. Secondly, draw the Line 8 1, and 'tis the Perpendicular required.

Secondly, Let A D, *Fig.* VI. be a given Line, and A the given Point.

Operation. Open your Compaffes to any Diftance, and fetting one Foot in the given Point A, fet down the other at pleafure, as on the Point B, fo that the Foot in the Point A, may be capable to interfect the given Line, as in the Point C. Alfo on the Point B, defcribe an Arch, as A G F, over the given Point A. Lay a Ruler from C to B, and it will cut the Arch A G F, in G: draw the Line G A, and 'tis the Perpendicular required.

Thirdly, Let N O, *Fig.* VII. be the given Line, and N the given Point.

Operation. Firft, from a Scale of equal Parts, as *a c d, Fig.* I. take 6 Parts in your Compaffes, and on the given Point N, defcribe an Arch, as M M. Secondly, take 8 Parts in your Compaffes, and fet them from N to I. Thirdly, take 10 Parts, and on the Point I, interfect the Arch M M, in the upper N, and draw the Line N N, the Perpendicular required.

Now as 64, the Square of 8, and 36 the Square of 6, are together equal to 100, which is the Square of 10 by 10; therefore N N is a Perpendicular to the given Line N O. Fourthly, let *b a, Fig.* VIII. be a given Line, and *a* the given Point.

Operation. With 60 Degrees of a Scale of Chords, on *a*, the given Point, defcribe an infinite Arch, as *b d*; and then fetting 90°, from *b* to *c*, draw *c a*, the Perpendicular required.

PROB. IV. *Fig.* IX.

To erect a Perpendicular on an angular Point.

Let *b a c* be the angular Point given.

Operation. (1) Affign two Points, as *b c*, at any equal Diftance from the given Point *a*. (2) On the Points *b* and *c*, by Prob. II. find a Point of Interfection, as *d*; and draw *d a*, the Perpendicular required.

PROB.

Prob. V. *Fig.* X. and XI.
To erect a Perpendicular on the Convexity, and in the Concavity of an Arch of a Circle.

First, Let *e f*, *Fig.* X. be the given Arch, and *a* the given Point.

Operation. Set off two Points, as *b d*, at any equal Distance from *a*, and thereon, by Prob. II. find a Point of Intersection, as *c*; draw *c a*, the Perpendicular required.

Secondly, Let *b a d*, *Fig.* XI. be the given Arch, and *a* the given Point.

Operation. (1) Set any equal Distances on each Side of *a*, the given Point, as in the last Problem, and thereon, by Prob. II. find the Point of Intersection, as *b*. (2) Draw *b a*, the Perpendicular required.

Prob. VI. *Fig.* XII.
To bisect a given right Line, by a Perpendicular.

Let *a b* be the given Line.

Operation. On the Points *a* and *b*, by Prob. II. find a Point of Intersection on each Side of the given Line, as *d* and *e*, and then drawing the Line *d e*, it will be a Perpendicular to the given Line *a b*, and bisect or divide it into two equal Parts at the Point *c*.

Prob. VII. *Fig.* XIII.
To erect a Perpendicular on the Extremity of a Concave Arch, whose Center is unknown.

Let *a d b* be the given Arch, and *a* the given Point.

Operation. Assign three Points in any Parts of the Arch, as *g d b*, and between them draw right Lines, as *g d* and *d b*, which by the last Prob. bisect or divide by Perpendiculars, which will intersect each other in *c*, the Center of the Arch; from whence draw *c a*, the Perpendicular required.

Prob. VIII. *Fig.* XIV. and XV.
To let fall a Perpendicular from a given Point, on a given right Line.

Let *a p*, *Fig.* XV. be the given Line, and *b* the given Point.

Operation. Open your Compasses to any Extent greater than the Distance from the given Point to the Line, and on *b*, the given Point, describe an Arch intersecting the given Line in the Points *m* and *b*, whereon find the Point of Intersection *g*, and laying a Ruler from *b* to *g*, draw the Perpendicular *b i*, as required.

Note, This Operation is to be used when the given Point is over, or nearly over, the Middle of a Line; and the following when the given Point is over, or nearly over, the End of a Line, as the Point *e*, *Fig.* XIV.

Operation. From the given Point *e*, draw an oblique Line, as *e c*, which by Prob. VI. bisect in the Point *f*, whereon with the Radius *f c* describe a Semicircle, cutting the given Line in the Point *n*, and draw *e n*, the Perpendicular required.

Prob. IX. *Fig.* XVI.
To let fall a Perpendicular, from a given Point, on a Concave Circular Arch, whose Center is unknown.

Let *b* be the given Point, and *d e f* the given Arch.

Operation. Assume three Points in the given Arch at pleasure, as *d e g*, and draw the Lines *g e* and *e d*, which bisect in the Points *o* and *c*, and thereon erect the Perpendiculars *o b* and *c b*, which will intersect each other in the Point *b*, the Center of the Arch. Lay a Ruler from *b*, the given Point, and draw *a n*, the Perpendicular required.

Prob. X. *Fig.* XVII.
To divide an Angle into two equal Parts, by a Perpendicular.

Let *b a e* be the given Angle.

Opera-

Operation. Set any equal Diftance on each Side the Angle, as from *a* to *d*, and *e*, whereon find a Point of Interfection, as *n*, through which, from the angular Point *a*, draw the Perpendicular *a n*, as required.

Prob. XI. *Fig.* XVIII. and XIX.
To make an Angle equal to a given Angle.

'Tis required to make the Angle *k f h*, equal to the Angle *e a b*.

Operation. Draw a right Line, as *k f*, and open your Compaffes to any Diftance, and on the angular Point *a*, defcribe an Arch, as *d c* ; with the fame Opening on the Point *f*, defcribe an Arch at Pleafure, as *n g* : make the Arch *n g*, equal to the Arch *d c* ; through the Point *g*, from the Point *f*, draw the right Line *f g h*, and then the Angle *k f h* will be equal to the Angle *b a c*. In the fame Manner, the Angle *e d f*, *Fig.* XX. is made equal to the Angle *b a c*, *Fig.* XXI.

Prob. XII. *Fig.* XXII.
To continue a right Line to a greater Length than can be drawn by a Ruler at one Operation.

Let *a* be the given right Line, which cannot be made longer at one Operation, by reafon of the Ruler being of the fame Length.

Operation. With the Length of the Line *a*, on the Point *a*, defcribe an Arch, as *c d* ; on which, from the End of the given Line, fet off two Points, as *e f*; whereon find a Point of Interfection, as *b* ; unto which, from the End of the given Line, lay a Ruler, and continue the given Line at Pleafure.

Prob. XIII. *Fig.* XXIII.
To draw a right Line, parallel to a right Line, at an affigned Diftance.

Let *i k*, *Fig.* XXIII. be the given right Line, and A B the given Diftance. Take the given Diftance A B in your Compaffes, and on any two Points, near the Ends of the given Line, as *r* and *p*, defcribe two Arches, as *n n* and *o o*, unto which lay a Ruler, fo as but juft to fee their Convexities, and draw the Line *m*, which will be parallel to *i k*, at the Diftance of A B, as required.

Prob. XIV. *Fig.* XXIV.
To draw a right Line, parallel to a right Line, which fhall pafs through a given Point.

Let *e h* be the given Line, and *b* the given Point.

Operation. From the given Point *b*, draw an oblique Line, as *b g*, at Pleafure, to cut the given Line in any Point, as *g*. By Prob. XI. make the Angle *e b g*, equal to the Angle *b g f*, and from the Point *c*, to the Point *b*, draw the Line *d b*, which will be parallel to the given Line, as required.

Prob. XV. *Fig.* XXV.
To defcribe a Circle, concentric to a given Circle, at a given Diftance.

Let the given Circle be *b*, and *e d* the given Diftance.

Operation. Draw a right Line through *a* the Center of the given Circle, as *e f*, and make *e d* equal to the given Diftance ; on *a*, with the Radius *a e*, defcribe the Circle *e g c*, as required.

Prob. XVI. *Fig.* XXVI.
Between two given Points to find two others directly interpofed.

Let *a d* be the two Points given, to find two others directly interpofed, as *b* and *c*, by the Help of which a right Line may be drawn from the Point *a* to the Point *d*, with a Rule whofe Length is lefs than the Diftance of *a* to *d*.

Operation. With any Diftance greater than half the Length of *a d*, on the Points *a*, *d*, find two Points of Interfection, as *e* and *f*, on which with any Diftance greater than half the Diftance between the two Points of Interfection, find two other Points of Interfection, as *b* and *c*, which will be directly interpofed between the given Points *a* and *d*, as required.

Prob.

PROB. XVII. *Fig:* XXVII.

To divide a right Line into any Number of equal Parts.

LET E F be the given Line, to be divided into 4 equal Parts.

Operation. Draw a right Line at pleasure, as *a b*, and thereon let four equal Parts of any Bigness, as 1 2 3 4, on the Points of *a* and 4, with the Distance *a* 4, make the Section *n*, and from *n*, through the Points *a* 1 2 3 4, draw right Lines out at pleasure. This done, take the given Line in your Compasses, and set it from *n* to *b*, and to *f*, and draw the Line *b f*, which will be equal to the given Line, and will be divided into 4 equal Parts by the Lines *n c*, *n d*, *n e*, as required.

A RIGHT Line may also be divided into any Number of equal Parts as following, *viz.* let *a b*, *Fig.* XXIX. be the given Line to be divided into five equal Parts.

Operation. From the End *b*, draw a right Line as *b d*, making any Angle at pleasure. By Problem XIV. draw *a c* parallel to *b d*, or by Prob. XI. make the Angle *b a c*, equal to the Angle *d b a*. On the Lines *b d* and *a c* set off four equal Distances of any Magnitude, as at the Points 1 2 3 4 on the Line *b d*, and at 5 6 7 8, on the Line *a c*. This being done, draw the Lines 4 5, 3 4, 2 3, and 1 2, which will divide the given Line *a b*, into 5 equal Parts at the Points *h g f e*, as required.

PROB. XVIII.

To divide a given right Line into unequal Parts in the same Proportion as another Line is divided.

LET the right Line A under *Fig.* XXV. be given to be divided in the same Proportion as the Line *b c*, next below it.

Operation. On the Points *b c* with the Distance *b c*, make the Section *a*, from whence draw right Lines through every of the Divisions *f g i n m*. Make *a d*, *e a 6*, each equal to the given Line A, and draw the Line *d 6*, which will be equal to the given Line A, because the Triangle *d a 6* is equilateral, and which will be divided by the Lines *a f*, *a g*, &c. in the same Number of Parts, and in the same Proportion as the Line *b c*.

PROB. XIX. *Fig.* XXVIII.

A Circle being given, to find its Center.

LET *f a b* be a given Circle, to find its Center.

Operation. Assign three Points in any Part of its Circumference, as *f a b*, and draw the Chord Lines *f a*, and *a b*, which bisect in the Points *z x*, whereon erect the Perpendiculars *z c*, and *x c*, which will intersect each other in *c*, the Center of the Circle.

PROB. XX. *Fig:* XXX.

To find the Center and Diameter of a Tower, &c. whose Base is a Circle; being without the same.

LET the Circle *f i l* represent the Out-line of a Cylinder or round Building, whose Center and Diameter is known.

Operation. Apply the straight Side of a ten-foot Deal against the Outside of the Building, as *b n*, or, for want thereof, strain a packthread Line, so as just to touch the Building, as the Line *b n*, touching in the Point *k*. Set any certain Distance (suppose 10 Feet) from *k* to *b f*, and from *k* to *n*, at which Points erect Perpendiculars continued until they meet the Building, as *b i*, and *n l*, and measure their Lengths exactly, which suppose to be each 6 Feet. This being done, make a Scale of equal Parts, as *Fig.* I. and let every Part represent 1 Foot. Draw a right Line to represent *b n*, which make equal to ten Parts of your Scale, and on the Ends *b* and *n* erect two Perpendiculars, making the Length of each equal to 6 Parts, and draw the Lines *i k* and *k l*. Lastly, bisect the Lines *i k* and *k l* in the Points *x z*, and thereon erect the Perpendiculars *x a*, *z a*; which by the last Problem will intersect each other in *a*, the Center of the Building, on which with the Radius *a k*, describe a Circle, which will represent the Out-line of the given

L. Building,

Building, and whofe Diameter being meafured on your Scale of equal Parts, will fhew the Number of Parts, which are the Feet contained therein.

P R O B. XXI. *Fig.* XXXI.

To find the Center and two Diameters of an Oval or Ellipfis.

LET *h a i e*, be a given Oval, whofe Center *p*, and two Diameters are to be found.

Operation. Draw at pleafure two parallel Lines, as *e e* and *m g*, which bifect in the Points *n* and *m*, through which draw a right Line, as *l n m k*, which bifect in *p*, whereon defcribe any Circle that will interfect the Sides of the Oval, as *c b f d*, in the Points *c b f d*; through the Interfections *b d*, draw the right Line *b d*, which bifect in *x*; then through the Points *x p* draw the longeft Diameter, and through the Point *p*, draw the fhorteft Diameter parallel to *b d*, and *p* is the Center, as required.

P R O B. XXII. *Fig.* XXX. *Plate* III.

To draw a right Line through a given Point, that fhall be a Tangent Line to a given Circle.

LET *d* be the given Point, through which the Tangent *d b* is to be drawn.

Operation. Draw a right Line from *d* the given Point, to *a* the Center of the Circle, which bifect in *m*, whereon with the Radius *m d*, defcribe the Semi-circle *a c d*, interfecting the given Circle in *c*, through which, from *d*, draw *d b*, the Tangent Line required.

THE fame is alfo to be underftood of a Tangent Line to an Ellipfis, as *Fig.* XXXII.

P R O B. XXIII. *Fig.* XXXIII. *Plate* IV.

A right Line being given, as c d, *to find another right Line equal thereto.*

LET *d c* be the given Line.

Operation. From the End *c* draw a right Line at pleafure, as *a c*, and on the Points *a* and *c*, with the Opening *a c*, find the Point of Interfection *b*, and draw *a e* and *a b* out at pleafure; on *c* with the Radius *c d* defcribe the Arch of a Circle *d c*, cutting the Line *a c*, continued in *e*. On *a* with the Radius *a e* defcribe the Arch *e f*, cutting the Line *a b* continued in the Point *g*; then is *b g* equal to *c d*, as required.

P R O B. XXIV. *Fig.* XXXIV. and XXXV. *Plate* III.

To divide the Circumference of a Circle into Degrees, Minutes, Hours, and Rhumbs.

Let the Circle *b a c d*, *Fig.* XXXIV. be given to be divided into 360 Degrees, the Circle *d a c e*, *Fig.* XXXV. into 60 Minutes, the Circle *d b c e*, *Fig.* XXXVI. into 12 Hours, and the Circle *e r* 8 *n*, *Fig.* XXXVI. into 32 Rhumbs or Points of the Compafs.

FIRST, in *Fig.* XXXIV. and XXXV. draw the two Diameters at right Angles, as *a d*, and *b c* in *Fig.* XXXIV. and *d c*, and *a e* in *Fig.* XXXV. Set the Radius of each Circle from *c* to *g*, and from *a* to *n*, and then will thofe Quadrants be each divided into three equal Parts. In the fame Manner divide the remaining three Quadrants in each Figure. This being done, divide *c n*, *n g* and *a g* in *Fig.* XXXIV. each into three equal Parts, and every Part into ten equal Parts, and then the Quadrant *a e c*, will be divided into 90 equal Parts. In the fame Manner divide the Quadrants *a b c*, *b e d*, and then the Circle will be divided into 360 Degrees, as required. Alfo divide *c n*, *n g*, and *a g*, *Fig.* XXXV. each into 5 equal Parts, and then the Quadrant *a g n c*, will be divided into 15 equal Parts. In the fame Manner divide the Quadrants *a d*, *d e*, and *e c*; and then that Circle will be divided into 60 Minutes, as required.

SECONDLY, *To divide the Circle of* 12 *Hours, Fig.* XXXVI.

DRAW two Diameters at right Angles, as *d c*, and *b e*, which will divide the Circle into 4 Quadrants, fet the Radius *a d*, from *d* to *n* and to *i*, alfo from *e* to *f* and to K, alfo from *c* to *m* and to *b*, and laftly from *b* to *o* and to *x*, and then will the Circle *d b c e* be divided into 12 equal Parts, as required.

THIRDLY,

THIRDLY, *To divide the* 32 *Points of the Compass, Fig.* XXXVII.

DRAW two Diameters at right Angles, as *e* 8, and *r n*, divide each Quadrant into two equal Parts, and then the whole will be divided into 8 Parts; divide each 8th Part into 2 equal Parts, and then the whole will be divided into 16 Parts. Lastly, divide each 16th Part into 2 equal Parts, and the whole will be divided into 32 equal Parts, as required.

To proportion the Height of the Figures to the Hours.

DIVIDE the Semi-diameter of the outer Circle of your Dial-Plate into 12 equal Parts, give one to the outer Margin for the Minutes, five to the Margin for the Hour's Figures, and the next one to the Margin for the Divisions of the Quarters.

THE Figures by which the twelve Hours are numbered, are the Capital Letters I, V, and X, which are proportioned and made as following:

To proportion the Breadth of the Figures, divide their Height into 8 equal Parts, and give one Part to the Breadth of the full Stroke in every Figure, and one Quarter of a Part to the Breadth of the fine Stroke in the V and the X.

THE Distance of the I's from each other is equal to their Breadth. The Breadth or Opening of a V at its Top, is 4 Parts, and of an X is 5 Parts, as may be seen in Figure XXXVIII. by the dotted parallel Lines. If the Figures stand very high above the Eye, their Graces, which is their arched Finishings at their Tops and Bottoms, must have a Breadth equal to the fine Stroke of an X, that is, of one Quarter of a Part. But when the Dial is near to the Eye, there need not be any Breadth given to them, as in the Figures is represented.

THE Curvature of every Grace begins at half a Part above the Bottom and below the Top of every Figure, as expressed by the Lines *c d*, and *a b*, and their Projections are half a Part also. The Graces to the I's are all Quadrants of a Circle, as *b d p*, and whose Centers are always on the Lines *c d* and *a b*, but the Graces of the V's and X's, are Arches less and more than a Quadrant, and whose Centers are found by this

GENERAL RULE.

FROM the Point *e Fig.* X. where the Out-line of the Figure cuts *c d*, the Line of the Height of the Graces, erect the Perpendicular, as *e m*. Make 4 *g* equal to half a Part, for the Projection of the Grace, and draw the Line *e g*, which bisect in *x* A, on which erect the Perpendicular *x m*, interfecting the Line *e m* in *m*, the Center, on which with the Radius *m e*, describe the Arch *e g*, which is the Grace required.

LECTURE IV.

On the Construction of Plane Figures.

PROB. II. *Fig.* E. *Plate* IV.

TO *describe an equilateral Triangle, as* a b c, Fig. E, *whose Sides shall be each equal to* d a, *a given Line*; *also an Isosceles Triangle, as* a b c, Fig. F, *whose Base and Sides shall be equal to the given Lines* d *and* e ; *and likewise a Scalenum Triangle, as* Fig. G, *whose three Sides shall be equal to three given Lines*, d e f.

FIRST, make *b c, Fig.* E, equal to the given Line *d*, on the Points *b* and *c*, with the Opening *b c*, make the Point of Interfection *a*, draw the Lines *a b*, and *a c*, and they will complete the equilateral Triangle, as required. Secondly, make *b c, Fig.* F, equal to the given Line *e*, on the Points *b* and *c* with an Opening equal to the given Line *d*, make the Point of Interfection *a*, draw the Lines *a b*, and *a c*, and they will complete the Isosceles Triangle, as required. Thirdly, make *b c, Fig.* G, equal to the Line *f*, on *b*, with an Opening equal to the Line *e d*, and on *c* with an Opening equal to the Line *d* made the Section *a*. Draw the Lines *a b* and *a c*, and they will complete the Scalenum Triangle, as required.

PROB. II. *Fig.* H, and I. *Plate* IV.

To make a geometrical Square, as Fig. H, *whose Sides shall be each equal to a*

L 2 *given*

given Line, as e, *and a Parallelogram as* Fig. I, *whose Length and Breadth shall be equal to two given Lines, as* e *and* f.

FIRST, Make e d, *Fig.* H, equal to the given Line e, on d, by Problem III. Lect. III. erect the Perpendicular d b equal to e d, on the Points b and e, with the Opening e d, make the Point of Interfection a. Draw the Lines a b, and a e, and they will complete the geometrical Square, as required.

SECONDLY, Make a b, *Fig.* I, equal to the given Line e, on the Point a, erect the Perpendicular a c, equal to the given Line f, on c, with an Opening equal to a b; and on the Point b, with an Opening equal to e a, make the Point of Interfection d. Draw the Lines d b, and d c, and they will complete the Parallelogram, as required.

PROB. III. *Fig.* K, and L. *Plate* IV.

To make a Rhombus, as a b c d, *Fig.* K, *whose Sides shall be each equal to the given Line* e, *also a Rhomboides, as* a c b d, *Fig.* L, *whose Sides and Ends shall be equal to the given Lines* e f, *and whose acute Angles shall be each equal to the given Angle* M.

FIRST, Make a d, *Fig.* K, equal to the given Line e, on d, with the Radius d a, describe the Arch a b e; make a b, and b c, each equal to a d. Draw the Lines a b b c, and c d, and they will complete the Rhombus, as required.

SECONDLY, Make a d, *Fig.* L, equal to the given Line e, by Problem XI. Lect. III. make the Angle d a c equal to the Angle b a c, and make c a equal to the given Line f, on the Point c, with an Opening equal to a d, and on the Point d, with an Opening equal to c a, find the Point of Interfection b; draw the Lines c b and d b, and they will complete the Rhomboides, as required.

PROB. IV. *Fig.* N, and O. *Plate* IV.

To make a Trapezoid, as a b d h, *Fig.* N, *whose Height, Top and Base shall be equal to the three given Lines* e z f, g, *and* h; *also a Trapezia, as* a c f g, *Fig.* O, *whose Sides shall be equal to* 4 *given Lines, and one of its Angles, as* e a g, *equal to* Q; *an Angle given.*

FIRST, Make a b equal to the given Line g, and bisect it in n, whereon erect the Perpendicular n e equal to b the given Height; by Problem XIII. Lect. III. draw d parallel to a b, bisect e f in z, and make c b and c d each equal to z e; draw the Lines d b and b a, and they will complete the Trapezoid a b d h, as required.

SECONDLY, Make a g, *Fig.* O, equal to the given Line d, by Prob. XI. Lect. III. make the Angle e a g, equal to the given Angle Q, and make e a equal to the given Line d. On the Point e with an Opening equal to the given Line f, and on the Point g with an Opening equal to the fourth given Side, find the Point of Interfection f. Draw the Lines c f, and f g, and they will complete the Trapezia, as required.

Note, If the Angle had been required to have been made an internal Angle, then the two Sides f e and f g, must have been drawn to the Point of Interfection h, as in *Fig.* P, which is a quite different Figure from *Fig.* O, although the given Angle and Sides are the same.

IT is also to be noted, when four right Lines are proposed to be the Bounds of a Trapezium, that those two Lines which make the Interfection, must be longer than the Distance contained between the Extremes of those Sides which make the given Angle, otherwise there cannot be a Trapezium made; for if the aforefaid two Lines, f e and f g, *Fig.* O, were but equal to the Distance contained between g and c, the Extremes of the Angle g a c, they would make but one Line, and consequently the Figure would be a Triangle, instead of a Trapezium; and if those two Lines were less than the Distance from e to g, then there could not be any Figure produced. Therefore 'tis plain, that to make a Trapezium, the two Sides which make the interfectional Point, must be greater than the Distance contained between the Extremes of those Sides which contain the given Angle.

PROB. V. *Fig.* A, B, C, D, and S. *Plate* IV.

To describe a Circle of any given Diameter, suppose ten Feet, and to describe Ovals of the first, second, third, and fourth Kinds, to any Length required.

Operation. First, make a Scale of equal Parts, as Z, and let each Part represent one Foot. Take 5 Parts in your Compasses, and on *a* describe the Circle, whose Diameter *c d*, will be equal to ten Feet, as required.

Secondly, Divide *a f*, *Fig.* B, the given Length of an Oval, into 3 equal Parts at *e* and *b*, whereon with the Radius *b f*, describe two Circles intersecting each other, in *c* and *g*, from which two Points, through the Centers *e* and *b*, draw the Lines *g e d*, *g b k*, *e b m*, and *c e n*; on the Points *g* and *c*, with the Radius *g d*, describe the Arches *d k*, and *n m*, which will complete an Oval of the first Kind.

Thirdly, Let *d f*, *Fig.* C, be a given Length, as before.

DIVIDE *d f* into four equal Parts, at *c e b*; on the Points *c b*, with the Radius *c d*, describe two Circles, touching each other in the Point *e*; on *e b* make the two equilateral Triangles *a c b*, and *n c b*, continuing their Sides out both ways at pleasure, as to 5 8 6 and 7; on the Points *a* and *n*, which with the Radius *n* 5, describe the Arches 5 6, and 8 7, which will complete an Oval of the second Kind.

Fourthly, Let *a k* be a given Length, as before.

DIVIDE *a k* into 24 equal Parts, and draw *b d* and *f i*, parallel thereto, each at the Distance of 10 Parts; draw *e b* through the Middle of *a k*, at right Angles to *a k*, and make *c b*, *c d*, also *g f*, and *g i*, each equal to 10 Parts, and then will you have completed two geometrical Squares, *viz.* *b c f g* and *c d g i*. Draw their Diagonals, and on their Centers *y* and *z*, with the Radius of *z d*, or *z i*, describe the Arches *f a b* and *d k i*. On the Points *c* and *g*, with the Radius *g d*, describe the Arches *b e d*, and *f b i*, which will complete an Oval of the third Kind.

It is here to be noted, That as the Proportion that the Side of a geometrical Square bears to its diagonal Line is yet unknown to all Mathematicians, the Difference between them cannot be ascertained. But however, the nearest Proportion that the Side has to the Diagonal, is, as Five is to Seven; that is, if the Side be five, the Diagonal is seven, and a little more. And therefore when the Length of the Oval is divided into 24 equal Parts, or twice 12, then *c d*, *&c.* being 5, *z k* will be 7, and a little more; and therefore when the Arches *d k i*, and *b a f*, are described on the Centers *y z*, they will exceed the Points *a* and *k*, some small Matter.

Fifthly, Let *e* 4, *Fig.* S, be a given Length, as before.

DIVIDE the Length *e* 4; into four equal Parts, at the Points 1, 2, 3; and through them draw the Lines *r t*, *b n*, and *s v*, at right Angles, to the Line *e* 4: make 1 *r*, 1 *t*, also 2 *b*, 2 *n*, and 3 *s*, 3 *v*, each equal to one-fourth of *e* 4, *viz.* to *e* 1, and complete the three geometrical Squares, *e r 2 t*, *b t n 3*, and *s 2 v 4*, continuing the Sides *n* 1, and *b* 1, as also the Sides *b* 3, and *n* 3, out at pleasure. On the Centers 1 and 3, with the Radius *e* 1, describe the Arches *m e b*, and *d* 4 *o*. On the Centers *b* and *n*, with the Radius *n h* or *n d*, describe the Arches *h d*, and *m o*, which will complete an Oval of the fourth Kind, as required.

PROB. VI. *Fig.* V, W, X, R, T, and Y. *Plate* IV.

To make an Oval of any Length and Breadth required, by divers Methods.

LET the Lines *z z*, *x x*, *Fig.* V, be the given Length and Breadth.

Operation. First, make *d l* equal to *z z*, and by PROB. VI. LECT. III. divide *d l* in two equal Parts, by the Line *a r*. Make *x c* and *x n*, each equal to half *x x*. Make *d e* equal to *x c*; divide *e x* into 3 equal Parts, and make *e h* equal to 1 Part. Make *x t* equal to *x k*, and by PROB. I. hereof, on the Line *b t*, complete the two equilateral Triangles, *b d t*, and *r b t*, continuing their Sides through the Points *b* and *t*, at pleasure. On the Points *b* and

t, with

t, with the Radius *t l*, deſcribe the Arches *k l m*, and *b d q*; alſo on the Points *a* and *r*, with the Radius *r b*, deſcribe the Arches *b c k*, and *q n m*, which will complete the Oval, as required.

Secondly, by a Diviſion of two Circles, Fig. W.

LET the given Length and Breadth be the Lines *x x*, *z z*, as before.

Operation. Make the Line 1 2, equal to the given Line *z z*, and divide it into two equal Parts by the Perpendicular 3 6. On *a*, the Point of Interſection, with the Radius *a* 1, deſcribe the Circle, 1 3 2 6; alſo on *a*, with a Radius equal to half the Line *x x*, deſcribe the concentrick Circle 7, 4, 8, 5. Divide the Circumference of each Circle into any and the ſame Number of equal Parts, (the more the better) as in the Figure where each Circle is divided into 24 Parts. Draw right Lines from the Diviſions in the ſmall Circle, parallel to the Line 1 2, to the right and to the left, at pleaſure. Alſo draw right Lines from the Diviſions as *s r t x z*, in the outer Circle parallel to the Line 3 6, and through the Points of Interſection, that they make with the other Lines before drawn, as *c d e h i*, &c. trace the Circumference of the Oval, whoſe Length 1 2, is equal to *z z*, and Breadth equal to *x x*, as required.

Thirdly, by the Ordinates of a Circle, Fig. X.

LET the given Length and Breadth be as before.

Operation. Make *b e* and *a d*, at right Angles to each other, and equal to the given Length and Breadth. On *c*, the Point of Interſection with the Radius *c d*, deſcribe the Circle *a* 5 *d*, &c. Divide the Semi-diameter *c f*, into any Number of equal Parts, ſuppoſe 4, as at the Points 1 2 3; through which draw right Lines, parallel to *a d*, as 1 *g*, 2 *i*, 3 *k*, which are called Semi-ordinates of the Circle. Divide *b c* and *c e*, each into the ſame Number of equal Parts, as *f c*, at the Points 4, 5, 6, through which draw Lines parallel to *a d*. Make 4 7, 4 *m*, (which are Semi-ordinates of the Ellipſis) each equal to 1 *g*, the Semi-ordinate of the Circle. Make 5 8, and 5 *n*, each equal to the Semi-ordinate 2 *i*; alſo 6 9, and 6 *o*, each equal to the Semi-ordinate 3 *k*; then from the Point *a*, through the Points 7, 8, 9, *e o n m d*, trace one half Part of the Ellipſis. In the ſame Manner ſet off Ordinates on the other Side, and complete the Ellipſis, as required.

Fourthly, by the Help of a Line, *or* String, *Fig.* T.

LET the given Line *b* be the Length, and the Line *w* the Breadth.

Operation. Make *b f*, the long Diameter, equal to the Line *b*, and *d n*, equal to the Line *w*, and at right Angles to *b f*. Set *e f*, half the tranſverſe Diameter, from *d* to *a*, and to *g* on the tranſverſe Diameter, which are called the Focus Points of the Ellipſis, wherein fix two Nails, &c. and about either of them, ſuppoſe the Nail at *a*, put a double Line of Packthread, &c. which ſhall reach unto the Point *f*; then with a Pencil, &c. applied within the ſaid Line, and held upright, trace about the Circumference of the Ellipſis, which will paſs through the Points *b d n*, as required.

Fifthly, by Help of a Tramel, *Fig.* R.

LET *b h* and *e n* be the given Diameters, drawn at right Angles.

Operation. Firſt, make a Tramel, which is nothing more than two Pieces of Wood, as *k i*, and *x g*, fixed together at right Angles, with a Groove in the midſt of each, wherein the Pins *g e* of the Deſcribent *g a* move, as the tracing Point *a* deſcribes the Ellipſis. The tracing Point *a*, is generally a fixed Point, but the Points *e* and *g*, are moveable Points, and are made to ſlide on the Deſcribent at pleaſure. The Diſtance of the Point *e*, from the Point *a*, is always equal to *f c*, half the conjugate Diameter, and the Diſtance of the Point *g*, from the Point *a*, is always equal to half the tranſverſe Diameter. Fix down the Tramel over the two given Diameters, ſo that the middle Line of each Groove may lie directly over them; and the Points *g e* and *a*, being fixed as aforeſaid: Then putting the two Points *e g*, into the Grooves, with one Hand move the tracing Point *a*, (wherein generally is fixed a black Lead Pencil) and with the other guide the Pins or Points *e g*, in their reſpective

Grooves,

Of GEOMETRY. 83

Grooves, whilſt the tracing Point *a*, makes one Revolution, which will deſcribe the Ellipſis required.

PROB. VII. Fig. Y. Plate IV.
To deſcribe an Elliptical Polygon, about a Plantation of Trees, or Piece of Water.

LET *d l* be the given Length, and *e d* the given Breadth.

Operation. Make a Parallelogram, as *h b c* 9, whoſe Length is equal to *g f*, and Breadth to *e d*. Biſect the Sides *h b* and *c* 9, in the Points *e d*; alſo the Ends *h c*, and *b* 9, in the Points *g* and *f*. Divide every Half of the Sides and Ends into any (and the ſame) Number of equal Parts, the more the better. In this Example, *d* 9, and *f* 9, are divided each into 9 equal Parts, as at the Points 1 2 3 4, &c. in each Line. Draw right Lines from *d* to 8, in *f* 9, as alſo from 1 to 7, from 2 to 6, from 3 to 5, from 4 to 4, from 5 to 3, from 6 to 2, from 7 to 1, and from 8 to *f*; and they will form one fourth Part of the Elliptical Polygon. Proceed in the ſame Manner, to deſcribe the remaining three Parts, and they will complete the whole, as required.

Note, In Practice this Figure may do near enough to repreſent an Oval; but ſtrictly conſidered it is a Polygon of 4 Times the Number of Sides, as are Parts in each half Side.

PROB. VIII. Fig. Z. Plate IV.
To deſcribe an Egg ovallar Polygon, about an irregular Piece of Water, by the Interſection of right Lines.

LET the given Length be *f h*.

Operation. Erect Perpendiculars on the Points *f* and *h*, as *a c*, and *b d*, which continue both Ways at pleaſure. Make *f c*, and *f a*, each equal to one-third of *f h*; alſo make *b h* and *h d*, each equal to three-fourths of *a c*, and draw the Lines *a b* and *c d*. Biſect *c d* in *g*, *d b* in *h*, *a b* in *e*, and *a c* in *f*. Then by the laſt Problem, divide each half Side, and half End, into equal Parts, and draw right Lines thereto, which will form the Curvature of the Egg ovallar Polygon, as required.

P. Pray, Sir, why do you call theſe two laſt Figures Polygons? for, if I miſtake not, there are ſome Authors who call them Ovals or Ellipſes.

M. 'Tis very true, and ſo an equilateral Triangle is, by the ignorant, called a three-ſquare Figure; and an Octagon, an eight-ſquare Figure, which is ridiculous and abſurd, becauſe neither of thoſe Figures have any ſquare Angles. And as all Ovals are compoſed of Arches of Circles, how is it poſſible that right Lines, which form the Bounds of the aforeſaid Figures, can produce Arches of Circles? Therefore if this be conſidered, 'tis plain, that the Bounds of the aforeſaid, and all ſuch other Figures, are compoſed of a Number of right Lines, which make very large obtuſe Angles; and therefore they are either regular Polygons, or Parts thereof; and though they come very near to the Bounds of Circles, or Ellipſes of the ſame Diameters, yet in fact they are neither. But however, as 'tis cuſtomary to call them Arches, I will therefore do ſo too, in the following Problems.

PROB. IX. Fig. A C. Plate IV.
To deſcribe a Semi-circle by the Interſection of right Lines.

LET *a c* be the given Diameter.

Operation. Biſect *a c* in *b*, whereon erect the Perpendicular *b h*, equal to *a b*, by PROB. X. LECT. III. Divide the Angle *h b c*, into two equal Parts, by the Line *b e*. Divide *b c* into 7 equal Parts, and make *b e* equal to 9 of thoſe Parts. Draw the Lines *h e* and *e c*, which divide into any Number of equal Parts, as in PROB. VII. hereof, and then drawing the Lines *c* 1, 1 2, 2 3, &c. they will form the Quadrant *h n c*. Proceed in the ſame Manner, to form the Quadrant *a h*, and it will complete the whole, as required

PROB.

Prob. X. *Fig.* A B. *Plate* IV.
To deſcribe a Scheme Arch, without any Reſpect being had to its Center.

Let *a c* be the given Length of its Chord Line, and one Half of the Perpendicular *b*, its given Height.

Operation. Biſect *a c*, and erect the Perpendicular *b*, equal to twice the given Height. Draw the Lines *a b*, and *b c*, which, as in Prob. VII. divide into equal Parts, and draw right Lines of Interſection, which will complete the whole, as required.

Prob. XI. *Fig.* A D, and A E.
To deſcribe a Gothick Arch for the Head of a Door or Window, by the Interſection of Lines.

Let *a g*, *Fig.* A D, be the given Breadth, and *e c*, the given Height.

Operation. Make *a g*, equal to the given Breadth, which biſect in *e*, whereon erect the Perpendicular *e c*, equal to the given Height. Draw *a b*, and *g d*, parallel to *e c*, and each equal to half *e c*. Draw the Lines *c b*, and *c d*. Divide the Lines *a b*, *b c*, *c d*, *d g*, each into equal Parts, as in Prob. VII. and draw the interſecting Lines, which will complete the whole, as required.

Fig. A E, is another Example, whoſe Height is leſs than *Fig.* A D, but its Conſtruction is all the ſame.

Note, If 'tis required to have the Curvature of the Hanſes of this Kind of Arches, to be more or leſs flat, the Height of the Lines *a b* and *d g*, muſt be encreaſed or decreaſed at pleaſure, which a very little Practice will make you perfect in.

Prob. XII. *Fig.* A G. *Plate* IV.
To deſcribe a Gothick Arch, compoſed of real Arches of Circles.

Let *n g* be the given Breadth.

Operation. Divide *n g* into 3 equal Parts, at *m o*, whereon with the Radius *o g*, deſcribe the Semi-circles *g m* and *o n*. On the Points *n m o g*, with the Radius *m g*, deſcribe the Arches *g r*, *m t r*, *o q*, and *n q*. From *q*, through *o*, draw the Line *q o d*, at pleaſure. Alſo from *r* through *m*, draw through the Line *r m b* at pleaſure ; alſo, on the Points *q* and *r*, with the Radius *q o*, more *o g*, deſcribe the Scheme Arches on each Side of *e*, which will meet the aforeſaid Semi-circles, at the Lines *b r* and *d q* ; and then will *n e g* be the Gothick Arch required.

Note, The Arches *a b c*, and *c d f*, are concentrick to the former, as being deſcribed at any given Diſtance on the ſame Centers.

A Gothick Arch may alſo be deſcribed, as in *Fig.* A F, as follows.

Let *c o* be the given Breadth.

Operation. Divide *c o* into five equal Parts. On the firſt Part, at each End, as on *b* and *n*, with the Radius *n o*, deſcribe the Semi-circles *c d e*, and *m l o*. On the Points *o n c b*, with the Radius *o b*, deſcribe the Arches *b q*, *c p*, and *n p*, *o q*, interſecting each other in the Points *p* and *q* ; from whence, through the Points *b* and *n*, draw the Lines *q b g*, and *p n i*, at pleaſure. On the Points *p* and *q*, with the Radius *p l*, deſcribe the Arches *l k*, and *d k*, interſecting each other in *k*, which will complete the Arch, as required.

Note, The concentrick Arch, *a g h i f*, is deſcribed on the ſame Centers as *b n*, and *p q*.

Prob. XIII. *Fig.* C. *Plate* V.
To deſcribe an Arch, whoſe Height is greater than half its Chord Line.

Let *c d* be the given Breadth, and *e b* the given Height.

Operation. Biſect *c d* in *e*, and thereon erect the Perpendicular *e a*, of Length at Pleaſure. Make *e b* equal to the given Height ; alſo *b a* equal to *e b*, and draw the Lines *c a* and *a d*, which divide into equal Parts, and draw the interſecting Lines, which will form the Arch as required ; and which is of very great Strength, and much ſtronger than a Semi-Elliplis of the ſame Breadth and Height, as I ſhall demonſtrate to you hereafter, when I come to explain the Strength and Abutments of all Kinds of Arches.

Prob.

Prob. XIV. *Fig.* A I. *Plate* IV.

To deſcribe a rampant Semicircular Arch, by the Interſection of right Lines.

Let *a p* be the given Diameter, and *a b* the Height of the Ramp. *Operation.* Biſect *a p* in *n*, whereon erect the perpendicular *n e*, of Length at pleaſure. From the Point *a*, draw *n b*, parallel to *n e*, and equal to the given Height of the Ramp; and draw the oblique Line *b p*. By Prob. X. Lect. III. divide the Angle *e n w* into two equal Parts, by the Line *n f*. Divide *n p* into ſeven equal Parts, as in Prob. IX. hereof, and make *n f* equal to nine of thoſe Parts. Set up *q e* equal to *a n*, and draw the Lines *e f*, *f p*, on the Points *b* and *e*, find the Point of Interſection *c*, by making *e c* equal to *e f*, and *c b* to *f p*, and draw the Lines *c b* and *c e*. Divide the Lines *b e*, *c e*, *e f*, and *f p*, into equal Parts, and draw the interſecting Lines; they will complete the Semicircle, as required.

Prob. XV. *Fig.* A L. *Plate* IV.

To deſcribe a rampant Semi-Ellipſis, by the Interſection of Lines.

Let *c h* be the tranſverſe Diameter, *f d* equal to half the conjugate Diameter, and *a b* the Height of the Ramp. *Operation.* Make *c h* equal to the given tranſverſe Diameter, which biſect in *g*, whereon erect Perpendiculars, as *g d*, at pleaſure. Draw *c a* and *e h*, parallel to *g d*, of Length at pleaſure; make *c b* equal to the given Height of the Ramp; alſo make *b a* and *h e*, each equal to half the given conjugate Diameter; and draw the Line *a e*. Divide *b a*, *a d*, *d e*, and *e h*, into equal Parts, and draw the interſecting Lines, which will complete the whole as required.

Prob. XVI. *Fig.* A H, and A K. *Plate* IV.

To deſcribe a rampant Circle, and a rampant Ellipſis, by the Interſection of right Lines.

Firſt, to deſcribe the rampant Circle, *Fig.* H.

Let *d f* be the Diameter given. *Operation.* Make *g i* equal to *d f*, and by Prob. III. hereof, complete the Rhombus *a e g i*. Biſect *a e* in *b*, *c i* in *f*, *a g* in *d*, and *g i* in *h*; then divide *a b*, *b e*, *e f*, *f i*, *i h*, *h g*, *g d*, and *d a*, into equal Parts, and draw the interſecting Lines, which will complete the whole, as required.

II. *To deſcribe the rampant Ellipſis, Fig.* A K.

Let *e d* be the tranſverſe, and *b h* the conjugate Diameters; alſo let the Angle *d i h* be a given Angle. *Operation.* Make *g i* equal to *e d*, and the Angle *d i h*, be equal to the given Angle. By Prob. III. hereof complete the Rhomboid *a e g i*, whoſe Sides and Ends biſect in the Points *e b d h*. Divide *a b*, *b e*, *e d*, *d i*, *i h*, *h g*, *g e*, and *e a*, into equal Parts, and then drawing the interſecting Lines, they will complete the whole, as required.

Prob. XVII. *Fig.* A. *Plate* V.

To deſcribe a rampant Scheme Arch, by the Interſection of right Lines.

Let *e d* be the Chord Line, or given Breadth, *c f* the given Height of the Arch, and *e a* the Height of the Ramp. *Operation.* Make *e d* equal to the given Breadth, which biſect in *g*, whereon erect the Perpendicular *g h*, of Length at pleaſure. Draw *e a* parallel to *g h*, and equal to the given Height of the Ramp. Draw the Line *a d*, and make *f c*, and *c b*, each equal to the given Height of the Arch. Draw the Lines *a b* and *b d*, which divide into equal Parts, and drawing the interſecting Lines, they will complete the whole, as required.

M Prob.

P R O B. XVIII. *Fig.* B. *Plate* V.
To defcribe a rampant Gothick *Arch, by the Interfection of right Lines.*
LET *i e* be the given Breadth, and *g b* the given Height.

Operation. Make *i e* equal to the given Breadth, which bifect in *f,* whereon erect the Perpendicular *f b,* of Length at pleafure ; from the Point B, draw the Lines *i a* and *e d,* parallel to *f b,* of Length at pleafure ; make *i b,* equal to the given Height of the Ramp, and draw the Line *b e* ; make *b a* and *e d,* each equal to half the given Height, alfo make *e b* equal to *e g,* draw the Lines *a b* and *b d.* Divide the Lines *a b, a b,* alfo *b d* and *d e,* each into equal Parts ; and draw the interfecting Lines, which will complete the whole, as required.

P R O B. XIX. *Fig.* D. *Plate* V.
To defcribe a rampant Semicircle by Ordinates.
LET *e b* be the given Diameter, and *q a* the Height of the Ramp.

Operation. Make *q d b* equal and parallel to the given Diameter *c e,* on the Points *c e,* erect the Perpendiculars *c a* and *e b,* each of Length at pleafure. Divide the Diameter *c e* into any Number of Parts either equal or unequal, as at the Points 1 4 6 8, *&c.* On *l,* with the radius *l c,* defcribe the Semicircle *c d c,* and from the Points 1 4 6 8, *&c.* draw right Lines parallel to the Line *c a,* of Length at pleafure. Make *q a* equal to the Height of the Ramp, and draw the Line *a b.* Take the Ordinates 1 2, 4 3, 6 5, 8 7, *&c.* in the Semicircle D, and fet them on the Line *a b,* from 1 to 2, from 4 to 3, from 6 to 5, from 8 to 7, *&c.* and from the Point *a,* through the Points *a* 2 3 5 7 *f, &c.* trace the Curve *a f b,* the rampant Semicircle required.

Fig. E is a given regular Scheme Arch, from whofe Ordinates, the rampant Scheme Arches *d g f, k l,* and *n m p,* are produced at different Heights of ramping, as *e f, b l,* and *l n,* where every refpective Ordinate is equal in each, unto thofe in the regular Scheme Arch *a b c, Fig.* E.

Fig. F is a given regular Semi-Ellipfis, from whofe Ordinates, the rampant Semi-Ellipfis *f g e,* and *l m i,* are produced at different Heights in the fame Manner.

P R O B. XX. *Fig.* G H. *Plate* V.
To defcribe a Parabola.
Note, When a Cone has a Section cut parallel to its Side, the curved Boundary of the Superficies, made by the Section, is called a Parabola.

LET *x f f* be a given Cone, and *b e* the Perpendicular of the given Section.

Operation. Bifect the Diameter of the Bafe *f f* in *p,* and from *x* the Vertex of the Cone, draw *x p,* its Axis, which continue downwards at pleafure towards *d,* in *Fig.* I ; in any Part of the faid Line *x p,* continued as at 5, draw *l q,* parallel to *f f,* and make 5 *z* equal to *b e.* Divide *b e* into any Number of equal Parts, fuppofe four (but the more the better) as at the Points *o p m s* ; and from thofe Points draw right Lines parallel to the Bafe *f f,* meet the Side of the Cone in the Points *g r b i k.* Alfo divide 5 *z,* in *Fig.* H, into the fame Number of equal Parts at the Points 1, 2, 3, 4, and through thofe Points draw right Lines, to the right and left at pleafure, and parallel to *l q.* In *Fig.* I, make 5 *n* equal to *f p,* the Semi-diameter of the Cone, and with the Radius *n* 5, on the Point *n,* defcribe the Circles *l a m b,* on *n* in *Fig.* I ; with the Radiufes *k s, i w, b u, e g q,* in *Fig.* G, defcribe the Circles *d f g i,* and from the Points *o p m s,* in *Fig.* G, draw right Lines parallel to *x z d,* interfecting the outward Circle in *Fig.* I, in the Points *a b,* the next in the Points *c d,* the next in the Points *e f,* and the next in the Points *b g,* interfecting the Diameter *l m,* in the Points *o p q.* Then will the Lines *a b, c d, e f, b g, k i,* be the feveral Ordinates of the Parabola that paffes through its Perpendicular, at its divided Points, 1 2 3 4 ; and therefore making 5 *l,* 5 *q,* each equal to *o a,* or *o b,* in *Fig.* I, alfo 4 *z,* 4 *u,* each equal to *c n* or *n d,* alfo 3 *y,* 3 *t,* each equal to *p e* or *p f,* alfo 2 *x,* 2 *s,* each equal to *b q* or *q g,* and from the Point *l,* in *Fig.* H, through the Points *z y x z s i u,* to *q,* trace the Curve of the Parabola required.

Note,

Note, It is to be observed, that to describe the upper Part of the Curve with Exactness, 'tis necessary to find the Points *r* and *w*, as following; divide *b p*, on *b e*, in *Fig.* G, in two equal Parts in *o*, and draw *o r* parallel to *x d*, also divide *x 2*, on the Line *x d*, in *Fig.* H, into two equal Parts at 1, and draw *w r*, parallel to *x s*; on *n*, with the Radius *i p m*, in *Fig.* G, describe the Circle *k i*, and from the Point *o* draw the Line *o k i*, parallel to *x d*, cutting *l m* in the Point *r*, make 1 *r*, 1 *w*, in *Fig.* H, each equal to *k r*, and through the Points *r w*, trace the Curve. By the same Method you may find more Points if required.

P R O B. XXI. *Fig.* K, L, M. *Plate* V.
To describe an Hyperbola.

Note, When a Cone has a Section cut parallel to its Axis, the curved Boundary of the Figure, made by the Section, is called an *Hyperbola.*

Let *a c b* be the given Cone, and *d n* the Perpendicular of the given Section.

Operation. Bisect the Base *c b* in *t*. Continue the Axis *a t*, downwards at pleasure, as to *m*, in *Fig.* M, and in any Part thereof, as at 5, draw *y x*, parallel to *c b*, and make 5 *m* equal to *d n*. Divide *d n* and 5 *m*, each into the same Number of equal Parts, as at *x f g e*, and 1 2 3 4. From the Points *e x f g*, draw right Lines parallel to *c b*, cutting the Side of the Cone in the Points *i k l m*. Make 5 *n* equal to *c t*, and through the Point *n*, draw the Line *o t*, parallel to *y x*, and equal to *c b*; on the Point *n*, with the Radius *c t*, describe the Circle *o 5 t m*, also with the Radiuses *m s*, *l r*, *k q*, and *i p*, describe the Circles *p q r s*. Continue *d n* the Perpendicular of the Section parallel to the Axis *a m*, intersecting the several Circles in the Points *a b c d e g h i k l*. Through the divided Points 1 2 3 4, in the Line *m 5*, *Fig.* L, draw right Lines parallel to *y x*, to the right and left at pleasure. Make 5 *y* and 5 *x* in *Fig.* L, each equal to *f a*, or *f l* in *Fig.* M, also make 4, 8; 4, 12; each equal to *f b*, or *f k*, also make 3, 7; 3, 11; each equal to *f c*, or *f i*, also make 2, 6; 2, 10; each equal to *f d* or *f h*; and lastly, make 1, 5; 1, 9; each equal to half *e g*, from the Point *y* through the Points 8, 7, 6, 5, *m g*, 10, 11, 12, to *x* trace the Hyperbola required.

P R O B. XXII. *Fig.* N. *Plate* V.

Upon a given right Line to describe any Polygon, from a Hexagon to a Duodecagon.

Let *a n* be the given Line.

Operation. Bisect the Line *a n*, in the Point *o*, whereon erect the Perpendicular *o m*, upon the Points *a* and *n*, with the Radius *a n*; describe the Arch *x n*, which divide into six equal Parts at the Points 1 2 3 4 5; make *x* 6, equal to *x n*, also *x m* to *x 5*, *x i* to *x 4*, *x e* to *x 3*, *x d* to *x 2*, and *x c* to *x 1*. Then will the Points *x c d e i m* 6, be the Centers of the Circles 6, 7, 8, 9, 10, 11, 12, which are capable of containing the given Line, six, seven, eight, nine, ten, eleven, and twelve times, and therefore will be a Hexagon, Septagon, Octagon, &c.

But to make this more intelligible, I will illustrate each Polygon singly in the following Problems.

P R O B. XXIII. *Fig.* A. *Plate* VI.
To describe a Pentagon, whose Sides shall be each equal to f g, *a given Line.*

Operation. On the Points *g* and *f*, with the Radius *f g*, describe the Arches *n g*, and *n f*; make *n z* equal to *b n*, the Chord Line of one sixth Part of the Arch *n f*, and on *z*, with the Radius *z f*, describe the Circle *a b e g f*; then making *f a*, *a b*, *b c*, *c g*, *g a*, each equal to *g f*, draw the Lines *a f*, *f b*, *f c*, and *c g*, which will complete the Pentagon, as required.

P R O B. XXIV. *Fig.* B. *Plate* VI.
To describe a Hexagon, whose Sides shall be each equal to h g.

Operation. On the Points *h* and *g*, with the Radius *h g*, find the Point of Intersection *n*, whereon with the Radius *n g*, describe the Circle *a b c d g h*, make *h a*,

M 2 *a b*,

a b, b c, c d, d e, and *e f,* each equal to *h g,* and draw the Lines *h a, a b, b c, c d, d e,* and *e f,* which will complete the Hexagon, as required.

Prob. XXV.　*Fig.* C.　*Plate* VI.

To describe a Heptagon or Septagon, whose Sides shall be each equal to a given Line, as y f.

Operation. Bisect *y f* in *x,* whereon erect the Perpendicular *x* 7, on the Point *f,* with the Radius *y f,* describe the Arch *y s,* make *s x* equal to one sixth Part of the Chord Line of the Arch *y s,* on *x :* with the Radius *x f,* describe the Circle *y a* 3 7 *d e f,* wherein from the Point *y,* set the given Line *y f,* from *y* to *a,* from *a* to 3, from 3 to 7, *&c.* and drawing the Lines *y a, a* 3, 3 7, *&c.* they will complete the Septagon, as required.

Prob. XXVI.　*Fig.* D.　*Plate* VI.

To describe an Octagon, whose Sides shall be each equal to a given Line, as p q.

Operation. Bisect *p q,* in *o,* whereon erect the Perpendicular *o r,* on the Point *q,* with the Radius *q p,* describe the Arch *p x* ; make *x r,* equal to *x m,* the Chord Line of one third Part of the Arch *p x* ; and on *r,* with the Radius *r p,* describe the Circle *a b c d e f g p,* wherein set the given Line *p q,* from *p* to *a,* from *a* to *b,* from *b* to *c, &c.* and drawing the Lines *p a, a b, b c, &c.* they will complete the Octagon, as required.

Prob. XXVII.　*Fig.* E.　*Plate* VI.

To describe a Nonagon, whose Sides shall be equal to a given Line, as e f.

Operation. Bisect *e f,* in *b,* whereon erect the Perpendicular *b d,* on *f,* with the Radius *f e,* describe the Arch *e a.* Make *a d* equal to the Chord Line of half the Arch *e a,* as *a x* ; on *d,* with the Radius *d f,* describe the Circle *e t s r g m e n,* wherein set the given Line *e f,* from *e* to *t,* from *t* to *s,* from *s* to *r, &c.* and drawing the Lines *e t, t s, s r, &c.* they will complete the Nonagon, as required.

Prob. XXVIII.　*Fig.* F.　*Plate* VI.

To describe a Decagon, whose Sides shall be equal to a given Line, as p e.

Operation. On *e* and *p,* with the Radius *e p,* describe the Arches *a p,* and *a e,* and on *a* erect the Perpendicular *a e* ; make *a e* equal to the Chord Line of two third Parts of the Arch *a p,* and on the Point *e,* with the Radius *e p,* describe the Circle *a n g h i k l m o e,* wherein set the given Line *p e,* from *p* to *n,* from *n* to *g,* from *g* to *h, &c.* and drawing the Lines *p n, n g, g h, &c.* they complete the Decagon, as required.

Prob. XXIX.　*Fig.* G.　*Plate* VI.

To describe an Undecagon, whose Sides shall be equal to a given Line, as e d.

Operation. On the Points *e* and *d,* with the Radius *d e,* describe the Arches *e a,* and *d a,* make *a g* equal to the Chord Line of five-sixths of the Arch *e a,* on the Point *g,* with the Radius *g e,* describe the Circle *i k l m, &c.* wherein set the given Line *e d,* from *e* to *i,* from *i* to *k, &c.* and drawing the Lines *e i, i k, &c.* they will complete the Undecagon, as required.

Prob. XXX.　*Fig.* H.　*Plate* VI.

To describe a Duodecagon, whose Sides shall be equal to a given Line, as g f.

Operation. Make *g a* and *a d* each equal to *g f* on *d,* with the Radius *d f,* describe the Circle *g b i k, &c.* wherein set the given Line *g f* ; from *g* to *b,* from *b* to *i,* from *i* to *k, &c.* and drawing the Lines *g b, b i, i k, &c.* they will complete the Duodecagon, as required.

Having thus shewn the Construction of each Polygon separately, you will easily understand how to make any Polygon from twelve to twenty-four Sides, by the following

Prob. XXXI.　*Fig.* O.　*Plate* V.

To make a Polygon of any Number of Sides from twelve to twenty-four, upon a given Line, as b c.

Operation.

Operation. Bisect *b c* in *d*, whereon erect the Perpendicular *d, a,* 24, of Length at pleasure, on the Point *c* describe the Arch *b a*, which divide into 12 equal Parts. Take as many of the 12 Parts of *b a*, as are Sides in the Polygon required more than 12. Suppose, for Example, a Polygon of six Sides ; upon the Point *a* with a Radius equal to four Parts, describe the Arch 12, *because the* 12 *Parts in the Arch* b a, *and the four set from* a *to* 2, *are equal to* 16 *Parts.* Upon the Point 2, with the Radius of 4 Parts, describe the Arch *e* 8, on the Point 8, with the Radius 8 *c* describe the Circle 16, the Circumference of which will contain the given Line *b c* sixteen Times, and thereby complete the Polygon, as required.

The like is also to be performed for any other Polygon.

PROB. XXXII. *Fig.* I. *Plate* VI.

To make an equilateral Triangle, Geometrical Square, Pentagon, Hexagon, Septagon, Octagon, Nonagon, or Decagon, within a given Circle.

LET *i d a z*, be the given Circle.

Operation. Draw the Diameters *i a* and *d z*, at right Angles to each other, also draw the Line *d a*, which bisect in the Point 2, and from *b* through the Point 2, draw the Line *b* 2 *b* ; through the Point 2 draw *c m*, parallel to *d z*, or make *a c* and *a m*, each equal to *a h*, also draw *b a* ; make *a e* equal to *a d*, and draw *d e*, divide the Arch *m a c* into three equal Parts, and make *x m* equal to one of those Parts. Then *c m* is the Side of an equilateral Triangle ; *d a*, of a geometrical Square ; *d e*, of a Pentagon ; *d h*, of a Hexagon ; *f m*, of a Heptagon ; *b a*, of an Octagon ; *m x*, of a Nonagon ; and *e h*, of a Decagon ; which may be made within the given Circle, *i d a z*, or Circles equal thereto ; as in the Circles, K L M N O P, which are equal to the Circle *Fig.* I, and which contain the following Polygons, *viz.* In the Circle K is a Pentagon, in L a Hexagon, in M a Septagon, in N an Octagon, in O a Nonagon, and in P a Decagon.

PROB. XXXIII. *Fig.* A D. *Plate* VI.

To describe any regular Polygon on a given Side, by the Help of the Line of Chords, and knowing the Quantity of Degrees contained in an Arch, whose Chord Line is the Side of the given Polygon.

THE number of Degrees contained in an Arch, whose Chord Line is the Side of an equilateral Triangle, are 120, of a geometrical Square 90, of a Pentagon 72, of a Hexagon 60, of a Septagon 51 ¾, of an Octagon 45, of a Nonagon 40, of a Decagon 36, of an Undecagon 32 $\frac{7}{11}$, and of a Duodecagon 30.

To prove that the aforesaid Degrees are the Quantity contained in an Arch, whose Chord Line is the Side of a Triangle, geometrical Square, *&c.* divide 360, the Number of Degrees in a Circle by the Number of Sides contained in the Figure proposed, and the Quotient is the Number of Degrees contained in the Arch of every such Chord Line, which is the Side required.

LET it be required to describe a Pentagon, as *Fig.* A D.

Operation. With 60 Degrees of your Line of Chords, on *z* describe the Circle *a b d i h*, make *a b, b d, d i, i h*, and *h a*, each equal to 72 Degrees, and draw the Lines *a b, b d, d i, i h*, and *h a*, they will complete the Pentagon, as required.

Note, If your Line of Chords should be of too large or too small a Radius, then proceed as follows, *viz.* suppose 'tis required to describe the small Pentagon *p k l n m.*

FIRST, complete the Pentagon, *a b d i h*, as before taught, and draw the Lines *z h, z a, z b, z d*, and *z i*. Bisect any Side of the Pentagon, as *b d*, in *u :* make *u t* and *u* each equal to half one Side of the given small Pentagon, and draw *t k* and *u p*, at right Angles, to *a b*, meeting the Lines *a z*, and *b z*, in the Points *p* and *k*. Make *z l, z n, z m*, each equal to *z k*, or *z p*, and drawing the Lines *l k, k p, p m, m n*, and *n l*, they will complete the Pentagon, as required.

EXAMPLE II.

AGAIN, suppose the small Pentagon *p k l n m* is given, and 'tis required to describe the large Pentagon *a b d i h*, with a small Line of Chords.

FIRST,

First, Complete the fmall Pentagon, and from its Center draw right Lines through the angular Points at pleafure. Continue any Side of the fmall Pentagon at both Ends, at pleafure, as the Side *k p*, towards *q* and *r*; bifect *k p* in *s* : make *s q*, and *s r*, each equal to half of one Side of the large Pentagon. Draw the Lines *q b*, and *r a*, at right Angles to *q r*, and continue them to meet the Lines *z a*, and *z b*, in the Points *a* and *d*; make *z d*, *z i*, and *z h*, each equal to *z b*, or *z a*, and draw the Lines *a b*, *b d*, *d i*, *i h*, and *h a*, which will complete the large Pentagon, as required.

PROB. XXXIV *Fig.* R. *Plate* VI.

To defcribe any Polygon, on a given Side, having the Number of Degrees given, that are contained in each Angle of the Polygon.

THE Number of Degrees in the Angle of a regular Pentagon are 108, in a Hexagon 120, in a Septagon 128 ⁴⁄₇, in an Octagon 135, in a Nonagon 140, in a Decagon 144, in an Undecagon 147 ³⁄₁₁, and in a Duodecagon 150.

LET *a b* be the given Side.

Operation. On the Points *a* and *b*, with 60 Degrees of Chords, defcribe the Arches *g f* and *h i* ; make *h z*, and *g z*, each equal to 90 Degrees, and *z i*, and *z f*, each equal to 18 Degrees, then will the Arches *g f*, and *h i*, be each equal to 108 Degrees ; through the Points *f* and *i*, draw the Lines *a e* and *b a*, each equal to *a b*, by PROB. XI. LECT. III. make the Angles *a e m*, and *b a m*, each equal to the Angle *a b a*, and draw the Lines *e m* and *a m*, which will meet in *m*, and complete the Pentagon, as required. And fo the like for any other Polygon.

THE Number of Degrees, that are contained in the Angle of any Polygon, is found by fubtracting the Number of Degrees contained in the Arch, whofe Chord is a Side of the Polygon, from 108, and the Remains is the Quantity of the Angle required.

PROB. XXXV. *Fig.* Q. *Plate* VI.

To find the Radius of a Circle capable to contain any Polygon, whofe Sides fhall be each equal to a given Line, as a c.

Operation Bifect *a c* in *b*; whereon erect the Perpendicular *b m*; make *a h* equal to *a c*, and on *b*, with the Radius *b a*, defcribe the Arch *a d c*, which divide into 6 equal Parts at the Points 1 2 d 3 4, make *h n*, *n o*, *h p*, *p g*, *g r*, *r s*, *s t*, and *t m*, each equal to the Chord Line of the Arch *a n*, *a p*, *a g*, *a r*, *a s*, *a t*, *a m*, *a 1*, and draw the Lines *a o*, which are the Semi-diameters of Circles that will contain all the Polygons from a geometrical Square unto a Duodecagon, *viz.* the Line *a o* is the Radius of a Circle that will contain a geometrical Square, the Line *a n*, the Radius for a Pentagon ; *a h*, for a Hexagon ; *a p*, for a Heptagon ; *a g*, for an Octagon ; *a r*, for a Nonagon ; *a s*, for a Decagon ; *a t*, for an Undecagon ; *a m*, for a Duodecagon. In the like Manner any greater Number of equal Parts being fet above *m*, all other Polygons of more Sides than 12 may be defcribed.

LECTURE V.

On the infcribing and circumfcribing of Geometrical Figures.

PROB. I. *Fig.* T. *Plate* VI.

To infcribe a Circle, as c a b, *in any right-lined Triangle, as* i l k.

OPeration. By PROB. XI. LECT. III. divide any two Angles of the Triangle, by Perpendiculars, as *i d* and *k e*, interfecting each other in *f* ; from whence, by PROB. VIII. LECT. III. let fall a Perpendicular, as *f a*, on *f* : with the Radius *f a*, defcribe the Circle *a b c*, which will touch the Sides *l i* and *k l*, in the Points of Contact *b* and *c*, and therefore is infcribed, as required.

PROB. II. *Fig.* S. *Plate* VI.

To infcribe a Circle, as n l m e, *within a geometrical Square, as* b c a d.

Operation.

Operation. Draw the diagonal Lines *b d*, and *a c*, from the Center *b*; let fall the Perpendicular *b e*; on the Center *b*, with the Radius *b e*, defcribe the Circle *n l m e*, which will touch the Sides in the Points *n l m e*, and therefore is infcribed, as required.

P R O B. III. *Fig.* V and W. *Plate* VI.
To infcribe a Circle, as h k l i g, *within any regular Polygon, as the Pentagon* a b c d f.

Operation. Let fall a Perpendicular from the Center *d*, to any Side, as *d g*, on *f e*; with the Radius *d g* defcribe a Circle, which will touch the Sides of the Pentagon, in the Points of Contact, *h k l i g*, and therefore is infcribed, as required.

Fig. W, is a fecond Example of a Hexagon, which hath a Circle infcribed within it, in the fame manner.

P R O B. IV. *Fig.* X. *Plate* VI.
To infcribe a geometrical Square, as e f d z, *within any right-lined Triangles, as* a b c.

Operation. On the Point *e* erect the Perpendicular *e z*, equal to *e b*. From the angular Point *a*, draw *a g*, parallel to *z e*, meeting the Bafe *b c* in *g*. Draw *z g*, cutting *a c* in *f*; draw *f z*, parallel to *a g*; alfo *f e*, parallel to *b c*; and *e d*, parallel to *f z*; then will *e f d z*, be a geometrical Square, infcribed within the Triangle *a b c*, as required.

P R O B. V. *Fig.* Y. *Plate* VI.
To infcribe an equilateral Triangle, as a b e, *in a geometrical Square, as* c a d g.

Operation. Draw the Diagonal *a g*, which bifect in *n*. On *n*, with the Radius *n a*, defcribe the Circle *c a d g*; on *g*, with the Radius *g n*, defcribe the Arch *b n f*. Draw right Lines from *n* to *b*, and to *f*, which will interfect the Sides of the Square *c g* and *d g*, in the Points *b* and *e*. Draw the Line *b e*, and the Triangle *a b e* will be equilateral and infcribed, as required.

P R O B. VI. *Fig.* A D. *Plate* VI.
To infcribe an equilateral Triangle, as b e g, *within a regular Pentagon, as* a b d i h.

Operation. Bifect any Side, as *b i*, in two, and erect the Perpendicular *z b*; alfo divide the Angle *a b i*, into two equal Parts, by the Line *b z*, cutting *b z* in *z*, the Center of the Pentagon. On *b*, with the Radius *b z*, defcribe the Arch *z z c*; divide the Arches *z z* and *z c*, each into two equal Parts, in the Points *o* and *m*, through which draw the Lines *b o e* and *b m g*; alfo draw the Line *e g*, then will *b e g* be the equilateral Triangle infcribed, as required.

P R O B. VII. *Fig.* A. *Plate* VII.
To infcribe a regular Pentagon, as n d e h k, *within an equilateral Triangle, as* a i u.

Operation. Let fall the Perpendicular *a k*, on *v*; with the Radius *v i*, defcribe the Arch *i t s o*, at pleafure. Draw *v p*, perpendicular to *v i*, cutting the Arch *i t s o* in *p*. Divide the Arch *i p* into 5 equal Parts, and make *p o* equal to one Part, and draw the Lines *a o* and *v o*, bifect *v o* in *l*, and draw the Line *l k*, continued to *f*; make *v a* equal to *i f*, and draw the Line *a k*, cutting the Line *a o* in *h*. Make *k n* equal to *k h*. Make *n d* and *h e*, each equal to *k h*, and then drawing the Lines *d n*, *h e*, and *d e*, the Pentagon *n d e h k* will be infcribed with *s* in the Triangle *i a v*, as required.

P R O B. VIII. *Fig.* C. *Plate* VII.
To infcribe a geometrical Square, as c b h f, *within a Pentagon, as* d a e n g.

Operation. Draw the Line *d e* and *e k* at right Angles thereto. Make *e k* equal to *e d*, and draw the Line *a k*, which will interfect *e g*, the Side of the Pentagon

Pentagon in *f*. Draw *f h* parallel to *n g*. On the Points *f* and *h*, erect the Perpendiculars *f b* and *h c*, meeting the Sides of the Pentagon *a e* and *a d*, in the Points *c* and *b*. Draw *c b*, and *c b h f* will be the geometrical Square inscribed, as required.

PROB. IX. *Fig.* B. *Plate* VII.
To find the Sides of a Penta-Decagon, or regular Polygon, of 15 Sides, which may be inscribed in a given Circle.

LET *c a b f n* be the given Circle.

Operation. By PROB. XXXII. LECT. IV. inscribe the equilateral Triangle *a d g*, and Pentagon *c a b f n*, so that one Angle of each Figure meet in the Point *a :* then will *f g* or *n d*, be one third Part of *f b*, or *n c* ; and as *f b* and *n c*, are each one fifth Part, therefore *n d* and *f g* are each one fifteenth Part, as required.

PROB. X. *Fig.* G. *Plate* VII.
To circumscribe a Circle, as a b c e, *about a geometrical Square, as* a b c e.

Operation. Draw the Diagonals, and on the Center *d*, with the Radius *a d*, describe the Circle *a b c e*, as required.

PROB. XI. *Fig.* E. *Plate* VII.
To circumscribe a geometrical Square, as a b c d, *about a given Circle, as* g f i e.

Operation. Draw two Diameters at right Angles to each other as *f e* and *g i*. Through the Points *f e*, draw the Lines *a b* and *c d*, parallel to *g i* ; also through the Points *g* and *i*, draw the Lines *a c* and *b d*, parallel to *f e*, which will meet each other in the Points *a b c d*, and form the geometrical Square, circumscribing the Circle, as required.

PROB. XII. *Fig.* F. *Plate* VII.
To circumscribe a Pentagon, as c b a e d, *about a Circle, as* x w h f g, *and a Circle about a Pentagon.*

Operation. First, by PROB. XXXII. LECT. IV. describe the Pentagon *e b a e d*, within the given Circle, and bisect its Sides in the Points *x w h f g*, to which, from the Center *z*, draw right Lines to meet the given Circle in the Points *d c b a e*. Draw the Lines *d c*, *c b*, *b a*, *a e*, and *e d*, and they will form the circumscribing Pentagon, as required.

Secondly, Bisect any two Sides, as *a b* and *b c* in the Points *h* and *w*, from which draw two right Lines at right Angles to those Sides, which will intersect each other in *z*, the Center of the Pentagon, whereon with the Radius *z a* describe the circumscribing Circle *c b a e d*, as required.

PROB. XIII, *Fig.* C. *Plate* VI.
To inscribe any Polygon within any Circle.

LET it be required to inscribe the Septagon *a 3 7 d e f y*.

GENERAL RULE.

Draw the two Diameters *z b* and *7 c*, at right Angles, dividing the Circle into four Quadrants. Divide any of these Quadrants into the same Number of equal Parts as there are Sides in the given Polygon; then four of those Parts will be the Side of the Polygon that may be inscribed, as required : so here the Arch *z 7*, being divided into 7 equal Parts, the Side 3 7 contains 4 Parts.

PROB. XIV. *Fig.* D. *Plate* VII.
To circumscribe any regular Polygon, about another Polygon of the same Kind.

LET it be required to circumscribe the Hexagon *e c a l i x e*, about the Hexagon *d b m k h f*.

Operation.

Operation. Draw the Diagonal Lines *d k*, *b h*, *m f*, to which draw right Lines at right Angles, *e c*, *c a*, *a l*, and *x e*, which by their meeting in the Points *e c a l i x*, will conſtitute the circumſcribing Polygon, as required.

PROB. XV. *Fig.* H. *Plate* VII.

To circumſcribe a Pentagon, as o a c y z, *about a geometrical Square, as* l 5 v w.

Operation. Continue the Side *w* 5 towards *d*; biſect 5 *l* in *i*, erect the Perpendicular *i b* on the Points *w* and *v*, with the Radius 5 *i*, deſcribe the Arches *q r* and *s t*, at pleaſure. On the Point 5, with the Radius 5 *i*, deſcribe the Arch *i d*; which divide into 5 equal Parts, at the Points *b g f e*. Make the Angles *i* 5 *a*, and *i l a*, each equal to two Parts of *i d*. Make the Arches *q r*, and *s t*, each equal to one Part, and continue the Line *w r* towards *a* and *y*; alſo *v t* towards *m* and *z*; alſo *a* 5 towards *b*, and *a l* towards *p*, which will interſect each other in the Points *o* and *c*. Make *c y*, and *o z*, each equal to *a c*, and draw *z y*, which will complete the circumſcribing Pentagon *o a c y z*, as required.

PROB. XVI. *Fig.* I. *Plate* VII.

To circumſcribe a Pentagon, as f a o r v, *about an equilateral Triangle, as* a k p.

Operation. On the angular Points *a k p*, with any Radius deſcribe Arches, as *q x o*, *l h f*, and *e d b*. Divide the Arch *d e* into 5 equal Parts. Make the Arch *c b* equal to four Parts of *d c*. Through the Point *b* draw the Line *a b* at pleaſure. Make the Arch *g e* equal to the Arch *c b*, and through *e* draw the Line *a f*, at pleaſure. Make the Arch *s x o*, and *b f*, each equal to the Arch *b d*, and from the Points *k* and *p*, through the Points *f* and *o*, draw Right Lines both Ways at pleaſure; which will meet the Lines *a o*, and *a f*, in the Points *o* and *f*. Make *o r*, and *f v*, each equal to *a f*, or *a o*, and join *v r*, then will *f a o r v*, be the circumſcribing Pentagon, as required.

PROB. XVII. *Fig.* Z, *and* A B. *Plate* VI.

To circumſcribe a geometrical Square, about any Scalenum, or Iſoſceles Triangle. THIS may be done two Ways.

LET *e n b*, *Fig.* Z, be a Scalenum Triangle given.

Operation I. Continue the Side *e n* towards *d*, and through the angular Point *b* draw the right Line *a c*, parallel to *e d*. On *e* erect the Perpendicular *e a*, to meet the Line *a c*, in the Point *a*. Make *a c*, and *e d*, each equal to *a e*, and draw *c d*, which will complete the circumſcribing geometrical Square, as required.

Operation II. *Fig.* A B. Draw *c a* through the angular Point *b*, and parallel to the Side *x n*. From the Points *n* and *x* let fall Perpendiculars to the Line *a a*. Make *c m*, and *a h*, each equal to *c a*, as required, which will complete the circumſcribing geometrical Square, as required.

LECT. VI.
Of proportional Lines.

PROB. I. *Fig.* N. *Plate* VII.

To find a mean proportional Line, between two given Lines.

A Mean proportional Line, is that which being multiplied into itſelf, its Product is equal to the Product of the two given Lines multiplied into each other; or it is the Side of a geometrical Square, whoſe Area is equal to the Area of a Parallelogram, whoſe Length and Breadth is equal to the two given Lines.

LET *d* and *g* be the two given Lines.

Operation. Draw a right Line, as *a e*, at pleaſure, make *a b* equal to the Line *r d*, and *b c* equal to the Line *e*. Biſect *a c* in *x*, and deſcribe the Semi-

N   circle

circle *a b c*; on *b* erect the Perpendicular *b h*, which is the mean proportional Line required.

P R O B. II. *Fig.* O. *Plate* VII.

To cut from a given Line, a Part that shall be a mean Proportional between what remains, and a Line proposed, as the Line n.

L et *n* be the given Line, and *m* the Line proposed.

Operation. Draw a right Line, as *a g*, at pleasure; make *a e* equal to the Line *n*, and *e g* equal to *m*. Bisect *a g* in *r*, and on *r* describe the Semi-circle *a x g*; and on *e* erect the Perpendicular *e x*. Bisect *e g* in *h*, make *h e* equal to *h x*, then *e e*, the Part cut off from *a e*, equal to the given Line *n*, is a mean Proportional between *e a*, the Part remaining, and *m*, the Line proposed. For making *l i*, in *Fig.* Q, equal to *a e*, and *i k* equal to *m*; and the Semi-circle *k b l* being described, the Perpendicular *i h* (which by the last P rob. is a mean Proportional to the Lines *k i*, and *i l*) will be equal to *e e*, the Part cut off.

P r o b. III. *Fig.* P. *Plate* VII.

Two Lines being connected into one Line, and their mean Proportion separate, being given, to find the Lengths of the given Lines, which are called Extremes.

L et *a c* be the given Extremes, connected together without Distinction, and the Line *d*, the mean Proportional.

Operation. Bisect *a c* in *b*; on *b* describe the Semi-circle *a g c*; on *c* erect the Perpendicular *c i*, equal to the Line *d*; draw *i g* parallel to *a c*, cutting the Semi-circle in *g*. Draw *g h* parallel to *i c*, which will divide *a c* in *b*; then are *a b*, and *b c*, the two extreme Lines required; for by P rob. I. *h g* is a mean Proportional to *a h* and *h c*, and is equal to the Line *d* also.

P r o b. IV. *Fig.* R. *Plate* VII.

Two right Lines being given, to find a third Proportional.

L et *k* and *m* be two given Lines.

Operation. Make an Angle at pleasure, as *d n e*. Make *n f* equal to *k*, and *n b* and *f a* each equal to *m*, and draw the Line *f b*; also draw the Line *a i*, parallel to *b f*; then will *a i* be the third Proportional required.

P r o b. V. *Fig.* S. *Plate* VII.

The right Lines being given, to find a fourth Proportional.

L et the Lines 1, 2, 3, be three given Lines, and 'tis required to find a fourth, which will be to 3, the third, exactly the same, as 2, the second, is to the first.

Operation. Make an Angle at pleasure, as *n g b*, make *g f* equal to the Line 1, and *g i* equal to the Line 2, and *f n* equal to the Line 3. Draw *i f*, and parallel thereto, the Line *n m*; then will *i m* be the fourth Proportional required; for *i m* is to *i g*, the same as *n f* is to *f g*, and therefore *m i* is to *n f*, exactly the same as *i g* is to *f g*.

Note, *This Problem is nothing more than the Golden Rule, or Rule of Three, geometrically performed.*

P r o b. VI. *Fig.* T. *Plate* VII.

The Mean of three Proportionals, and the Difference of the Extremes being given, to find the Extremes.

L et *b c* be the mean Proportional, and *g e* the Difference of the Extremes.

Operation. On *e* erect the Perpendicular *e d*, of Length equal to *b c*. Bisect *g e* in *b*; on *b*, with the Radius *b d*, describe the Semi-circle *l d a*; and then *l e*, and *e a*, are the Extremes required.

PROB. VII. *Fig.* V. *Plate* VII.
To find the Extremes b *and* f, *having two mean Proportionals, as the Lines* g *and* h *given.*

LET the given Line g be equal to 8, and the Line h equal to 4.
Operation. Draw a c at pleafure, and on a erect the Perpendicular a 6, which make equal to 8 the given Line g. Make a c equal to twice a 6, and draw the Line 6 c 6 out at pleafure. Draw c d perpendicular to a c, and of Length at pleafure; to which draw a parallel Line, at the Diftance of the given Line h, which will cut the Line 6 c in the Point e; from which Point draw the Line e d n parallel to a c, cutting the Line c d in d; then the Lines a c, and c d, equal to the Lines b and f, are the two Extremes required; for a c equal to 1 6, and c d equal to 2, multiplied into each other, produce 32, the fame as a 6, equal to 8, multiplied into d e 4, equal to 32 alfo.

PROB. VIII. *Fig.* V. *Plate* VII.
To find the two Means g *and* h, *having the two Extremes* b *and* f *given.*

Operation. Draw a c equal to the given Length of the Line b, fuppofe 1 6, and erect the Perpendiculars a 6, and c d. Make c d equal to the given Length of the Line f, fuppofe 2. Make a 6 equal to half a c, and draw the Line 6 c e, of Length at pleafure. Through the Point d draw the Line n e, parallel to a c, cutting the Line 6 c in e; then a b equal to the Line g, and d e equal to the Line h, are the two Means required.

PROB. IX. *Fig.* W. *Plate* VII.
To cut two Lines, each into two Parts, fo as that the four Segments may be proportional.

LET b and q be the two given Lines.
Operation. Make a right Angle at pleafure, as a z x. Make x z equal to b, and a z equal to q; and draw the Line a x. Bifect z x in g, and on g defcribe the Semi-circle x c z. From the Point c d draw the Line c b, parallel to z x, and c y parallel to a z. Then will x y be to y c, as y c is to c b, and y c will be to c b, the fame as c b is to b a.

PROB. X. *Fig.* X. *Plate* VII.
To divide a right Line into extreme and mean Proportion.

LET a b be the given Line.
A LINE is faid to be divided into extreme and mean Proportion, when the Area produced by the whole Line multiplied into one of its Parts, is equal to the Area produced by the other Part multiplied into itfelf.
Operation. Erect the Perpendicular a d, and produce it towards c. Make a c equal to half a b. Make c d equal to c b, and a e equal to a d; then will the Line a b be divided at e, in extreme and mean Proportion, as required.
Demonftration. Complete the Parallelogram c d a b, and draw the Diagonal c a. Make b h equal to b e, and draw h g parallel to b a: alfo from e draw e f parallel to c b. Now the Parallelogram h g b a, whofe Length is equal to a b the given Line, and Breadth h b to b e, one of the Parts of the given Line, is equal to the geometrical Square d f a e, whofe Sides are each equal to e a, the other Part of the given Line. For as the Diagonal c a, divides the Parallelogram c d a b, into two equal Parts, and as the oppofite Triangles, on each Side the Diagonal, are each equal to its oppofite, therefore the Parallelogram g f muft be equal to the geometrical Square e b; and therefore, if to the Parallelogram e g, we add the Parallelogram g f, which together make the geometrical Square d f a e, it will be equal to the Parallelogram g h a b, which is the geometrical Square e b, added to the Parallelogram g e; becaufe in both thefe Equalities, the Parallelogram g e is common, as well to the Parallelogram g f, as to the geometrical Square e b.

PROB

PROB. XI. *Fig.* Y. *Plate* VII.
To divide a given Line in any Ratio or Proportion required.

LET *i a* be a given Line to be divided according to the Proportion of the given Lines *k l* and *n*.

Operation. From one End of the given Line, as *a*, draw a right Line, as *a e*, making any Angle at pleasure. And thereon make *a b* equal to *k*, *b c* equal to *l*, *c c* equal to *m*, *d e* equal to *n*, and draw the Line *e i*. From the Points *d e b*, draw the Lines *d h*, *g*, and *b f*, parallel to *e i*, which will divide the given Line *i a*, as required.

PROB. XII. *Fig.* Z. *Plate* VII.
To make upon a given right Line, two Parallelograms that shall be in any given Ratio, or Proportion to another.

LET *b a* be the given Line, upon which 'tis required to make two Parallelograms, which shall be to one another as the Line *x* to the Line *z*.

Operation. From the Point *b*, draw the Line *b d*, making any Angle at pleasure, and thereon make *c b* equal to the Line *x*, and *c d* equal to the Line *z*, and draw the Line *a d*, also draw *c e* parallel to *a d*; then will the Parts *b e*, and *e a*, the Parts of the given Line, be to each other, as the Line *x* is to the Line *z*; and Parallelograms made thereon of any equal Heights, as *b f*, *e a*, and *g b*, *b e*, will be to one another, as the given Line *x* is to the Line *z*.

PROB. XIII. *Fig.* A B. *Plate* VII.
The Difference between the Side and Diagonal of a geometrical Square being given, to find the Side of the Square.

LET *b a* be the given Difference.

ERECT the Perpendicular *b c* equal to the Difference *b a*, and draw the Line *a c*, continued towards *d* : make *c d* equal to *c b*; then will *a d* be the Side of the Square required.

PROB. XIV. *Fig.* I. *Plate* VIII.
To cut from a Line any Part required.

'TIS required to cut off two ninth Parts of the given Line *b c*.

Operation. Make an Angle as *e a h*, at pleasure, and on any Side thereof, as on *a e*, set off nine any equal Parts, as from *a* to *d*, make *a h* equal to *b c*, and draw the Line *d h*; also at two Parts from the Point *d* draw the Line *g*, parallel to *d h*, then will *g h* be equal to two ninth Parts of *a h* (which is equal to *b c*), as required.

PROB. XV. *Fig.* II. *Plate* VIII.
From a given Point without a Circle as e, to draw a Chord Line as i n, in a given Circle, that shall be equal to a given Line, as a b.

Operation. Assume any Point in the Circumference as *g*, and thereon with the Length of the given Line *a b*, make the Section *l*, and from *g* through *l* draw the Line *g l n*, of Length at pleasure. On the Center *e* with the Radius *e e* describe the Arch *e p*, on the Point *e* with the Radius *p g*, describe the Arch *m k*, cutting the Circle in *n* and *d*. Draw the Lines *d e* and *e n*, cutting the Circle in *h* and *i*; then will either of the Lines *d h*, or *n i*, be a Chord Line equal to the given Line *a b*, as required.

PROB. XVI. *Fig.* IV. *Plate* VIII.
To describe a Part or Portion of a Circle, capable of containing an Angle equal to an Angle given, upon a given Line.

LET *g h k* be the given Angle, and *f e* the given Line.

Operation. Make the Angle *f e i* equal to the given Angle *g h k*; at *e* on the Line *i b* erect the Perpendicular *e b*, bisect the Line *e f* in *g*, and erect the Perpendicular *g d*, cutting the Line *b e* in *d*; whereon with the Radius *d e*, describe the Portion of a Circle *f b a e*, then all the Angles that can be made in this Segment, as *e c f*, *f a e*, &c. will be equal to the given Angle *g h k*.

PROB.

Pᴙᴏʙ. XVII. *Fig.* III. *Plate* VIII.
To cut off a Segment of a Circle, capable of containing an Angle equal to an Angle given.

Lᴇᴛ *d c b a* be a given Circle, from which a Part is to be taken, that shall contain the given Angle *q p f.*

Operation. Draw the Semi-diameter *g e*, and Tangent Line *b e*, make the Angle *d e b* equal to the given Angle *q p f*, cutting the Circle in *d.* Then is *d b c a c*, the Segment required, and all Angles made therein, as *d c c*, *d b c*, &c. will be equal to the given Angle *q p f*, as required.

Pᴙᴏʙ. XVIII. *Fig.* VI. *Plate* VIII.
To describe a spiral Line, at any given Distance.

Lᴇᴛ *a b* be the given Distance.

Operation. First draw a right Line, as *b b*, at pleasure, and assume a Point therein, as *d*, at pleasure. Make *d c* and *d e* each equal to half *a b*, and on *d* describe the Semi-circle *c e*, on the Point *c* describe the Semi-circle *e f*, and on *d* the Semi-circle *f i*; again, on the Point *c* describe the Semi-circle *i g*, and on *d* the Semi-circle *g k*. In like manner on the Points *c* and *d* describe as many other Revolutions as may be required. Secondly, spiral Lines may be described concentrick to each other, as in *Fig. p h*, next below *Fig.* VI. as follows.

Lᴇᴛ *q r* be the given Distance.

Operation. Draw a right Line, as *p b*, and therein assume two Points, as *a* and *b*, whose Distance must be equal to the given Distance *q r*; on the Point *a* describe the Semi-circle *b i*, and on *b* the Semi-circles *a c*, and *i d*; then on the Point *a* describe the Semi-circles *c k* and *d l*, and on the Point *b* the Semi-circles *k c*, and *l f*. Proceed in like manner, as in the last Problem, to make as many other Revolutions as may be required.

Pᴙᴏʙ. XIX. *Fig.* V. *Plate* VIII.
To describe an Artinatural Line.

Operation. First trace by Hand the several Curvatures or Turnings at pleasure, which divide into as many Parts as seem each to be the Segment of a Circle, as *e c a*, *n b g*, &c. This done, in each Arch assume 3 Points, as *e c a*, and *n b g*, and then by Pᴙᴏʙ. XIX. Lᴇᴄᴛ. III. find the Centers *f* and *m*, and describe the Curves *e c a*, and *n k b g a.* In the like manner proceed throughout the whole, to describe all the various Meanders remaining, which will appear with the utmost Beauty.

Sᴇʀᴘᴇɴᴛɪɴᴇ Rivers, and Walks through Wildernesses, &c. being laid out in this Manner, are the nearest to Nature, and the most agreeable of all others.

PART III. Of Aʀᴄʜɪᴛᴇᴄᴛᴜʀᴇ.

LECTURE I.

Of the Description and Construction of Moldings.

Tʜᴇ several Members or Moldings of which the five Orders are composed, are of three Kinds, *viz.* square, circular, and compound.

First, Square Members are Plinths, Fillets, Dados, Cinctures, Annulets, Abacuses, Fascias, and Tenias of Architraves, Freezes, Denticules, Dentuls, and Regulas.

Secondly, Circular Members are Beads, Torules, Astragals, Ovolos, Cavettos, and Apophyges.

Thirdly, Compound Members are those which are composed of two or more Arches, as Scotias, Cyma Rectas, Cyma Reversas, Plancers of Modillions, &c. As square Members are nothing more than Parallelograms, I need not
say

say any Thing of their Conftructions, and therefore I fhall proceed to fingle
and compound Moldings, and give the Etymology of fquare Members as
they come in their Order.

P R O B. I. *Fig.* B. *Plate* VIII.

To defcribe a Torus.

Let *w x* be the given Height.

Operation. Draw *x r* at pleafure, and the Line *w* parallel thereto, at the Diftance of the given Height; in any Part, as at *n*, erect the Perpendicular *n a*,
make *n c* equal to half the given Height, and on *c*, with the Radius *n c*, defcribe
the Torus required.

This Member is called a Torus from the *Greek Toros*, a Cable, which its
Swelling refembles, or rather from the *Latin Torus*, a Bed, or Cufhion, becaufe it
feems to fwell by the impofed Weight. It is generally placed on a Zocolo or
Plinth. D, which is fo called, from *Plinthos*, a fquare Brick or Table, placed the
very lowermoft of all, to preferve the Foot of the Column from rotting; for originally Columns were made of the Tapering Bodies of Trees.

P R O B. II. *Fig.* C. *Plate* VIII.

To defcribe an Aftragal with its Fillet.

Let *d f* be the given Height.

Operation. Draw *f z* at pleafure, and in any Part, as at *f*, erect the Perpendicular *f d*, equal to the given Height *f d*, which divide in 3 equal Parts at *e*
and *a*, through the Points *d a e*, draw the Lines *d w*, *n c*, and *e x*, parallel to *f z*;
make *f b* and *f g* each equal to *e f*. On *a* defcribe the Semi-circle *d e*, and on *g*
the Quadrant *f k*, which will complete the Aftragal, as required.

This Member is called an Aftragal from the *Greek Aftragalos*, the Bone (or
more properly the Curvature) of the Heel, and for which Reafon the *French* call
it *Talon*, either of which I think is very proper, when employed in a Pedeftal or
Bafe of a Column, but not when placed on the Shaft of a Column, when it does
the Office of a Collar, and is therefore by many called *Collarino*.

P R O B. III. *Fig.* O. *Plate* VIII.

To defcribe the Apophyges of a Pilafter or Column.

The Apophyges of a Column or Pilafter is that curved Part of the Shaft, which
rifes or flies from the Cincture, and ends in the Upright of the Shaft, as the Arch
b d; it is alfo by fome Mafters ufed at the lower Part of the Corinthian Freeze,
and of the Dado of a Pedeftal. This Member takes its Name from the *Greek*
Word 'Αποφυγη, becaufe in that Part the Column feems to emerge and fly from
its Bafe. In the *Tufcan* Order, this Member is nothing more than a Quadrant,
as *b a*, *Fig.* B, whofe Height is equal to its Projection, but in all other Orders it
is not fo, and is thus defcribed.

Operation. Divide the Projection of the Cincture *e d*, *Fig.* O, before the Upright
of the Column into 5 equal Parts, make its Height *e b* equal to fix of thofe Parts;
draw *a b* parallel to *e d*, alfo draw *b d*, which bifect in *g*, whereon erect the Perpendicular *g a*, cutting *b a* in *a*; on *a* defcribe the Arch *b d*, the Apophyges
required.

Note, The fame Rule is to be obferved in defcribing the Hollow under the Fillet
of the Collarino, at the Top of a Shaft of a Column in every of the Orders.

P R O B. IV. *Fig.* F *and* G. *Plate* VIII.

To defcribe an Ovolo of any given Height.

Let *a c*, *Fig.* F, be the given Height.

Operation. Firft, draw *c d* at pleafure, on any Point, as *c*, erect the Perpendicular *c a* equal to the given Height, through the Point *a* draw *b c*, parallel to
d c, on *a*, with the Radius *a c* defcribe the Arch *c b*; which is the Ovolo required.

Secondly, Let *b c*, *Fig.* G, be the given Height.

Operation. Divide the given Height into 4 equal Parts, and give 3 of thofe Parts
to the Projection. Draw the Lines 3 *c*, which bifect in *d*, on which erect the
Perpendicular *d a*, on *a* defcribe the Arch *c* 3, which is the Ovolo required.

6

This

THIS Member is called an *Ovolo*, from the *Latin Ovum*, an Egg, which 'tis generally carved into, intermixed with Darts and other Devices, symbolizing Love, &c. It is also called *Echinos*, or *Echinus*, from the *Greek*, as being something like the thorny Husk of a Chesnut, which being opened, discovers a Kind of Oval Kernel, something dented a little at the Top, which the *Latins* call *Decacuminata Ova*, and Workmen Quarter Round.

P. *I remember, that, in the last Problem, you was speaking of the Apophyges taking its Rise from the Cincture; pray what is a Cincture?*

M. A Cincture is the first Part of a Shaft of a Column, as *a w*, in *Fig.* B, *Plate* VIII. which always is placed on the Base of every Column, and anciently was nothing more than a broad Iron Ferril or Hoop, to confine and strengthen the lowermost Part of the Shaft, which the *Italians* call *Listello*, or *Girdle*. The Shaft of a Column is that round plain Part, which is contained between the Base and the Capital, of which I shall give you a more full Account, when I come to treat of the Parts of an Order. It is also called *Fust* from the *Latin Fustis*, a Club; *Vitruvius* calls it *Scapus*, and by some Masters 'tis called *Vivo*, *Fige*, and *Trunk*.

PROB. V. *Fig.* D and E. *Plate* VIII.
To describe a Cavetto of any given Height.

LET *a c*, *Fig.* D, be the given Height.

Operation. First, Draw *e f* at pleasure, and in any Part thereof, as at *c*, erect the Perpendicular *c a*, equal to the given Height, and through the Point *a* draw the Line *b g*, parallel to *e f*; make *c e* equal to *c a*, and on *e* with the Distance *e c*, describe the Cavetto *b c*, as required.

Note, If 'tis required to make a Fillet on the Cavetto, as *b n*, then the given Height must be divided into 4 equal Parts, and the Fillet made equal to one Part. The Projection of its under Part *c d* is equal to one 8th of the whole Height, which is half of *b d*, or of one Part.

THIS Member is called *Cavetto*, from the *Latin Cavus*, a Hollow; and Workmen call this Member a Hollow also, though I believe not with Respect to the *Latin*, but because it is a real Hollow; and as an Ovolo is generally made a Quadrant, they therefore call that Member a Quarter Round.

To describe a Cavetto a second Way.

Secondly, Let *b y*, *Fig.* E, be the given Height.

Operation. Divide *b y* into 5 equal Parts, and give the upper 1 to the Fillet, make the Projection 1, 3, equal to 4 Parts, and *y n* equal to 1 Part, and draw the Line *a n* parallel to *b y*; continue *y n* out at pleasure, and draw the Line 3 *x n*, which bisect in *x*, and thereon erect the perpendicular *x p*. On *p* describe the Cavetto *n* 3, as required.

PROB. VI. *Fig.* H. *Plate* VIII.
To describe a Bed-Molding of any Height required.

LET *a x* be the given Height.

Operation. Divide the given Height into 8 equal Parts, give 3 to the Cavetto, 1 to the Fillet, and four to the Ovolo, and then by Problems IV. and V. describe their Curves, as required.

PROB. VII. *Fig.* I. *Plate* VIII.
To describe a Cymatium of any given Height.

LET *a g* be the given Height.

Operation. Divide the given Height into 4 equal Parts, as at 4 *h*, and give the upper 1 to the Height of the *Regula.* Draw right Lines from the Points 4, 3, and *h*, at right Angles to the Line 4 *h*, of Length at pleasure, and draw *a g* at any Distance from 4 *h*, and parallel thereto make *n c* equal to *n g*, and draw the Line *c g*, which bisect in *e*, on *e c*, and *e g*, make the equilateral Sections *d* and *f*, whereon describe the Arches *c e* and *e g*, which completes the Cymatium, as required.

THIS Member with its Regula is called a *Cymatium*, from the *Greek* Κυμάτιοι, *Undula*, a rolling Wave, which it resembles, or *Kymation*, a Wave. *Vitruvius* calls it it *Epiſtheates*, and the *Italians* and *French*, *Gola*, *Geule*, or *Doucine*. But when we ſpeak of this Molding ſingly, without its Regula or Fillet, we call it a *Cyma Reeta*, and Workmen oftentimes call it a *Fore Ogee*, to diſtinguiſh it from *Cyma Inverfa*, which they call a *Back Ogee*.

P R O B. VIII. *Fig.* K. *Plate* VIII.

To deſcribe a Cyma inverfa, as b r, *of any given Height.*

Operation. Draw the Line n r, at pleaſure, in Part, as at r, erect the Perpendicular r b equal to the given Height, which divide into 4 equal Parts, and give the upper 1 to the Fillet. Through the Points a and b draw right Lines, as d b, and c a, parallel to n r, and of Length at pleaſure. Make a c equal to a r, divide c a in 6 equal Parts, and make n r, and e c, each equal to one of thoſe Parts; draw the Line *e g n*, which biſect in g, on the Points n g, and g e; make equilateral Sections, and deſcribe the Arches e g, and g n, which completes the *Cyma Inverfa*, as required.

P R O B. IX. *Fig.* L. *Plate* VIII.

To deſcribe a ſingle Cornice of any given Height.

LET a b be the given Height.

Operation. Firſt, divide the given Height into 5 equal Parts, give the lower 1 to the Cyma Inverfa f; one third of the ſecond to the Fillet c, and the upper 1 to the Regula e; and the remaining two Parts and ⅓, to the Cyma Reeta d. Secondly, by PROB. VII. and VIII. deſcribe the Curves of the two Cymas, and the Cornice will be completed, as required.

Note, That the Projection of the *Cyma Reeta*, and of the *Cyma Inverfa*, which is alſo called *Cyma Reverfa*, is always equal to their own Height.

P R O B. X. *Fig.* B A. *Plate* VIII.

To divide and proportion Dentuls to any given Height.

LET n s be the given Height.

Operation. Divide the given Height into 8 equal Parts, give the upper one to n s, the Height of the Fillet, the next ſix to s v, the Height of the Dentuls, and the lower one to v x, the Margin of the *Denticule*.

To proportion the Breadths of the Dentuls and Intervals between them, make v q equal to s v, and dividing v q into 3 equal Parts, give two to the Breadth of a Dentul, and one to its Interval, which is called *Metoche*, which with two Pair of Compaſſes, the one opened to the Breadth of a Dentul, and the other to the Breadth of an Interval, ſet off thoſe Diſtances reciprocally throughout the whole Length of your Molding.

IF it is required to make Eye-Dentuls in the Intervals, as A A, divide the Height of the Dentul into 5 equal Parts, and give the upper one to the Height of the Eye-Dentul.

Note, This Ornament is generally begun at the projecting Angle, over an angular Column, with the Form of a Pine-Apple, or rather, the Cone of a Pine-Tree, as at k g, which is thus deſcribed.

MAKE its Breadth x n, equal to the Breadth of a Dentul, which divide in 4 equal Parts; make k g equal to n x, and draw x g; make n d, x b, each equal to half n x; and draw d b, which biſect in e. On e, with the Radius e d, deſcribe the Semi-Circle d m b. On the Points d f, and b f, with the Radius f d, deſcribe the dotted Sections next above the Line d b, on which, with the ſame Opening, deſcribe the Arches b f, and f d, which will complete the whole, as required.

THESE Ornaments are called Dentuls, from *Dentelli*, Teeth, which they repreſent. The *Denticulus* is that flat or ſquare Member, on which the Dentuls are placed.

P R O B. XI. *Fig. 11*, next under *Fig.* A B, aforeſaid *Plate* VIII.

To proportion and deſcribe an Ionick Medallion, of any given Height required.

LET a b be the given Height.

Operation. Divide the Height into 8 equal Parts, as r q, give the upper 2 to the Height of the Cyma Inverfa, with its Fillet, and the next 5 to the

Depth

Depth of the Modillion. Draw *d c*, for the Side of a Front Modillion, make *e e* equal to *c d*, and *d f* equal to *d c*, then is *d f* the Breadth of the Modillion in Front. Divide *d f* in 4 equal Parts; make *f l*, the Projection of the Modillion in Profile, equal to 6 of those Parts. Divide the Projection of the Modillion in Profile into 6 equal Parts, at the Points 1, 2, 3, 4, 5. Through the Points 2 and 5, draw the Lines *o m*, and 5 *t*, parallel to *f p*. Make 5 *t* equal to two Parts and half, and 2 *o* equal to one Part : Also make *o m* equal to 5 *t*, and draw the Line *m s t*. On the Points *m* and *t*, with the Radius *t* 5, describe the Arches *o s*, and *s* 5; also on 2, with the Radius 2 1, describe the Arch 1 0, which will complete the Modillion, as required.

This Member is called *Modillion*, from the *Italian Modiglioni*, a plain Support to the Corona of the Corinthian and Composite Cornice, to which they only belong, although now falsely introduced into the Ionick.

Prob. XII. *Fig.* N *and* M. *Plate* VIII.
To describe Scotias of any given Heights.

First. Let *a g*, *Fig.* M, be the given Height.

Operation. Draw the Line *f g*, and on any Part thereof, as at *g*, erect the Perpendicular *g a* equal to the given Height, and through the Point *a* draw the Line *a x*, parallel to *g f*. Divide *a g* in 3 equal Parts, at the Points *d z*, and through the Point *d* draw the Line *c d e*, parallel to *a x*. Make *d e* equal to *d a*. On the Point *d* describe the Quadrant *a c*; and on the Point *e* the Quadrant *c f*, which together form the Curve of the Scotia, as required.

This Member is called *Scotia*, from the *Greek* Σκοτια, *Skotos*, Darkness, which the upper Part causes by its Projecture. 'Tis also, by some, called *Trochilus*, from the *Greek Trochilos*, Τροχιλος, or Τροχια, a Rundle or Pully, whose hollow Part within the Rope-works hath some Resemblance of this Member; and with respect to its Darkness, 'tis by many, though improperly, called a Cavetto. The *Italians* call it *Bastone*. This kind of Scotia is adapted to the Attick Base.

Secondly. Let *a d*, *Fig.* N, be the given Height.

Operation. Draw the Lines *k a* and *n d*, parallel to each other, at the Distance of *a d*, and draw *a d* at right Angles thereto. Divide *a d* in 3 equal Parts, and through *c*, the third Part down, draw *h c*, parallel to *a k*. Make *c h*, and *d n*, each equal to *a c*; and draw *i h n*, parallel to *a d*. Make *h i* equal to *h n*, and from *i* through *c*, draw the Line *i c m*. On the Point *c* describe the Arch *a m*, and on *i* the Arch *m n*, which completes the Scotia, as required.

Prob. XIII.

The Diameter, or Breadth of a Door, or Window, being given, to find the Breadth of an Architrave, that will be proportionable thereto.

A General Rule.

Divide the Diameter, or given Breadth, into 6 equal Parts, and take one for the Breadth of the Architrave required; and that you may also know how to divide the Architrave into its proper Members, I have given you in *Plate* VIII. and IX. thirty and one kinds of Architraves, of which those marked A B C D E F, are Tuscan; G H I K L M N O, are Dorick; P Q R S T V, are Ionick; W X Y Z, A B, A C, are Corinthian; and A D, A E, A F, A G, and A H, are Composite, which in general have the Heights of their several Members proportioned by equal Parts. As for Example. In *Fig.* A, the Height or Breadth of that Architrave is divided into 10 equal Parts, of which the upper 2 and ½ is the Height of the Tenia *a*, and the Remainder is the great Fascia, with its Hollow. In *Fig.* D, the Height is divided into six equal Parts, of which the upper 1 is the Height of the Tenia ; the lower 2 the Height of the small Fascia *c*, and the other 3 is the Height of the great Fascia *h*. In the same manner you are to understand all the others ; and as the principal Parts into which the Height of every Example is divided, are signified by the equal Divisions and Figures against them ; and as the Manner of describing all the Moldings of which they are composed has been already taught, to say any thing further on the manner of describing them is

O

needless ;

needlefs; as indeed is what I have already faid, the whole being fo very plain, as to be underftood by the meaneft Capacity, at the firft View.

LECT. II.

Of the making of Scales of equal Parts, for the delineating of Plans and Elevations of Buildings.

THE neceffary Scales for our Purpofes, are thofe reprefenting, firft, Feet; fecondly, Feet and Inches; thirdly, Modules and Minutes; and fourthly, Chains and Links. Thofe of Feet, and Feet and Inches, are ufed in the making of Plans and Uprights, or geometrical Elevations of Buildings. Thofe of Modules and Minutes are for proportioning of the feveral Members of the five Orders of Columns in Architecture; and thofe of Chains and Links are for making Surveys of Lands, as Farms, Parks, &c. whofe feveral Ufes will be fully illuftrated in their proper Places.

P R O B. I. *Fig.* I. *Plate* IX.
To make a Scale of Feet.

Operation. Make a Parallelogram at pleafure, as *a d m e*; open your Compaffes to any fmall Diftance, and fet off 10 equal Parts, from *m* to *x b*; alfo make *x b*, and *b e*, &c. each equal to *m x b e*; then will the Line *m e* be a Scale of equal Parts, which may reprefent Inches, Feet, Yards, &c. and which muft be thus numbered, *viz.* As *x b* is equal to the 10 Parts between *m x*, therefore at *b* place the Number 10, at *e* the Number 20, &c. being fo many Parts from *x*. To take off any Number of Feet, lefs than 10, fet one Foot of your Compaffes on *x*, and extend the other to the Number of Feet required.

To take off any Number of Feet more than 10, fet one Foot of your Compaffes in *b*, and extend the other to the Number of odd Feet that is contained in the given Length more than 10. Suppofe 17 was the given Length: extend your Compaffes from *b* to 7 Parts beyond *x* towards *m*, which is 17 Feet, as required; and fo the like of any other Number of Feet, more than 10, 20, &c.

To make a Variety of Scales of equal Parts, which it is neceffary to have, as fome Works require a leffer or a greater Scale than others; therefore, if from the 10 equal Parts, in *m x*, you draw right Lines unto the Point *a*, and afterwards draw right Lines parallel to *m e*, at any Diftances, as *f r*, *g q*, *h p*, *i o*, *k n*, and *l m*, you will have made other Scales of equal Parts, of various Sizes, which may fit all Purpofes required.

P R O B. II. *To make a Scale of Feet and Inches.* *Fig.* VI. *Plate* IX.

Operation. Make a Parallelogram, as *a b c d*, fet off 12 fmall equal Parts, from *e* to *e*, reprefenting the Inches in a Foot; make *e* 10, 10 20, 20 30, &c. each equal to the 12 Parts, then is your Scale of Feet and Inches completed; for *e* 10, 10 20, are Feet, and the Parts in *c c*, are Inches. To take off a Length of Feet and Inches, is the fame here, as before in the Feet: fo the Diftance of 3 10, is 15 Inches, of 6 10, is 18 Inches, of 9 10, 21 Inches. Scales of Feet and Inches are alfo made on two-foot Rules, as *Fig.* II. in manner following, *viz.*

MAKE a Parallelogram, as *c a z b*, at pleafure, and let the Diftance of *z f* be made to reprefent one Foot. Make *f* 3, 3 1, and 1 *b*, on the Line *z b*, each equal to *z f*; that is, each equal to one Foot. **Draw** *f g*, parallel to *e z*. Bifect *e g* in *e*, and draw the Lines *e z*, and *e f*. Divide *g f* in 6 Parts, at the Points *l k i b g*, and draw right Lines through them, parallel to *z b*, and then is the Scale completed; and the Diftance of *z f*, which is the given Foot, is divided into 12 Inches, *viz.* The Diftance of *g* 1, is one Inch; *b* 2, two Inches; *i* 3, three Inches; *k* 4, four Inches; *l* 5, five Inches; *g* 6, fix Inches; *l* 7, feven Inches; *k* 8, eight Inches; *i* 9, nine Inches; *h* 10, ten Inches; *g* 11, eleven Inches; and *f z*, one Foot, as before.

THESE kind of Scales may be made either bigger or lefs, at pleafure, in the very

very fame manner, as may be feen at the Eud *a b*, where the Foot is made but half the aforefaid.

PROB. III. *Fig.* IV. *Plate* IX.
To make a Scale of Chains and Links, for the plotting of Lands, &c.

Operation. Make a Parallelogram, as *a v u w*, and let the Diftance *b e* reprefent one Chain, which is equal to four Statute Poles, each 16 Feet and half, or to 66 Feet. Make *e d* equal to *e b*, then *d e* is one Chain alfo. Divide *a b* into 10 equal Parts, and through them draw right Lines parallel to *b w*. Divide *a f*, and *b e*, each into 10 Parts, and draw the diagonal Lines *f* 10, *h* 20, &c. then your Scale is completed; and the Diftance of 1 *k* is one Link; 2 *l*, two Links; 3 *m*, three Links; 4 *m*, four Links; 14 *n*, fourteen Links; 19 *s*, nineteen Links; 20 *e*, twenty Links, &c. to which, one or more Chains-length may be added, as occafion requires. At the right Hand End, the Parallelogram *e v g w* is another diagonal Scale of Chains and Links, made to half the Magnitude of the aforefaid.

PROB. IV. *Fig.* III. *Plate* IX.
To make a Scale of Minutes, or to divide the Diameter or Module of a Column into 60 Minutes.

Operation. Divide the Length of the Diameter into 10 equal Parts, as at the Points 6, 12, 18, &c. on its Ends erect Perpendiculars, whereon fet up any 6 equal Parts, and draw right Lines parallel to the given Diameter, which will complete a Parallelogram, as *Fig.* III. whofe upper Side muft be divided into 10 equal Parts, as the given Diameter, as at the Points 6, 12, 18, &c. This done, draw the diagonal Lines, 6, 1; 12, 6; 18, 12; which will complete the whole; and the Diftances taken from the left Hand, perpendicular to the Points 1, 2, 3, 4, &c. are the Minutes required.

PROB. V.
To make divers Scales of Chords of any Length or Radius required,
LET *c e*, at the left Angle of *Plate* IX. be a given Scale of Chords, divided as before taught.

Operation. Erect the Perpendicular *c a*, of Length at pleafure, and draw the Hypothenufal Line *a e*. At any Diftances from *c*, draw divers right Lines parallel to *c e*, as *d d*, *e e*, &c. Draw right Lines from the feveral Degrees in *c e*, unto the Point *a*, and they will divide all the intermediate parallel Lines *d d*, *e e*, &c. in the fame Proportion as the given Line of Chords *c e*, and confequently each of them will be a Line of Chords, as required.

LECT. III.
Of the principal Parts of an Order, and of the Orders in general.

AN ENTIRE ORDER confifts of three principal Parts, *viz.* a Pedeftal, a Column, and an Entablature.

A PEDESTAL is the firft or lowermoft Part of an entire Order, as *e h*, *Fig.* I. *Plate* XIX. which confifts of three principal Parts, *viz. g h* its Bafe, *g f* its Dado, or Die, and *f e* its Cornice. Its Name comes from the *Greek Stylobutes*, the Bafe of a Column; 'tis alfo called *Stereobate*, or *Stylobate :* but, as Mr. *Evelyn* in his Parallel obferves, our Pedeftal is *Vox Hybrida* (a very Mungrel), not *à Stylo*, as fome imagine, but *à Standa.*

A COLUMN is the fecond principal Part of an entire Order, as *b e*, *Fig.* I. *Plate* XIX. which confifts of three principal Parts, alfo, *viz.* its Bafe *d e*, its Shaft *c d*, and its Capital *b c*. The Bafe receives its Name from the *Greek* Verb βαίνω, importing the Suftent or Feet of a Thing ; and the Capital from the *Latin*, *Capitellum*, the Head or Top. The Architrave is called by the *Greeks*, *Epiftileum ;* that is to fay, *Epi* upon, and *Stylos* a Column, which, from a mungrel Compound of two Languages (Αρχυ) *Trabs*, as much as to fay, the principal Beam, or rather from *Arcus*, Chief, and *Trabs*, a Beam, we call Architrave. The Freeze takes its Name either from the *Greek* Ζωοφόρ, *Zophorus*, importing the imaginary Circle of the Zodiack, depicted with its 12 Signs, or is derived either from the *Latin Phrygio,* a Border, or from the *Italian Phrygio,* an embroidered or fringed Belt. The Cornice receives its Name from the *Latin, Coronis,* a Crowning, from whence its Fascia is called *Corona,* also called *Supercilium,* or rather *Stillicidium,* the Drip *(Corona elucolata Vite),* and with more Reason 'tis called by the *French, Larmier.* The *Italians* call it *Gocciolatoio,* and *Ventale,* from its protecting the Building both from Water and Wind; and for which Reason the *Latins* call it *Mentum,* a Chin, because its Projection carries off the Rains from the lower Part of the Entablature, as the Prominency of that Part in Men's Faces prevents the Sweat of the Face from trickling into the Neck.

An Entablature, from the *Latin, Tabulatum,* a Cieling, and by some called Ornament, is the third, and uppermost Part of an entire Order, as *a b,* which likewise consists of three principal Parts, namely, its Architrave, Freeze, and Cornice.

The principal Parts of Pedestals, Columns, and Entablatures, are subdivided and proportioned in such manners, that the Results of their Compositions shall give such Usefulness, Grace and Beauty, that are agreeable to the Order they are made to represent.

The Orders in Architecture were originally but three, *viz.* Dorick, Ionick, and Corinthian, invented by the ancient *Greeks;* to which two more have been since added, called Tuscan and Composite.

The Tuscan Order, for its being the most robust and masculine, is therefore placed before the Dorick, and the Rear of the whole is brought up with the Composite.

The Tuscan Order is so called, from the *Asiatick Lydians,* who are said to have first peopled *Italy,* and raised Buildings thereof, in that Part called *Tuscany.* This Order, for its Simplicity, or native Plainness, when well performed, and employed at the Entrances of Cities, Magazines, and other Buildings of Strength, is not in the least inferior to any of the other Orders. The general Proportions of this Order are as follow, *viz.* The Height of the Pedestal is one fifth of the whole, its Column 7 Diameters, and the Entablature one fourth of the Column, or one Diameter, 45 Minutes, as exhibited in *Fig.* I. *Plate* XIX.

The Dorick Order is so named from *Dorus,* King of *Achaïs,* who, 'tis reported, built a magnificent Temple of this Order in the City of *Argos,* which he dedicated to the Goddess *Juno,* and which, *Vitruvius* saith, was the very first Model of the Kind.

This Order, for its Masculine, or rather, as *Scamozzi* calls it, *Herculean* Aspect, with regard to its excellent Proportion, is to be employed where Strength and Grandeur are required, as at the Gates of Noblemen's Palaces, *&c.* The general Proportions of this Order are as follow, *viz.* The Height of the Pedestal is one fifth of the whole, its Column 8 Diameters, and its Entablature one fourth of the Column, or two Diameters, as exhibited in *Plate* XXIII.

The Ionick Order is said to have been invented by *Ion* King of *Ionia,* a Province in *Asia,* who erected a Temple of this Order, and dedicated it to the Goddess *Diana:* and as this Order is a Mean between the *Herculean Dorick,* and Feminine *Corinthian* Extremes, it ought therefore to be employed in Porticoes, Frontispieces, *&c.* at the Entrances into Noblemen's and Gentlemen's Houses. The general Proportions of this Order are as follow, *viz.* The Height of its Pedestal is one fifth of the whole, its Column 9 Diameters, and its Entablature one fifth of the Column, or one Diameter, 48 Minutes, as exhibited in *Plate* XXVIII.

The Corinthian Order received its Name from the luxurious City of *Corinth,* where it was invented and made by *Callimachus,* an ingenious Statuary of *Athens,* who took the first Hint thereof from a Basket, placed on the

the Grave of a young Lady of *Corinth*, wherein the Nurfe having put her Play-Toys, according to the Cuftom of thofe Times, and covered the Bafket with a fquare Tyle, a Root of *Acanthus*, or *Branca Urfina*, Bears-Foot, happened to grow under it ; which putting forth its Leaves around from under the Bafket, as in *Fig.* V. *Plate* XXXIV. they turned up the Sides, and enclofed the whole at Bottom ; whilft the Flower-ftalks in advancing higher were repulfed by the projecting Tyle, and obliged to turn under it, in a curved Manner. To form this Capital, he made a *Vafe* or Bell, to reprefent the Bafket, and about it placed fixteen Leaves, in two Heights ; from which, in Imitation of the curved Flower-ftems, he fprung Stalks enriched, whofe Curvatures he finifhed with Volutes, and covered the Whole with a horned Abacus of Moldings, in Imitation of the Tyle. This Order being the moft rich and delicate of all the Orders, it fhould therefore be employed within Buildings, as in Rooms of State, *&c.* where Magnificence and Beauty are required. The general Proportions of this Order are as follow : Its Pedeftal is one fifth of the whole Height, its Column ten Diameters, and its Entablature is equal to one fifth of the Column, as exhibited in *Plate* XXXII.

THE COMPOSITE ORDER, called by fome the *Roman* or *Italian* Order, is generally made, of all others, the very worft ; for its Capital is nothing more than the lower Part of the *Corinthian* Capital, covered with the *Ionic* Capital for an Abacus ; is much lefs elegant than the *Corinthian*, as its Entablature is alfo : and if to thefe be added the Lownefs of its Shaft, which has very little Diminution, and of equal Height with the *Corinthian ;* upon a juft View of the Whole, it will appear to be rather a Difgrace than a Credit to the Inventor, or, at leaft, a full Proof of a great Barrennefs of Invention : and that I may not be thought to find Fault with the Endeavours of others, and at the fame Time give no better Example, I therefore, in *Plate* XLI. have given the *Compofite* Entablature, by *Andrea Palladio*, with a *Compofite* Entablature of my own Invention, for infide Works, which I fubmit to the Judgment of the Judicious. The general Proportions of this Order are exhibited in *Fig.* I. *Plate* XXXIX.

To thefe five Orders we may add many more, *viz.* Firft, the Orders of the *Perfians* and *Cariatides*, as *Fig.* II. III. and IV. *Plate* XLII. where the Statues of Men and Women are ufed inftead of Columns, of which the firft is crowned with a *Dorick* Entablature, and the laft with an *Ionick*. Secondly, the *French* and *Spanish* Orders, which are only different from the *Corinthian* in their Capitals, and Enrichments of their Freezes. Thirdly, the Grotefque and *English* Orders of my Invention, *vide Plates* 302, to 310, of my ancient Mafonry. And laftly, the *Gothick* Order, which makes twelve Orders in the Whole.

L E C T. IV.

Of the Manner of proportioning the particular Parts of the Tufcan *Order, by Modules and Minutes, according to* ANDREA PALLADIO, *and by equal Parts, compofed from the Mafters of all Nations.*

P R O B. I.

To find the Diameter, or Module of an Order, proportionable to any given Height.

BEFORE an Order can be delineated, the Diameter muft be found ; and as Columns are employed in four different Manners, *viz.* Firft, alone, without either Pedeftal or Entablature : Secondly, with the Pedeftal only : Thirdly, with the Entablature only : And laftly, with both Pedeftal and Entablature : Therefore, to find the Diameter in every of thefe four Cafes, this is the Rule, *viz.* Divide the given Height into the fame Number of equal Parts, as there are Minutes coftained in the Height of the principal Parts that are to be employed ; and take fixty of thofe Parts for the Diameter of the Column.

THE Height of the Column alone, *o q, Fig.* I. *Plate* XIX. is 7 Diameters ; therefore one feventh of the given Height, where the Column only is to be employed,

employed, is the Diameter required. The Height of the Pedestal and Column, as *b b*, equal to *n x*, *Fig.* I. *Plate* XIX. is 9 Diameters eighteen Minutes and ¾, which are equal to 558¾ Minutes. Now admit the given Height to be 12 Feet, reduced into Inches, equal to 144, and the Inches reduced again into 10ths, equal to 1440. Then say, by the Rule of Three direct, As 558 Minutes, the Number of Minutes contained in the Height of the Pedestal and Column (rejecting the ¾ of a Minute), is to 60, the Minutes contained in the Diameter of the Column : So is 1440, the tenths of an Inch contained in the given Height of 12 Feet, to 151 ¼⅞, which is very little more than one Quarter Part of one tenth. Now 151 tenths of an Inch reduced, is equal to 15 Inches, one tenth, one fourth of a tenth, and a very small Matter more, and is the Diameter required. And if 15 Inches, one tenth, and ¼ of a tenth, be divided into 60 equal Parts, omitting the small Matter more than the ¼ of a tenth (which will be near enough for Practice), they will be the Minutes of the Diameter, by which the Heights and Projections of the Order may be proportioned.

In the same Manner the Diameter may be found, when the Column and Entablature only are employed, whose Height *i p*, *Fig.* I. *Plate* XIX. is 8 Diameters, 45 Minutes ; as also may the Diameter of the entire Order, whose Height *a b* is 11 Diameters, 3 Minutes, and ¾, as expressed on the Line *l w*.

This being understood, and a Diameter being thus found and divided, the delineating of this Order is easily performed, as follows.

Prob. II.
To delineate the Tuscan *Pedestal, by Modules and Minutes.*

Let A, *Plate* XIX. be a Diameter found, or given (which is also called a Module), and divided into 60 Minutes.

Before we proceed to this Operation, it is to be observed, that the Heights of the Members are expressed on the central Line, to be read upwards, and their Projectures are placed against them, to be read level with the Eye, either on the right or left Hand Side.

Operation. First, Draw a base Line, as *k r*, *Fig.* III. *Plate* XIX. and in any Part, as at *k*, erect the Perpendicular *k k*. Make *k f* equal to 37 Minutes and ½, as expressed between *k* and *f*; also make *f e* equal to 2½ Minutes ; *e d* to 5 Minutes ; *d c* to one Diameter, 9 Minutes, ⅔ ; *c a* to 4 Minutes, ¼ ; *a b* to 2 Minutes, ½ ; *b k* to 17 Minutes, ⅓ ; and through the Points *k b a c d e f*, draw right Lines to the right and left, parallel to the base Line *k r*. Secondly, Make *k r*, and *f s*, each equal to 47 Minutes and ½ ; and draw the Line *s r*. Make *f t*, and *e v*, each equal to 45 Minutes, and draw the Line *v t*. Make *d w* equal to 41 Minutes. Make *d x*, and *c y*, each equal to 40 Minutes, and draw the Line *y x*. Make *c* 41 equal to 41 Minutes. Make *a z*, and *b* 45, each equal to 45 Minutes, and draw the Line 45 *z*. Make *b r*, and *k b*, each equal to 47 Minutes and ½, and draw the Line *b r*. Then by Prob. V. of Lect. I. hereof, describe the Cavettos *y z*, and *z v* ; and the very same being repeated on the left Hand Side of the central Line, will complete the Pedestal, as required. And as the Members in the Base and Capital of the Column, as also the Members in the Entablature, are all delineated in the very same Manner, there needs no more to be said thereof, and therefore the next Work is, How to diminish the Shaft of this, or any other Column.

But before we can proceed to this Work, it must be observed, First, that the Heights of the Bases of Columns in general are all equal to half a Diameter, or 30 Minutes ; as is also the Height of the *Tuscan* and *Dorick* Capitals. Secondly, That the Cincture *b*, *Fig.* I. *Plate* X. and the *Astragal*, or *Collerino k k*, are both Parts of the Shaft. Thirdly, That since the whole Column in the *Tuscan* Order, including its Base and Capital, is 7 Diameters high ; therefore taking the Base and Capital from it, which together are equal to one Diameter, the Remains, 6 Diameters, is the Height of the Shaft. Fourthly, That Columns in general are diminished but in the two upper third Parts of their Height, the lower third Part being a Cylinder. Fifthly, That the *Tuscan* Co-

5   lumn

lumn is diminished one fourth of the Diameter of its cylindrical Part; the *Dorick* one fifth, the *Ionick* one sixth, the *Corinthian* and *Composite* one seventh; and therefore the Diameter of the *Tuscan* Column, at its Top, is but 45 Minutes, the *Dorick* 48 Minutes, the *Ionick* 50 Minutes, the *Corinthian* and *Composite* each 51 Minutes, ⅓.

PROB. III. *Fig.* I. *Plate* X.
To diminish the Shaft of the Tuscan, *or any other Column.*

Operation. Draw *l b* for its Height, ⅓ of which is its Diameter. Divide *l b* into three equal Parts, at *q* and *C;* through the Points *l C* and *b* draw right Lines, at right Angles, to the central Line *l b*. Make *C y*, and *C* 7, each equal to 30 Minutes, and *l h, l k,* and *C D, C E,* each equal to 22 Minutes and a half, and draw the Lines *h D,* and *l E* on the Point *C;* with the Radius *C y*, describe the Semicircle *y w* 7. Divide *l C*, into any Number of equal Parts, suppose four, at the Points *u q v,* and through them draw the right Lines *m o, p r,* and *s t,* of Length at pleasure. Divide the Arches *y* 2, and 3 7, each into as many equal Parts, as you divide the Line *l C*, which here is 4, as at the Points 1 2 3, and 4 5 6, and draw the Ordinates 1 4, 2 5, 3 6. Make *v s,* and *v t,* each equal to the half Ordinate *B* 6; also *q p,* and *q r,* each equal to the half Ordinate *A* 5; and *n m,* and *u o,* each equal to the half Ordinate 9 4. From the Points *h k,* through the Points *m p s,* and *o r t,* unto the Points *y* 7, draw the Lines *h y,* and *k* 7, so as not to make an Angle at any Point, and they will diminish the upper Part of the Shaft, as required. As this Method is general for diminishing the Shafts of all the other Orders, no more need be said on this Subject.

IN Plate XX. *Fig.* I. and II. are exhibited the particular Members of every principal Part of this Order, with their respective Measures of Heights and Projections.

PROB. IV. *Fig.* II. *Plate* XIX.
To proportion the Heights of the principal Parts of the Tuscan *Order, by equal Parts.*

Operation. Divide *a l,* the given Height, into 5 equal Parts; the lower one *g l,* is the Height of the Pedestal, and the remaining 4 Parts, *a g,* equal to *n r,* divided into 5 equal Parts, the upper one is the Height of the Entablature, and the lower 4, the Height of the Column, which being divided into 7 equal Parts, 1 is equal to its Diameter; and thus are the Heights of all the principal Parts determined.

PROB. V.
To divide the Height of the Tuscan *Pedestal, into its Base Die and Cornice, and them into their respective Members.*

Operation. Divide *g l, Fig.* II. *Plate* XIX. the given Height, into 4 equal Parts, as *s v;* give the lower 1, to the Height of the Plinth, one third Part of the next 1, to *i k,* the Height of the Moldings to the Base, and half the upper 1 to *g h,* the Height of the Cornice.
To divide the Moldings of the Base and Cornice of the Tuscan *Pedestal.*
Fig. IV. *Plate* XX.

Operation. First, Divide *k* 3, the Height of the Moldings on the Base, into 3 equal Parts; give the upper two to the Cavetto, and the lower one to the Fillet. *Secondly,* Divide *a d,* the Height of the Cornice, into three equal Parts; also the upper 1, *b c,* into two Parts, and the lower 1, *e g,* into three Parts. Then giving the upper 1 of *b c,* to the Regula, and the upper 1 of *e g,* to the Fillet, the two Remains will be the Plat-band and Cavetto.
To determine the Projections of these Members.

FIRST, Make the Projection of the Dado *k k,* equal to half the Height of the Dado and Moldings on the Plinth taken together, thereby forming a geometrical Square, as in *Fig.* II. *Plate* XIX. wherein is a Circle inscribed. *Secondly,* Make the Projection of the *Plinth* and *Regula,* before the upright of the Dado, equal to the Height of the Cavetto and Fillet on the Plinth.

Thirdly,

Thirdly, Divide *f h*, the aforefaid Projection, into 6 Parts, the firſt 1 ſtops the two Cavettos at *n* and *o*; the third, the upper Fillet *m*, and the 5th the Plat-band and lower Fillet *p*.

PROB. VI.

To divide the Height of the Tuſcan *Column, into its Baſe, Shaft and Capital, and them into their reſpective Members.*

Operation. Firſt, Divide *b g* into 7 equal Parts, and take 1 for the Diameter. Make *e g*, and *b f*, each equal to half a Diameter, for the Heights of the Baſe and Capital. This done, ſuppoſe *G q*, and *a c*, in *Fig.* XX. to be the Heights of the Baſe and Capital, as before found.

To proportion the Baſe of the Tuſcan *Column.*

DIVIDE *d f*, equal to its Height *a c*, into 7 equal Parts; give 4 to the Height of the Plinth, and 3 to the Height of the Torus; alſo make *e d*, the Height of the Cincture, equal to 1 Part.

To determine the Projections of the Members of the Tuſcan *Baſe.*

Divide *c* 3, equal to the Semi-diameter, into 3 equal Parts, and make *e* 4, equal to 4 of thoſe Parts. Divide the Part 3 4, into 5 equal Parts, and a Line, as 5 *h i*, being drawn from the ſecond Part, parallel to the central Line of the Order, will cut the central Line of the Torus in *i*, its Center, and ſtop the Cincture at *n*. This being done, and the Shaft of the Column erected on the Baſe, as before taught, proceed we now

To proportion the Tuſcan *Capital.*

DIVIDE its Height *G q*, equal to *A B*, into 3 equal Parts. Divide the upper 1, as *E F*, into 4 Parts, give the upper 1 to the Regula, and the lower 3 to the Abacus. Divide the middle 1 into 6 Parts; give the upper 5 to the Ovolo, and lower 1 to the Fillet. The lower 1 is the Height of the *Hypotrachelium*, or Neck of the Capital. *Now to find the Projectures of theſe Members*, make *g i* equal to half *G g*, and divide *k l*, equal to *g i*, into 6 Parts; the firſt 1 ſtops the Fillet, the 4 Parts and ¼ the Ovolo, the fifth Part the Abacus.

The Aſtragal, to the Top of the Shaft, is thus proportioned.

Make *q r* its Depth, equal to half *k n*, the Height of the Necking, which divide into 3 Parts; give 2 to the Aſtragal, and 1 to the Fillet. The Projecture of the Aſtragal *o*, is equal to *m n*, *viz.* to half the Height of the Neck, which is equal to ½ of the whole Capital's Height, and its Fillet to ⅔ thereof.

PROB. VII.

To divide the Height of the Tuſcan *Entablature, into its Architrave, Freeze, and Cornice, and them into their reſpective Members.*

Operation. Divide *a A*, equal to its Height *k G*, *Fig.* III. *Plate* XX. into 7 Parts: give 2 to the Height of the Architrave, 2 to the Height of the Freeze, and 3 to the Height of the Cornice. *To divide the Architrave*, divide *C D*, its Height, into 6 Parts, and give the upper 1 to the Tenia, which is alſo called *Diadema*, a Bandlet or Fillet to bind the Head, whoſe Projection *d c*, is equal to its own Height. Continue its Face to *f* and *b*, making each equal to its Projection, and deſcribe the Quadrant *a c*, above the Tenia, for the immediate carrying the Rains from it, and the other below it, to ſtrengthen its Projection.

To divide the Tuſcan *Cornice into its Members.*

ITS Height being before divided into 3 Parts, divide the lower 1, *d e*, into 2 Parts, give the upper 1 to the Height of the Ovolo, and the lower 1, *h f*, divide into 4 Parts; give the upper 1 to the Fillet, and the lower 3 to the Cavetto. Theſe three Members taken together, form that which Workmen call the Bed-Molding of a Cornice. Divide the upper two Parts of the Cornice into 24 equal Parts, as *b e*; give nine Parts and a half to the Height of the Corona, and to the Height of the Ovolo, and the Remains between them *i g*, being divided into 3 Parts, give 2 to the Aſtragal, and 1 to the Fillet. The Projection of of this Cornice *m l* is equal to its Height ; therefore make *n o*, againſt the Freeze, equal to its whole Proje[ction, and divide it into 3 Parts. Divide the firſt Part into 8 Parts, as at *p ;* the firſt 1 Part ſtops the Proje[ction of the Foot of the Cavetto, the 4th Part its Fillet, the 7th the Ovolo, and the 8th, its Fillet next under the Corona. The middle Part being divided into 4 Parts, the third Part from the left ſtops the Drip of the Corona, and the fourth Part the Face of the Corona. The third or outer Part being divided into 2 Parts, and the firſt 1 Part into 4 Parts, the firſt 1 ſtops the Fillet *x*, and the next 1 the Aſtragal *y ;* and thus is the whole Order completed, by equal Parts, as requ'red.

Now to proportion any Part of this Order to any given Height, theſe are the Rules, *viz.*

I. *To proportion the Column and Entablature only, to any given Height, and to find the Diameter.*

Rule. Divide the given Height into 5 equal Parts, the upper 1 is the Height of the Entablature, and the lower 4 of the Column, which divide into 7 Parts, and take 1 for the Diameter of the Column.

II. *To proportion the Pedeſtal and Column only, to any given Height, and to find the Diameter.*

Rule. Divide the given Height into 21 equal Parts, give 5 to the Height of the Pedeſtal, and 16 to the Column, which divide in 7 Parts, and take 1 for the Diameter.

III. *To proportion the Height of the* Tuſcan *Cornice to any given Height.*

This admits of two Varieties, *viz.* Firſt, being conſidered as the Cornice of an entire Order ; and laſtly, as the Cornice of an Entablature, to a Column only.

In the firſt of theſe Caſes, divide the given Height into 35 equal Parts, and take 2 $\frac{1}{2}$, for the Height of the Cornice ; and in the laſt Caſe take 3 Parts, which divide into 3 Parts, *&c.* as before dire[cted in the Cornice of the *Tuſcan* Entablature.

The Intercolumniation of this Order, that is the Diſtance at which the central Lines of the Columns are to be placed from one another, is of divers Kinds, and thoſe according to the Uſes they are applied to. As for Example, in a Colonnade, as *Fig.* I. *Plate* XXII. the Diſtance between the central Lines is 5 Diameters. In the Frontiſpieces, *Fig.* I. and II. *Plate* XXI. and in the Arcades *A B C, Plate* XXII. whoſe Columns are on Subplinths, they are at 6 Diameters Diſtance. And in Arcades of Columns on Pedeſtals, as *Fig.* IV. *Plate* XXI. they are at 7 Diameters Diſtance.

When *Tuſcan* Columns are placed in Pairs, as *a b e f, Fig.* II. and *d e f g h i, Fig.* D and E, *Plate* XXII. the Diſtance of their central Lines is 1 Diameter, 45 Minutes.

The Intercolumniation of Columns, in *Tuſcan* Porticos, are of two kinds, *viz.* the Middle 5 Diameters, as *c d, Fig.* II. *Plate* XXII. and the Sides 4 Diameters each, as *b c* and *d e.*

LECT. V.

Of the Manner of compoſing Frontiſpieces, Arcades, Colonnades, and Por'icos of the Tuſcan *Order.*

FRONTISPIECES to Doors are either ſtraight or circular headed, which laſt is either Semi-circular or Semi-elliptical.

Semi-circular headed Doors are more graceful than thoſe that are Semi-elliptical, which laſt is ſeldom uſed but at ſuch times when the Height will not admit of a Semi-circle, as being either too high or too low. When the given Height that an Arch muſt riſe above the Impoſts from which it ſprings is more than half the Breadth of the Opening, the Arch muſt be a Semi-elliplis, made on the conjugate Diameter, as *Fig.* X. *Plate* LXIII. But when the given

P

Height

Height is less than half the Breadth of the Opening, the Arch must be a Semi-ellipsis, made on the transverse Diameter, as *Fig.* IX. *Plate* XXIII.

It is always to be observed in making of Doors with arched Heads, that their Imposts be placed sufficiently above a Man's Height, that they may not obstruct any Part of the Entrance.

Prob. I. *Fig.* I. *Plate* XXI.

To make a Tuscan square-headed Door, with a circular pitched Pediment.

Draw the Base Line, and at any Point, as *b*, erect the Perpendicular *b e*, and draw *g h*, and *k i*, parallel to the central Line *b e*, each at 3 Diameters Distance. Set up the Subplinths *g* and *k*, each 1 Diameter in Height, and on them erect two Columns with their Entablature, by Prob. II. or IV. Lect. IV. and give the Subplinths 42 Minutes Projection on each Side of their central Lines. Make the Margins *m m* 30 Minutes in Breadth, from the cylindrical Parts of the Columns, and from the under Part of the Architrave. Divide the whole Extent of the level Cornice into 9 equal Parts, as is done in *Fig.* D, *Plate* XV. and set up two of those Parts, from *a* to *c*, and draw the line *e i*, for the upper Part of the raking Cornice.

To proportion the raking Members to the raking Cornice, Fig. VII. *Plate* XV.

From the Point *y* draw *d y*, parallel to *t w*, also *x z*, parallel to *d y*. On any Part of *x z*, as at *a*, erect the Perpendicular *a t*, which continue through the level Moldings. Make *a b* equal to *o p*; *b c* equal to *p q*; *c d* equal to *q r*; *d e* equal to *r s*; and *e f* equal to *s t*; and through the Points *a b c d e f*, draw right Lines parallel to *x z*, which will be the Members required; and which will have the same Proportion to the raking Cornice, as the level Members have to the level Cornice.

To make a circular Pediment.

Let *g i, Fig.* E, *Plate* XV. represent the Extent of the whole Entablature. Make *x e* equal to 2 Ninths of *g i*, draw *e g*, or *e i*, which bisect in *f* or *h*, whereon erect the Perpendicular *f h*, or *h k*, which will cut *e x*, continued in *k* the Centre, which in *Fig.* I. *Plate* XXI. is the Point *f*, on which describe the Members found as aforesaid.

Prob. II. *Fig.* IV. *Plate* XV.

To find the Curvature or Mold of the raking Ovolo, that shall mitre with the level Ovolo.

Let *a p* be a Part of the level Cornice, and *a n* the Points from which the raking Cornice takes its rise; also let *f a* and *g n*, represent a Part of the raking Cornice. On *n* erect the Perpendicular *n b*, and continue *l a* to *b*; divide *b n* into any Number of equal Parts, at the Points 1 2 3, *&c.* and from them draw the Ordinates 1 2, 3 4, 5 6, *&c.* In any part of the raking Ovolo as at *c*, draw the Perpendicular *c m*, and make *c d* equal to *b n*, the Projection of the level Ovolo. Divide *c m* into the same Number of equal Parts as are in *b n*, as at the Points 1 3 5 7, *&c.* from which draw Ordinates equal to the Ordinates in *b n*, and through the Points 2 4 6, *&c.* trace the Curve required. In the same Manner the Curvature or Mold may be found when the upper Member is a Cavetto, Cyma Recta, or Cyma Reversa, as is exhibited in *Fig.* V. VI. and VII.

Prob. III. *Fig.* IV. *Plate* XV.

To find the Curvature or Mold of the returned Molding, in an open or broken Pediment.

Let the Point *f* be the given Point, at which the raking Molding is to return. Continue *n p* towards *b* at pleasure, and from the Point *f*, let fall the Perpendicular *f h*; draw *f e* parallel to *b p*, and make *f e* equal to *b a*, the Projection of the level Cornice. Draw *e i* parallel to *f h*, and divide *e g* into the same Number of equal Parts, as are contained in *b n*, as at the Points 1 3 5 7, *&c.* from which draw the Ordinates 21, 43, 65, *&c.* equal to the Ordinates in *b n*, through the Points 2 4 6 8, *&c.* trace the Curve required. In the same manner the Curvature or Mold may be found when the upper Member is a Cavetto, Cyma Recta, or Cyma Reversa, as is exhibited in *Fig.* V. VI. and VII. *Plate* XV.

Prob.

PROB. IV. *Fig.* II. *Plate* XXI.

To make a Tuscan *circular headed Door with a pitched Pediment, or Balustrade.*

SET up two Columns with their Entablature as before taught, making the Distance of the central Lines equal to 6 Diameters. Divide *a b*, the Height of the Columns, into 3 equal Parts, and set down 1 Part from *n* to *g*, for the Center of the Arch, and draw the Line *g r*. Make the Breadth of the Pilasters *p q*, each 30 Minutes, from the cylindrical Part of the Columns, and delineate the Imposts and Architrave of the Arch as follows, *viz.*

IN *Fig.* III. *Plate* XXI. *a* 3 represents the Breadth of a Pilaster; make *a b* equal to *a* 3, and divide *a b* in 3 equal Parts at *i* and *g*, then the upper 1 is the broad Regula or Fillet, and the lower 1 the Neck of the Impost. Divide the Middle Part in 4, give the upper 3 to the Ovolo, and the lower 1 to its Fillet. Make *b c* equal to half *g b*, and divide *b c* in 3 Parts, give 2 to the Astragal and 1 to the Fillet: and thus are the Heights of all the Members determined. The Projection of the Regula on the Ovolo is equal to its Height, as is the Fillet under the Ovolo. The Projection of the Astragal is equal to the Height *t v*, and its Fillet to ½ thereof. To divide the Architrave of the Arch, divide *a* 3 into 3 Parts, the inward 1 is the Breadth of 2 3, the first Fascia, half the outer one is the Breadth of *a n*, the Fillet, and the Remains is the Breadth of *n* 2, the great Fascia. The Breadth of the Key-stone *n m*, on the lower Part of the Architrave, is one eleventh Part of the Semicircle. Now if 'tis required to finish this Door with a Pediment either straight or circular, proceed therewith as before taught in PROB. I. hereof, and if with a Baluftrade as on the left Side, then by PROB. V. LECT. IV. divide *d s*, the Height, which is equal to the Height of the Pediment, into the same Parts as the Tuscan Pedestal, making the Breadth of the Dado of the Pedestal, equal to the Diameter of the Column at its Astragal, then the Cornice and Base being continued, and the Dado Part filled with Banisters, the whole will be completed, as required.

To divide the Distances of the Banisters. Divide the Distance between the Dado of the Pedestal and the central Line *a b*, into 33 equal Parts, give 2 to the half Banister against the Pedestal, 2 to the Intervals or Distances between the Banisters, 4 to the Breadth of each Banister, and 1 to the half Interval at the central Line *a b*.

THE Banister proper to this Order is exhibited in *Fig.* A B C, *Plate* LXVIII. with the Proportions of their Members adjusted by equal Parts.

Note, If 'tis required to complete this Frontispiece strictly, according to ANDREA PALLADIO's Measures, then, instead of the preceding Impost, we must insert either of the Imposts A or B, in *Plate* XLII. where are exhibited all the imposts to the five Orders by this great Master.

Note also, If to such a Semi-circular-headed Door, 'tis absolutely necessary to set the Columns on Pedestals, then the Distance of the central Lines of the Columns must be increased unto 7 Diameters, as in *Fig.* IV. *Plate* XXI.

PROB. V. *Plate* XXII.

To make a Tuscan Arcade.

ARCADES are made in three different Manners, *viz.* First, of single Columns as A B C; secondly, with Columns in Piers as D E; and lastly, with Rustick Piers instead of Columns as F G and H I K.

To form the two first Kinds of Arcades is no more than to place Columns at such Distances as is expressed between their central Lines, and to complete them with their Pilasters, Imposts, and Arches, as taught in the last Problem.

ARCADES with Piers have their Piers of the same Breadths as are equal to the Breadths of the Pilasters and Columns in the two former Kinds, as is evident by the dotted Lines continued down to them; and the Height of the level Rusticks from which the Arches spring, is the same as the Height of the Imposts in the former. The Rusticks in the Arches are divided in different Manners, as *First, Fig.* D, where the Arch is divided into 11 Parts, and their Length made equal to half the Breadth of the Pier. *Secondly, Fig.* E, where the Key-stone *b* is 1 eleventh Part of the whole ; the Sides *a b*, and *c d*, each equal to half *b c*, and then the Side *o a*, divided into 4 Parts, give 1 to each Ruftick. *Thirdly, Fig.* C is divided in the fame manner as E, but its Pier G being but half the Breadth of the Pier H, the lower Ruftick on each Side is therefore omitted. *Fig.* B is divided the fame as *Fig.* D, with its lower Rufticks omitted for the aforefaid Reafon. *Fig.* A is divided the fame as *Fig.* E, and hath its lower Rufticks omitted as in *Fig.* C, but its Side Rufticks are fquared on their Sides by the central Line of each Pier, and at their Tops, by a Line drawn level from the upper Part of the circular Architrave. The circular Architraves in *Fig.* A B and C have their Heights equal to half the Thicknefs of their Piers, and their Fillet is equal to 1 fourth of their Height, as expreffed by the Divifions on the right Side of the Key-ftone in *Fig.* B.

PROB. VI. *Fig.* I. *Plate* XXII.
To make a Tufcan Colonnade.

To form a Colonnade is no more than to range Columns with their Entablature, at 5 Diameters Diftance, as expreffed between the central Lines of the Columns. The Intercolumniation of this Colonnade is called *Arœoftyle*, from the *Greek Aracos*, Rare, and *Stylos*, a Column, by which *Vitruvius* fignified the greateft Diftance that fhould be made between Columns that have not Arches between them to affift the bearing of the Architrave.

PROB. VII. *Fig.* II. *Plate* XXII.
To make a Tufcan Portico.

PORTICOS were anciently Porches formed by Columns, fupporting Parts of Roofs, continued out beyond the Uprights of the Ends of Temples, as the Portico of *St. Paul's, Covent Garden.* But now they are oftentimes placed againft the Fronts of Buildings fupporting a Pediment, to difcharge the Rains, and alfo in Gardens, to terminate the View of a grand Walk, &c.

DIVIDE the given Breadth into 35 Parts, and take 2 of thofe Parts for the Diameter of the Column. This done, fet out the central Lines of the Columns as expreffed between them, and complete the feveral Columns with their Entablature. But as the four middle Columns are finifhed with a Pediment to make the Portico, they muft advance 3 Diameters forward before the Range of the Columns *a* and *f*, and Pilafters muft be placed behind the Columns *b* and *c*, in range with *a* and *f*, which indeed fhould be Pilafters alfo.

A PILASTER is called by the *Greeks, Paraftate*, and by the *Italians, Membretti*, and is nothing more than a fquare Column, and is diminifhed the fame as a round Column, when ftanding with Columns; but when alone, it muft not be diminifhed, nor indeed even when with Columns, as in this Example when ftanding at an Angle, as thofe of *a* and *f*; becaufe the Quoins of all Buildings fhould be erect.

Examples for Practice in the Tufcan Order.

I. *The Height of the Tufcan Architrave being given, to find the Height of its Freeze, and of its Cornice.* RULE, Make the Height of the Freeze equal to the Height of the Architrave, and the Height of the Cornice, to 3 fourths of the Height of the Architrave and Freeze taken together.

II. *The Height of the Tufcan Cornice being given, to find the Height of the Architrave and of the Freeze.* RULE, Divide the Height of the Cornice in 3 Parts, and make the Height of the Architrave, and of the Freeze, each equal to two Parts thereof.

III. *The Height of a Tufcan Cornice being given, to find the Diameter of the Column.* RULE, By Example II. find the Height of the Architrave and Freeze, and add them to the Cornice ; multiply the Height of the Architrave, Freeze, and Cornice by 4, and divide their Product by 7, the Quotient is the Diameter required.

IV. *The Diameter of a Tufcan Column being given, to find the Height of the Cornice.* RULE, As 12 is to 9, fo is the given Diameter to the Height of the Cornice required.

V. *The*

V. *The Height of a* Tuscan *Architrave being given, to find the Diameter of the Column.* RULE, Double the Height of the Architrave, and it will be equal to the Diameter required; and so on the contrary, if the Diameter was given and the Height of the Architrave required, then half the given Diameter is the Height of the Architrave.

VI. *The Height of the* Tuscan *Entablature being given, to find the Height of the Capital.* RULE, Divide the Height of the Entablature into 7 Parts, and make the Height of the Capital equal to 2 of those Parts; and so on the contrary, if the Height of the Capital was given to find the Height of the Entablature, divide the Height of the Capital into 2 Parts, and make the Height of the Entablature equal to 7 of those Parts.

VII. *The Height of the Capital and Entablature being given, to find the Diameter.* RULE, Divide the given Height of both Capital and Entablature into 9 equal Parts, the Diameter will be equal to 4 of those Parts.

LECTURE VI.

Of the Manner of proportioning the particular Parts of the Dorick Order by Modules and Minutes, according to ANDREA PALLADIO; *and by equal Parts, composed from the Masters of all Nations.*

THE principal Parts of this Order by ANDREA PALLADIO are exhibited in *Fig.* I. and its Pedestal in *Fig.* III. *Plate* XXIII. The Base, Capital, Entablature, and Plancere of the Cornice are exhibited by *Fig.* I. and III. *Plate* XXIV. and as they are all proportioned by Modules and Minutes in the same Manner as the *Tuscan* Order, it is needless to say any more thereof.

PROB. 1.

To proportion the Heights of the principal Parts of the Dorick Order by equal Parts.
LET *a b, Fig.* II. *Plate* XXIII. be the given Height, divide *e f,* equal to *a b,* into 5 equal Parts, give the lower 1 to the Height of the Pedestal. Divide the 4 remaining Parts into 5 equal Parts, the upper 1 is the Height of the Entablature, and the lower 4 the Height of the Column, which divide into 8 Parts, and take 1 for the Diameter of the Column.

PROB. II.

To divide the Height of the Dorick Pedestal into its Base, Die, and Cornice, and them into their respective Members.

LET *a b, Fig.* IV. be the given Height and central Line of the Pedestal, divide *c d,* equal to *a b,* into 4 equal Parts, give *d* 1, the lowest Part to *b* L, the Height of the Plinth. Divide the next Part into 3, as *r s,* and give 1 to *t s,* the Height of the Moldings on the Plinth. Divide *t s* into 8 Parts, give 3 to the Cavetto G, 1 to the Fillet I, 4 to the inversed Cyma Recta K, and the lower 1 to its Fillet L. Make *e f* equal *e* to half the upper 4th Part of the Pedestal's Height, which divide into 2 Parts; divide *h g* equal to 1 Quarter of *e f* into 3 Parts, give 1 to the Fillet E, and 2 to the Astragal D. Divide *k i,* equal to half *e f,* into 4 Parts, give the upper 1 to the Regula A, and the other 3 to the Fascia B. The Remains is the Ovolo C.

To determine the Projections of the Members.

IN *Fig.* II. a Circle being inscribed within the Dado of the Pedestal, shews that its Height and Projection are equal, therefore draw the Line *q x,* parallel to *a b,* at the Distance of half the Height of the Dado F. Make *w w* equal to *v x,* and through the Point *w* draw the Line *w p,* which is the Projection of the Plinth M, and Regula A. Divide *p q,* the whole Projection before the upright of the Dado, into 8 Parts, and one half thereof, as *n o* into 3 Parts; the first Part of *n o* is the Projection of the Fascia B, and its last Part, or 4th Part of *p q,* of the Ovolo C, and the 6th and 7th Parts of *p q* terminate the Astragal D, and its Fillet E. The first Part of *p q* terminates the Fillet L, the 5th Part the Fillet I, and the 7th Part the Cavetto G.

3

PROB.

PROB. III.

To divide the Height of the Dorick Column into its Base, Shaft, and Capital, and them into their respective Members.

Divide the given Height into 8 Parts, 1 is the Diameter, and as the Height of the Base and Capital are each half a Diameter, therefore (as in *Fig.* II. *Plate* XXIII.) make *p q* the Height of the Base, and *m n* the Height of the Capital, each equal to half a Diameter.

To divide the Members of the Base.

LET *a f*, *Fig.* IV. *Plate* XXIV. be equal to a given Height of the Base. Divide *a f* into two Parts, the lower 1 is the Height of the Plinth : Divide *c e* equal to half *a f*, into 4 Parts ; give the lower 3 to the Torus, and the upper 1 to the Astragal, which divide into 4 Parts, and make *b c* the Height of the Cincture equal to two Parts.

To determine the Projection of the Base.

DRAW the Line *h* 3 parallel to *i k* the central Line, and, at the Distance of half a Diameter, divide *k* 3 into 3 Parts, and make *k* 4 the Projection of the Plinth equal to 4 of those Parts. The Projection of the Torus is always equal to the Plinth in every Order : The Projection of the Cincture is equal to a Perpendicular drawn through the Center of the Torus, as is the Center of the Astragal also.

To divide the Members of the Capital.

LET R W, *Fig.* II. be equal to a given Height of the Capital, divided into 3 equal Parts, as *q* 1 2 3, and the lower 1 Part is the Height of the Neck: the middle Part equal to *x y*, divided into 3 Parts, the upper 2 is the Height of the Ovolo, and the lower 1 divided into 3, as *a z*, the upper 2 is the Height of the Astragal, and the lower 1 the Fillet : the upper third Part, equal to *s w*, divided into 3 ; the lower two is the Height of the Fascia, and the upper 1 divided into 3 ; the upper 1 is the Height of the Fillet, and the lower 2 of its Cyma Reversa.

To determine the Projectures of these Members.

LET R W represent the central Line of the Column, to which draw the upright Line of the Column S A parallel to R W, at 24 Minutes Distance : make S T equal to half R S, and from any Part of the Neck of the Capital, as at A, draw the Line A B equal to S T, which divide into 4 equal Parts ; the 1st Part terminates the Projection of the Astragal under the Ovolo, and ¾ thereof its Fillet, the 3d Part terminates the Fascia of the Abacus, and ¼ thereof the Ovolo. The Astragal at C is proportioned in the same Manner as the Astragal to the *Tuscan* Column.

THE Shaft of the *Dorick* Capital is sometimes fluted, either according to the Manner of the Ancients, without Fillets, as on the right Hand of *Fig.* III. *Plate* X. or, according to the modern Manner, with Fillets, as on the left Side, in Manner of *Ionick* Flutes. 'Tis said, that the first fluted Columns were those of the renowned Temple of *Diana*, built at *Ephesus*, as some think by the *Amazons*, which were of Marble, 70 Feet in Height, and whose Flutings were made in Imitation of the Plaitings in Women's Robes this Building employed 200 Years to finish it at the Expence of all *Asia*. The Number of Flutes to the *Dorick* Shaft was originally but twenty, as they still should be made, that their Breadths may be greater than those of the *Ionick* and other Orders, which are always 24 in Number : And the Reason is, that as the *Dorick* Order hath a masculine Aspect, its Parts ought to be larger and bolder than the *Ionick*, which represents a feminine Slenderness. But how just the Precepts of the Ancients may be, some modern Architects take Liberty to decorate the *Dorick* Shaft with 24 Flutes with Fillets, thinking those of 20 too large. And indeed, when the Order is made within a Building, and near to the Eye, I think 24 to be better than 20, which are much better in Columns that stand abroad, and seen at a great Distance.

PROB.

Prob. IV.

To divide the Flutes, or Flutes and Fillets, in the Shaft of the Dorick *Column.*

First, According to the Manner of the Ancients, let *i b b*, *Fig.* IV. Plate XXIV. represent one Half of a Part of the *Dorick* Shaft; on *i* describe the Quadrant 1 2 3 4, &c. *b*, which divide into 10 equal Parts; divide any 2 of the Parts, as 3 4 5, each into 2 Parts, and on the Points 3 and 5, with three of those Parts, make a Section, on which describe the Curve 3 5. In the same Manner describe all the others. Now if from the Points 1 3 5 7 9, you draw right Lines parallel to the central Line *i k*, and terminate them with Arches, which shall end level with the upright Part of the Shaft, they will be the perspective Appearances of the several Flutings.

Secondly, According to the Manner of the Moderns, let *c z x x*, *Fig.* III. Plate X. represent a Part of the *Dorick* Shaft.

First, Draw *a b* the central Line, on *a* describe the Semicircle *c b z*, which divide into 12 equal Parts, to which draw right Lines from the Center *a*, and continue them out something beyond the Semicircle. In the Quadrant *b z*, on the Points *b* 5, 4, 3, &c. with a Radius equal to half one Part, describe the Quadrant *r* 3, and Semicircles 3 6 *t*, *t* 7 *v*, &c. on the Points *r* 6 7, &c. with the Radius *r* 3, describe the Arches *q* 3, 3 *t*, *t v*, &c. which are the Flutes without Fillets. *Secondly*, In the Quadrant *c b*, divide any one of those 6 Parts into 8 equal Parts, and with a Radius equal to 3 of those Parts on the Points *b*, 9, 13, 17, &c. describe the Arches *p q*, *n* 11 *o*, *l* 15 *m*, &c. which will be the Flutes, and the Intervals *o p*, *m n*, *k l*, &c. left between them will be the Fillets; and if from the Points *p o n m l k*, &c. right Lines be drawn parallel to the central Line, and terminated at the lower Part of the Shaft with Arches as before, they will be the perspective Appearance of the Flutes and Fillets, as required. In these several Manners, the Breadth of Flutes, or of Flutes and Fillets, may be found at the upper Part, and in any Part between the upper and lower Parts of a Column. It is also to be noted, that the Flutings of Columns are sometimes filled for one third Part of the Column's Height, with Staves or Cablings, which are thus described, *viz.* on the Points 15, 11, &c. with the Radius 11, 9, describe the Arches 10, 9, 12; 14, 13, 16, &c. which are the Plans of the Cablings, and which are sometimes enriched with Ribbons, Pearls and Olives, &c. as exhibited in the upper Part of this Plate.

Prob. V.

To divide the Height of the Dorick *Entablature, into its Architrave, Freeze, and Cornice, and them into their respective Members.*

Let *d* R, *Fig.* II. Plate XXIV. be the central Line and given Height, which divide into 8 equal Parts, give 2 to the Height of the Architrave, 3 to the Height of the Freeze, and 3 to the Height of the Cornice.

To divide the Architrave.

Divide *p*, the Height of the Architrave, into 6 Parts, give the upper 1 to the Height of the Tenia, the next 1 divide into 4, give the upper 1 to the Height of the Fillet, over the Drops, and the lower 3 into the Height of the Drops.

To divide the Triglyphs and Metopes in the Freeze, Fig. V. and VI. Plate XLIV.

Triglyphs are Ornaments placed in the *Dorick* Freeze, and were first used in the *Delphic* Temple, representing an *antique Lyre*, a musical Instrument invented by *Apollo*. The Word Triglyph comes from the *Greek* Τριγλυφ, signifying a three-sculptured Piece, *quasi tres habens Glyphos*, which the *Italians* call *Pian ssi*. A Triglyph consists of seven Parts, *viz.* two entire *Glyphes* or Channels, two *Semi-Glyphes*, and 3 Spaces or *Interstices* between them. The Breadth of a Triglyph is equal to 30 Minutes, and of a Metope 45 Minutes, which being equal to the Height of the Freeze, is therefore a geometrical Square.

Metopes are the Intervals or square Parts of the Freeze that are contained between the Triglyphs, and receive their Names from the *Greek Meta* and *Ope*, between three, which anciently was enriched with Oxes Skulls, Instruments of Sacrifice, Trophies of War, &c.

Let

LET *a* n*q* r be the Breadth of a Triglyph, which divide into 12 equal Parts, as at *a* u, from which draw the Lines 1 *t*, 2 2, 3 *t*, &c. which continue upwards through the Cornice unto *i* h, &c. and downwards through the Tenia and Fillet of the Architrave ; make *a* b and *n* z, each equal to 2 of the 12 Parts in *a* n, and draw the Line z z ; make b f, i e, k m, and z p, each equal to 1 of the 12 Parts, and draw the Miter Lines c f, d e, e g, b m, m k, and o p, which will complete the Triglyph as required.

To form the Drops under the Tenia of the Architrave.

FROM the Points x 2, 4, 6, 8, 10, 12, draw Lines towards the Points *t* t, &c. stopping them at the Fillet v w, and they will form the Drops, as required.

To form a Metop, as n b r a.

MAKE n b and r a, each equal to n r, and draw the Line b a, then n b r a is the Metope required. If it is required to make a hollow Pannel therein, as d e h i, divide r a in 6 Parts, and make the Margin about the Pannel equal to 1 of those Parts ; also divide the Margin into 5 Parts, as at A c, and make the Breadth of the Molding within the Pannel equal to 1 of those Parts ; then drawing the Diagonals d i and c e, their Interfection is the Center, about which Place a Rose, or any other Ornament at pleafure.

To divide the Cornice into its refpective Members, Fig. II. *Plate* XXIV.

THE Height of the Cornice being 3 Eighths of the whole Entablature, as afore-faid, divide the lower 1 into 3 Parts, give the lower 1 to the Height of the Capping to the Triglyph ; divide the remaining Height equal to b o in 4 Parts, and the lower 1 thereof into 6, then the lower 1 is the Height of the Aftragal under the Ovolo, and the next 4 is the Height of the Ovolo ; the fecond Part of b o being divided into 3, the loweft 1 is the Height of the Bells or Drops, the next 1 of their Fafcia I. and the upper 1 divided into 3, the upper 1 is the Height of the Fillet, and the lower 2 of the Cyma Reverfa ; the third 1 of b o divided into 6, the upper 1 is the Height of the Fillet to the Corona, and the lower 5 is the Height of the Corona ; laftly, the upper 1 of b o, divided into 4, the upper 1 is the Height of the Regula, and the lower 3 of the Cyma Reverfa.

To determine the Projections of the Members in this Cornice.

THE Upright of the Column and Freeze x O S being before drawn, make x M equal to half the Height of the whole Entablature, and from any Part of the Upright of the Freeze draw a Line, as O P, equal to the Projection x M, which divide into 4 equal Parts at 1 2 3 ; divide the 1ft Part into 3, the firft 1 is the Projection of the Tenia in Profile againft the Return, and of the Aftragal, under the Ovolo, which divide into 4, the firft 2 is the Projection of the Triglyph in return, the next 1 of the Capping to the Triglyph over the Freeze, and of the Fillet, and Drops under the Tenia of the Architrave.

THE remaining 2 Parts of the firft 1 of O P, divided into 6, the firft 3 terminates the Ovolo, and the next 1, the Platform K, againft which the Mutules are placed. The 3d Divifion of O P terminates the Fillet of the Cyma Reverfa, that crowns the Mutules, and this third Part divided into 3, and the laft 1 into 3, the firft 1 terminates the projecting Mutule L.   Laftly, the laft Part of O P equal to Q R, divided into 9, the firft 4 terminate the Projection of the Corona, and the next 1 its Fillet.

MUTULES are a Kind of Modillions, that are always placed perpendicularly over the Triglyphs, to fupport the Corona, as well of Pediments as of ftraight or level Cornices, and whofe Breadths are always equal to the Triglyphs, as exhibited in *Plate* XXVI. The Word *Mutule* comes from *Mutuli*, the *Latin* for Modillions.

THE Figure D E F G is the Plancere or Cieling, which the *Italians* call *Soffito*, of a Mutule, whofe Sides are each divided into 6 equal Parts, and parallel Lines drawn from them, divides the whole into 36 geometrical Squares, in whofe Centers the Drops or Bells are placed ; and if from their Centers right Lines be drawn up to the projecting Mutule K L, they will be the central Lines, over which the 6 Drops between K and L are to be placed.

THE

THE central Lines of the Drops to H I the Mutule in Front, are determined by the Continuation of the twelve Lines from the Triglyph, which also makes the Breadth of the Mutule equal to the Breadth of the Triglyph, *vide Fig.* IV. *Plate* XLIV. where *e d a b* is a complete Mutule in Front, and *Fig.* III. a Mutule in Profile, divided as aforesaid, whose Drops are drawn to the Points *n n, &c.* at the Interfections of their central Lines, with the Line *c d* drawn through the midst of the Fascia *a o.*

IN *Plate* XXV. are exhibited various Manners of making the Returns of the Planceres of the *Dorick* Cornice, wherein 'tis to be noted, that *Fig.* I. and V. which are Returns at external Angles, have but 18 Bells or Drops each, according to *Palladio,* and *Fig.* II. which is a Return at an external Angle, has 36, as at F. 2*dly,* That sometimes Mutules are made square, and shew but 28 Bells, as at B and D, *Fig.* IV. which is a Return at an internal Angle, as also is *Fig.* III. whose shaded Parts A B G C E F G represent Parts of Columns, whereby 'tis seen, that the Mutules D E in *Fig.* III. D F in *Fig.* II. and B D in *Fig.* IV. stand directly over their respective Columns. The Coffers or hollow Pannels. E A B C in *Fig.* II. and A C in *Fig.* IV. are to be enriched with Roses, as A, *Fig.* I. Examples of which are given in *Figures* A, B, C, D, E, *Plate* XXXVIII.

PROB. VI.

To determine the Intercolumniations of the Dorick *Order.*

Operation. As the Breadth of a Triglyph is always equal to 30 Minutes, and the Breadth of a Metope to 45 Minutes, therefore the Sum of the Minutes contained in the Triglyphs and Metopes, that are required between the central Lines of two Columns, is always the Intercolumniation, or Distance at which the Columns are to be placed. Therefore to have 1 Triglyph between, as *a b,* or *e f, Fig.* II. *Plate* XXVII. the Distance must be two Diameters, 30 Minutes; if 2 Triglyphs between, as *b c,* and *d e,* 3 Diameters, 45 Minutes; if three Triglyphs, as *c d,* 5 Diameters; if 4 Triglyphs, as over each of the Arcades, *Fig.* A B C, *&c.* 6 Diameters, 15 Minutes, *&c.* Hence 'tis plain, that in the making of Frontispieces, *&c.* to any given Height, the Breadth cannot be confined; and therefore when such a Case happens, the Triglyphs and Mutules must be omitted; and the Distance between the Columns should not exceed 4 Diameters.

IN *Plate* XXVI. *Fig.* I. and II. are Designs of Doors, the first with a square Head, with both circular and pitched Pediments over it, the other with a Semicircular Head, with a Balluftrade and pitched Pediment, which are given for Examples, as also is *Fig.* III. which is half of an Arcade on a Pedestal.

Fig. IV. is the *Dorick* Impost at large, whose Height, *a b,* divided into 3, the lower 1 is the Height of the Neck, the upper 1 divided into 4, the upper 1 is the Height of the Fillet or Regula, and the lower 3 of the Fascia. The middle 1, divided into 3, the upper 2 is the Height of the Ovolo; and the lower 1 divided into 3, the upper 2 is the Astragal, and the lower 1 its Fillet. The Distance *a i,* represents the Breadth of the Pilaster, and *i s* its upright. Make *i h,* the Projection, equal to one third of *a i.* Make 3 *g* equal to *i h,* which divide into 4, then the first one determines the Projection of the two Fillets, to the two Astragals; the third Part the Ovolo; and half the last Part, the Fascia of the Abacus.

THE Depth of the Astragal *b d* is equal to half the Height of the Neck, divided into 3, give 2 to the Astragal, and 1 to the Fillet. In *Plate* XXVII. *Fig.* I. is a Colonnade; *Fig.* II. a Portico; *Fig.* A B C D E Arcades, with single Columns, and Columns in Pairs, and F G H I K, are rusticated Arcades, which are given as Examples for Practice.

Examples for Practice in the Dorick *Order.*

I. *The Height of the* Dorick *Architrave being given, to find the Height of the Freeze, and of the Cornice.* RULE, Divide the Height of the Architrave into 2 equal Parts; make the Height of the Freeze, and of the Cornice, each equal to 3 of those Parts.

Q

II. *The*

II. *The Height of the* Dorick *Cornice being given, to find the Height of the Archi-trave, and of the Freeze.* RULE, Divide the Height of the Cornice into 3 equal Parts; make the Height of the Freeze equal to the Height of the Cornice, and the Height of the Architrave to two thirds of the Cornice.

III. *The Height of the* Dorick *Cornice being given, to find the Diameter of the Column.* RULE, Divide the Height of the Cornice into 3 equal Parts, and make the Diameter equal to 4 of those Parts.

IV. *The Diameter of a* Dorick *Column being given, to find the Height of the* Dorick *Cornice.* RULE, Divide the Diameter into 4 equal Parts, and make the Height of the Cornice equal to 3 of those Parts.

V. *The Height of the* Dorick *Architrave being given, to find the Diameter of the Column.* RULE, Double the Height of the Architrave, and 'twill be equal to the Diameter required.

VI. *The Height of the* Dorick *Entablature being given, to find the Height of the Capital.* RULE, Divide the Height of the Entablature into 4 Parts, and make the Height of the Capital equal to 1 of those Parts; and so on the contrary, if the Height of the Capital was given, and the Height of the Entablature required, 'tis no more than to make the Entablature equal to 4 times the Height of the Capital.

VII. *The Height of the Entablature and Capital being given, to find the Diameter.* RULE, Divide the Height of the Capital and Entablature into 10 Parts, and take 4 of those Parts for the Diameter required.

L E C T. VII.

Of the particular Parts of the IONICK ORDER, *proportioned by Modules and Minutes, according to* ANDREA PALLADIO, *and by equal Parts, composed from the Masters of all Nations.*

THE principal Parts of this Order are exhibited by *Fig.* I. *Plate* XXVIII. and the particular Parts by *Fig.* I. and II. *Plate* XXIX. which in general are determined by Minutes, as the preceding Orders.

PROB. I. *Fig.* II. *Plate* XXXII.

To proportion the Heights of the principal Parts of the Ionick *Order, by equal Parts.*

FIRST, Divide *d t*, equal to the given Height, into 5 equal Parts; give the lower 1 to *l s*, the Height of the Pedestal. Secondly, divide *a m*, equal to the Remains, into 6 equal Parts; give the upper 1 to the Height of the Entablature, and the lower 5 to the Height of the Column, which being divided into 9 equal Parts, take 1 for the Diameter of the Column.

PROB. II. *Fig* IV. *Plate* XXVIII.

To divide the Ionick *Pedestal into its principal Parts, and them into their respective Members.*

FIRST, Draw *q w* for the base Line, and *i w* for the central Line. Secondly, Divide *i q*, equal to *s w* the given Height, into 4 equal Parts; give half the upper 1 to the Height of the Cornice, and the lower 1 to the Height of the Plinth. Divide *o p* equal to the second Part, into 3 Parts, and the lower 1 equal to *x y*, into 8 Parts; give the upper 2 to the Cavetto, half the next 1 to its Fillet, the lower 1 to the Fillet on the Plinth, and the Remains to the inverted Cyma. Thirdly, Divide *k n*, equal to the Height of the Cornice, into 4 equal Parts, the lower 1 divided into 3, the upper 1 is the Height of the Astragal, half the next the Height of the Fillet, and the Remains is the Height of the Cavetto. The second Part of *k n*, is the Height of the Ovolo, the next 1 of the Platform or Fascia, and the upper 1 divided into 3, the upper 1 is the Height of the Fillet, and the lower 2 of the Cyma Reversa.

To determine the Projections of the Moldings.

THE Diameter being before found, by PROB. I. hereof, divide it into 6 equal Parts, and draw *m r*, parallel to *s w*, at the Distance of 4 Parts. Make *y z*, the Projection of the Plinth, and *m l*, the Cornice, equal to *y x*, and draw

l z,

l z, parallel to *m r*. In any place againſt the Upright of the Dado, as at *b*, draw *a b*, equal to *z y*, which divide into 4 equal Parts. The firſt 1 terminates the Projection of the Platform or Faſcia of the Cornice, the next 1 the Ovolo, the third 1 the Cavettos to both Baſe and Cornice; and which being divided into 3, as *c d*, or *g b*, the laſt 1 terminates their Bottoms, then half the firſt 1 terminates the Fillet *z* on the Plinth, which completes the whole, as required.

P R O B. III. *Fig.* II. *Plate* XXVIII.

To divide the Height of the Ionick *Column into its Baſe, Shaft, and Capital.*

THE Height *b n*, equal to *f l*, being divided into 9 equal Parts, give half the lower 1 to the Height of the Baſe. Divide *i g*, equal to the upper 1, into 6 Parts, give the upper 4 Parts to the Height of the Capital, the Remains between is the Height of the Shaft.

P R O B. IV. *Fig.* IV. *Plate* XXIX.

To divide the Baſe of the Ionick *Column into its reſpective Members.*

DRAW *o z* for the Baſe Line, and *a o* for the central Line. Divide *b m*, equal to the given Height, into 3 Parts. Divide *n l*, equal to the middle Part, into 6; then the lower 1, with the lower 1 Part of *b m*, is the Height of the Plinth, the next 1, the Height of the Fillet, and the upper 4 of the Scotia. Divide the upper 1 of *b m*, into 2 Parts; divide *i k*, equal to the lower 1, into 3 Parts, and give 1 to the Fillet under the Torus; the upper 2, with the upper 1 of *f g*, is the Height of the Torus. Make *c d*, the Height of the Cincture, equal to one 4th of *f g*. *To determine the Projectures.* Draw *f p*, parallel to *a o*, at the Diſtance of half the Diameter before found. Divide *o p* into three Parts, and make *p z*, the Projection of the Plinth, equal to 1 Part. Divide *p z* into 3 Parts, then the firſt 1 terminates the Projection of the Fillet *v*, the Center of the Torus *w*, and the Cincture *x*. Biſect the laſt Part in *r*, which terminates the Projection of the Fillet *s*, and completes the whole, as required.

P R O B. V.

To divide the Height of the Ionick *Capital into its reſpective Members.*

DRAW the Line 17, 19, repreſent the Top of the Aſtragal, to the Shaft of the Column, and 17 11 for the central Line. Divide *r q*, equal to the given Height, into 4 equal Parts; then the upper 3 of thoſe Parts is the Height of the Volute and Abacus. Divide the upper 1 Part into 8 Parts; give the upper 3 to the Ovolo, the next 1 to the Fillet, and the lower 4 to the Faſcia. Divide L M, the Height of the Volute, into 8 Parts; make the Height of the Ovolo equal to the fifth and ſixth Parts, the Aſtragal under it, to the fourth Part, and the Fillet under that, to the upper half of the third Part. Make *s t*, the Height of the Aſtragal on the Shaft, equal to one eighth Part of *r q*, which divide into 3 Parts, and give 2 to the Aſtragal, and one to the Fillet.

To determine their Projections.

CONTINUE the central Line towards I at pleaſure, and in any Part of it, as at I, draw a Line at right Angles, as I K, equal to three fourths of the Diameter, which divide into 9 equal Parts, each equal to 5 Minutes. Draw the Upright of the Column, at 25 Minutes Diſtance, parallel to the central Line, alſo the Line 13, 30, at 30 Minutes Diſtance, which terminates the Projection of the Aſtragal on the Shaft, and the Aſtragal to the Capital, whoſe End at 13 is the Eye of the Volute. Biſect the Height of the Aſtragal to the Capital, and draw its central Line 12, 29. Divide the Diſtance between 25 and 30, in I K, into 3 equal Parts, and from the ſecond Part draw the Line 2, 22, 16, parallel to the central Line, which will terminate the Projections of the two Fillets at 22 and 16, and being continued, will interſect the central Line of the Aſtragal 12, 13, in the Center of the Eye of the Volute. Make 11, 10, in the Capital, equal to 35 Minutes of I K, for the Projec-

tion

tion of the Ovolo. From the Points 40 and 45, in *i k*, draw the Lines N 40, and O K, parallel to the central Line, which will terminate the Projections of the Angles of the Abacus. In any Places, as at *a b*, and *c d*, draw two Lines, as *a b*, and *c d*, between the afore-drawn outward parallel Lines. Divide *a b* into 5 Parts, and *c d* into 2 Parts; then the third and 4th Parts of *a b* terminate the Projection of the Fascia and Fillet, the Abacus in Front, and half *c d* the Fillet of the returned Abacus; and as the Abacus of this Capital is made circular on each Side, as in the Quarter Plan underneath, 'tis neceffary to fhew how to defcribe the fame. The aforefaid Lines, for finding the Projection of the Capital, being defcribed, through any Part of the central Line, as at the Point 18, draw the Line Z 18 X, at right Angles, and make 18 Z equal to 18 X. On the Points Z and X, with the Radius Z X, make the equilateral Section F, on which, with the Radius F 32, defcribe the Arch 31, 32. Make 31 P equal to 11 10, the Projection of the Ovolo under the Abacus, then the Point P is the Center of the Plan; whereon, with the Radius 31 P, defcribe the Quadrant 31, 4. In a whole Plan of a Capital, continue the Lines 31 P, and P 4, the two Semi-diameters, out both ways at pleafure, and thereon fet the Diftance F I, which will give you the other 3 Centers, on which the Arches of the other 3 Sides may be defcribed; on the Center P, with the Radius *s*, equal to the Upright of the Shaft, the Projection of the Aftragal, and of its Fillet, defcribe the Arches 1 2 3; laftly, make X 33 equal to X 32, draw the Line 32, 33, whereon defcribe the equilateral Triangle 32, 33, 34, whofe Sides will be interfected by the Arches defcribed on the Center F, &c. and then right Lines being drawn from one refpective Interfection to the other, and the like being performed at every of the four Angles of the Capital, the Plan will be completed.

THE next Work in order to complete the Capital is to defcribe its Volutes, which may be done by either of the following Problems.

PROB. VI. *Fig.* P. *Plate* XII
To defcribe the Ionick *Volute.*

LET *a i* be the given Height.

DIVIDE the given Height into 8 equal Parts at the Points *b c d e f g h*, which are alfo numbered, 1 2 3 4 5 6 7; bifect the 5th Divifion *e f* in *x*, and on *x* with the Radius *x e* defcribe a Circle, as *w e v f*, which is the Eye of the Volute. Through *x* draw the Line *w v*, at right Angles to *a i*, and then complete the geometrical Square *w e v f*, and bifect its Sides in the Points 1 2 3 4. Draw the Diameters 2 4, and 1 3; and divide each Semi-diameter into three equal Parts at the Points 1 2 3 4 5 6 7 8 9 10 11 12, which are the Centers on which the Contour or Outline of the Volute is to be defcribed, as following, viz. the Point 1 is the Center of the Arch *a k*, the Point 2 of the Arch *k i*, the Point 3 of the Arch *i l*, the Point 4 of the Arch *l c*, the Point 5 of the Arch *c n*, the Point 6 of the Arch *n o*, the Point 7 of the Arch *o p*, the Point 8 of the Arch *p q*, the Point 9 of the Arch *q r*, the Point 10 of the Arch *r s*, the Point 11 of the Arch *s t*, and the Point 12 of the Arch *t e*.

To defcribe the inward Line, which diminifhes the Lift.

DIVIDE each third Part of every Semi-diameter of the geometrical Square *w e v f* into 5 equal Parts, as is done in *Fig.* L, which is the Eye of the Volute at large. The firft one, within each of the aforefaid 12 Centers, are the Centers for defcribing of the inward Line, which Centers are numbered, 13, 14, 15, 16, 17, 18, 19, 20, 21, 22, 23, 24.

PROB. VII. *Fig.* I. *Plate* XIII.
To defcribe the Ionick *Volute a fecond Way.*

LET K 8 be the given Height.

Firft, Divide the given Height into 8 equal Parts, and in the fifth Divifion defcribe the Eye of the Volute as in the preceding.

THROUGH E the Center, draw the Line 2 *b* E *f b*, alfo draw the oblique Lines 1, 5, and 7, 3, each at 45 Degrees Diftance from the Line *a* F E *d* 4, which is called the *Cathetus*.

Secondly,

Secondly, Draw B A, *Fig.* II. equal to 3 Parts and a half; on A erect the Perpendicular A C, which make equal to 4 Parts and half, and draw the Line C B, on A; with the Radius equal to half a Part, *viz.* equal to E 24, in *Fig.* I. describe the Quadrant E *g,* and draw the Line *g* B on B; with the Radius B *g* describe the Arch *g* D, which divide into 24 equal Parts, through which from B draw right Lines to meet the Tangent Line C A in the Points 1, 2, 3, 4, 5, &c.

Make E 1, E 2, E 3, E 4, E 5, E 6, E 7, E 8, &c. in *Fig.* II. equal to A 1, A 2, A 3, A 4, A 5, A 6, A 7, A 8, &c. in *Fig.* I. On the Points *a* and 1, in *Fig.* I. with the Distance 1 E, make a Section within the Eye of the Volute, on which describe the Arch *a* 1. On the Points 1 and 2, with the Distance 2 E, make a Section in the Eye as before, and thereon describe the Arch 1, 2. On the Points 2 and 3, with the Distance 3 E, make a Section as before, whereon describe the Arch 2, 3, proceed in like manner until the Outline be completed.

To diminish the Lift of the Volute

Let A F be its given Breadth.

Divide *a* F into 24 equal Parts, and make 1 *a* equal to 23 Parts of *a* F; 2 *b* to 22 Parts; 3 *c* to 21 Parts; 4 *d* to 20 Parts; 5 *e* to 19 Parts; 6 *f* to 18 Parts, &c. Proceed then to find Sections for the several Arches, which pass through the Points *a b c d,* &c. as was done for the outward Arch 1, 2, 3, 4, 5, &c. and they will complete the diminished Lift as required.

The Ionick Volute was anciently described by six Centers, as follows, *Fig.* III. *Plate* XIII.

Suppose *a f* to be the given Height.

Divide the given Height into 8 equal Parts, and make the Eye equal to the 5th Division, as in the preceding Examples.

Divide the Height of the Eye into 6 equal Parts, as at the Points 1, 3, 5, 6, 4, 2, which are the Centers on which you may describe the Outline as following.

On the Point		with the Radius		describe the Semi-circle		which together form the Outline of the Volute, as required.
	1		1 *a*		*a g f*	
	2		2 *f*		*f b b*	
	3		3 *b*		*b i e*	
	4		4 *e*		*e k c*	
	5		5 *c*		*c l d*	
	6		6 *d*		*d m* 1	

To describe the inward Line of this Volute.

Divide each 6th Part of the Eye into 4 equal Parts (as in *Fig.* A, which is the Eye of the Volute enlarged, for the better understanding of the Situation of the Centers), and take the next inward ones for the six other Centers, on which you may describe the inward Line, as required.

Note. It is best to begin the describing of this inward Line at the Eye, and work outwards; for if any Mistake should happen in Practice, 'tis much easier rectified in the outward Parts than in the inward, where the Parts are nearer together.

Prob. VIII. *Fig.* N. *Plate* XII.
To describe an Elliptical Volute of any Height and Breadth required.

Let *k m* be the given Height, and *f e* the given Breadth.

First, by either of the preceding Methods, describe a Volute, as *Fig.* H, whose Height is equal to the given Height, and its Breadth is always equal to ¼ of its Height, therefore make *e f* and *a b* equal to ¼ of *e a.* Divide *e a* and *f b* each into 8 equal Parts, and the Lines *a b* and *e f* each into 7 equal Parts, and draw the horizontal and perpendicular Lines, which will form 56 geometrical Squares. *Secondly,* Complete the Parallelogram *f e b a,* making its Height and Breadth equal to the Height and Breadth given. Divide *f b* and *e a* each into 8 equal Parts; also *f e* and *b a* into 7 equal Parts, and then drawing the several horizontal and perpendicular Lines, as in *Fig.* H, you will form 56 Parallelograms. Now as the Parts of the elliptical Volute must have the same Heights as the like Parts in the circular Volute; therefore make the Ordinate

d e,

d c, h g, i k, e l, p, r, t y, b z, &c. in *Fig.* N, equal to the Ordinates *d c, h g, i k, e l, p, r, t, y,* &c. in *Fig.* H, and then every Part of the elliptical Volute N will affect the 56 Parallelograms in the very same manner as the circular Volute H doth the 56 geometrical Squares: and as what is here said of the outward Line is to be also understood of the inward; therefore, when you have found all the preceding Points through which the Curves are to pass, apply unto them a thin pliable Ruler, or with a free Hand trace their Curves, as required.

This Ornament is called a *Volute,* from the *Latin Valuta, à volvendo,* as that it seems to be rolled upon an Axis or Staff; and the Eye is by some, from the *Latin,* called *Oculus.*

Prob. IX. · *Fig.* III. *Plate* XXIX.

To divide the Height of the Ionick *Entablature into its Architrave,* Freeze *and Cornice, and them into their respective Members.*

Divide *a x* equal to the given Height, into 10 equal Parts, give 3 to the Height of the Architrave, 3 to the Height of the Freeze, and 4 to the Height of the Cornice.

To divide the Architrave.

Divide the lower 1 of the Architrave into 4 Parts, give the upper 1 to the Bead, and lower 3 to the small Fascia. Divide the upper 1 into 4 Parts, give the upper 1 to the Tenia, the next 2 to the Cyma Reversa, and the Remains to the great Fascia; make D H the Projection of the Tenia equal to the Height of the Tenia and Cyma Reversa, which divide into 3 Parts, and give the first 1 to the Projection of the great Fascia.

Divide C D, the Height of the Freeze, into 4 equal Parts, and on the Points C and D, with the Radius of 3 Parts, make the Section E, on which, with the Radius E D, describe the swelling Freeze.

To divide the Cornice.

The Height of the Cornice consisting of four Parts, divide *h k* equal to the two lower Parts into 3 Parts, and the lower and upper Parts thereof each into 6 Parts, as *h m* and *i k*; give the lower 5 of *i k* to the Height of the Cavetto, and the upper 1 to the Margin of the Denticule below the Dentules: Give the upper 5 Parts of *h m* to the Height of the Ovolo, and the lower 1 to its Fillet. Divide *g f*, equal to 1 Quarter Part of the Height of the Cornice, into 4 Parts, give the lower 3 Parts to the Height of the Corona, and the upper 1 to the Height of its Cyma Reversa. Divide *h n,* equal to the upper 4th Part of the Cornice, into 4 Parts, give the upper 1 to the Height of the Regula, and then *d g,* equal to the lower 1, being divided into three Parts, give the lower 1 to the Fillet between the two Cymas. And thus are the Heights of all the Members determined.

To determine their Projectures.

The Upright of the Column B C D 19 being before drawn, make B A the Projection of the Regula equal to B C the Height of the Cornice, and from any Part of C D, as from *v,* draw a right Line, as *v w* equal to B A, which divide into 4 equal Parts; divide *c d,* equal to the 2d Part, into 6 Parts, and *a b,* equal to the 1st Part of *v w,* and the 1st Part of *c d,* into 5 Parts; then half the 1st Part of *a b* terminates the Projection of the Foot of the Cavetto, the 3d Part of the Denticule, and ⅓ of the next of its Fillet Half the 2d Part of *c d* terminates the Projection of the Ovolo, and the 3d Part of *v w* the Projection of the Corona: Divide *e f,* equal to the 4th Part of *v w,* into 4 Parts, the first 1 terminates the Projection of the Fillet between the two Cymas.

To divide the Dentules.

Divide *x y* into 10 Parts, and *y z* into 3 Parts, give 2 Parts to the Breadth of each Dentule, and 1 Part to each Interval between them. And thus are all the Parts of the Order proportioned, as required.

Prob. X. *Plate* XXX. *and* XXXI.

To determine the Intercolumniations of the Ionick *Order.*

It is to be observed, That although Dentules properly belong to the *Ionick* Order,

der, yet *Palladio* and some other Masters exclude them, and introduce Modillions in their Stead; and therefore, as the Intercolumniations of the *Dorick* Order are determined by the Number of Triglyphs, so here in this Order the Intercolumniations are determined by the Number of Modillions, or Dentules, that are required to be placed between them.

First, *To determine Intercolumniations when Modillions are employed.*

THE Distance between the central Lines of Modillions is either 30 or 32 Min. *Palladio* makes them 32 Minutes, and the Breadth of each Modillion 10 Minutes. When the Distance and Number of Modillions is resolved on, the Intercolumniations are easily found by this RULE, *viz.* As many Modillions as are required between the central Lines of any Columns, add so many times 30 or 32 Minutes together, and their total Sum is the Intercolumniation, or Distance at which the central Lines of the Columns are to be placed : Therefore taking 30 or 32. Minutes in your Compasses, set that Distance from one central Line towards the other, as many times as there are Modillions required; and if every 30 or 32 Minutes be considered as one Part, and as the Breadth of a Modillion is 10 Minutes, therefore setting 5 Minutes on both Sides of every Part so set off, they will determine the Breadth of every Modillion in their respective Places. When the Distance of Modillions is fixed at 32 Minutes, to have 3 Modillions between those over the central Lines of each Column, the Distance between the central Lines must be 128 Minutes, equal to 4 times 32, or 2 Diameters 8 Minutes: If 5 Modillions, then 192 Minutes, equal to 6 times 32, or 3 Diameters 12 Minutes : If 7 Modillions, then 256 Minutes, equal to 8 times 32, or 4 Diameters and 16 Minutes : If 9 Modillions, then 320 Minutes, equal to 10 times 32, or 5 Diameters and 20 Minutes, *&c.*

IN *Fig.* I. II. and V. *Plate* XXX. are three Examples, wherein *Fig.* I. contains 13 Parts or Modillions, and *Fig.* II. and V. 14 each, whose Modillions are at 30 Minutes Distance, as is seen by the Number of Diameters contained in their respective Intercolumniations.

IN *Plate* XXXI. *Fig.* I. is exhibited the Intercolumniation for the Colonnade, whose Columns are at 3 Diameters, 44 Minutes Distance, not 45 Minutes, as inserted in the Plate by Mistake of the Engraver, and have 7 Modillions between the central Lines of every two Columns each, at 32 Minutes Distance between their central Lines. The Portico, *Fig.* II. and the Arcades, *Fig.* III. and IV. have their Intercolumniations proportioned, so as to have the Distances of the central Lines of their Modillions each 30 Minutes.

Secondly, *To proportion Intercolumniations when Dentules are employed.* Fig. III. Plate XXIX.

As *x y* is equal to 25 Minutes, and being divided into 10 Parts, as aforesaid, two of which is the Breadth of a Dentule, and 1 of an Interval; 'tis therefore evident, that each Part is equal to two Minutes and a half: And therefore to make the Division of Dentules easy, the Distance between the central Lines of Columns must always contain some Number of Parts, each of five Minutes, as the Occasion may require; as one Diameter and ½, wherein there are 18 such Parts; or 4 Diameters, wherein there are 48 such Parts; and 5 Diameters, 60 such Parts, as in the several Intercolumniations of the Portico, *Fig.* II. *Plate* XXXI. Now, if each of these Parts be divided into 2 Parts, then each Part will be equal to 2 Minutes and a half; and then giving 2 of those Parts to the Breadth of each Dentule, and 1 to each Interval, the whole will be completed, as required.

Note, the raking Dentules, in all Kinds of Pediments, must stand exactly over those in the level Cornice, in the very same Manner as the Mutules in the *Dorick* Order. The like is also to be observed of Modillions; and as Modillions are always capped with a Cyma Reversa, or some other Molding, whose Curvatures, or Molds, on the upper and lower Sides, are both different from those of the Front raking Molding; 1 must, before I proceed any further, shew how to describe those returned Moldings to the Caps of raking Modillions.

PROB.

PROB. I. *Fig.* I. II. III. *Plate* XV.

To deſcribe the returned Moldings of the Caps of raking Modillions in Pediments.

1ſt, SUPPOSE the Ovolo C, *Fig.* III. to be the raking Molding in Front, with which a raking Modillion is to be capped; draw the Chord Line *a e*, and divide it into any Number of equal Parts, ſuppoſe 8, as at the Points 2, 4, 6, 8, 10, *&c.* and from them draw the Ordinates 1, 2; 3, 4; 5, 6; *&c. 2dly*, Suppoſe the Lines *h b* and *i c* to be the Bounds of the Front raking Ovolo, and let the Line *y i* repreſent the upper Side of a raking Modillion, and *d f* its lower Side. From the Point *y* draw the horizontal Line *n y*, and from the Point *o*, the Line *o p*; make *o p*, and *n y*, each equal to *a b*, the Projection of the Front Ovolo, and through the Points *n* and *p* draw the perpendicular Lines *h l* and *e p l*, cutting the upper Line *h b*, in *h*, and *e*, draw the two Chord Lines *h i* and *f e*, and divide each into the ſame Number of equal Parts, as the Chord Line *a e*, and from thoſe Parts draw Ordinates equal to the Ordinates in C. Through the Points 1, 3, 5, 7, *&c.* in *Fig.* A and B, trace the Curves *h* 7 *i*, and *f* 7 *e*, which are the true Curves of the returned Moldings on the upper and lower Side of the Modillion, as required.

Note, The ſame Method of working will find the Curvatures of all other Kinds of returned Moldings; as for Example, when the Front Molding is a Cavetto, as C, *Fig.* II. then A and B are the upper and lower Mold, or when a Cyma Reverſa, as C, *Fig* I. where A is the upper, and B the lower, as in the two other Examples.

PROB. XII.

To proportion the Ionick *Frontiſpieces, Colonnades, Porticos and Arcades.*

As by the Practice of the two preceding Orders, it is very reaſonable to believe that my Reader is now capable of inſpecting into this and the two ſucceeding Orders, that is, to readily underſtand what is meant by the Meaſures affixed to each Part with reſpect to the Intercolumniations, Number of Modillions, Breadth of Pilaſters, Height of Impoſts, *&c.* I ſhall therefore only explain the Impoſts, *Fig.* VI. *Plate* XXX. and then recommend him to the ſeveral Figures in *Plate* XXX. and XXXI. for his further Practice.

To proportion the Ionick *Impoſt by equal Parts.*

DIVIDE *a k*, its given Height, into 3 equal Parts, the lower 1 is the Height of the Neck. The lower Half of the middle Part divided into 4, the upper 1 is the Height of the Fillet, and the lower 3 of the Cavetto; the upper Half is the Height of the Ovolo, as is the lower Half of the upper 1, the Height of the Faſcia. Divide the upper Half into 3 Parts; give the upper 1 to the Regula or upper Fillet; and the lower 2 to the Cyma Reverſa.

To determine their Projections.

LET *a b* repreſent the Breadth of the Pilaſter, and *b p* the Upright thereof; divide *o p*, equal to the Breadth of the Pilaſter, into 3 Parts at *t* and *v*, make *p r* equal to *p v*, divide *p r* into 3 Parts at *x* and *s*, and make *r q* equal to *s r*. Then *p x* determines the Projection of the Cavetto, half *s r* the Ovolo, *p r* the Faſcia, and *p q* the Regula. The Aſtragal is determined in its Height and Projection, as that of the Dorick.

THE Height of the Impoſt in *Fig.* II. *Plate* XXX. is two thirds of the Height of the Column and Sub-baſe, but in *Fig.* V. 'tis at three Times the Height of the whole Pedeſtal, and the Key-ſtones, in both Examples, are one 15th Part of the Semi-circle. The length of Key-ſtones is generally made equal to 1 Diameter, and their Depth below the Architrave is always at pleaſure; but moſt generally about ¼ or ⅓ of their Breadth, at the lower Part of the Architrave. In *Plate* XXXI. *Figures* A B C D, are two Varieties of Conſoles or Key-ſtones, in Front and Profile, which may be uſed in the Ionick, Corinthian, or Compoſite Arches at Diſcretion.

Note, The Ionick Impoſt by ANDREA PALLADIO is exhibited by *Fig.* D, *Plate* XLII.

PROB. XIII.

To proportion the Dorick *and* Ionick *Cornices, to the Height of any Room,* &c.

FIRST, The *Dorick* Cornice. Divide the given Height into 50 equal Parts, and give 3 of those Parts to the Height of the Cornice, which is confidered as the Cornice to an entire Order. But being confidered as a Cornice to an Entablature on a Column, without a Pedeftal, then divide the Height into 40 equal Parts, and give 3 to the Height of the Cornice. Secondly, the *Ionick* Cornice. *To find the Height of a Cornice to an entire Order.* Divide the Height of the Rooms into 75 Parts, and give the upper 4 to the Height of the Cornice required. *To find the Height of the Cornice of an Entablature on a Column only.* Divide the Height of the Room into 60 Parts, and give the upper 4 to the Height of the Cornice.

Examples for Practice in the Ionick *Order.*

I. *The Height of the* Ionick *Architrave being given, to find the Height of the Freeze and of the Cornice.* RULE, Make the Height of the Freeze equal to the Height of the Architrave, divide the Height of the Architrave into 3 equal Parts, and make the Height of the Cornice equal to 4 of those Parts.

II. *The Height of the* Ionick *Cornice being given, to find the Height of the Architrave and of the Freeze.* -RULE, Divide the Height of the Cornice into 4 equal Parts, and make the Heights of the Architrave and of the Freeze, each equal to 3 of those Parts.

III. *The Height of the* Ionick *Cornice being given, to find the Diameter of the Column.* RULE, As 36 is to 50, fo is the Height of the given Cornice, to the Diameter required.

IV. *The Diameter of the* Ionick *Column being given, to find the Height of the* Ionick *Cornice.* RULE, As 50 is to 36, fo is the given Diameter, to the Height of the Cornice required.

V. *The Height of the* Ionick *Architrave being given, to find the Diameter of the Column.* RULE, As 27 is to 50, fo is the Height of the given Architrave, unto the Diameter required.

VI. *The Height of the* Ionick *Entablature being given, to find the Diameter of the Column.* RULE, As 9 is to 5, fo is the Height of the given Entablature, to the Diameter required.

VII. *The Height of the* Ionick *Entablature being given, to find the Height of the Capital of 20 Minutes in Height, according to* ANDREA PALLADIO. RULE, As 27 is to 5, fo is the given Height of an Entablature, to the Height of the Capital required, and which being doubled is the Height of the Capital of 20 Minutes, as given in *Fig.* II. *Plate* XXVIII.

VIII. *The Height of the* Ionick *Entablature and Capital according to* PALLADIO *being given, to find the Diameter.* RULE, As 37 is to 15, fo is the given Height of the Capital and Entablature, to the Diameter required.

LECT. VIII.

Of proportioning the particular Parts of the Corinthian Order, *by Modules and Minutes, according to* ANDREA PALLADIO, *and by equal Parts, composed from the Masters of all Nations.*

FIGURE I. *Plate* XXXII. exhibits the Proportions and Measures of all the principal Parts of this Order, by *Andrea Palladio,* and *Fig.* III. the particular Parts of the Pedeftal. *Fig.* I. and II. *Plate* XXXIII. exhibit the particular Parts of the Base to the Column, with its Capital and Entablature, which being in general determined by Modules and Minutes, nothing more, with refpect to the Formation of their Parts, need be faid, and therefore I fhall proceed to the Divifion of this Order, by equal Parts.

PROB. I. *Fig.* II. *Plate* XXXII.

To proportion the principal Parts of the Corinthian Order, *unto any given Height,*

R

DIVIDE

DIVIDE *d w*, equal to *b z* the given Height, into 5 equal Parts; the lower 1 is the Height of the Pedeftal. Divide *c s*, equal to *b r* the remaining Part, into 6 equal Parts; the upper 1 is the Height of the Entablature, the lower 5 Parts is the Height of the Column, and which being divided into 10 equal Parts, take 1 for the Diameter of the Column, which divide into 60 Minutes, *viz.* Firft, into 6 equal Parts, which will each contain 10 Minutes, and then the firft one of them into 10 Parts.

PROB. II. *Fig.* IV. *Plate* XXXII.

To divide the Height of the Corinthian *Pedeftal into its Bafe, Die and Cornice, and them into their refpective Meafures.*

To proportion and divide the Bafe, draw *m k*, the bafe Line, and *k c*, the central Line. Divide *f k*, equal to *c k* the given Height, into 4 equal Parts. Divide *d e*, equal to the fecond Part, into 3 Parts; and *z z*, equal to the lower 1 Part, into 4 Parts, and make *b a*, *x y*, and *x w*, each equal to 1 of thofe Parts. Divide *b a* into 3 Parts, then the upper 2 is the Height of the Cavetto F, and the lower 1 of its Fillet. The two middle Parts of *z z* is the Height of the inverted Cyma Recta G. Divide *w y* into 5 equal Parts; give the upper 1 to the Fillet of the Cyma, and the lower 4 to the Torus H. The Remains *i k* is the Height of the Plinth. *To proportion and divide the Cornice.* Make *b g*, equal to one 8th Part of *f K*, the whole Height of the Pedeftal for the Height of the Cornice, which divide into 6 equal Parts. Divide *r q*, equal to the lower 1 of *b g*, into 3 Parts; give the lower 2 to the Cavetto, and the upper 1 to its Fillet. Divide *o p*, equal to the third divided Part of *b g*, into 3 Parts; give the upper 1 to the Fillet, and the other 2, with the fecond Part of *b g*, is the Height of the Cyma Recta. Divide *k m*, equal to the 2 upper Parts of *b g*, into 6 equal Parts, and give the fecond Part below, to the Height of the Fillet on the Fafcia B. Divide the 2 upper Parts of *k m* into 3 equal Parts, as at *i*; give the upper 2 to the Regula, and the Remains is the Height of A, the Cyma Reverfa. *To determine the Projectures of the Moldings.* Draw the Line *b l*, parallel to *c k*, at the Diftance of 42 Minutes of the Diameter before found. Make *g b* equal to *g f*, and through the Point *b*, draw the Line *a m*, parallel to *b l*, which will determine the Projections of the Plinth I, and Cornice at *a*. From any Point in *d f*, the Upright of the Dado or Die, draw a horizontal Line, as *r s*, which divide into 4 equal Parts; then the firft 1 terminates the Fillet on the Torus and Fafcia in the Cornice; the third Part the two Cavettos in the Bafe and Cornice, and one third of the laft Part, the Feet of the Cavettos.

PROB. III. *Fig.* II. *Plate* XXXII.

To divide the Height of the Corinthian *Column into its Bafe, Shaft, and Capital.*

The Diameter being found as before taught, let *g r* be the given Height. Make *q r*, the Height of the Bafe, equal to half the Diameter; alfo *g l*, equal to 70 Minutes, for the Height of the Capital; then *l q* the Remains is the Height of the Shaft, which is diminifhed one 6th Part at *l*.

PROB. IV. *Fig.* IV. *Plate* XXXIII.

To divide the Bafe of the Corinthian *Column into its refpective Members.*

DRAW *k m* for the bafe Line, and *i k* for the central Line. Divide *a b*, equal to the given Height, into 3 equal Parts, the lower 1 is the Height of the Plinth. Divide *b g*, equal to the 2 upper Parts of *a b*, into 4 Parts, the upper 1 is the Height of the upper Torus. Divide *c f*, equal to the 3 lower Parts of *b g*, into 2 Parts, the lower 1 is the Height of the lower Torus. Divide *d e*, equal to the upper 1 of *c f*, into 6 equal Parts, the upper and lower Parts is the Height of the two Fillets, and the middle 4 Parts of the Scotia. Draw the Line *r l*, parallel to *i k*, at 30 Minutes Diftance, for the Upright of the Column; make *l m* equal to 12 Minutes, and *l n* equal to two third Parts of *l m*; then the Line *p n* terminates the Projection of the Fillet *t*, and the upper Torus *p*. Laftly, the Projection of the Cincture *s*, and Fillet

q, are

q, are each equal to the Projection of the Center of the upper Torus, which is found by setting half the Height of the upper Torus from *p*, towards the central Line. This Base is that which is called the Attic Base.

PROB. V. *Plate* XXXV.

To divide the Height of the Corinthian *Capital, into its respective Members.*

LET A B I be the central Line, and A B the given Height. Through the Points A and B, draw the Line *a* A *z*, and *b* B *y*, at right Angles to A B. At any Distance below the Point B, draw the Line O P Q R, parallel to *b* B *y*. On any Side of the central Line A B, draw the Line *z y*, parallel to A B, at such a Distance, as to be clear of the Projection of the Abacus. Divide *z y* into 7 equal Parts, as at the Points 1 2 3 4 5 6, then each Part will be equal to 10 Minutes, because the whole Height of the Capital is 70 Minutes. Divide the second, fourth, fifth, and sixth Parts, each into 2 equal Parts, at the Points Z *d c* and *b*, and from the Points Z Y X *d* W *c* V *b* T, draw right Lines parallel to *b* B *y*, as *q* Z, *p* Y, *o* X, *n d*, *m* W, *l c*, *k* V, *i b*, *h a*, and *g* T, which determines the Heights of the Leaves, Stalks, Helices, and Volutes. Divide the upper Part into 2, as on the left Hand Side, the lower 1 is the Height of the curved Fascia of the Abacus; and the upper 1, divided into 6 equal Parts, the lower 1 is the Height of the Fillet, and the upper 5 of the Ovolo. Make *p o*, the Height of the Astragal, equal to five Minutes, which divide into 3 Parts; give the upper 2 to the Height of the Astragal, and the lower 1 to the Height of the Fillet; and thus are the Heights of all the Members determined. *To determine the Projectures.* Make 25 P, and 25 Q, on the Line O R, each equal to 25 Minutes, which is equal to 2 Parts and half of *z y*; also make O P and Q R, each equal to two Parts of *z y* or 20 Minutes. Through the Points O P, Q R, draw the Lines O *a*, P *g*, Q *n*, and R *z*; then C *a*, and R *z*, will determine the Projections of the two Sides of the Abacus, and the Lines P *g*, and Q *n*, will be the two upright Lines of the Shaft of the Column. Divide O 10, on the left Hand Side, into 8 equal Parts; then O *w*, the first three Parts, determines the Projection of the Fillet in the Abacus at *r*; O *x*, the first 5 Parts, the Projection of the Fascia at *t*, and Ovolo at *d*; O *y*, the first 6 Parts, the Projection of the Fillet at *s*; and O *z*, the first 7 Parts, the Projection of the Fascia at *v*. Make the Projections on the right Hand, equal to those on the left, and then the Abacus will be completed.

MAKE *q*, the Projection of the Astragal, equal to *p o*; and *s r*, the Fillet, unto 2 thirds thereof. Divide *p t* into 3 Parts, and make *p v* equal to 4 of those Parts. Draw *v x* parallel to *p t*. Draw *t v*, which bisect in *w*, whereon raise the Perpendicular *w x*, cutting *v x* in *x*, whereon, with the Radius *x v*, describe the Arch *v t*. Make *h k m*, on the left Side, equal to *g t v*, on the Right, and then the Astragal will be completed.

On the Point B, with the Radius B *o*, describe the Semicircle *i* N G H I K L M *o*, which divide into 8 equal Parts, at the Points N G H I K L M, and from them draw the Lines N A, G C, H D, I B, K E, L F, parallel to the central Line A B, which continue upwards at pleasure, which are the central Lines of the several Leaves. Draw the Lines *a h*, and *z q*, which determines the Projecture of the two Out-Leaves in the second Range. Divide the Distance 12, 13, into 4 Parts, and from the third Part, at the Point 14, draw the Line 14 *q*, which determines the Projecture of the Out-Leaf in the lower Range, at the Point 15. This being done, proceed to delineate by Hand the several Leaves, Stalk and Helice, on the right Hand Side, and when the same is done, transfer every particular Part thereof unto the left Side, by taking their several horizontal Distances from the central Line, and set them from the central Line on the left Hand Side; or otherwise, draw parallel Ordinates through on both Sides, and make those on the left Hand equal to those on the right. By either of these Methods, you may make the two Sides of the Capital exactly the same.

Note, It will be best, first for to describe the Leaves in Gross, as is done

on

on the right Hand Side, wherein you muſt be very perfect in their Outlines, before you proceed to divide them into their Palms and Raffles; and for the eaſy dividing of Leaves into their Palms and Raffles, I have given 7 Examples of Leaves for Practice, in *Plate* XXXIV, of which the large Leaf D is in a Manner geometrically deſcribed, and whoſe Height is to its Breadth, as 7 is to 6, as may be ſeen by the equal Parts on its left Side, and at its Bottom, which Parts being ſubdivided, as in the Figure is expreſſed, the Points of the Palms in every Palm are exactly determined. *Note*, a Palm conſiſts of 5 Points, as *r q g y* D, or *m n t* A F, or *w x* C G H. *Note alſo*, that when the Learner has formed two or three Leaves in large thus divided, he may then proceed to make others of leſs Magnitude, by Hand, and omit all the aforeſaid Diviſions by Lines, as R W X Y, which are all Leaves in Front, ſerving as well for Pilaſters as the Front Leaves of Columns. *Fig.* S is a Leaf in Profile, and T in an oblique View, ſuch as thoſe that are between the middle or front Leaf, and outer or profile Leaf of a Column. The Figures M and Q, are two Examples of Stalks or Stems for Practice, of which Q is a Stalk only with its Leaves, and M is complete with its Volute and Helice. *Fig.* P is the ancient Ornament with which the Abacus is uſually charged, inſtead of which I have placed a Lion's Maſk, as an Emblem of Majeſty, Power, &c.

Prob. VI. *Fig.* G C D E. *Plate* XXXIII.

To divide the Height of the Corinthian *Entablature into its Architrave, Freeze, and Cornice, and them into their reſpective Members.*

Divide *h l*, equal to the given Height, into 10 equal Parts; give the lower 3 to the Height of the Architrave, the next 3 to the Height of the Freeze, and the upper 4 to the Height of the Cornice. Divide *z h*, equal to the Height of the Freeze, into 5 Parts, the lower 1 is the Height of the firſt Faſcia, with its Bead, which is 1 fourth Part thereof, the ſecond Part is the Height of the ſecond Faſcia. The third Part, equal to *e f*, divided into three Parts, the lower 1 is the Cyma Reverſa between the ſecond and third Faſcias. The fourth Part, equal to *c d*, divided into 4 Parts, the upper 1 is the Bead over the third Faſcia, and the 3 lower Parts, with the two remaining Parts of *e f*, is the Height of the third Faſcia. The upper or 5th Part equal to *a b*, divided into 3 Parts, the upper 1 is the Regula of the Tenia, and the lower 2 of its Cyma Reverſa. *To determine the Projectures of theſe Members in the Architrave.* Make *w x* equal to *w y*, which divide into 5 Parts, give 1 Part to the Projection of the ſecond Faſcia, and 2 to the third Faſcia. *To divide the Cornice.* Divide *k g*, equal to its Height, into 5 equal Parts, and *i m*, equal to the third Part, into 8 Parts. Make *y q* equal to the two lower Parts of *k g*, and the lower 1 Part of *i m*, which divide into 15 equal Parts; give the lower 4 Parts to the Height of the Cyma Reverſa, the next 5 Parts and half to the Height of the Denticule, againſt which the Dentules are placed, whoſe Depth are 5 Parts only; the next half Part to the Fillet on the Dentules; the next 1 Part to the Aſtragal, and the upper 4 Parts to the Ovolo. Divide *l p*, equal to the 3 remaining Parts of *k g*, into 3 Parts; the lower 1 divided into 4, the lower 3 Parts thereof is the Height of the Faſcia, againſt which the Modillions are placed, and the upper 1 of the Cyma Reverſa, with its Fillet, with which the Modillions are capped. Divide *n o* into 2, the lower 1 is the Margin below the Modillions. Divide *s r* into 3 Parts, the upper 1 Part is the Height of the Fillet, and the lower 2 Parts of the Cyma Reverſa. Divide *x t*, equal to the middle Part of *l p*, into 4 Parts, give the upper 1 to the Height of the Cyma Reverſa *d d d*, and the lower 3 to the Height of the Corona. Divide the upper Part of *l p* into 4 equal Parts, and the lower 1 Part thereof into 3 equal Parts; give the lower 1 Part, to the Fillet, and then the 4th Part of the upper 3d Part of *l p*, being given to the Regula, the Remains will be the Height of the Cyma Recta. *To determine the Projections of theſe Members.* Make *b* the Projection of the Cornice, before the Upright of the Freeze and Column,

equal

equal to *k g*, its entire Height. From any Part of the Freeze, as A, draw an
horizontal Line, as A B, which make equal to *k g*, the Projection of the Cornice, and draw the Line *b* B. Divide A B into 4 equal Parts. Divide *c d*, equal
to the firſt Part, into 6 Parts; then the firſt 2 Parts and half determine the Projection of the Denticule; the firſt four Parts and half, the outer Denticule; the
5th Part the Fillet over the Dentules, and the 5th Part and half the Aſtragal.
The ſecond Part of A B, divided into 5 Parts (which in the Plate is omitted by
Miſtake), the firſt 1 Part determines the Projection of the Ovolo, and one third
of the next Part the Projection of the Outſide of the outer Modillion. The third
Part of A B determines the Projection of the Modillion in Profile at *i*. Divide *e f*,
equal to the laſt Part of A B, into 5 equal Parts, and *g h*, equal to the 2d and
3d Parts of *e f*, into 3 equal Parts; then half the 1ſt one determines the Projection of the Corona at *c*, and the 2d Part the Fillet of the Cyma Reverſa: And
thus are the Heights and Projections of the ſeveral Members of this Order determined. The next Work, in order to complete this Cornice, is to divide out
the Dentules and Modillions, and to deſcribe the Modillion in Front and Profile.

Proв. VII. *Fig.* G C. *Plate* XXXIII.
To divide the Dentules in the Corinthian *Cornice.*

Divide the Diſtance between the central Line and the Upright of the Freeze
into 12 equal Parts, give 2 Parts to the Breadth of a Dentule, and 1 Part to an
Interval.

Proв. VIII. *Fig.* G C. *Plate* XXXIII.
To divide the Diſtances of Corinthian *Modillions.*

It is generally agreed on by the beſt Maſters to place the central Lines of
Modillions at 35 Minutes Diſtance, and to make the Front of each equal to 10
Minutes, whereby their Intervals or Diſtances between are each 25 Minutes, and
the Length or Projection of a Modillion is 20 Minutes, equal to double its Front
or Breadth. Now as over the central Line of every Column there muſt be a Modillion, therefore the Intercolumniation of this Order muſt be conformable to the
Number of Modillions that are to be between every two Columns; and to divide
the Diſtances of Modillions, is no more than to take 35 Minutes in your Compaſſes,
and to ſet off that Diſtance from the central Line of your Column, as often as
the Number of Modillions are required.

Proв. IX. *Fig.* III. IV. *and* V. *Plate* XIV.
To deſcribe the Front, Profile and Plan, or Plancere of the Corinthian *Modillion.*
I. *To deſcribe a* Corinthian *Modillion in Front.*

Let the geometrical Square *a b h i*, *Fig.* III. be the Outlines of a *Corinthian*
Modillion, with its Cyma Reverſa and Fillet, whoſe Breadth *h i*, and Depth *y i*
are given. Biſect *h i* in *d*, and draw the Perpendicular *e d*. Divide *h i* into 8 equal
Parts, and make the Fillets *h i* and 7 *i* each 1 Part. Biſect *y i* in *l*, and draw
k l parallel to *h i*. Draw the Lines *q m* and *v o* parallel to *e d*, each at the Diſtance of half the Breadth of the Fillet *h i*, and divide the Diſtance between them
into 8 equal Parts, as at *d*, and make the ſmall Fillets next within the Lines *q m*
and *v o*, each 1 of the 8 Parts. Draw the Lines *m o* and *q v* parallel to *k l*, and
each at the Diſtance of *m z*. Take the Diſtance to either of the Fillets, and on
the Points *x* and *z* deſcribe the two Semi-circles of the Bead. Draw the Lines *t q*,
v w, alſo *n m* and *o p*. Biſect *t q* in *f*, divide *f q* into 8 Parts; on *f* and *q*, with a
Radius equal to 5 Parts, make the Section *r*, on which deſcribe the Arch *f q*.
In the ſame Manner deſcribe the Arch *t f*, alſo the Compound Arches *v w*, *n m*
and *o p*; which completes the Modillion in Front, as required.

II. *To deſcribe a* Corinthian *Modillion in Profile*, Fig. V.

Divide the Length *m f* into 3 equal Parts, and the 1ſt one Part into 7 Parts;
make *m l* the Height, equal to 8 of thoſe Parts, and complete the Parallelogram
l b m f. From *p*, at 4 Parts and ½ Diſtance from *m*, draw the Line *p q* parallel
to *m f*. At 4 Parts from *m* draw the Line *k i* parallel to *l m*, whoſe Interſection
is the Center of the Eye of the greater Scroll, and whoſe Diameter is equal to the

6   5th

5th Divifion of *l m.*　*Fig.* D is the Eye of this Volute or Scroll at large, wherein the geometrical Square being inferibed, and each Semi-diameter divided into 2 equal Parts, as at the Points 7, 6, 8, 5, then the Points 1, 4, 3, 2, 5, 8, 7, 6, as they ftand in the Figure, are the Centers on which defcribe the Scroll, beginning at the Point *i.*　Divide *b c,* equal to 4 Parts of *l m,* into 8 equal Parts, and draw the Line *d c* for the Depth of the fmall Scroll. Make *b a* equal to 7 Parts of *b c,* and at 4 Parts from *b* draw the Line 4 *d* B parallel to *b f.*　At 4 Parts and ⅓ from *b* draw the Line *f r* parallel to *a b,* which will interfect the Line *o d* in the Center of the Eye of the fmall Scroll, whofe Diameter is equal to the 5th Divifion in *b c.*

INSCRIBE a Square within the Eye, and divide its Semi-diameters as before, as in *Fig.* D, and then the Points 3, 2, 1, 4, 7, 6, 14, as they ftand in *Fig.* D, are the Centers, whereon defcribe the fmall Scroll, beginning at the Point *o.* Draw the Line *o p,* which bifect in L; alfo bifect *i* L in *g,* and L *p* in *c.*　Erect the Perpendiculars *g* A and *e* B, cutting the Lines *k i* in A and *o d* in B.　On the Points A and B, with the Radius A *i* defcribe the Arches *i* L and L *p,* alfo the inward Arches which limit the Breadth of the Lift.

III. *To defcribe the Plan or Plancere of the* Corinthian *Modillion,* Fig. IV.

MAKE B C and *c f* each equal to *h i* in *Fig.* III. alfo make B *c* and C *f* each equal to *l b* in *Fig* V. and complete the Parallelogram B *c* C *f.*　Draw *o d* and *l k* parallel to C *f,* each at the Diftance of *h i* in *Fig* III. Draw the Lines *a n b* and *g h m* at the fame parallel Diftances from B *c* and C *f,* as are refpectively equal to the Projections of the Cyma Reverfa in *Fig.* III. before *b i* the Upright of the Modillion, which continue about at the End, and return from B and C. The Beads, with its Fillets *r t,* and the Cymas *d q r* and *t k,* &c. are defcribed exactly the fame as *n m z o p* in *Fig.* III.

Note, The Manner of dividing the Plancere of the *Ionick, Corinthian* and *Compofite* Cornices, and to make their Returns at external and internal Angles, is exhibited by *Fig.* VII. *Plate* XLIV. wherein B B reprefent the Plan of the two Modillions next to an internal Angle, and E E of two Modillions next an external Angle, as alfo are H H.　The geometrical Squares A C A A F G are hollow Pannels, called Coffers, which are to be enriched with Rofes, as thofe of *Fig.* A B C D E, *Plate* XXXVIII.

PROB. X.

To proportion the Corinthian *Cornice to the Height of any Room required.*

THIS admits of two Varieties, *viz. Firft,* To confider the Cornice as the Cornice to an entire Order; and, *laftly,* as the Cornice of an Entablature on a Column only.

To find the Height of a Cornice to an entire Order.

DIVIDE the Height of the Room into 75 Parts, and give the upper 4 to the Height of the Cornice.

To find the Height of the Cornice of an Entablature on a Column only.

DIVIDE the Height of the Room into 60 Parts, and give the upper 4 to the Height of the Cornice.

PROB. XI.

To proportion Frontifpieces, Colonnades, Porticos, Arcades, &c. *of the* Corinthian *Order.*

As the Intercolumniations of this Order are regulated by the Number of Modillions, whofe Diftances between their central Lines are 35 Minutes, as before obferved, therefore to make Frontifpieces, Colonnades, &c. the Diftances of the central Lines muft confift of as many Times 35 Minutes as the Nature of the Cafes requires. *Fig.* I. II. and III. *Plate* XXXVI. are Examples hereof, where the Columns in *Fig.* I. have 13 Modillions between, *Fig.* II. 12 Modillions, *Fig.* III. 14 Modillions.　In *Plate* XXXVII. *Fig.* I. confifts of 13 Modillions, and *Fig.* A of 12, between the two middle Columns, as before in *Fig.* I. and II. *Plate* XXXVI.　But as here in *Fig.* A, there are Columns in Pairs on each Side, their Diftances have but 3 Modillions between their central Lines, accounting the

two

two half Modillions on the Sides of the two central Lines as one Modillion. In *Plate* XXXVIII. the Colonnade, *Fig.* I. contains 6 Modillions between every two Columns, the single Arcades 11 Modillions, the Arcades of Columns in Pairs 3, and 11 Modillions, and the Portico, *Fig.* II. contains three Modillions between the central Lines *a* and *b*, 6 Modillions between *b* and *c*, and 8 Modillions between *c* and *d*.

Now from the preceding 'tis evident, that the Intercolumniations of this Order must be as follow, *viz.* If it have two Modillions between those over the two Columns, the Intercolumniation must be 1 Diameter 45 Minutes; if 3 Modillions, then the Intercolumniation must be 2 Diameters 30 Minutes; if 4 Modillions, then 2 Diameters 55 Minutes; if 5 Modillions, then 3 Diameters 40 Minutes; if 6 Modillions, then 4 Diameters 5 Minutes; if 7 Modillions, then 4 Diameters 40 Minutes; if 8 Modillions, then 5 Diameters 15 Minutes; if 9 Modillions, then 5 Diameters and 50 Minutes; if 10 Modillions, then 6 Diameters 25 Minutes; if 11 Modillions, then 7 Diameters; and if 12 Modillions, then 7 Diameters 35 Minutes: And so, by the continual adding of 35 Minutes, the Intercolumniation for any greater Number of Modillions may be found. *Note*, the Intercolumniations for Columns, which have 3, 5, 7, 9, 11 and 13 Modillions between them, as published in *Palladio Londinensis*, by Mr. *Salmon* of *Colchester*, and revised by Mr. *Edward Hoppus*, Surveyor of the *London* Insurance-Office, are in general false, and seem, as that neither of them knew what they were doing; for by the preceding 'tis plain, that the Intercolumniation for Columns that have 3 Modillions between them, is 2 Diameters 40 Minutes, not 2 Diameters 30 Minutes; and for Columns that have 5 Modillions between them, is 3 Diameters 30 Minutes, and not 3 Diameters 45 Minutes, as they have falsely published in *p.* 87, *&c.*

THE Height of Imposts in this Order are two Thirds of the Height from the Base Line unto the under Part of the Architrave, as in the preceding Orders, and the Breadth of the Key-stone is the 15th Part of the Semi-circular Architrave; and as Key-stones to this Order admit of Embellishments, I have therefore in *Figures a b c d e f g h i k*, given proper Examples thereof.

THE Impost to this Order, by *Andrea Palladio*, is exhibited by *Fig.* F, *Plate* XLII. and that by equal Parts, by *Fig.* V. *Plate* XLIII. which is thus proportioned.

To Proportion the Corinthian *Impost by equal Parts.*

DIVIDE *a h* the given Height into 3 Parts; the lower one is the Height of the Neck or Freeze of the Impost. Divide the Middle Part into 3 Parts, and the lower 1 into 3, give the lower 2 to the Cavetto, and the upper 1 to the Fillet. Divide the upper 1 into 3 Parts, and give the upper 1 to the Fillet on the Cyma Recta, and the Remains to the Height of the Cyma Recta. Divide *a k*, the upper third Part of *a h*, into 2 Parts, and the upper 1 into 3 Parts, give the lower 2 to the Height of the Cyma Reversa, and the upper 1 to the Height of the Regula or upper Fillet.

To determine the Projections of these Members.

DRAW *b e* parallel to *a h*, at a Distance equal to the Breadth of the Pilaster. Divide *d e*, equal to the Breadth of the Pilaster, into 3 equal Parts; make *e g* equal to one of those Parts, and *g f* equal to one Third of *e g*: Divide *e g* into 3 Parts, and the first and third Parts thereof each into 3 Parts, then the first Part from *e* determines the Projection of *z* the Bottom of the Cavetto, the next 1 the Fillet of the Astragal *c*, and the next 1 the Astragal at *b*, and the Fillet on the Cavetto at *y*.

THE 2d Part of the third Part of *e g* determines the Projection of the Cyma Recta at *x*, and *e g* the Projection of the Fascia at *w*: Lastly, *b c* being made equal to *e f*, completes the whole, as required.

THE Height of the Astragal *o h*, divided into 3 Parts, is equal to half *m h* the Height of the Neck.

THE Architrave *a b* of the Arch is thus divided, *viz. d e* being already divided into 3 Parts, divide the outer 1 Part into 3 Parts: give the 1st Part to *v t*, the Breadth of the Regula; the next 1 to the Ovolo with its Fillet, which is equal

to

to ⅓ thereof, and the laſt Part to the Cavetto and Bead, which is ⅓ thereof. The middle Part of *d e* is the Breadth of *r p* the great Faſcia; and the outer Part divided into 6 Parts, the firſt 1 Part is the Breadth of the Cyma Reverſa, and the other 5 of the ſmall Faſcia.

Examples for Practice in the Corinthian *Order.*

I. *The Height of the* Corinthian *Architrave being given to find the Height of the Freeze and of the Cornice.* RULE, Make the Height of the Freeze equal to the Height of the Architrave. Divide the Height of the Architrave into 3 equal Parts, and make the Height of the Cornice equal to 4 of thoſe Parts.

II. *The Height of the* Corinthian *Cornice being given, to find the Height of the Freeze and of the Architrave.* RULE, Divide the Height of the Cornice into 4 equal Parts, and make the Height of the Freeze and of the Architrave, each equal to 3 of thoſe Parts.

III. *The Height of the* Corinthian *Cornice being given, to find the Diameter of the Column.* RULE, Divide the Height of the given Cornice into 4 equal Parts, and make the Diameter equal to 5 of thoſe Parts.

IV. *The Diameter of the* Corinthian *Column being given, to find the Height of the* Corinthian *Cornice.* RULE, Divide the Diameter into 5 equal Parts, and make the Height of the Cornice equal to 4 of thoſe Parts.

V. *The Height of the* Corinthian *Architrave being given, to find the Diameter of the Column.* RULE, Divide the Height of the Architrave into 3 equal Parts, and make the Diameter of the Column equal to 5 of thoſe Parts.

VI. *The Height of the* Corinthian *Entablature being given, to find the Diameter of the Column.* RULE, One half Part of the Height of the given Entablature is equal to the Diameter required.

VII. *The Height of the* Corinthian *Entablature being given, to find the Height of the Capital.* RULE, Divide the Height of the Entablature into 12 equal Parts, and make the Height of the Capital (excluſive of the Aſtragal, which is a Part of the Shaft) equal to 7 of thoſe Parts.

VIII. *The Height of the* Corinthian *Capital and Entablature being given, to find the Diameter of the Column.* RULE, Divide the whole Height of the Capital and Entablature into 19 equal Parts, and make the Diameter of the Column equal to 6 of thoſe Parts.

LECTURE IX.

Of the Manner of proportioning the Compoſite Order by Modules and Minutes according to ANDREA PALLADIO, *and by equal Parts compoſed from the Maſters of all Nations.*

THE principal Parts of this Order, according to *Andrea Palladio,* are exhibited by *Fig.* I. and the particular Parts of the Pedeſtal by *Fig.* III. *Plate.* XXXIX. the particular Parts of the Baſe to the Column and of the Entablature, are exhibited by *Fig.* I. and II. *Plate* XLI. which being in general proportioned by Modules and Minutes as the preceding Orders, nothing more need be ſaid thereof; and therefore I ſhall proceed to the Manner of proportioning the Parts of this Order by equal Parts.

PROB. I. *Fig.* II. *Plate* XXXIX.

To proportion the principal Parts of the Compoſite Order by equal Parts.

DIVIDE *t r,* equal to the given Height, into 5 equal Parts, the lower 1 Part is the Height of the Pedeſtal. Divide *s p,* equal to the remaining Part, into 15 equal Parts, and the 11th Part into 6 equal Parts, the 2 upper Parts and ⅓ of the next lower Part is the Height of the Entablature, and the Remainder *v p* is the Height of the Column, and which being divided into 11 equal Parts, 1 of thoſe Parts will be equal to the Diameter of the Column. And its Height to 11 Diameters.

PROB. II. *Fig.* IV. *Plate* XXXIX.

To divide the Height of the Compoſite Pedeſtal into its principal Parts, and them into their reſpective Members.

DRAW *w d,* for the Baſe Line, and *f d,* for the central Line, divide *k e,* equal

equal to the given Height into 4 equal Parts, and the 2d Part into 3 equal Parts; divide z a, equal to ⅓ of the 2d Part, into 12 equal Parts, and make a b equal to 5 of those Parts, and draw v b, for the Height of the Plinth; at 3 Parts above a draw the upper Line of the Torus, and make the Height of its Fillet equal to 1 Part; give the upper 2 Parts to the Height of the Cavetto, and the next 1 to the Height of the Fillet, then the Remains will be the Height of the inverfed Cyma Recta. Half the upper Part of k e is the Height of the Cornice; divide b l into 3 equal Parts, and the lower 1 Part into 6 Parts, give the lower 2 to the Height of the Cavetto, and the next 1 to the Height of its Fillet. Divide the middle 1 of b l into 6 Parts, give the 3d Part to the Height of the Fillet on the Cyma reverfa, and the Remains of that, and the lower Part, will be the Height of the Cyma Reverfa. Divide the upper 1 Part of b l into 4 equal Parts, give the upper 2 Part to the Regula, and the next 2 to the Cyma Reverfa.

To determine the Projections of thefe Members.

THE Diameter found as before, being divided into 60 Minutes, draw b x, parallel to f d, at 42 Minutes Diftance, make x w, and b a, each equal to a z, and draw a w, which will determine the Projection of the Plinth at $v.w$, and the Cornice at a. From any Part of b x, the Upright of the Dado, draw a right Line as 1, 2, which divide into 4 equal Parts; the firft 1 determines the Projection of the Fafcia c d, ⅔ of the next 1 the Projection of the Cyma Recta at d; the third 1, the Fillet on the Cavetto, and on the Cyma in the Bafe at p, and ⅔ of the laft 1, the Foot of the Cavetto in the Cornice, and in the Bafe; laftly, the Projection of the Fillet q, in the Bafe, is equal to the Projection of the Center of the Torus.

P R O B. III. *Fig.* II. *Plate* XXXIX.

To divide the Compofite *Column into its Bafe, Shaft and Capital.*

THE Height d b, being divided into 11 Parts, one of which being the Diameter as aforefaid make b g, the Height of the Bafe, equal to half the Diameter; and d e the Height of the Capital, equal to the Diameter, and one fixth Part thereof.

P R O B. IV. *Fig.* IV. *Plate* XLI.

To divide the Bafe of the Compofite *Column into its refpective Members.*

DRAW k f for the Bafe Line, and c f for the central Line. Divide a f into 3 equal Parts, the lower 1 Part is the Height of the Plinth. Divide the middle 1 into 5 equal Parts, the lower 3 Parts is the Height of the lower Torus, the next 1 of the Aftragal, and half the next 1 of its Fillet. Divide the upper 1 of a f into 5 equal Parts, the upper 2 is the Height of the upper Torus; half the next 1 is the Height of the Fillet under the Torus, and the Remains is the Height of the Scotia. *To determine the Projectures of thefe Moldings.* Draw i b, parallel to a f, at the Diftance of 30 Minutes, and make k b equal to 12 Minutes. Divide k b into 5 equal Parts; the firft 1 Part and half determines the Projection of the Aftragal on the lower Torus, the fecond Part its Fillet, the third Part the Fillet under the upper Torus, and its Center alfo; and the third Part and half, the Center of the Aftragal on the upper Torus, and its Fillet alfo. The Height of the Aftragal on the upper Torus is equal to half the Height of the upper Torus, and the Fillet on the Aftragal to half the Height of the Aftragal.

P R O B. V. *Plate* XL.

To proportion the Parts of the Compofite *Capital by equal Parts.*

FIRST, fet up the Height of the Capital, proportion its Aftragal, Leaves, and Abacus, exactly the fame as in the *Corinthian* Capital; and the 20 Minutes contained between d, the lower Part of the Abacus, and i, the Top of the upper Range of Leaves, divide as follows, viz. Divide g s into 8 equal Parts, give the fixth and feventh Parts, to the Height of the Fillet E. Divide the 5 Minutes between 50 and 55 into 2 equal Parts at f; then g f is the Height of the Aftragal D, which is alfo the Height of the Eye of the Volutes N and N. Divide the upper 5 Minutes contained between 55 and 60 into 4 equal Parts;

S   give

give the upper 1 to the Height of the Fillet under the Abacus, and the remaining Part *e f* to the Height of the Ovolo C. Now as the Volutes N N are elliptical, and have the Centers of their Eyes in that Point of the Line *t* X, the upright Line of the Shaft that is cut by the central Line of the Astragal D, and as they are comprized within a Parallelogram, formed by the upright Lines proceeding from *v*, the Projection of the lower Part of the Abacus and *w* P, as also by *d t v*, the under Line of the Abacus, and *i r* the Top of the second Range of Leaves; therefore by Pron. VI. or VII. Lect. VII. hereof, describe a circular Volute, whose Height is equal to the Breadth of your Parallelogram; and then from that Volute so made, by Prob. VIII. Lect. VII. aforesaid, describe an elliptical Volute in the aforesaid Parallelogram, which will be the Volute to this Capital, and which being in like Manner performed on both Sides, the Capital will be completed, as required.

Prob. VI. *Fig.* III. *Plate* XLI. and *Fig.* I. *Plate* XLII.
To divide the Height of the Composite *Entablature into its Architrave, Freeze, and Cornice.*

As I have given two Examples of Entablatures in this Order, the one for the Inside of Buildings, to be seen at a small Distance, and the other for the Outsides of Buildings, to be seen at a considerable Distance, I shall therefore speak particularly thereof.
I. *Of the* Composite *Entablature, to be used within Buildings* *Fig.* III. *Plate* XLI.
Divide *l* A, equal to the given Height, into 8 equal Parts; give 2 to the Height of the Architrave, 3 to the Height of the Freeze, and the same to the Height of the Cornice.

To divide the Height of the Architrave.
Divide *t c*, its Height, into 50 equal Parts; give 8 to the Height of Z the lower Fascia, 1 and half to its Bead, 10 to Y the middle Fascia, 4 to the double Bead X, 15 to the upper Fascia, of which 5 must be given to the Drops V, 3 to the Cavetto T, 1 to its Fillet, 2 to the Astragal S, 4 to the Tenia R, and 1 to its Fillet.

To divide the Height of the Freeze.
Divide *n v*, equal to its Height, into 12 equal Parts, and give the upper 1 to P, its Capital.

To divide the Height of the Cornice.
Divide *k m*, equal to its Height, into 70 equal Parts; give 1 to the lower Fillet, 2 to the Astragal O, 4 and half to the Cavetto N, 1 to its Fillet, 6 to the Denticule, of which the upper 5 is the Height of the Dentules; then give 1 to their Fillet, 2 to the Astragal L, 4 and half to the Ovolo K, and 6 to the Platform of the Modillions, of which the upper 5 is the Height of the Modillions. Give 2 to the Cyma Reversa H, 7 to the Super-Modillions G, and 1 to the Fillet. Give 2 to the Astragal F, 4 to the Super-Astragal E, and 1 to its Fillet. Give 8 to the Corona D, 3 to the Cyma Reversa C, and 1 to its Fillet. Give 2 to the Astragal B, 8 to the Cyma Recta A, and 3 to its Regula.

To determine the Projections of these Moldings.
Make *q* E, and C D, each equal to the Semi-diameter of the Column at its Astragal, and draw the Line *e d* for the Upright of the Freeze, which continue up through the Cornice. Make the utmost Projection before the Upright of the Freeze, equal to *k m* the Height of the Cornice.
From any Part of the Upright of the Freeze, as at E, draw a horizontal Line, as E F, which divide into 4 equal Parts. Divide the first 1 Part into 3 Parts; then the first 1 Part thereof determines the Projection of the Cavetto and Astragal at *w*, and two thirds thereof, the Capital of the Freeze, whose Fillet Projects equal to its Height. The second Part of the first Part E F, determines the Projection of the Fillet *v*; and one fourth of the next third Part the Denticule *t*. E *b*, one fourth Part of E F, determines the Projection of the Fillet

Fillet *s*, and Center of the Aſtragal *r*; as alſo the Bottom of the Ovolo K. Divide *b d*, the ſecond Part of E F, into 8 Parts; or *b e* its Half, into 4 Parts; then the ſecond Part determines the Projection of the Outſide of the Modillion at *n*. Biſect *d f*, the third Part of *e f*, in *e*. Divide *d e* into 4 Parts, then the firſt Part determines the Projection of the Modillion in Profile at *m*; the ſecond Part, the Super-Modillion at *l*, and *d e* the Super-Aſtragal at *i*. Divide *f* F, the fourth Part of E F, into 7 equal Parts; then *f* 2, equal to 3 of thoſe Parts, determines the Projection of the Corona, and *f h*, equal to ⅓ of *f* F, the Fillet of the Cyma Reverſa C. Make *y z* the Tenia of the Architrave, equal to ⅓ of ⅔ of E *b*. Make *q r*, and *t x* in the Freeze, equal to half the Diameter at the Baſe of the Column. Divide *t x* into 6 Parts, and give 2 Parts to the Breadth of each **Drop**, as in the *Dorick* Order.

To divide the Dentules in the Cornice.

Divide *a b* into 24 equal Parts; give 2 Parts to the Breadth of each Dentule, and 1 to each Interval. The Breadth of an upper Modillion is equal to 10 Minutes, and of an under Modillion unto 5 Minutes. The Diſtance in the Clear between the upper Modillion is 30, and between their central Lines 40 Minutes; ſo that to adjuſt the Diſtances of Columns in this Order, we muſt place them at 3, 4, 5, &c. times 40 Minutes, and then the Modillions will happen at their true Diſtances. This Entablature, without Oſtentation, is the richeſt and moſt magnificent, that has yet appeared in the World.

II. Of the Compoſite *Entablature, to be uſed againſt the Outſides of Buildings.* Fig. I. Plate XLII.

Divide *r s*, equal to the given Height, into 20 equal Parts; give the lower 3 to the Height of the Architrave; the next 3 to the Height of the Freeze, and the upper 4 to the Height of the Cornice.

To divide the Height of the Architrave.

Divide *t v*, equal to the given Height, into 5 equal Parts; divide the lower 1 Part into 4 Parts; give the lower 3 to C the lower Faſcia, and the upper 1 to B the Bead. The ſecond Part of *t v* is the Height of A, the middle Faſcia. Divide the third Part of *t v* into 3 equal Parts, and give the lower 1 to *z* the Cyma Reverſa. Divide *y x*, the 4th Part of *t v*, into 4 equal Parts; give the upper 1 to the Height of the Bead *x*, and the Remains, with the Remains of the third Part, will be the Height of *y* the upper Faſcia. Divide the upper Part of *t v* into 3 equal Parts; give the lower 2 to the Height of the Cyma Reverſa, and the upper 1 to the Height of *q* the Regula.

To divide the Height of the Freeze.

Divide the upper third Part into 5 equal Parts, and the upper 1 of thoſe Parts into 3 Parts; give the upper 2 Parts to the Height of the Aſtragal *n*, and the lower 1 to the Height of its Fillet *o*. This Freeze may be made either upright or ſwelling, at the Pleaſure of the Architect.

To divide the Height of the Cornice.

The Height, conſiſting of 4 principal Parts, divide *i n*, the firſt Part, into 8 equal Parts; give the lower 4 Parts to the Cyma Reverſa *m*, and the upper 4 Parts to the Platform of the under Modillion, of which the upper 3 Parts muſt be given to the Height of the Modillion. Divide *f i*, the ſecond Part of the Height, into 4 Parts; give two thirds of the lower 1 to the Height of the Cyma Reverſa *i*, and the upper 1 being divided into 3 Parts, give the upper 2 to the Ovolo, and the lower 1 to the Fillet. Divide *e f*, the third Part of the Height, into 4 equal Parts, and the upper 1 thereof into 2 Parts; give the under 1 to the Height of the Fillet *d*, and the 3 remaining Parts will be the Height of the Corona *e*. Divide the upper fourth Part of the Height of the Cornice into 4 equal Parts, and the lower 1 thereof into 3 equal Parts, add the lower 1 to the Remains of the third principal Part, which together make the Height of the Aſtragal C. The upper 4th Part is the Height of the Regula *a*,

To

To determine the Projections of these Moldings.

DRAW F O parallel to the central Line Q R, make F G equal to F M, from any Part of the Upright of the Freeze, as at K; draw the horizontal Line K L equal to F G, which divide into 4 equal Parts, and each Part into 6 equal Parts, then the 1st Part of K 1 determines the Projection of the Fillet and Center of the Astragal, the 4th Part the under Modillion; the 5th Part the upper Modillion, and K 1 the Ovolo or Capping of the upper Modillion; the 2d Part of K L being divided into 6 Parts, 4 Parts and ¼ determines the Projection of the lower Modillion in Profile, 5 Parts and ⅘ the Super-Modillion in Profile, and 5 Parts ⅔ its Fillet; the first half Part, between 2 and 3, determines the Projection of the Ovolo under the Corona, whose Projection is determined by the 3d Part of K L, and its Fillet by the next half Part.

THE Projection of the Tenia O P is equal to 4 Parts of K 1, and which being divided into 5 equal Parts, give ¾ of the first 1 to the Projection of the middle Fascia, and the first 2 to the upper Fascia. The Breadth of a Super-Modillion is 10 Minutes, and the Interval between every two is 25 Minutes, and which being in every respect equal to the Modillions of the *Corinthian* Order; therefore when this Entablature is used, the Intercolumniations must be the same as those of the *Corinthian* Order, of which *Fig.* I. II. and IV. *Plate* XLIII. are Examples, and as the first and last of these Examples are arched Doors, I must therefore proceed to explain the Impost and circular Architrave, *Fig.* V. which is used therein.

To divide the Composite Impost and Architrave.

DIVIDE *a h* the Height into 3 Parts, the lower 1 is the Height of the Neck, or Freeze of the Impost. Divide the middle 1 into 3 equal Parts, and the lower 1 into 3, give the lower 2 to the Cavetto, and the upper 1 to its Fillet; divide the upper 1 into 3, and giving the upper 1 to the Fillet, the two lower Parts, together with the middle Part, is the Height of the Cyma Recta. Bisect *a h* in *i*; divide *a i* into 3 Parts, give the lower two Parts to the Cyma Reversa, and the upper one to the Regula. The Astragal and its Fillet is equal to half *m h* the Neck of the Impost.

The Projections of these Members are thus found.

DRAW *b e* for the Upright of the Pilaster; divide *d e*, the Breadth of the Pilaster, into 3 equal Parts; make *e g* equal to one Part, and *g f* equal to ⅓ of *e g*; make *b c* equal to *e f*; divide *e g* into 3 Parts, and the first 1 Part into 3 equal Parts; then the first 1 Part determines the Bottom of the Cavetto at *z*, the 2d Part the Fillet of the Astragal at *c*, and the third the Astragal and Fillet *y*; divide the last 3d Part of *e g* into 3 Parts, the first 2 Parts determines the Projection of the Fillet at *x*, and *e g* of the Fascia at *w*.

To divide the Architrave.

DIVIDE *d e*, equal to *a b* the Breadth of the Architrave, into 3 equal Parts; divide the first 1 into 3 equal Parts, the outer one is the Breadth of the Regula, the middle 1 of the Ovolo, with its Fillet, which is a fifth Part thereof, and the third 1 is the Breadth of the Cavetto, with its Bead, which is ⅓ Part thereof; the middle 3d Part of *d e* is the Breadth of *r p* the great Fascia, and the next Part of the small Fascia, and Cyma Reversa, which is ⅟₇ thereof.

LECTURE X.

Queries on the five Orders of ANDREA PALLADIO, *recommended to the Consideration of his Advocates.*

I, *Of the* Tuscan *Order. Plate* XX.

Quere, 1. CAN the Cincture, which is absolutely a Part of the *Tuscan* Shaft, be justly considered as a Part of the Base?

2. 2. Are the Parts in the Heights of the Members of *Palladio's Tuscan* Base, *Fig.* II. similar to the Number of Diameters contained in the Height of the Column?

2. 3. Are not the Parts in the Heights of the *Tuscan* Base, *Fig.* III. similar to the Number of Diameters, in the Height of its Column?

$\mathcal{Q}$. 4. Is not the Neck of this *Tuscan* Capital too low, and the Projection of its Ovolo and Abacus too little ?

$\mathcal{Q}$. 5. Is not his Abacus, and Ovolo under it, too massive for the Fillet ?

$\mathcal{Q}$. 6. If, in the Execution of the *Dorick* Order, the Triglyphs and Drops are left out, as often is done, how are the *Tuscan* and *Dorick* Architraves to be known from one another, since that, in both these Orders, he has divided each Architrave into two Fascias ?

$\mathcal{Q}$. 7. Is not the Height of his *Tuscan* Freeze, which he has made equal to $\frac{1}{4}$ of the Entablature, too little ; for a great Part of its Height being eclipsed, by the Projection of the Tenia, the Remains has more the Look of a Fascia than of a Freeze ?

$\mathcal{Q}$. 8. Should any compound Members, as the Cyma Recta of the Cornice, be used in this Order, since that its native Simplicity (which consists in the plainness of its single Moldings) is thereby destroyed ?

$\mathcal{Q}$. 9. Which is most agreeable to the Character of the Order, *viz.* To finish the Entablature with the Cyma Recta and Regula, as *Fig.* II. or with the plain and bold Ovolo, as in *Fig.* III ?

II. *On the* Dorick *Order.*   Plate XXIV.

$\mathcal{Q}$. 10. Is not the *Attick* Base, which he has given to this Order, much too extravagant, and more especially as that anciently this Order was made without any Base ? Is not the modest Addition of an Astragal on the Torus, as in *Fig.* IV. sufficient to distinguish it from the *Tuscan* ?

$\mathcal{Q}$. 11. Are the Annulets proportionate or disproportionate to the Ovolo and Abacus ? Have they so noble an Aspect as the Astragal under the Ovolo in the Capital, *Fig.* II ?

$\mathcal{Q}$. 12. Can the Annulets be seen distinctly, at so great a Distance, as the aforesaid Astragal ?

$\mathcal{Q}$. 13. Is it good Architecture, to make the same Bed-Molding in the *Dorick* Entablature, as in the *Tuscan* ?

$\mathcal{Q}$. 14. Is a dripping or oblique Plancere, as A, the most agreeable, or the most disagreeable of all others ?

III. *Of the* Ionick *Order.*   Plate XXVIII.

$\mathcal{Q}$. 15. Is not the Plinth of his Pedestal, *Fig.* III. much too low ?

$\mathcal{Q}$. 16. Should the *Ionick* Architrave be divided into the same Number of Fascias as the *Corinthian* Architrave ?

$\mathcal{Q}$. 17. Is it good Architecture, to make the same Bed-Molding in the *Ionick* Entablature, as in the *Tuscan* and *Dorick* ?

$\mathcal{Q}$. 18. To which of the Orders do Dentules properly belong ?

$\mathcal{Q}$. 19. Should the *Dorick* and *Ionick* Cornices be alike finished with a Cyma Recta and Reversa, as in *Plates* XXIV. and XXIX. ?

IV. *Of the* Corinthian *Order.*   Plate XXXII.

$\mathcal{Q}$. 20. Is not the Plinth to his Pedestal much too low for the Stateliness of the Order ?

$\mathcal{Q}$. 21. Is it good Architecture to make the Shaft of the *Corinthian* Column, *Fig.* 1. 20 Minutes shorter than the Shaft of the *Ionick* Column, *Fig.* I. *Plate* XXVIII. ?

V. *Of the* Composite *Order.*   Plate XXXIX.

$\mathcal{Q}$. 22. Is not the Plinth to his Pedestal much too low for the Stature of the Order ?

$\mathcal{Q}$. 23. As the *Corinthian* Order, which is more delicate than the *Composite* Order, has its Shaft made 20 Minutes shorter than the Shaft of the *Ionick*, why doth he make the Shaft of the *Composite* Order, whose Capital and Entablature are more massive than the *Corinthian*, 30 Minutes higher than the Shaft of the *Ionick* ?

Q. 24. Has the double Aftragal *d*, in *Fig*. I. *Plate* XLI. any Similarity or Proportion to the other Members of the Bafe ?

Q. 25. Is it good Architecture to proportion the Architrave and Freeze of this Order the fame (½ a Minute only excepted) as the *Tufcan* ?

Q. 26. Can any Perfon believe, that the Fillet on the Freeze, and its Aftragal, fhould be made equal ?

Q. 27. Are not the Greatnefs of the Members in the whole Entablature more proportionate to a *Tufcan* Column of feven Diameters in Height, than to a flender Column of ten Diameters, which he has affigned ?

To thefe I could add much more ; but let thefe fuffice to fhew, that this great Mafter is no more free from Miftakes than another, although fo very much applauded by many, who, for want of knowing better, have believed him immutable.

LECTURE XI.
Of the Grotefque *Order, Fig.* I. *Plate* XLVII.

THIS Order is a degree below the *Tufcan :* It confifts chiefly of Square Members, and is to be ufed in Grottos, &c.

To proportion the Parts of this Order

DIVIDE *a l*, equal to the given Height, into 3 equal Parts, and the lower 1 Part into 7 Parts, give two Parts and ¼ to the Subplinth ; divide the upper 1 Part of *a l* into 7 equal Parts, and give the upper 1 to the Height of the Ovolo ; divide *b k* into 5 Parts, the lower 4 Parts is the Height of the Column ; and which being divided into 7 Parts, is the Diameter of the Column ; divide *b e*, the upper 1 Part of *b k*, into 3 Parts, the upper 1 is the Height of the Corona and Fillet, which is ¼ of the whole; divide *f g* into 7 Parts, give 3 to the Architrave and 4 to the Freeze ; make *g h* the Capital equal to ⅝ the Diameter, as alfo the Height of the Bafe ; make the Height of the Cincture on the Bafe, and the Fillet under the Capital, each equal to ¼ of the Height of the Bafe.

To rufticate the Shaft.

DIVIDE its Height into 7 equal Parts, and make each Ruftick and each Interval equal to one Part. The Projection of the Bafe is 40 Minutes, and of the Subbafe 45 Minutes, from the central Line of the Column. The Projection of the Cincture, from the Upright of the Column, is equal to its own Height, and the Projection of the Ruflicks is equal to that of the Cincture. The Shaft is diminifhed ⅛ of its Diameter at the Bafe, and its Capital projects, before the Upright of the Shaft, ⅛ of its Diameter at the Capital. The Projection of the Ovolo, from the central Line *c m*, is 1 Diameter 37 Minutes and ⅓.

LECTURE XII.
Of the Attick *Ord.r, Fig* VIII. *Plate* XLV.

THIS Order is never ufed, but when an *Attick* Story is placed over the Cornice of fome one of the preceding Orders, and is thus proportioned.

DIVIDE D G the Height into 9 equal Parts, give the upper 1 Part to the Height of the Cornice.

To divide the Members of the Cornice, Fig. II.

DIVIDE the Height into 10 equal Parts, give the firft 3 Parts to *k m* the Height of the Denticule, the next 2 to the Height of the Cavetto *x*, the next 3 to the Height of the Corona *w*, and the upper 2 to *v*, the Cyma Reverfa, with its Fillet *t*.

NOTE, *In the Plate the Cyma Reverfa is, by Miftake, made a Cyma Recta, which the Reader is defired to correct.*

The Height of the Denticule, divided into 6 Parts, the Depth of the Dentules muft be made 5 of thofe Parts, their Breadths 3 Parts, and the Intervals each 1 Part

2   Part

Part and ½. The Projection of the Cornice is equal to its Height. The Height of the Plinth is 12 Parts and ½, as alfo is the Breadth of the Pilafter, of thofe 10 Parts into which the Height of the Cornice is divided, and the fmall Torus and Fillet on the Plinth is 2 Parts and ¼.

If 'tis required to place Balls on the Necks over the Pilafters of this Order, the Height of the Neck muft be equal to the Height of the Cornice; which being divided into 5 Parts, give 2 to the Plinth, ¼ the next 1 to its Fillet, and ½ of the upper 1 fo the upper Fillet. The Diameter of the Ball is equal to the Diameter of the Pilafter, and the Diftances of the Pilafters are always the fame, as of the Columns over which they ftand.

LECTURE XIII. *Fig* II. *Plate* X.
Of wreathed Columns.

AS at fome Times, the Shafts of the *Ionick* and *Corinthian* Columns have been wreathed or twifted, it is therefore neceffary to fhew,
How to defcribe a wreathed or twifted Column.

LET *a b c r* be a given Shaft, 1ft, Bifect *a b* in G, and draw the Line G *e*, make *r p* equal to *r c*, and draw *w p* parallel to *c r*. Draw the Diagonal Lines *c p*, and *d r*, and make the Triangle *d z c* equal to the Triangle *p g r*, on the Points *z* and *g*; with the Radius *g r*, defcribe the Arches *p r*, and *d c;* 2dly, Make *p o* equal to *p w*, and draw *e o* parallel to *c r*, alfo draw the Diagonals *e p*, and *o w*. Make the Triangle *o p g* equal to the Triangle *e b w*, on the Points *b* and *g*, with the Radius *b d*, defcribe the Arches *d c*, and *p o*. 3dly, Make *o n* equal to *o v*, draw the Diagonals *s o*, and *e n*, make the Triangle *s f e* equal to the Triangle *n i o*, and on the Points *f* and *i*, with the Radius *i o*, defcribe the Arches *s e*, and *n o;* 4thly, Make *n l* equal to *n t*, &c. and fo proceed to repeat thefe Operations, until the whole be completed, as required.

LECTURE XIV. *Plate* XI.
Of the Manner of dividing the Flutes and Fillets, on the Surfaces of real Pilaf-ters, and Columns.

PILASTERS are fluted in two different Manners, *viz.* either with Fillets only, as *Fig.* N. or with Fillets and Beads at their Angles, as in *Fig.* M.

THE Number of Flutes in the Front of a Pilafter fhould be feven precifely, al-though fome make lefs, and others more, but thofe are never done by an Artift or Workman.

THE Breadth of a Flute is to the Breadth of a Fillet, as 3 is to 1. In *Fig.* N. there are 8 Fillets, and 7 Flutes, which are thus found, *viz.* divide the given Breadth of your Pilafter into 29 equal Parts, give 1 to each Fillet, and 3 to each Flute.

In the other Example, *Fig.* M divide the given Breadth into 31 equal Parts, give 1 to each Bead, and the other 29 to the 8 Fillets and 7 Flutes, as in *Fig.* N.
To readily divide the Flutes and Fillets of a Pilafter.

DRAW a Line at pleafure, as *a b*, *Fig.* N, and therein fet off 29 any equal Parts from *a* to *b*. Make the equilateral Triangle *a z b*, and from the 29 Divi-fions draw Lines to the Point *z:* This being done, fet the given Diameter of your Pilafter from *z* to *d*, and to *c*, and draw the Line *c d*, which will be divided at the Points *e f g h i*, &c. into its Flutes and Fillets, as required. For as *c d* is parallel to *a b*, therefore the Triangle *c d z* is fimilar to the Triangle *z a b*, and confequently the Line *c d* is divided in the fame Proportion as the Line *a b*.

In the fame Manner a Pilafter with Beads and Fillets is readily divided by an equilateral Triangle of 31 Parts, as *d a b*, *Fig.* M.
To divide at once the juft Breadths of Flutes and Fillets, on the Surface of a real Column.

LET *Fig.* F. *Plate* XI. be the Plan of the Bafe, and *Fig.* E. of the Top of a given Column, to be fluted with Fillets.

Operation.

Operation. Draw a right Line, as *p q*, *Fig.* I. at pleasure, and having two Pair of Compasses, open one Pair to any small Distance, suppose *q r*, and the other Pair to one third Part thereof; now these two Openings of the Compasses are to one another, as the Breadth of a Fillet is to the Breadth of a Flute, therefore from *p* towards *q*, set off the two Openings, each 24 Times reciprocally, that is interchangeably, as first *p r*, then *r s*, then *s t*, equal to *p r*, *&c.* but you must observe that the two Openings aforesaid are such, that when you have set each 24 Times from *p* to *q*, that the Length from *p* to *q* be less than the Girt or Circumference of your Column that is to be fluted, otherwise your Labour will be in vain. From the several Divisions so set off, on the Line *p q*, draw right Lines perpendicular to *p q*, of Length at pleasure, and then you may proceed to the finding of the true Breadths of your Flutes and Fillets as following.

1st, Strike a perpendicular Chalk Line from the Astragal to the Cincture on the Surface of the Column, and being provided with a narrow streight-edged Piece of Parchment, *&c.* girt about the Column at its Base, and cut the Parchment exactly to its Girt. This being done, apply one End of the Parchment to one Side of *Fig.* I. suppose at *x*, and its other End unto the other outer Line, as at *a*; then will *x a*, the streight Edge of the Parchment, be divided by the aforesaid perpendicular Lines at the Points *b c d e f g h i k l m*, *&c.* which are the true Breadths of the several Flutes and Fillets for your Column, and which being marked on the Edge of the Parchment with a Black-lead Pencil, apply the said Parchment about the Base of your Column, laying one End unto the chalk Line aforesaid, as at B, and prick off the Breadth of every Flute, as at *a b, c d, e f, g h, i k, l m, &c.*

2dly, Take the Girt of the Column under its Astragal, and apply it to *Fig.* I. as from *n* to 1, whereon mark the Breadths of every Flute as in the former, and applying one End of it unto the aforesaid perpendicular Line, as at A; prick off the Breadth of each Flute, as at the Points 1 2, 3 4, 5 6, 7 8, 9 10, 11 12, *&c.* and then chalk Lines being struck on the Surface of the Column, from the Divisions under the Astragal to those at the Base, the whole Surface of the Column will be set out ready for working, as required.

Note, To know when a Flute is worked truly Semicircular in a Pilaster, apply a Square within it, and if the angular Point and Sides of the Square touch the Surface, and Extremes of the Flute, at the same Time, as at *p q r*, *Fig.* G. *Plate* XI. the Work is true, otherwise 'tis false. And Flutes, that are less than Semicircles, are proved by the very same Method, only instead of applying a Square, you must apply a Bevel in the Manner following.

As for Example, Let a b c, *Fig.* H. *Plate* XI. *be the Plan of a Flute whose Depth is less than the Radius of the Circle, of which the Flute is a Segment.*

Operation. Assume a Point in any Part of the Flute, as at *b*, and draw the Lines *b c d*, and *b a f.* Nail together two streight Pieces of Lath, *&c.* so as to make an Angle equal to the Angle *f b d*, and to prevent its opening or shutting, to a greater or lesser Angle, tack on a Brace, as the Piece *g e*, then will your Bevel be prepared for Use, as the Square aforesaid.

Note, By this Method, the Height and Extent of any Scheme or rather circular Arch being given, may be described without any Recourse being had to the Center, for if the Sides of the Bevel be kept to *a* and *c*, the Extent of the Flute, the angular Point *b*, by P ᴿ ᴼ ᴮ. XVI. LECT. VI. PART II. will always fall on some Part or other of the Arch *a b c*; and consequently if the Point *b* be applied to the Point *a*, and then moved on towards *b*, thence to *c*, (the Sides of the Bevel being always kept sliding close to the Points *a* and *c*,) it will describe the Arch *a b c*, which is a Segment of a Circle, and without any Regard being had to its Center.

Fig. II. and III. *Plate* XI. Shews the Manner of making an Instrument on Pasteboard, or Ivory, for the ready setting off the Breadths of Flutes of Columns on a Drawing, without the Trouble of describing and dividing of a Semicircle, as before taught, which is an Invention of Mr. *Edward Stephens*, Cabinet-maker, and thus made.

Operation. First, Describe a Semi-circle, as *c g*, of a larger Size than the Diameter of any Column that you may defign to draw; divide its Circumference into its proper Flutes and Fillets, as before taught, and then drawing right Lines from them to the Center *a*, the Inftrument is completed.

Secondly, Suppofe you have the Drawing of a Column to be fluted, whofe Semi-diameter is equal to P *a*. On the Center *a c* defcribe the fmall Semi-circle *d* 1, 2, 3, 4, 5, &c. which will cut the central Lines of the Inftrument, in the Points 1 2 3 4 5 6, &c. from which draw right Lines with Black-lead, at right Angles to *c g*, and they will divide *d a* into unequal Parts, which are the true Appearances of the Breadths of the feveral Flutes required. And the Edge *d a*, being applied to the Diameter of the Column in your Drawing, prick off the feveral Divifions, which will be the Breadths of your Flutes and Fillets, as required.

Fig. III. is another Inftrument of the fame Kind, made for fetting off the Flutings of *Dorick* Columns, according to the Manner of the Ancients.

LECTURE XV.

Of the Manner of placing Columns againft Walls, and over one another, as the Dorick *on the* Tufcan, *the* Ionick *on the* Dorick, &c.

COLUMNS are placed either againft Walls, with a fourth Part of their Diameters inferted, as *Fig.* III. and IV. *Plate* XXX. when three Quarters of the Body of the Shaft project before the Upright of the Walls; or entirely clear from the Wall, as *Fig.* III. *Plate* XLIII. in which laft Cafe, a Pilafter is always inferted in the Wall, as C and E, before the Columns D E; and the Intercolumniation or Diftance of the Column from the Pilafter, is always the fame as when Columns are placed in Pairs. The Quantity of Infertion of Pilafters muft be fuch as will be agreeable to the Parts of their Capitals. In the *Tufcan* and *Dorick* Orders the Pilafter may project before the Wall, a half, a third, a fourth, a fifth, a fixth, or feventh Part of its Diameter: but in the *Ionick, Corinthian,* and *Compofite* Orders, they fhould be half a Diameter precifely, otherwife the Ornaments of their Capitals will be unevenly divided, and have a very bad Appearance.

When Columns are to be placed over one another, as was the Cuftom of the Ancients, who placed an Order in every Story, we are to obferve, firft, That the Diameter of the Column in the fecond Story be at its Bafe, equal to the Diameter of the lower Column at its Aftragal and that they ftand exactly perpendicular over each other, that the upper Solid may ftand on the lower. Secondly, To place the upper Columns on a continued Pedeftal, whofe Height fhall be fo agreeable to the Windows, as to make the Cornice of the Pedeftal do the Office of Stools to the Windows; for when Columns have their Bafes placed below the Bottoms of Windows, fo that their Stools being continued ftop againft the Shafts of the Columns, as thofe do at the Royal *Banqueting-Houfe* at *Whitehall,* they have a very ill Effect. The Intercolumniation of Orders placed over one another muft be governed by the Triglyphs and Modillions, and therefore to place the *Dorick* over the *Tufcan,* regard muft be had to the Number of Triglyphs in the upper Order, to which the *Tufcan* muft be conformable, as indeed muft the *Ionick* to the *Dorick* in fome Cafes, when the Diftances of its Modillions muft be made a little more or lefs to bring them into Order; and when the *Corinthian* is placed over the *Ionick,* the Modillions of the *Ionick* muft be conformable to thofe of the *Corinthian.*

When an open Gallery is made over an Arcade, the Openings between the Columns may be quite down to the Bottom of the Pedeftal in the upper Order, as in *Fig.* I. *Plate* XLIV. but at fuch Times 'tis beft to place a Baluftrade between the Pedeftals, which will be a Security and an Ornament alfo.

T

LECTURE

LECTURE XVI.

Of the various Kinds of Ornaments for the Enrichment of the several Members of which the Five Orders of Columns are composed.

THE Ornaments that are, and may be invented for the Enrichments of Moldings, are endless; but those that are now in the greatest Esteem, I have introduced in the several Members of the last four Orders; not that every Order must be so fully enriched as I have expressed, but such Parts of them only, as shall be judged sufficient; and that the Learner should not be at a loss to know what Ornaments are proper for such Members, as he may be inclined to enrich, I therefore have been so profuse, as to give every Member an agreeable Enrichment. And as oftentimes 'tis required to enrich Pannels, Picture-frames, and other Parts of Buildings, I have therefore, in *Plates* XVI. XVII. and XVIII. given a great Variety of Ornaments at large, together with the Sections of divers curious Moldings for such Purposes, of which take the following Account:

I. THE *Figures* E F I are Ornaments called *Vitruvian Scrolls*, I suppose from *Vitruvius*, who might be the Inventor of them. The Distances of the Spirals is at pleasure; but their Height being divided into two Parts, their Distance is generally equal to 3 of those Parts, and their Spirals are described by the Methods before taught.

II. THE *Figures* G H K L M are *Interlacings*, or *Guilochis* of various Kinds, of which G H K and L are composed of the Arches of Circles, as is evident by Inspection, and that of *Fig.* M, of parallel right Lines, which form geometrical Squares of any Magnitude connected together, by Quadrants on the Outsides. The fret Ornament of the Ancients is by some called *Guilochi*, of which in *Plate* XVIII. I have given Examples of 15 Kinds, for the Practice of the young Student, and whose Number of Parts into which the Breadth of each is to be divided are signified by Divisions, and Numerical Figures against each.

III. THE Eggs and Darts, commonly called Eggs and Anchors, as *Fig.* I. *Plate* XVI. are thus described. Divide the Height 7 P into 9 equal Parts, at the Points 1 2 3 4 5 6 7 8 9. First, Draw *a* C and *k* B, parallel to 7 P, each at the Distance of 7 Parts; and divide *a* 7 and 7 *k*, each into 7 Parts. Through the Point *f* draw *e m*, parallel to C B; make *f e* and *f m*, each equal to 4 Parts, and draw the Lines *e* 3 and *m b*. Through the Point 3, on the central Line 7 P, draw the Lines *e* 3 *y*, and *m* 3 *v*. On the Point *f*, with the Radius *f* 12, describe the Semi-circle *o* 12 *p*. On the Points *e* and *m*, with the Radius *m o*, describe the Arches *o v* and *p y*; and on the Point 3 with the Radius 3 *y*, describe the Arch *v* 1 *y*, which will complete the Outline of the Egg. *Secondly*, Draw the Line *d l*, through the Point 7, on the Line 9 P, and divide the Distance between the Points 3 and 4, on the Line 9 P, into 2 equal Parts, and draw the Lines *d z* and *l w*. On the Points *d* and *l*, with the Radius *d h*, describe the Arches *h z* and *b w*; and on the middle Point, between 3 and 4, on the Line 9 P, describe the Arch *w z*. *Thirdly*, Draw *c g* through the Point 8; make *c* 8 and 8 *g* each equal to 3 Parts. From the Points *c* and *g* draw the Lines *g x* and *c* A, through the middle Point between the Points 4 and 5, on the Line 9 P. On the Points *c* and *g*, with the Radius *c i*, describe the Arches *i* A and 1 *x*; also on the middle Point between 4 and 5 aforesaid, describe the Arch *x* P A. *Fourthly*, Through the Point 2 on the Line 9 P, draw the Line 2 *r s*; as also draw the Lines *i* B, stopping at *r*; also 12 B, and *q r*; then one half Part of a Dart will be completed; and in the same Manner complete the other Half, and all others. Now from hence 'tis plain, that to set out the Distances of Eggs and Darts, you must first divide the Height of the Ovolo into 9 equal Parts. *Secondly*, Take 7 of those Parts, and set that Distance along your Molding, and then Lines being drawn from those Points, square to the Top and Bottom of the

Ovolo,

Ovolo, every other Line will be the central Line of an Egg, and the others of the Darts, which divide as aforesaid. Eggs in Ovolos are oftentimes enriched with Leaves, Husks, &c. instead of Darts, as between N O P, *Plate* XVI.

IV. *The several Moldings for Pannels and Picture Frames*, Plate XVII. *are thus divided.*

I. Of Moldings for Pannels, *Fig.* I. divide the Height into 3 Parts; give two Thirds of the upper 1 to A the Regula; the remaining 3d Part, and the middle great Part to B the Cyma Reversa; half the lower Part to C the Astragal; and the remaining half Part, divided into 3 Parts, give 2 to E the Cavetto, and 1 to D its Fillet.

THE Distances of the central Lines *a k, c d, e f*, &c. of the Leaves, &c. is equal to the Height of the Cyma B. *Secondly, Fig.* II. Divide the Height into 4 Parts, give the upper 1 to A the Regula; the next 2 to B the Cyma Recta; and the lower 1 divided into 3 Parts, give the upper 1 to C the Fillet, and the lower 2 to D the Cavetto. Divide *b d* into 5 Parts, and set off the central Lines of the Leaves, as *a c*, &c. each at the Distance of 7 Parts. *Thirdly, Fig.* IV. Divide the Height into 5 Parts; give the upper 1 to A the Regula, two Thirds of the next 1 to B the Cavetto; the next 2 Parts, with the Remains of the 4th Part, to C the Cyma Reversa, and the lower Part divided into 3 Parts, give 1 to the Fillet E, and 2 to the Astragal D. The Distance of the central Lines of the Leaves, &c. *b d, a e, c f*, &c. is equal to the Height of the Cyma Reversa. *Fourthly, Fig.* V. Divide the Height into 5 Parts, give the upper 1 to the Regula, the next 1 to the Ovolo, 1 Third of the next to its Fillet, the remaining 2 Thirds, and the next 1 to the Cavetto; and lastly, the lower 1 divided into 3, give the upper 2 to the Astragal, and the lower 1 to the Fillet. Divide *a d* into 9 Parts, and make the Distance of *a b, b c*, &c. equal to 7 of those Parts, as aforesaid. *Fifthly, Fig.* VI. Divide the Height into 3 equal Parts, and the upper 1 into 3; give the upper 2 Parts to the Regula A, and the Remainder, with the middle great Part, to the Ovolo B. The lower great Part divided into 2 Parts, give the upper 1 Part to the Astragal C, and the lower Part being divided into 4 Parts, give the lower 3 Parts to the Cavetto D, and the other 1 Part to its Fillet. The Distances of the central Lines of the Eggs, &c. are to be found as aforesaid.

II. *Of Moldings for Picture Frames.*

FIRST, *Fig.* III. Divide the Height into 4 Parts; the upper 1 divide into 3, give 1 to the Regula A, and 2 to the Cyma Reversa B. Divide the upper Half of the next Part into 2 equal Parts; give the lower Part to the Cavetto E, and the upper Part being divided into 3 Parts, give the upper 2 to the Astragal C, and the lower 1 to the Fillet D. Divide the lower 4th Part into 3 equal Parts, and the lower 1 Part into 3 Parts; give the lower 2 Parts to the Cavetto K, and the upper 1 to the Fillet I. Divide the upper 3d Part into 2 Parts; give the upper 1 to the Fillet G, and the Remains to the Astragal H. Divide *b d* into 5 Parts, and make the Distance of the central Lines of the Leaves, as *a c*, &c. equal to 6 of those Parts, the central Line of the Roses to the *Vitruvian* Scroll in the Freeze F, is directly in the Midst of the Freeze, and the Distance of the Centers of each Rose, as *e f*, is equal to the Height of the Freeze.

SECONDLY, *Fig.* VII. Divide the Height into 3 equal Parts, and each Part into 4 equal Parts; give the upper 1 Part to the Regula A, the next 2 Parts to the Ovolo B, and the next 1 to the Fillet C and Cavetto D. Give the middle great Part, and 1 Fourth of the lower great Part, to E the Freeze. Give the next fourth Part of the lower great Part to the Cavetto F, and Fillet G; and then the Remains *x* being divided into 4 Parts, on *z* describe the Quadrant *y x*, and then making *e b* equal to *y z*, describe the Curves *y a*, and *a b*, which with the Quadrant *y x*, forms that Molding which Workmen call the *Welsh Ogee*. The Manner of describing the *Guilochi* in the Freeze is plain to Inspection, as also are the Distances of the Eggs, in B the Ovolo, and Leaves in H the *Welsh Ogee*.

T 2   THIRDLY,

THIRDLY, *Fig.* VIII. Divide the Height into 3 Parts, and each Part into 4 Parts, as before; give the upper 1 Part to the Regula A, the next 2d Part and 1 Third of the third Part to the Ovolo B, the second third Part to the Fillet C, and the Remains of the upper 1 great Part, to the Cavetto D. The middle great Part is the Height of the Freeze E. The lower great Part being divided into 4 equal Parts, give the upper 1 to the Cavetto F, and Fillet G; the next 1 to the Aftragal H. The remaining 2 Parts, divided into 8 Parts, give 1 to the Fillet I, 5 to the Cyma Recta K, and the lower 2 to the Fillet. To these Examples many more might be added; but as I must not fwell the Work to a much greater Bulk and Price than is proposed; and as he that is Master of thefe, will be able to invent others without End, I fhall therefore proceed to

LECTURE XVII.

Of the Manner of ruſticating the Shaſts of Columns and Pilaſters, Plate XLV.

THE Orders ufually rufticated are the *Tuſcan, Dorick,* and *Ionick.*

To ruſticate the Tuſcan *Column, Fig.* A *and* B.

DIVIDE the Height of the Column into 7 equal Parts, and give 1 Part to each Ruſtick, whofe Projections may be made equal to the Projection of the Cincture, as in *Fig.* A, or equal to the Projection of the Plinth, as in *Fig.* B, and which in both Cafes may be made diminifhing with the Column, or Upright, as expreffed by the dotted Lines; but this laft has a very heavy Appearance, and feems contrary to Reafon, by over-charging the fmalleft Part of the Shaft with the greateft Rufticks.

To ruſticate the Dorick *Column, Fig.* C *and* D.

DIVIDE the Height of the Column into 8 equal Parts; give 2 to each Ruſtick, as *b b* and *d d,* and the fame to the Intervals *c c.* The Projections of thefe Rufticks are determined as thofe of the *Tuſcan.*

To ruſticate the Ionick *Column, Fig.* E *and* F.

DIVIDE the Height into 9 equal Parts, give 1 to each Ruſtick, and to each Interval, and determine their Projectures, as in the *Tuſcan* and *Dorick.*

To ruſticate Tuſcan *Pilaſters, Fig.* G *and* H.

PILASTERS are rufticated in two different Manners, *viz.* either champhered, as *Fig.* G, or rabbeted as *Fig.* H.

To ruſticate a Tuſcan *Pilaſter, with champhered Ruſticks, as Fig.* G.

DIVIDE the Height of the Column into 7 equal Parts, and any one of the Parts, as *h y,* into 8 equal Parts, give 6 Parts to the Height of the Face of each Ruſtick, and 1 to each of its Champhers. The Projection *x y* of the Rufticks, before the Upright of the Pilaſter, is equal to 1 Part.

To ruſticate a Tuſcan *Pilaſter, with Rabbet Ruſticks, as Fig.* H.

DIVIDE the Height into 7 equal Parts, as before, and one Part into 12 Parts, as at *a c.* Make the Height of each Rabbet equal to two Parts, and then the Height of the Face of each Ruſtick will be 10 Parts; or if every two Parts be confidered as 1 Part, then each Rabbet will be 1, and each Ruſtick will be 5, as expreffed by *Figures* on the right-hand Side. The Projection of the Rufticks, before the Upright of the Pilaſter, may be made equal to the Projection of the Cincture, or to the Height of a Rabbet; but this laft is rather too great, for then the Rufticks will have a very heavy Appearance.

LECTURE XVIII.

Of Block Cornices and ruſtick Quoins, Fig. II. III. IV. V. VI. *and* VII. **Plate XLVII.**

DIVIDE *a z, Fig.* II. the given Height into 9 equal Parts, and give the loweft 1 to the Height of the Plinth. Divide the upper 8 Parts into 14 Parts; give the upper 2 to the Height of the Cornice, and the lower 12 to the 12 Rufticks. Divide the Height of each Ruſtick into 4 Parts, give 3 to the

5

Face

Face of each Ruſtick, and ½ of 1 Part to each Champher. Divide *b x*, the Height of the Cornice, into 4 equal Parts, and give to each Member, as each Part doth expreſs. The Projection of the Cornice is equal to 2 Parts and ⅔ of the Cornice's Height. The Length of the ſtretching Ruſticks are equal to 3 Parts, and of the heading Ruſticks to 2 Parts of the Cornice's Height, ſet back from the Upright of the Quoin, *Fig.* III. IV. V. VI. and are five different Examples, whoſe Parts are proportioned in the ſame Manner as their ſeveral Diviſions and Numbers expreſs.

LECTURE XIX. *Fig.* I. II. III. IV. V. VI. *Plate* XLVI.

Of the Manner of proportioning the principal Parts of Doors, Windows, and Niches.

TO proportion Doors to any given Height, *Fig.* IV. V. and VI.
 Firſt, Divide the given Height in *Fig.* IV. and VI. into 5 equal Parts, the upper 1 Part is the Height of the Architrave, Freeze, and Cornice, and the lower 4 of the Door. Make *g h*, in *Fig.* IV. and *i k*, in *Fig.* VI. each equal to 2 Parts for the Breadth of the Openings, and ⅛ Part thereof is the Breadth of the Architraves *x g*, and *k x*.

Secondly, Fig. V. Divide the Height into 4 equal Parts, and the upper 1 Part into 4 Parts, then the upper 3 Parts is the Height of the Architrave, Freeze, and Cornice, and the Remainder is the Height of the Door, whoſe Breadth is equal to 1 great Part and a Half, and its Architrave to ⅙ of the Breadth. The Breadth of the open Pilaſters *l x*, againſt which Truſſes are fixed as at *k*, to ſupport the Cornice, is equal to ⅔ of the Breadth of the Architrave. Divide the lower 4th Part, of the upper great Part, into 2 equal Parts, and that gives the Depth from the Cornice, at which the Foot of the Truſs is to be placed. The proper Truſs for the Support of theſe Kinds of Cornices is exhibited in *Fig.* I. *Plate* XIV. and is thus deſcribed.

To deſcribe a ſpiral Truſs, for the Support of Cornices over Doors, Windows, and Niches.

DIVIDE A B, the given Height, (including the Height of the Architrave, Freeze and Cornice) into 15 equal Parts, give the upper 4 to the Height of the Cornice, and the lower 11 to the Height of the Truſs. Let the Line M z repreſent the Upright of the Face of the open Pilaſter, againſt which the Truſs is fixed. Draw W *e n* parallel to M z, at the Diſtance of two Parts and ⅓; alſo draw B z the Baſe Line at Right Angles to M z. From the Points 3, 4 and 2 in the Line A B, draw the Lines 8 *g*, 4 G and 2 E, parallel to B z, and of length towards the Right Hand at pleaſure: theſe Lines laſt drawn determine the Heights of the greater and leſſer Spirals or Scrolls. Divide *a e*, the under Part of the Cornice, into 8 equal Parts, and *a g* into 7 equal Parts; alſo divide G E into 7 equal Parts, and make G *y* and E 8 equal to 8 of thoſe Parts; this being done, proceed in every reſpect to deſcribe the two Spirals, as you did thoſe in the *Corinthian* Modillion, *Fig.* V. PROB. IX. LECT. VIII. hereof.

Fig. II. Is the Front View of this Truſs, whoſe Breadth H I is equal to B F, *viz.* to 1 Part and ⅛ of the Parts in A B, and which being divided into 8 equal Parts, is deſcribed in every Particular the ſame as *k n*, *m z o p l*, in *Fig.* III. the Face or Front of the *Corinthian* Modillion.

To divide the Heights of the Members in the Cornice.

THE Height being divided before into 4 equal Parts, divide the lower 2 Parts into 4 equal Parts, give the firſt 1 Part to the Height of the Cavetto V, the next 2 Parts to the Fillet T, the Dentule S, and Fillet R, and the 4th, or upper Part, to the Ovolo Q. The 3d great Part is the Height of the Corona P, and the next and laſt Part is the Height of the Fillet O, the Cyma Recta N, and Regula M. The Projection of the Cornice W X is equal to its Height W *e*.

To divide the Dentules.

DIVIDE *x x* the Height of the Denticule into 6 Parts, and make the Length of a Dentule equal to 5 Parts. Make the Breadth of a Dentule and an Interval equal

equal to the Height of a Dentule, which divide into 3 Parts, give 2 to a Dentule and 1 to the Interval.

    II. *To proportion Windows and Niches to any given Height, Fig.* I. II. *and* III. *Plate* XLVI.

    Divide the given Height into 5 equal Parts, the lower 1 Part is the Height of the Pedestal, whose Parts are to be divided according to the Pedestal of any Order required. The remaining 4 Parts being divided into 5 equal Parts, the upper 1 Part is the Height of the Entablature, and their Breadths, if for Windows, into 2 Parts. The Breadths of their Architraves, as *m n, Fig.* III. is equal to ¼ of the Opening, and of their open Pilaster, to ⅔ of the Architrave, as likewise are the Margins *o p* and *q r, Fig.* II. when made into Niches. The proper Entablatures to be placed over Doors, Windows and Niches, are exhibited by *Figures* A B C D E F and G, *Plate* XLVII. But as sometimes the Quoins and Heads of Windows are rusticated, I have therefore in *Plate* XLV. given five Examples thereof, with the Divisions of their Parts, which explains them to the meanest Capacity.

LECTURE XIX.

Of PEDIMENTS.

PEDIMENTS are employed either for Ornament and Use, or for Ornament only. Pediments for Ornament and Use are those which are made on the Outsides of Buildings, and which must be entire, that thereby the Buildings underneath may be wholly protected from the Injuries of Rains. Entire Pediments are made in three different Manners, *viz. 1st,* Straight, as *Fig.* II. *Plate* XLIII. which Workmen call a raking Pediment. *2dly,* Circular, as *Fig.* I. *Plate* XLIII. And, *3dly,* Compounded of three Arches, as *Fig.* II. *Plate* XLIX.

    The Manner of finding the Height of the *Fastigium,* or Pitch of a raking and circular Pediment, being already taught in 1 ROB. I. LECT. V. hereof, I shall therefore proceed to shew

       How to describe a compound Pediment, as Fig. II. *Plate* XLIX.

    A COMPOUND Pediment has the same Pitch as a raking Pediment, therefore to describe a Pediment of this Kind, draw the raking Bounds of a pitched Pediment, as B A and A C, bisect B A in *b,* and A C in *d,* also bisect A *d* in *e,* and thereon erect the Perpendicular *e* F, cutting the central Line A F in F. Bisect B *b* in *a,* and *d* C in *e;* on the Points *a* and *e* erect the Perpendiculars *a* E and *e* D, which will cut the Perpendiculars C D and B E in the Points E and D. On the Points E D and F, with the Radius E B, describe the Arches B *b, b* A *d,* and *d* C, and concentrick thereto, at the respective Heights of the several Members of the Pediment, describe the whole as required.

    PEDIMENTS for Ornament are those which are imperfect, and are vulgarly called *Broken* or *Open Pediments,* as *Fig.* I. II. III. *Plate* XLVIII. and *Fig.* I. and III. *Plate* XLIX. These Sort of Pediments should never be used without Buildings, because being open in the Middle, they let in the Rains on the Cornice, in the same Manner as if no Pediment was there. It is therefore that these Kinds of Pediments must be used within Doors for Ornament only, and whose Opening is generally made for the Reception of a Busto, Shield, Shell, &c. Now seeing that to make an open Pediment without Doors is absurd, to make an entire Pediment within Doors, where no Rains come, must be absurd also.

    IN the *Tuscan* Order, the Length of the raking Cornice, as A G, *Plate* XLVIII. being divided into 5 equal Parts, as at 1, 2, 3, 4; the Length of the Regula 5 G is equal to the 4 lower Parts. The same is also to be observed in a circular open Pediment, as *Fig.* I. *Plate* XLIX. But in a *Dorick* Pediment, the Length of the raking Cornice is to be regulated by the Mutules, for as the raking Mutules, as H I, in the Pediment, must be directly over A B, in the level Cornice, therefore the Distance *f h,* the Projection of the Cornice beyond the Upright of the level Mutule K, being set from 4 to *b,* and the Line *b* 20 being drawn, it

cuts

cuts the raking Line *s a* into 9, making the Length of the raking Cornice required.

THE Length of the raking Cornice of an *Ionick* Pediment is determined by placing a Modillion in Profile against a raking Modillion, as H against G, equal in Projection to *f* 5, the level Modillion in Profile, and making 5, 1; the Projection of the raking Cornice beyond the Upright of 1, 13, the Upright of the raking Modillion in Profile, equal to the Projection of the level Cornice beyond the level Modillion in Profile.

THE laſt raking Modillion in the Pediment is always at pleaſure, according as the Breadth of the Opening of the Pediment is required; and therefore it might have been either that over E or F, inſtead of at G over A.

Note, The ſame is alſo to be underſtood of Pediments of the *Corinthian* and *Compoſite* Orders.

PEDIMENTS are ſometimes finiſhed with Scrolls, as *Fig.* III. *Plate* XLIX. which are thus deſcribed. Let A B C be the Extent and Pitch of a raking Pediment. Biſect B A and A C, in *b* and *g*, find the Centers H D G, in the ſame Manner as you found the Centers E F D, in *Fig.* II. Draw the Lines *b* D, and *g* D, and on the Points H and G deſcribe the ſeveral Members on each Side, as was done in *Fig.* II.

DIVIDE *b* A into 8 equal Parts. From the third Part draw the Line C D, and on the Center D deſcribe the Arch *b c*, and Members concentrick thereto; make *e e* equal to 3 Parts and ⅔ of *b* A. Divide *e e* into 8 equal Parts; and on the 5th Part from *e* deſcribe a Circle, as the Eye of a Volute or Spiral, and therein find the Centers as before taught, on which turn about the two Cymas, and finiſh the Eye with a Roſe, &c. at pleaſure.

Note, Sometimes the Cyma Recta is left out of the Scroll, and the Cyma Reverſa with the Corona only, are turned about to form the Scroll, which has a very good Effect; and then in ſuch a Caſe the Cyma Recta is ſtopt, and returned as in an open Pediment.

LECTURE XXI.

Of truſſed Partitions.

WHEN Partitions have ſolid Bearings throughout their whole Extent, they have no need to be truſſed; but when they can be ſupported but in ſome particular Places, then they require to be truſſed in ſuch a Manner that the whole Weight ſhall reſt perpendicularly upon the Places appointed for their Support, and no where elſe. As Partitions are made of different Heights, to carry one, two or more Floors, as the Kinds of Buildings require, therefore in *Plate* L, I have given ſix Examples, of which *Fig.* II. V. and VI. are of one Story in Height, and *Fig.* III. IV. and VII. of two Stories.

THE firſt Things to be conſidered in Works of this Kind, is the Weight that is to be ſupported; the Goodneſs and Kind of Timber that is to be employed; and proper Scantlings neceſſary for that Purpoſe.

THE Strength of Timber in general is always in proportion to the Quantity of ſolid Matter it contains. The Quantity of ſolid Matter in Timber is always more or leſs, as the Timber is more or leſs heavy; hence it is, that all heavy Woods, as *Oak*, *Box*, *Mahogany*, *Lignum Vitæ*, &c. are ſtronger than *Elder*, *Deal*, *Sycamore*, &c. which are lighter, or (rather) leſs heavy, and indeed, for the ſame Reaſon, Iron is not ſo ſtrong as Steel, which is heavier than Iron; and Steel is not ſo ſtrong as Braſs or Copper, which are both heavier than Steel. To prove this, make two equal Cubes of any two Kinds of Timber, ſuppoſe the one of *Fir*, the other of *Oak*; weigh them ſingly, and Note their reſpective Weights; this done, prepare two Pieces of the ſame Timbers, of equal Lengths, ſuppoſe each 5 Feet in Length, and let each be tried up as nearly ſquare as can be; but to ſuch Scantlings, that the Weight of a Piece of *Oak* may be to the Weight of the Piece of *Fir*, as the Cube of *Oak* is to the Cube of *Fir*; then thoſe two

Pieces

Pieces being laid horizontally hollow with equal Bearings, and being loaded in their Middles with increafed equal Weights, it will be feen, that they will bend or fag equally, which is a Demonftration, that their Strengths are to each other, as the Quantity of folid Matter contained in them.

As the whole Weight on Partitions is fupported by the principal Poft, their Scantlings muft be firft confidered; and which fhould be done in two different Manners, *viz*. Firft, when the Quarters, commonly called *Studs*, are to be filled with Brick Work, and rendered thereon; and laftly, when to be lathed and plaiftered on both Sides.

WHEN the Quarters are to be filled between with Brick Work, the Thicknefs of the principal Pofts fhould be as much lefs than the Breadth of a Brick, as twice the Thicknefs of a Lath; fo that when thofe Pofts are lathed to hold on the rendering, the Laths on both Sides may be flufh with the Surfaces of the Brick Work; and to give thefe Pofts a fufficient Strength, their Breadth muft be increafed at Difcretion; but when the Quarters are to be lathed on both Sides, or when Wainfcotting is to be placed againft the Partitioning, then the Thicknefs of the Pofts may be made greater at pleafure. The ufual Scantlings for principal Pofts of *Fir*, of 8 Feet in Height, is 4 or 5 Inches fquare; of 10 Feet in Height, 5 or 6 Inches fquare; of 12 Feet in Height, 6 or 7 Inches fquare; of 14 Feet in Height, 7 or 8 Inches fquare; of 16 Feet in Height, from 9 to 10 Inches fquare. But thefe laft, in my Opinion, are full large, where no very great Weight is to be fupported. As *Oak* is much ftronger than *Fir*, the Scantling of *Oak-Pofts* need not be fo large as thofe of *Fir*; and therefore the Scantlings affigned by Mr. *Francis Price*, in his Treatife of Carpentry, are abfurd; as being much larger than thofe that he has affigned for *Fir Pofts*. To find the juft Scantling of oaken Pofts, that fhall have the fame Strength of any given *Fir Pofts*, this is the RULE:

As the Weight of a **Cube** of *Fir* is to the Weight of a Cube of *Oak* of the fame Magnitude, fo is the Area of the fquare End of any *Fir Poft*, to the Area of the End of an oaken Poft; and whofe fquare Root is equal to the Side of the oaken Poft required.

THE Diftances of principal Pofts is generally about 10 Feet, and of the Quarters about 14 Inches, but when they are to be lathed on both Sides, the Diftances of the Quarters fhould be fuch as will be agreeable to the Lengths of the Laths, otherwife there will be a very great Wafte in the Laths. The Thicknefs of ground Plates and Raifings are generally from 2 Inches and Half to 4 Inches, and are fcarfed together, as expreffed in *Fig.* I. K L M N O P Q R.

IN the feveral Examples aforefaid the principal Pofts have their Inter-ties and **Braces** framed into them, as expreffed in *Figures* F B G H C D A E, whofe refpective Places the feveral Letters in each refer to.

LECTURE XXII.
Of naked Flooring.

THE principal Things to be obferved in naked Flooring are, firft, the Difpofition of Girders, or Manner of placing them in the moft fecure and advantageous Manner. Secondly, their Scantlings; and laftly, the Manner of truffing them, when their Lengths require it.

THERE are fome Carpenters, who infift that Girders fhould be laid on ftrong Lentils over Windows, and who allege that Girders, being laid on Lentils in Piers, the Piers are endangered at the Decay of thofe Lentils. Others infift, that 'tis beft to lay Girders in Piers, as being the moft folid Bearings, and that if found oaken Lentils are laid under them, they will endure as long as the Brick Work will remain found.

In Buildings, whofe Piers are narrow at the renewing of Lentils, the Piers will be endangered in both thefe Cafes; for Lentils laid over Windows muft be laid into the Piers, on both Sides of a Window, and which, when taken out, will make large Fractures, that will be very little lefs dangerous than the

other,

ether, and therefore I shall submit this Point to the Discretion of the Workmen.

LENTILS laid in Piers between Windows, for the Support of Girders, should have their Lengths equal to the Breadths of the Piers: and those laid in Party-Walls, or Gable Ends of Building, should be equal in Length to the Distance that is contained between every two Girders. The Thickness of Lentils should always be equal unto the Height of 2 or 3 Courses of Bricks, and their Breadth unto a Brick's Length; so that in every of those Particulars, they may be conformable to the Brick Work in which they are placed, and to that which is raised on them. And for the better disposing of the Weight imposed on Girders, Lentils should always be firmly bedded on a sufficient Number of short Pieces of *Oak*, laid across the Walls, vulgarly called Templets, which are of excellent Use.

LET Girders be laid in Piers, or in Lentils over Windows, it will, in both these Cases, be commendable to turn small Arches over their Ends, that in case their Ends are first decayed, they may be renewed at pleasure, without disturbing any Part of the Brick Work; and for their Preservation, anoint their Ends with melted Pitch and Grease, *viz.* of Pitch 4, of Grease 1; and indeed, were Lentils to be covered with Pitch and Grease also, it would contribute very greatly to their Duration.

IT is always to be observed, that the shortest Girders bend down, or sag, as Workmen term it, the least, and therefore 'tis always best to lay Girders over the narrow Parts of Rooms, and whose Ends should always have, each, at least 14 Inches bearing in the Walls, excepting in small Buildings, where the Front, *&c.* Walls are but a Brick and half in Thickness, when to prevent the Ends of the Girders from being seen without-side, their Bearings cannot much exceed 11 Inches.

IT is also to be observed, that Girders be so disposed of, that the Boards of every Floor be parallel throughout the whole Floor; for 'tis as disagreeable to the Eye, to see the Joints of Boards in the same Floor, lie different ways, as 'tis to see Steps out of one Room into another, which should always be avoided.

IN the carrying up the several Walls of Buildings, it should be carefully observed, to lay in Bond Timbers on Templets, as aforesaid, at every 6 or 7 Feet in Height, cogged down, and braced together with diagonal Pieces at every Angle, which will bind the whole together, in the most substantial Manner, and prevent Fractures by unequal Settlement.

THE Distances of Girders should never exceed 12 Feet, and their Scantlings must be proportioned according to their Lengths; as by Experience 'tis known, that a Scantling of 11 Inches, by 8 Inches, is sufficient for a *Fir* Girder of 10 Feet in Length, the Area of whose End is 88 Inches, it is very easy to find the proper Scantling for a Girder of any greater Length, suppose 20 Feet, by this Rule: As 10 Feet, the Length of the first Girder, is to 88; the Area of its End, so is 20 Feet, the Length of the second Girder, to 176, the Area of its End.

Now, to find its Scantlings, that being multiplied into each other, shall produce 176 Inches, the Area found, one of them must be given, *viz.* either the Depth, or the Thickness. In this Example, the given Depth shall be 12 Inches; therefore divide 176 by 12, and the Quotient is 14 Inches and 2 Thirds, which is the other Scantling or Breadth required.

To prevent the sagging of short Girders, 'tis usual to cut them *Camber*, that is, to cut them with an Angle in the Midst of their Lengths, so that their Middles shall rise above the Levels of their Ends, as many half Inches as the Girder contains Times 10 Feet. And indeed, Girders of the greatest Length, although trussed, should be cut Camber in the same Manner.

IN *Plate* LII. I have given three different Examples for the trussing of Girders; and in *Plate* LIII, *Fig.* I. a fourth, which being in general plain to Inspection, I therefore submit the Choice to the Discretion of the Workman.

V

TRE

THE next in Order are *Joists*, of which there are five Kinds, *viz*, *Common-Joists*, *Binding-Joists*, *Trimming-Joists*, *Bridging-Joists*, and *Cieling-Joists*. First, Common Joists are used in ordinary Buildings, whose Scantlings in *Fir* are generally made as follow, *viz*. Joists of 6 Feet in Length, to be 6 and half by 2 and half; of 9 Feet, 6 and half by 2 and half; of 12 Feet, 8 by 2 and half. But in large Buildings, the Scantlings are made larger, where 'tis common to make Joists of 6 Feet, 5 by 3; of 9 Feet, 7 and half by 3; of 12 Feet, 10 by 3.

As *Oak* is much heavier than *Fir*, 'tis customary to make the Scantlings of *Oak-Joists* larger than those of *Fir*; but I believe it to be entirely wrong, for the Reason before given, relating to the Strength of Timber. Secondly, *Binding-Joists* are generally made half as thick again as *Common-Joists* of the same Lengths, which are represented in *Fig.* V. and VI. *Plate* LI. by *n m q p*, *&c.* and which are framed flush with the under Surfaces of Girders, to receive the *Cieling-Joists*, and about three or four Inches below their upper Surfaces, for to receive the *Bridging-Joists*; so that the upper Surfaces of the *Bridging-Joists* may be exactly flush or level with the Girder to receive the Boarding. In *Fig.* IV. *Plate* LI. A represents the Section of a Girder; *b b*, *&c.* Parts of two *Binding-Joists*, tenon'd into the Girder, *a a*, *&c.* the Ends of *Bridging-Joists*; *e e* boarding on the Bridgings; *d d*, *&c.* Mortises in the *Binding-Joists* to receive the Tenons of *Cieling-Joists*; as also are the Mortises *b e*, *b e*, *&c.* But these last are those which are called Pulley Mortises, into which the *Cieling-Joists* are slid. To understand this more plainly, the Figures *f f f f* are added, which represent the Sections of so many *Binding-Joists*; *g g*, *&c.* the Sections of small Joists between them; *x x* a Side View of a *Bridging-Joist*, and *h h h Cieling-Joists*, tenon'd in the *Binding-Joists*, flush with their Bottoms, as aforesaid, to receive the Lath and Plaister. The Distance that *Binding-Joists* should be laid at, should not exceed 6 Feet, though some lay them at greater Distances, which is not so well, because the *Bridging* and *Cieling-Joists* must be made of larger Scantlings, to carry the Weights of the Cieling and Boarding, and consequently a greater Quantity of Timber must be employed. But however, as this Particular is at the Will of the Carpenter, I shall only add, that the Scantlings for Bridgings of *Fir*, having 6 Feet Bearing, should be 4 by 3 Inches; those of 8 Feet bearing, 5 and half by 3; and those of 10 Feet, 7 by 3. Their Distance from each other is generally about 12 or 14 Inches. The *Fig.* A B C D E F G H I, exhibits different Kinds of Tenons for *Binding-Joists*, which are to be practised as Occasions require. The Figures V. and VI. exhibit the View of a Floor over two Rooms, wherein the Girders F F are laid in the Piers C A D B. In *Fig.* VI. the *Binding-Joists n m q p*, *&c.* and *Trimming-Joists* are represented singly, without the *Bridging-Joists*; and in *Fig.* V. the *Bridging-Joists* are laid on the *Binding-Joists*, as when ready for to receive the Boarding. This Example is given, only as a Specimen of these Kinds of Plans, that from thence the young Student may the better know how to represent Plans of Floors, when required.

THE *Figures* II. and III. are Examples of Floors made of short Lengths, which I have given for the Diversion of the curious.

L E C T. XXIII.
Of Roofs and their Coverings.

BEFORE we can proceed herein, a Plan of the Building to be covered must be made, by which we may acquire a just Knowledge of the Dimensions of every Part that will be contained in the whole Design, before any Part of the real Work be begun; and by which we shall also be taught, how to perform every Operation at once in the least Time, and to account for, or estimate the Quantity of Timber that will be employed.

SUPPOSE *a m r s*, *Fig.* II. *Plate* LII. be the Plan of a regular Building to be covered, which is 50 Feet by 25 Feet in the Clear within; first, make a Parallelogram,

by

by a Scale of equal Parts, whose Length shall be 50 of those Parts, and Breadth 25 Parts, which will represent the Inside of the Building. Secondly, without the Side and Ends of this Parallelogram, draw right Lines parallel thereto, at the Distance of the Breadth of the Raising, suppose 1 Foot, equal to 1 Part of the Scale. Thirdly, as the Distance at which Beams are laid, should not exceed 10 Feet, on account of the Lengths of *Cieling-Joists* which are framed in between them ; therefore divide the Length of the Plan, with as many Beams as are necessary, as at the Points *b i k l*, and *t v x y*; and draw the central Lines of the Beams *b t*, *i v*, *k x*, and *l y*; as likewise the central Lines of the Plan 1 10, and *z w*; and the Bases of the Hips *a 2*, *r 2*, and 8 *m*, 8 *s*. Fourthly, consider the Height of the Pitch, which let be equal to 6, 5 ; then the Lines 5 *k*, and 5 *x*, are the Lengths of a Pair of principal Rafters, the Angle 5 *k* 6, is the Angle or Mold for their Feet, and the Angle 6 5 *k*, for their Tops. On the Points 2 and 8, erect the Perpendiculars 2, 3 ; 2, 4 ; and 8, 7 ; 8, 9. Draw the Lines *a* 3, *r* 4, *m* 7, *s* 9, which are the Lengths of the four Hip Rafters; the Angle 2 *a* 3, is the Angle or Mold for all their Feet, and the Angle *a* 3 2, for all their Tops, and which, with the Lengths of the principal Rafters being measured on your Scale of equal Parts, will give you their true Lengths in Feet and Parts of Feet. This being done, make your Raising equal to the Magnitude of the Building, and brace its Angles, as *n n*, &c. which will be a very great strengthening to them. Divide out the Distances of the Beams, and cog them down on the Raisings, as at *c d e f*, which is a secure Method to tie the Building together. Set out the Mortises for the *Cieling-Joists* in the Beams, so that the under Surfaces of the Joists may be flush with the under Surfaces of the Beams, and observe, that the Distances of the *Cieling-Joists* be agreeable to the usual Lengths of Laths, that no Waste be made thereby in the Lathing. The like Caution should also be taken in the Distance of Rafters, for very often the Tiler is injured very greatly in the Waste of his Laths.

WHEN the Lengths and Angles of the principal and Hip Rafters are thus discovered by the Plan, we must then consider the proper Scantlings for them, and for the Beams on which they stand. When Beams exceed 20 Feet Extent, 'tis always best to truss them up in one or more Places, as their Lengths may require. Beams should never exceed 15 Feet in their Bearings, nor Rafters more than 10 Feet, and especially in Roofs of very low Pitch, whose Covering has a much greater Pressure on their Rafters, than those of higher Pitches, and which may therefore in some Cases exceed 10 Feet. The Height or Pitch of a Roof should be agreeable to the Building it covers, and to the Kind of Materials it is to be covered with.

THE Kinds of Covering in *England* are four, *viz. Lead, Pantiles, Plain Tiles,* and *Slates*. First, *Coverings of Lead* are, of all others, the most beautiful, but the Expence being the greatest, it is therefore never used, but for to cover magnificent Buildings. The Height of Roofs, covered with Lead is at pleasure, but now 'tis generally used for Roofs that are very low, and which is commonly 2 Ninths of the Building's Breadths, which is called *Pediment Pitch*. Secondly, *Coverings of Pantiles* may be also used to low Roofs, but the general Pitch is 3 Eighths of the Building's Breadth. Thirdly, *Coverings of plain Tiles and Slates* have generally the highest Pitch, on account, that when they are laid on low Roofs, the driving Rains will enter between them. The Pitch allowed for these Kinds of Coverings is that, whose Rafter's Length is equal to 3 Fourths of the Building's Breadth, and which is called *true Pitch*.

To form the Trusses for principal Rafters, we must divide the Length of the Rafter into some Number of equal Parts, each to contain about 10 Feet ; and at those Parts place such Collar-Beams, Prick-Posts, and Struts, as are sufficient to support them. In *Plate* LIII. are 15 Designs for the trussing of principal Rafters, whose Beams extend 15, 30, 45, 60, and 75 Feet, and whose several Pitches are made agreeable to the aforesaid Coverings. *Fig.* Q and R are Extents 15 Feet each, the first for Lead, the last for Pantiles, which

require

require no Help from Collar-Beams, &c. but *Fig.* T, of the same Extent, being higher, and consequently has longer Rafters, must be helped by a Collar-Beam placed between them ; and for the same Reason, *Fig.* K, whose Beam extends 30 Feet, must have two Collar-Beams, whilst *Fig.* C and D, of the same Extent, whose Pitches are lower, and Rafters are shorter, will each do with one Collar-Beam.

When the Extent of Beams is such, that the Length of Collar-Beams will be too great, which should never exceed 15 Feet at the most, the Weight of the Rafters and their Coverings must be supported by Prick-Posts and Struts, framed into King-Posts, by means of which the Beams will be trussed up secure, and the whole Weight strongly sustained. For this Purpose all the remaining Examples in this Plate, and those in *Plate* LIV. are given, which being in general conspicuous, requires very little more Explanation.

In *Plate* LIV. the *Figure* E exhibits the Manner of framing the Foot of a principal Rafter into the End of a Beam, where *a* is a Part of the Rafter, *f f*, a Part of the Beam, and *c d*, the Tenon of the Rafter's Foot in its Mortise. The *Fig.* C exhibits the upper Part of a King-Post, with its Joggle *d d*, into which *e e*, the upper Parts of two principal Rafters, are framed, whose Shoulders *b b* must be made truly square to the Joggle. The *Fig.* B exhibits the Manner of framing the lower Parts of Struts, as *b e*, into the Joggle of a King-Post, as at *a b d*, whose Shoulders should also be square to the Joggle, or as nearly square as possible ; *n n* is an Iron Strap, to bind the Beam *g g* unto the King-Post B, which is bolted through the King-Post at *n n*.

As the common Method of framing the Trusses of principal Rafters of large Roofs, is to lay the whole Weight of the Beam and Covering upon their Feet, they therefore should be secured at the Beam with Iron Straps, to prevent their flying out, in case that their Tenons should fail. According to this Method all the Trusses in *Plate* LIII. are made; but as I apprehend this Method was capable of Improvement, I therefore considered, that if under the lower Parts of principal Rafters, there be discharging Struts framed into the Beams and Prick-Posts, as *a b*, *e f*, *Fig.* A, *Plate* LIV. they will discharge the principal Rafters from the greatest Part of the whole Weight.

The Truss, *Fig.* F, hath its Struts turned the contrary Way to all the preceding, and the whole Weight is taken off the Rafters, by the discharging Struts *e e* and *b g*, for the whole Weight that hangs on the King-Post is sustained by the Struts *a d* and *b f*, which are sustained by the Prick-Posts *c d* and *b f*, which are sustained by the discharging Struts *e e* and *b g*. In the same Manner the Weights of the Trusses, *Fig.* G, M, R, P, S, and T, are discharged by their discharging Struts, which are shaded to distinguish them from the others. The Trusses H L N are for Buildings that have arched Cielings, which are tied in by their Hammer-Beams *l i*, in *Fig.* H, *e k*, and *f i*, in *Fig.* L, and *d i*, and *d g*, in *Fig.* N, which must be made very secure by Straps and Bolts, as at *k* and *e*, in *Fig.* H. The Trusses G and I admit of Garrets. But the Top of *Fig.* I, which is called a Trunk Roof, must be covered with Lead. The Trusses O Q R and S are Trusses for M Roofs; those of O R and S are wholly supported by their King-Posts and Struts, but that of Q must have its Gutter at *a*, supported either with a Party-Wall, or trussed Partition, as *Fig.* K, whose principal Posts are *a a*, &c. the Gutter Plate *d d*, &c. and Struts *c c*. The Truss, *Fig.* D, as also *Fig.* B, *Plate* LV. are for the Roofs of Churches, which are supposed to be supported within-side by Columns at *b* and *e*.

The next and last Kind of Roofing whose Timbers are straight, is that of Spires on the Towers of Country Churches, as *Fig.* G, *Plate* LVI. The Height or Pitch of Spires is from 4 to 5 of the Towers Diameter on which they stand. And as the several Hips have an equal Inclination, they do therefore truss up each other. The Base of a Spire is generally an Octagon, whose Manner of framing is exhibited by *Fig.* A, which if made of good *Oak*, and securely bolted down on the Heads of eight principal Posts, fixed in the Sides of the Tower,

Tower, will ſtand unto the End of Time, could the Materials endure ſo long. The ſecond Example, *Fig.* C, has its Spire placed on an *Ogee* Roof at *e f*, framed together as *Fig.* B, which is repreſented at large, and whoſe Baſe *g h* is framed together as *Fig.* D. The third Example *Fig.* H, whoſe Spire is placed on a Lanthorn, is ſomething more difficult than the preceding, and therefore *Fig.* F is given to ſhew the Manner of framing the Lanthorn, and *Figure* E the Kirb to the Lanthorn's Head.

As I have thus given a brief Explanation of theſe ſeveral Sorts of Truſſes for ſtraight Rafters, it will be neceſſary to ſay ſomething of the Scantlings of Beams and Rafters before I proceed any further.

I. *Of the Scantlings for Beams.*

	Feet.			Inches.
If the Length of a Beam of Fir be	30 45 60 75 90	Its Scantlings ſhould be		6 by 7 9 7 10 8½ 10½ 10 12 10½

II. *Of principal Rafters.*

	Feet.		Inches.			Inches.
If the Rafter be of Fir, and its Length	24 36 41 60 72	Its ſcantlings at Top ſhould be	5 by 6 7 6 9 7 10 7½ 10 9	and at its Bottom		7 by 6 9 7 10 7½ 10 9 11 9½

III. *Of ſmall Rafters.*

	Feet.		Inches.
If the Length of the Rafter be	8 10 12	Its Scantlings ſhould be	4½ by 3 5 3 6 3

CIRCULAR Roofs are the next that come under our Conſideration, which are *Firſt*, Cylindrical, as *Fig.* A, *Plate* LV. *Secondly*, Spherical, as *Fig.* G and N. *Thirdly*, Spheroidical, as *Fig.* D, which two laſt are vulgarly called Domes. *Fourthly*, Trumpet-mouth'd, as *Fig.* C A. *Fifthly*, Bell Roofs, as *Fig.* I K. *Sixthly*, Bottle or Ogee Roofs, as *Fig.* M. And *Laſtly*, Compound Roofs, as *Fig.* C and L. And as by Inſpection 'tis plain, that theſe Roofs in general have their Truſſes formed by the ſame Principles as the preceding, I need only add, that *Fig.* F is the Plan of a Spheroidical Dome whoſe ſeveral Truſſes are connected together at their Tops, by the horizontal Braces, *a b c d*, on which the Lanthorn D is erected.

Fig. H is a half Plan of the ſpherical Roof or Dome, *Fig.* G, whoſe Purloins *c f d*, and *e h g i k*, are repreſented by the concentrick Semi-circles 5 3 4 8, and 6 1 2 7, and the Baſe of each Truſs by the central Lines *q w*, *r x*, *s x*, *t a*, and *y v*. The ſeveral Ribs, or principal truſſed Rafters, muſt diminiſh as their Baſes *a t*, *x s*, &c. and may either be framed into a horizontal Kirb at Top, as *w z x a y*, or connected together as in *Fig* F, on which the Lanthorn F may be erected.

Now as by the preceding we have taught how to find the Lengths of our ſeveral Rafters, to give them their proper Scantlings, and to ſupport them and their Beams, in ſuch a Manner as the Nature of the Work ſhall require, I ſhall now proceed to ſhew

How to lay out Roofs in Ledgement, Fig. IV. *Plate* LVII.

To lay out a Roof in Ledgement is no more than to lay out the Skirts and Ends; but thereby is taught how to find the Lengths and Angles of every particular Part, and conſequently the Quantity of the whole.

5

Example I.

LET *a b c d*, *Fig.* IV. *Plate* LVII. be the Plan of a Raifing to a fingle regular hip'd Roof, wherein *z y*, 1 3, *z z*, *n p*, are Beams; *o n* and *o p* the Outlines of a Pair of principal Rafters; *o r* the Height of the Pitch; *r b* and *r d*, alfo *a m* and *c m*, the Bafe of the four Hips; *r s* and *r q*, each equal to *r o*, the Height of the Hip-Rafters, whofe Lengths are *s b* and *q d*. On the Ends *a c* and *b d* make the Ifofceles Triangles *b e d* and *a f c*, whofe Sides *b e*, *d c*, and *a f*, *f c*, are each equal to *s b*, the Length of a Hip-Rafter. Continue the central Lines of the Beams *z y* and *n p* to *l* and *s*, and to *k* and *w*, making *k z*, *l m*, *y w* and *p x*, each equal to the Length and Breadth of a principal Rafter; and draw the Lines *a k*, *k l* and *l k*, alfo *c w*, *w x* and *x d*: This being done, draw in fuch other principal Rafters as are requifite, and between them the Purloins, as 8, 9, 6, 5, 7, &c. at Difcretion, obferving not to place any two Purloins directly oppofite, whofe two Mortifes would weaken the principal very much. Laftly, between the principal Rafters draw in the fmall Rafters, and then the Lengths and Angles of every particular Part of the whole Roof will be determined, and from which a juft Eftimate of the Quantity of Timber that will be employed therein (Regard being had to the Dimenfions or Scantlings of the feveral Parts as aforefaid) may be made. In *Fig.* VI. the Angle O P R being equal to the Angle *o p r* in *Fig.* IV. therefore the Angle at P is the Bevel of the Feet of the principal Rafters, as the Angle at O, for the fame Reafon, is the Bevel of their Tops; and the Angle S B R, *Fig.* V. being equal to the Angle *s b r* in *Fig.* IV. therefore the Angle at B is the Bevel of the Feet of the Hip-Rafters, and S is the Bevel of their Tops. The *Fig.* A B on the Left-hand exhibits a Joint made by a Purloin and a Hip, as by *a k*, and the Purloin 12, 14, the Meafure of whofe Angle is the Arch 13, 15. *Fig.* VII. reprefents a Pair of principal Rafters truffed up, on whofe Prick-Pofts is placed a Cupola, as *e f i g h*.

THE next in Order is, to find the Angles of the Jack-Rafters againft the Hips, and to back the Hip-Rafters.

As Jack-Rafters are parallel to one another, therefore all their Angles againft the Hips are the fame.

To make the End of a Jack-Rafter fit to the upright Side of a Hip-Rafter.

THERE are two Angles to be formed, that is, the one upon the upper Surface of the Jack-Rafter, the other on its Sides from the Ends of the former. The Angle on its upper Surface is the Angle made by the upper Edges of the Jack and Hip; and which is that, that every Jack-Rafter makes with the Hip-Rafter in the Ledgement, as every of the Angles between *e* and *d*. Therefore from your drawing in Ledgement, fet your Bevel to one of thofe Angles, and the feveral Jack-Rafters being cut to their refpective Lengths, at their upper Ends on their upper Surfaces, apply that Bevel, and defcribe the upper Angles. This done, take the Mold S, made for the Tops of the principal Rafters, and apply it againft the Sides of each Jack-Rafter, at the Ends of the Angle on their upper Surfaces, and by its upper Edge draw Lines; then from the Line of the upper Angle, through the Lines on the Sides, faw through the Rafter, and that Cut will be the Angle required.

To find the Angle of the Back of a Hip-Rafter.

FROM the Point *e* let fall a Perpendicular, as *e h*, on the Hip *f a*; make *e g*, equal to *e h*; alfo make *a i* equal to *a e*; draw the Lines *e g* and *g i*, and the Angle *e g i* will be the Angle or Back of the Hip required.

EXAMPLE II. *Fig.* V. *Plate* LIX.

THIS fecond Example is of a regular double Roof, which is hip'd as the preceeding, with Valleys within-fide.

THE Outlines of this Plan are *a f g k*, wherein *h* B, B E, E *i* and *i h*, are the Ridges, *a* B, E *f*, *i k* and *h g* are the Hips, *h* A C, B A C, D A E and D A *i* are the Valleys, A C, D A the Gutter, *f q* the Height of the Pitch, *p q* and *q r* a Pair of principal Rafters, *v f* and *t k* Hip-Rafters. By the laft Example, lay out the Ends *f e i k*, and *a* B *b g*, alfo the Skirts *a b e f* and *g* A I *k*; continue *g* H to *f*, *k* I to *d*, *a b* to *c*, and *f e* to *d*, and becaufe the Lengths of the Valleys are

equal

equal to the Lengths of the Hips, therefore make H *e*, I *d*, *b c*, and *d e*, each equal to one of the Hips, as I *k*, and draw the Lines *c d* and *c d*: this being done, draw in all the principal and small Rafters at Discretion, and then the whole will be completed, as required.

Example III. *Plate* LX.

This third Example is of an irregular double Roof, whose Ends are hip'd, and whose Plan is *t p z z y z*, wherein *r s, s o, o* 1, 1 *m, m v* and *v r* are its Ridges, *t s, p o,* 2 1, *z m, o y* and *r x* are its Hips, *r q, s q* and *o v* are the Valleys, *o q* a Gutter, and *m* 1 *o n* a Flat; 3 4 5 and 5 7 8 are two Pair of principal Rafters, *t s, r x* are the Bases of the Hip-Rafters, *t,* 1 2, and 1 3, *x, p o* and 2 1 are the Bases of the Hip-Rafters 2, 1 4, and *p o; z m* is the Base of the Hip-Rafter *z,* 1 6, and *v y* of the Hip-Rafter *y* 1 7.

On the Points *s* and *r* erect the Perpendiculars *s,* 1 2, and *r* 1 3, each equal to the Height of the Pitch, and draw the Lines 1 2, *t,* and 1 3, *x,* which are the Lengths of those two Hip-Rafters. In the same Manner, on the Points *o,* 1, *m, v,* erect Perpendiculars of the same Height, and draw the other Hip-Rafters: this done, by the first Example lay out the whole in Ledgement, and fill up the several Skirts and Ends *f g h i, l k, e a* and *d e,* with their principal and small Rafters, which will complete the whole, as required.

Note, If the Drawing be made on thick Paper, and the whole be cut out, by the Outlines, you may, by bending the Drawing on the Lines of the Eaves and Ridges, fold up the whole, and thereby form a real Model of the Work to be done.

Example IV. *Plate* LVIII.

This Example is of an irregular Roof, whose several Angles are Bevel, wherein *t s a q* is the Plan, 1 1, *e;* 1 2, *k;* 1 3, *l;* and 1 4, *o;* are the Beams over which the principal Rafters are to stand.

Let the Line *e n* be the Base of the Ridge, which is to be placed at pleasure, and let *t e, a c* and *n s, n q* be the Bases of the 4 Hips; on the Points *c g k n* erect the Perpendiculars *c d, g f, k i,* and *u m,* which make each equal to the Height of the Pitch, and draw the Lines *d* 11, *d e; f* 12, *f h;* 1 13, *i l; m* 14, *m o;* which will be the Lengths of the several principal Rafters. At the Points *c* and *n,* erect the Lines *n r, n p,* and *c v, c b,* perpendicular to the Bases of the Hips, and each equal to the Heights of the Pitch, and draw the Lines *t v, a b,* and *r s, p q,* which are the Lengths of the several Hip-Rafters; make *s x,* and *x q,* the Sides of the Scalenum Triangle *s x q,* equal to *r s* and *p q,* also *t w* and *w a,* equal to *t v* and *a b,* which will complete the Ledgement of the Ends. Make 1 4 *x,* equal to the principal Rafter 1 4 *m,* and *s z* equal to the Hip *r s,* also make *o z* equal to the principal Rafter *o m,* and *q z* equal to the Hip *p q;* also make *e y* equal to the principal Rafter *d e,* and *a y* equal to the Hip *w a;* also make 8 *y* equal to the principal Rafter *d* 8, and *t y* equal to the Hip *t v.* Make *y* W and *y* Y each equal to *c g;* also W X and Y Z each equal to *g k;* also X *z* and Z *z* each equal to *k n.* Draw the principal Rafters 12 W, 13 X, and *b* Y, *l* Z. Lastly, draw in the Purloins 21, 22, 20, 23, 24, at Discretion, and they will complete the whole Ledgement, as required.

As the Beams lie oblique to the Raisings, therefore all the principal Rafters must be backed, which is thus performed:

Let *d e, Fig.* E, represent that Part of the Raising, that is at the Foot of the principal Rafter *d e;* also let C E represent a Part of the Beam 1 1 *e;* and *b* the lower Part of the Rafter *d e;* and make the Angle D E C be equal to the Angle *d e c.*

From the Point *y* in *Fig.* E, erect the Perpendicular *y x;* then the Foot of the Rafter being made equal to the Angle D E C on the left-hand Side, set off the Distance *z x,* and from the Point *z* strike a Chalk Line up the Side of the Rafter parallel to its upper Edge, and then a Fletch being cut off from *y* the right-hand Angle to the Chalk-Line aforesaid, the Rafter will be backed as required.

In the same Manner the other Rafters *f h, i l, m o,* &c. must be backed, as expressed

expreſſed by the *Figures* H I. and O. And the Angles D E C and E D C, in *Fig.* E, being equal to the Angles *d e c* and *e d e*, *&c.* are the Molds for the Top and Foot of the Rafter *d e*, *&c.* The ſame is alſo to be underſtood of the Molds of the ſeveral Hip-Rafters in *Figures* T V C, R N S, D C E and P N Q, whoſe Angles are equal to the reſpective Angles of the Feet and Tops of thoſe Hip-Rafters againſt which they are placed. The next and laſt Work is to back the Hip-Rafters, which is done by this general Rule.

THROUGH any Part of the baſe Line of a Hip-Rafter, as the Point 10 in *n q*, draw a right Line as *g* 8, at right Angles, cutting the Outlines of the Raiſing in the Points *g* and 8. From the Point 10 let fall a Perpendicular on the Hip-Rafter *p q*, as 10, 0; make 10, 2, equal to 10, 0, and draw the Lines *g* 2 and 2 8, then the Angle *g* 2 8 is the Angle of the Back of the Hip *p q*, as required.

LECTURE XXIV.

Of the Manner of deſcribing Angle-Brackets and Hip-Rafters in polygonal Roofs.

AS Brackets are uſed very frequently in Buildings, I ſhall therefore ſhew how to find the Curvature of any Angle-Bracket by one general Rule, as follows:

LET A in *Fig.* VI. *Plate* LIX. be a Front Bracket given, whoſe Height is *d b*, its Projection *a b*, and its Curve a Cavetto; and let the ſhaded Parts *b d* repreſent an Angle of a Building, againſt which the Cove is to be fixed.

DRAW the Lines *a h* and *h i* parallel to the two Sides of the Building, at the Diſtance of the Projection of the Front Bracket, and draw 7 *d* the Baſe of the Front Bracket, and *f h* the Baſe of the Angle Bracket; divide 7 *c* into any Number of equal Parts, as at the Points 6, 5, 4, 3, 2, 1, and draw the Ordinates 6, 8; 5, 9; 4, 10; 3, 11; *&c.* divide *h f* into the ſame Number of equal Parts as 7 *c* is divided, which will be done by continuing the Ordinates of 7 *c*, until they meet *h f* in the Points 6, 5, 4, 3, *&c.* whereon erect the Ordinates 1, 13; 2, 12; 3, 11, *&c.* equal to the Ordinates 1, 13; 2, 12; 3, 11; *&c.* on the Line 7 *c*; and through the Points 13, 12, 11, 10, 9, 8 *h*, trace the Quarter of an Ellipſis, which is the Curve of the Angle-Bracket required.

BY the ſame Rule, all other Kinds of Angle-Brackets may be deſcribed, and which is very evident.

BY *Fig.* I. II. III. IV. VII. VIII. IX. which exhibits all the Varieties of Brackets, at acute, right and obtuſe Angles, and wherein the Front Bracket in each Example is expreſſed by the Capital A, and the Angle-Bracket by the Capital B.

THE Curvatures of Hip-Rafters to polygonal Roofs, that is, thoſe whoſe Plans are Polygons, as the *Figures* I L M N, *Plate* LVI. are alſo found by tranſpoſing the Ordinates of a principal Rafter (which muſt be given) upon the Baſe of a Hip-Rafter.

SUPPOSE, in *Fig.* I. *a d* to be the Baſe, over which the Cavetto principal Rafter *c d* is to ſtand, and let *a e* be the Baſe of a Hip-Rafter. Divide *a d* into equal Parts, and draw the Ordinates 2, 1; 4, 3, *&c.* on the Line *a d*; divide *a e* in the ſame Manner as *a d*, and on the Line *a e* draw the Ordinates 1, 2; 3, 4; 5, 6, *&c.* and from the Point *b*, through the Points 2, 4, 6, 8, *&c.* trace the Curve of the Hip-Rafter as required. In the ſame Manner in *Fig.* L, the principal Rafter *c d* being given, the Hip-Rafter *b e* is found; as alſo are the Hip-Rafters *b e* in *Fig.* M, and *c e* in *Fig.* N, the principal Rafters being firſt given.

LECTURE XXV.

Of the Formation of the Heads of Niches.

NICHES, *quaſi Nidi*, or Neſts, of old *Concha*, were a Kind of *Pluteus*, or ſmall Tribunals, and are ſo called by the *Italians* to this Day, wherein Statues are placed to protect them from the Injuries of Weather. The Heads of *Niches* are made four different Ways, as, *firſt*, with Bricks; *ſecondly*, with Stone; *thirdly*,

thirdly, with Ribs or Quarters, lathed and plaistered, or covered and lined with slit Deal, &c. and, *lastly*, with divers Thicknesses of Plank glewed upon one another.

Those made with Bricks or Stone are built upon Centers of Wood, which are the very same as those which are covered with slit Deal, and are of two Kinds, *viz.* the one semi-circular, the other semi-elliptical.

I. *To make the Center for the Head of a semi-circular Niche*, Fig. VII. Plate LX.

Make a semi-circular Raising, equal to the Plan of the Niche, and cut out as many Ribs as are necessary, each equal to half the Curve of the Raising, and of the same Curvature; cut out the curved Front, whose Breadth is at pleasure, and whose Curve must be equal to that of the Raising: This done, fix your Front-piece on the Ends of the Railing, and then the Distances of the several Ribs being set out on the Railing, as at the Points *e d e f g h i k l*, fix thereon the several Ribs, which connect together at *a*, and then will they be ready to receive their Covering and Lining also, if required.

To cover or line the Head of a Niche, Fig. K. Plate LVI.

Let *a f c* be the Plan of the Head of a semi-circular Niche, and complete the Circle *a f c d*. Draw the Diameters *a b c*, and *d b f*, continued out towards *e* at pleasure. Make *f r*, and *f s*, each equal to 1 fourth of *a f*; then *f s* will be equal to half *a s*, and draw the Lines *h b* and *s b*. Divide *b d* into any Number of equal Parts, and draw the Ordinates 1, 8; 2, 9; 3, 10, &c. and on the Points where those Ordinates cut the Semi-diameter *b d*, with the Radius of each Semi-ordinate, describe Semi-circles, as the dotted Semi-circles in the Figure. Make *e p* equal to the Curve *a f*. Make *f p* equal to *a* 1; *f o* equal to *a* 2, *f n* equal to *a* 3, *f m* equal to *a* 4, *f l* equal to *a* 5, *f k* equal to *a* 6, and *f q* equal to *a* 7. On the Point *e* describe the Arches 13, 14; 11, 12; 9, 10, &c. Bisect the half Part of each of the dotted Semi-circles, as *f c* in *i*, 1 8 in 2, 3 9 in 4, 5 10 in 6, 7 11 in 8, 9 12 in 10, 11 13 in 12, and 13 14 in 14. Make *f h*, and *f g*, each equal to half the Arch *f i*; *p* 1, and *p* 2, each equal to half the Arch 1 2; *o* 3, and *o* 4, each equal to half the Arch 3 4; and so in like Manner, *n* 5, and 5 6, to half the Arch 5, 6, &c. From the Point *e*, through the Points 12, 11, 9, 7, &c. and 14, 12, 10, &c. trace the Curves *e h* and *e g*; then four such Pieces, as *e h g*, will cover the Head of the Niche, as required.

Note, If the Niche be to be lined, then the Diameter of the Circle, being made equal to the inside Diameter of the Niche, the Lining may be found in the same Manner The same Method is also to be used, for the Covering or Lining of a Semi-elliptical-headed Niche, as is plainly seen by *Fig.* O, where every of the same Operations is performed on the Plan of an Ellipsis, and where *e h s* is the Covering for 1 eighth of the whole Hemispheroid.

As sometimes the Niches are made semi-polygonal, it is necessary to shew their Covering also, and which is of great Use in the Covering of polygonal Roofs, as those of Banqueting-Houses, Turrets, &c.

Let *Fig.* L, *Plate* LVI. be a Plan given, whose principal Rib or Rafter is *e d*, and Hip *b e*. Make the Length of *k f* equal to the curved Length of *e d*, and draw the Lines *g a* and *h a*. Draw the Ordinates to the principal Rib *e d* on its Base *a d*. Make the several Distances *k i*, 1, 2; 2, 3, on the Line *k f*, equal to the several Parts of the Principal *e d*, as they are divided by the Ordinates, making *k i* equal to the first Part from *d*; 1, 2, equal to the second Part, 2, 3 equal to the third, &c. Divide *k a* in the same Proportion as *a d*, at the Points 1, 2, 3, &c. through which draw right Lines parallel to *g b*, to terminate at the Lines *g a* and *h a*; also through the Points 1, 2, 3, in the Line *k f*, draw right Lines at pleasure, and parallel to *g b*. Then making the Lines 1, 7; 2, 8; 3, 9, &c. on the Line *k f*, equal to the Lines 1, 7; 2, 8; 3, 9, &c. on the Line *k a*; and from *f*, through the Points 13, 12, 11, &c. to *b*, trace the Curve *f h*. In the same Manner trace the Curve *f g*. Then the Piece *f g h*, being bended up, and laid on the two Hips that stand over the Line *g a*

X   and

and *h a*, will be the Covering for that Side of the Roof or Niche, as required.

Note, The Coverings to the two Ogee Roofs M and N, and the Cavetto Roof I, are found in the same Manner, as is evident to Inspection.

II. *To make the Center of the Head of a semi-elliptical-headed Niche*, Fig. IX. X. XI. Plate LX.

LET *b f d*, *Fig.* XI. or *e b g*, *Fig.* X. be the Plan of an elliptical-headed Niche. First, Make the Raising and Front, each equal to the Plan, and fix them together. Secondly, Cut out the middle Rib, which is a Quadrant, whose Radius is equal to *a f*, and fix it on the Raising at *f*, and to the Front-Piece at *a*, as in *Fig.* IX. which will keep the Front-Piece in its true Position. This done, set out the several Distances of the other Ribs, as at *g h i k*, &c. in *Fig.* XI. and draw the Lines, *g a*, *h a*, *i a*, and *k a*. Thirdly, If the Lines *g a*, *h a*, *i a*, and *k a*, be each considered as the semi-transverse Diameters of so many Ellipses, whose several semi-conjugate Diameters are each equal to the semi-conjugate Diameter *a f*, then one half Part of every of those Semi-ellipses will be the true Curves for the several intermediate Ribs, that are to stand on the Raising, at *g h i k*, &c. and which being connected together, as at *a*, in *Fig.* IX. and either covered or lined, by the Rule before delivered, the whole will be completed, as required.

III. *To make a semi-circular-headed Niche, with the Thicknesses of Boards, Planks, &c. glewed upon one another*, Fig. XIV. Plate LX.

FIRST, let *c a e* be the Face of the Niche, described on a Wall or flat Pannel, &c. Divide its Height *1 a*, into such equal Parts as will be agreeable to the Thickness of your Plank, as at the Points 4, 7, &c. through which draw right Lines parallel to *c e*. On the Edge of your Plank fix a Center, and describe a Semi-circle thereon, equal to the Plan of your Niche; apply a Square to the Center, and draw a Line on the Edge to the other Side, to find the opposite Center, whereon, with a Radius equal to + 6, describe another Semi-circle; then with a turning Saw, cut through from 1 Semi-circle to the other, and then your first Thickness is made. Secondly, on the Edge of your next Piece of Plank fix a Center, and thereon describe a Semi-circle equal to the last. Apply a Square to the Center, and find the opposite Center as before, whereon with the Radius 7 *g*, the half Length of the Line that passes through the next equal Part, describe another Semi-circle; and with a turning Saw, cut through from one Semi-circle to the other, and then is your second Thickness made. Proceed in like Manner with all the remaining Thicknesses, observing to make the under Semi-circle of every Piece, equal to the upper Semi-circle of the next last, and which being glewed together, when the whole is dry, clear off the Inside with a circular smoothing Plane, whose Curve is something quicker than the Curve of the Niche.

IV. *To make a semi-elliptical-headed Niche, with the Thickness of Boards, Planks, &c. glewed upon one another*, Fig. XV. Plate LX.

LET *d b e* represent the semi-elliptical Niche required. Divide its Height *a b* into equal Parts as before. Make *a b c*, **Fig.** XIII. equal to *b a e*, *Fig.* XV. Make *a c*, and *c d*, at right Angles, and each equal to *a b*, the Height of the Niche, *Fig.* XV. and on *c* describe the Arch *a 3*, which represents the middle Depth of the Niche. Divide *a c*, *Fig.* XII. and *a b*, *Fig.* XIII. (which are each equal to *b a*, the Height of the Niche, *Fig.* XV.) into the same Number of equal Parts, and from those Parts draw Lines parallel to *c d*, and *b e*; then will the Parallels in *Fig.* XIII. be semi-transverse Diameters, and the Parallels in *Fig.* XII. will be semi-conjugate Diameters of the several Ellipses, which are to be described on the upper and under Surfaces of the several Thicknesses of Planks, &c. in the very same Manner as the Semi-circles in the preceding Example, and which being glewed together in like Manner, will form a semi-elliptical-headed Niche, as required.

L E C.

LECTURE XXVI.

Of Timber Bridges.

BRIDGES of Timber differ very little in their Truffes from thofe of Roofs, as is evident by the feveral Defigns in *Plate* LXI. and LXII. In *Plate* LXI. I have 3 Defigns; that of *Fig.* IV. is an Aperture equal to 30 Feet; that of *Fig.* I. to 45 Feet; and that of *Fig.* V. to 60 Feet: The *Fig.* II. is a Section of the feveral Profiles, whofe Breadth is equal to 50 Feet. The Piles that fupport the Truffes of thefe feveral Defigns are fuppofed to rife a fufficient Height above the Flowing of the Water, fo that the Joints in the feveral Truffes erected thereon may not be affected thereby; and when the Depth of a River is fo great, that the Length of Piles above the Bed of the River muft exceed, when driven, 25 or 30 Feet, then Super-Piles muft be erected upon horizontal Beams, mortifed down upon the Heads of the lower Piles, as in every of thefe Examples. The Scantlings proper for Piles to fuch Bridges fhould not be lefs than one Foot in Diameter, at the Middle of their Lengths. The *Fig.* III. reprefents Part of the Plan, with the Bafe of two Truffes, *a* and *b*, whofe Diftances in the Clear fhould not exceed 10 Feet; becaufe on them the Joifts which carry the Floor of the Bridge are laid: The under Piles muft be fhod with Iron, that they may the better penetrate through the feveral Stratums of Earth, into which they are to be driven. Before Piles are driven, the whole Weight of the Framing that is to come on them, and the Weight of the Planking on the Joifts, Clay, Gravel, Pavement, &c. fhould be eftimated nearly to the Truth; otherwife the Piles cannot be driven with any Certainty, and which is thus to be performed, *viz.* Divide the total Weight to be fuftained, by the neceffary Number of Piles, and the Quotient will be the Weight that each Pile is to fupport. Then each Pile being driven until it refift a Force much greater than the Weight it is to fupport, it may be depended on, that afterwards there cannot be any Settlement by the Weight it is to fuftain.

THE Scantlings for the Beams of Truffes fhould be about 12 Inches by 9 Inches, as alfo fhould be the feveral King-Pofts. But the Struts and Joifts need not exceed 9 by 6 Inches, and the Plank on the Joifts being made 3 Inches in Thicknefs, will be fufficient. Before the Timbers are worked (which is fuppofed to be of the beft Oak), 'tis beft to cut them out to their Scantlings, and lay them in a running Water for a Month at the leaft, to foak out the Sap, which is very deftructive, and then dry them thoroughly over a Saw-duft Heat, &c. before they are worked. If this be carefully done, and the Work kept dry whilft working, and being truly framed, there will be no fagging in the Work, as ufually happens by the fhrinking of the Timbers, when they are not thus fhrinked before working; nay, I have experienced, that Timbers fo prepared have always fwelled afterwards, and made the Joints much clofer than when firft put together. It is alfo advifable, for the better preferving of the Tenons, that every Mortife and Tenon be well covered over with a good Body of White Lead, and boiled Linfeed Oil, which will endure a long Time, and will not permit any Rains to enter the Mortifes, to the Prejudice of the Tenons. The Ends of the Joifts fhould alfo be covered with brown Paper, dipped in Pitch, and Sheet Lead laid over the Paper. And for the more effectual preferving of the Plank and Joifts, the Plank ought to be covered with a ftrong Clay, firmly rammed down unto about 9 Inches in Depth, on which the Road of Gravel and Pavement, or Gravel only, of a fufficient Thicknefs is to be laid, with a Rifing in the Middle, to difcharge hafty Rains to the Sides, as exhibited by B, in *Fig.* I, *Plate* LXII.

IN *Plate* LXII. are two other Defigns, each of 100 Feet Opening, which I. made for the New Bridge at *Weftminfter*; but believing that Intereft was predominant to real Merit, I therefore declined to trouble the Honourable Commif-

fioners

fioners therewith, as I have now the Public, in hopes that they may be of fome Help to Invention, if not worthy of being put into Practice, over Rivers, where large Openings are required.

The Defign, *Fig.* II. is of prodigious Strength, as being a double Trufs, and whofe Timbers are fo fixed together, that not any Part of the whole can fag the hundredth Part of an Inch, they being prepared, before worked, as aforefaid.

Fig. I. is a Section of the Breadth of the Bridge, wherein A A, &c. reprefents the feveral Truffes, for the Support of the Joifts and Roads. A and C reprefent the Foot-ways, each 10 Feet in Breadth; and B, the Horfe-way, 30 Feet in Breadth. As the Offices of the Struts *a d e t b l e k i*, &c. are obvious to every difcerning Eye, I need not fay any Thing thereof.

The *Fig.* V. contains a double Defign, the Struts on the Side G being different from thofe on the Side H. Both thefe Defigns are of immenfe Strength; and as the whole is laid on Stone or Brick Piers, which rife above the Flowing of the higheft Tide, a Bridge of this Kind will be of very great Duration. As there is fome Difficulty to lay Foundations for Stone Piers in Rivers that are affected by Tides, and as in wooden Bridges the moft early Decay is in that Part of the Piles that are affected by the rifing and falling Waters of the Tides, therefore to avoid both thefe Inconveniences, fuch Piers may be thus erected, viz. Confider the Weight of a Pier, and the Weight that the Pier is to carry. Affign the Place in the River where the Pier is to ftand: bore the Ground for 15 or 20 Feet in Depth, that a Judgment may be formed, how long the Piles muft be. This done, drive a Range of Piles, dove-tailed together, at about 15 Inches, without the Upright that the Stone Pier is to be erected, all round the Limits of the Pier, and the like exactly under the Upright of the Pier. Thefe two Ranges of Piles form within the Ground a ftrong Enclofure, about the encompaffed Earth on which the Pier is to ftand. Within the Limits enclofed drive as many Piles as fhall be thought fufficient to carry the Weight, and which fhould be driven nearly all equally; that is, Firft, to drive them all to fuch a Depth, as to keep them upright in their Places. Secondly, to drive them all about 2 Feet lower, and then all two Feet lower again; and fo on, until each Pile be firmly driven, as aforefaid. By this regular driving down all the Piles together, they will caufe the enclofed Earth into which they are driven to be equally compreffed, and of much greater Compactnefs than it was before, as being confined by the double Ranges of Piles firft driven. When all the Piles are thus driven, their Heads muft be fawed level, at about 18 Inches below the Surface of the low Water; and to render them imperifhable, the whole muft be filled up with ftrong Clay, let down in large fquare Pieces, worked very ftiff, and well rammed, which is a Work eafy to be performed, although the Depth of Water fhould be 20 Feet. When this is done, prepare a double Floor of Oak Timbers, free from Sap, each Floor about 10 Inches in Thicknefs, pinned down one on the other, fo that the upper Timbers lie at right Angles acrofs the lower. Fix this Floor on the Piles, and thereon erect the Stone-work, to any Height required. The next Work is to fill up the Space between the outer Range of Dove-tailed Piles, and the next inner Piles, to preferve the inner Range from being injured by the Flux and Reflux of the Tide; and which being firmly performed, the whole Foundation will be rendered as imperifhable, as were all the Piles driven into the very Bed of the River, as being fecured from the Actions of both Air and Water. The outward Range of Dove-tailed Piles are all that are liable to decay; and as their Office is no more than to fupport the outward Cafe of Clay, which is there placed to preferve the next inner Range of Piles, they are eafily and foon repaired, as their Decays occur.

Note, The outer Range of Piles muft be made of fuch a Length, as to rife fomething above the Level of High-Water; and horizontal Beams being mortifed down on their Heads, with horizontal Ties laid through the Thicknefs of the

Pier

Pier in fmall Arches turned for that Purpofe, being cogged down on the Beams, they will be a lafting Prefervative and Defence to the Piers, againft all the Infults of tempeftuous Weather and Navigation that can happen.

Note, If the Depth of Low-Water be any Thing confiderable, it will be a very fecure Way to drive a Range of oblique Piles, juft within the Limits of the up-tight Piles, as Braces, to fteady the next within, from inclining either Way by the Weight of the Pier.

If inftead of Timber Truffes, 'tis required to make Arches of Stone, a fuf-ficient Number of Piles muft be added within every Pier, that, with the others, will be capable to carry the additional Weight of the Arches.

Note alfo, That Piers built with well burnt Bricks, laid in Terrace, on a Bafe-ment of large Blocks of Stone, about 3 Feet in Height, will be much cheaper than being made entirely of Stone, and of longer Duration : For well burnt Bricks do not decay fo faft as *Portland* Stone, which is very evident by St. *Paul's* Cathedral, where the Stone, in many Parts of the *South* Side, is already decayed more than the 10th Part of an Inch.

LECTURE XXVII.
Of Brick and Stone Arches to Windows, Doors, &c.
I. *Of ftraight, circular, elliptical, Gothick and rampant Arches in ftraight Walls,* Plate LXIII.

IN this Plate are exhibited 13 Kinds of Arches, of which *Fig.* I. II. III. IV. V. VII. VIII. and IX. are Arches of Brick Work, and the others of rufticated Stones. In *Fig.* I. and III. the Diftance of the Center, to which all the Joints have their Sommering, is equal to the Breadth of the Window ; but thofe of *Fig.* II. and IV. is the Center of a geometrical Square, whofe Side is equal to their Breadth. *Fig.* V. is a femi-circular Arch, whofe Joints fommer to its Center. *Fig.* VII. and IX. are femi-elliptical Arches, the firft on the conjugate Diameter, and the laft on the transferfe Diameter. The Courfes in *Fig.* VII. are divided on the inner Curve *b f m,* and outer Curve *a e n,* into the fame Number of equal Parts, as alfo is the right-hand Side of *Fig.* IX. whofe left-hand Side has its Courfes fommering to *c* and *l* the Centers of the Ellipfis. *Fig.* VIII. is a *Gothick* Arch, whofe Courfes have the fame Sommerings as thofe of *Fig.* IX.

In all thefe Cafes the only Thing to be obferved is, that the Number of Courfes into which each is divided be an odd Number, that thereby the Middle Courfe may be perpendicular, and that the Breadth of each Courfe on the upper Part of the Arch be fomething lefs than the Thicknefs of a Brick, to allow for rubbing. The rufticated Arches, *Fig.* VI. X. XI. and XII. have the fame Sommering as thofe of *Fig.* V. VII. VIII. and IX.

To divide their Key Stones and Ruflicks.

DIVIDE each half Arch into 9 equal Parts, as in *Fig* V. give 1 to half the Key Stone, the next 1 *g* to its Counter Key, and 2 to each Ruftick and Interval, as the Figures exprefs. The like is alfo to be obferved in all the other Arches.

THE Arch, *Fig.* XIII. is a rampant Semi-circle, whofe Curvature may be de-fcribed by PROB. XIX. LECT. IV. PART II. or as following. Let *f b* be the Breadth, and *f g* the Height of the Ramp ; draw *g b,* and in the Middle of *f b* erect the Perpendicular *q a,* of Length at pleafure ; alfo draw the Line *q r* parallel to *f b.* From the Point of Interfection made by the Lines *g b* and *f b,* fet up half the Breadth of the Opening to *a,* and draw the Lines *a g* and *a b.* Bifect *g a* in *m,* and *a b* in *o,* and erect the Perpendiculars *m n* and *o p ;* then the Point *n* is the Center of the Arch *g d,* and *p* is the Center of the Arch *d b,* which divide in-to Rufticks, as in *Fig.* VI. Then the Length of the Rufticks muft be equal to ⅔ of the Opening, and of the Intervals to ¼ of the Ruftick, as exhibited by *k l i, Fig.* VI.

II. *Of ftraight, circular and elliptical Arches in circular Walls,* Plate LXIV.

THE firft Work to be done is the making of the Centers to turn thefe Kinds of Arches upon, which may be thus performed. Let G H I K be the Plan of a

circular

circular Building, and at *Fig.* VI. 'tis required to make a Center for a semi-circular Arch to the Window, whose Diameter without is *a d*, and within *n m*. Bisect *a d* in *f*, and describe the Semi-circle *a p d*. Divide *a d* into any Number of equal Parts at the Points 6 4 2, &c. and draw the Ordinates 6, 6; 4, 4; 2, 2; &c. Divide *n m* into the same Number of equal Parts, and make the Ordinates 6, 5; 4, 3; 2, 1, &c. equal to the Ordinates 6, 6; 4, 4; 2, 2, &c. and through the Points 5 3 1 *k*, &c. trace the Curve *n k m*, then *a p d* and *n k m* will be the two Ribs for the Center: This being done, place the Ribs perpendicular over the Lines *a d* and *n m*, and cover them, as Centers usually are, and then applying the Edge of a Plumb-rule to the divers Parts of the Inside and Outside of the Window's Bottom, the Top of the Rule will give the several Points at which the Inside and Outside of the Covering is to be cut off, so as to stand exactly over the Inside and Outside of the Building, and then the Center will be completed as required.

To divide the Courses in the Arch of this Window.

On a flat Pannel, &c. draw a Line, as *b e*, *Fig.* VII. make *a f o* equal to the Curve *a c d*, also make *a b* and *o e* each equal to the intended Height of the Brick Arch. Make *f p* in *Fig.* VII. equal to *e p* in *Fig.* VI. also make *a b* and *d e* in *Fig.* VI. each equal to *b a* in *Fig.* VII. then the Points *b* and *e* will be the Extremes of the Arch. Make *p r* in *Fig.* VII. equal to *b a* the given Height of the Arch, and through the Points *b r c* and *a p o* describe two Semi-ellipses, which divide into Courses as before taught, and which will be the Face of the Arch required.

To find the Angles or Bevels of the Under-part of each Course.

Continue the Splay-Backs of the Window *m d* and *n a* until they meet in F. On F, with the Radius F *n* and F *a*, describe the Arches *n y v* and *a f s*, making *n y v* equal to the Girt of the Arch *n k m*. Make *n* 6, *n* 4, *n* 2, *n y*, &c. on the Arch *n y v*, equal to *n* 6, *n* 4, *n* 2, *n y*, &c. on the Curve *a k m*, and draw the Lines 6 F, 4 F, 2 F, *y* F, &c. make the Ordinates 6, 5; 4, 3; 2, 1; *y x*, &c. on the Lines 6 F, 4 F, &c. equal to the Ordinates 5, 6; 3, 4; 1, 2; *b 1*, &c. on the Line *n m*, and through the Points 5, 3, 1, *x*, &c. trace the Curve *v x n*. In the same Manner transfer the Ordinates 5, 6; 3, 4; 1, 2; *c, f*, &c. on the Line *a d* to the Arch *s f a*, as from 5 to 6, from 4 to 3, &c. and trace the Curve *s c a*; and then will the *Figure n y v s c a* be the Soffito of the Window laid out, and which being divided into the same Number of equal Parts, as the under Part of the Arch *a p o*, *Fig.* VII. and Lines drawn to the Center F, as is done in *Fig.* II. to the Center A, by the Lines 2, 2, &c. those Lines will give the Bevel of every Course in Soffito, as required. *Fig.* V. is another Example of a semi-elliptical Arch, whose Front is *Fig.* IV. Also *Fig.* II. is a third Example of a Scheme Arch, whose Front is *Fig.* I. And *Fig.* VIII. is a fourth Example of a straight Arch, which in general are performed by the aforesaid Rule.

To find the Curvature of every Course in Front.

Suppose the rusticated semi-circular-headed Window, *Fig.* IX. be standing in the Side of a Cylinder, whose Sides are the Lines Q T and P V, continue out the Sides of each Rustick until they cut the Sides of the Cylinder in the Points Q R S T and N O P, &c. then the Lines Q N, R O, Q N, &c. will be transverse Diameters of so many Ellipses, whose conjugate Diameters are each equal to the Diameter of the Cylinder, which describe as in *Fig.* X. and draw their conjugate Diameters *k l*, *i m* and *n o*; make the Distances *o* 5, *m* 3, *l* 1, on each Ellipsis, equal to *a g* the Semi-diameter of the Window, *Fig.* IX. also make the Distances 5 6, 3 4, 1 2, on each Ellipsis, equal to *g* 10 the Height of the rustick Arch; then the Segments of the several Ellipses, 5, 6; 3, 4; 1, 2; at Z X A, will be the Curves of the several Courses, as required.

Fig. III. represents the Manner of covering the Outside of a Cone, the Arch *c a* being made equal to the Circumference of the Circle *e*, which is equal to the Base of the Cone: This Figure is exhibited here to shew, that the Soffito of a semi-circular-headed Window, whose Splay is continued all round, is no more than

than the lower Superficies of a Semi-cone ; for if the Splay was continued in every
Part, it would meet in a Point, as the Lines *k d h* and *i c h*, *Fig.* VIII. and form
a Semi-cone as aforefaid.

This is illuſtrated by *Fig.* V. *Plate* LXVII. where *s o w* repreſents the Section of a Wall, in which is placed a circular Window, as *Fig.* A, whoſe Splay is
expreſſed by *a c* and *f h :* Now, if *c a* and *h f* be continued, they will meet in *i*,
on which, with the Radius *i c*, deſcribe the Arch *c l*, alſo the Arch *b m*. Make
the Length of the Curve *c l* equal to the Circumference of *d p*, the outer Circle
of the Splay, and draw the Line *l m :* then the ſhaded Figure *k* being bent about
and fixed within the Splay, it will exactly fit every Part thereof : But as the bending of Stuff of any conſiderable Thickneſs is impracticable, therefore divide the
whole into Parts, as at 1, 2, 3, 4, 5, 6, &c. which glew, or otherwiſe fix together,
equal to the Curvature of the Window, at pleaſure.

Fig. XI. exhibits the ancient Manner of making ſtraight Arches of Stone, in
Places where no Abutments can be had, whoſe Vouſſoirs are joggled together,
and their ſpreading prevented by Iron Bars toothed into the Head of each, run in
with Lead, as at *e c e*, and *c*.

LECTURE XXVIII.

Of Centering to Arches and Groins, Plate LXIV.

TO deſcribe the Curvatures of Groins is the chief Thing to be done in Works
of this Kind, which is moſt eaſily performed, as follows .

EXAMPLE I. *Fig.* A.

LET *a c e f* be a ſquare Plan, whoſe Vault is to be interſected by two concave
Semi-cylinders. Deſcribe the Semi-circle *a b c*, which divide into Ordinates, as
1, 2, 3, &c. Draw the Diagonal *a c*, which divide into the ſame Number of
Ordinates, and make them equal to the Ordinates of the Semi-circle, and through
their Extremes trace the Semi-ellipſis *a g c*, which is the Curve of the Groin required. In the ſame Manner the Groin *k g e* is found, whoſe interſecting Arches
are *k h i* and *i d e* ; as alſo are the Groin Curves of *Fig.* Q S and B. The Figures D and E are both ſingle ſemi-cylindrical Vaults, in whoſe Sides are ſmall interſecting Vaultings over the Heads of Windows or Doors, which are thus deſcribed, *Fig.* D. Draw as many Ordinates in the given Arch at one End as are
neceſſary, as the Ordinates 1, 2, 3, 4, 5, which continue until they meet *d e* the
Side of the Baſe of the ſmall Arch, and from thoſe Points draw Lines perpendicular thereto, of Length at pleaſure. On *d i*, the given Breadth of the ſmall
Arch, deſcribe the interſecting Curve of the ſmall Vault of any Kind, as re-
quired, as *a b i* ; divide the Baſe of one Groin, as *e i*, into the ſame Number
of equal Parts as *d x*, the ¼ Breadth, and erect Ordinates thereon, equal to the
Ordinates on *d x*, and through their Extremes trace the Curve *i f*, which is the
Curve of that Groin required. By the ſame Rule all other Kinds of interſecting
Arches may be found, although they cut the ſtraight Vault on any oblique
Angle inſtead of a right Angle, the Baſe of the ſhorter and of the longer
Groin being divided into the ſame Number of equal Parts, and the Ordinates in
each being made reſpectively equal. The other Examples at *q n*, in *Fig.* D, and
at *k g* and *r p*, are given for a further Inſpection, to illuſtrate the Truth of this
Rule.

To find the Lengths and Angles of Boards for the Covering of Centers, Fig. N O P.

Suppoſe *b d k l*, to be the Plan of a Vault, whoſe interſecting Arches are the
Semi-circle *b c d*, and the Semi-ellipſis *d h l* ; continue *b d*, both Ways, and make
it equal to the Girt of the Semi-circle *b c d*, and from the Center *i* draw the Lines
i a and *i g* ; then the Triangle *a i g* is the Covering for one End, and the Boarding being cut with Angles, equal to the Angles made by dotted parallel Lines,
and the Lines *a i*, and *i g*, will be the Bevels ; and their Lengths being taken from
the Lines *a i* and *i g*, unto the Line *a g*, will be their Lengths, as required.
Continue *d m*, both Ways, and make *e m* equal to the Girt of the Semi-ellipſis

d h m,

d h m, and draw the Lines *i c,* and *i m*; then the Triangle *i e m;* is the Covering for one Side, whose Bevels and Lengths are to be found as before.

Note, The Figures R T V X Y, exhibit a Method for describing the Cieling of a Vault in Plano, as published in Mr. *Price's* Treatise of Carpentry, which is as follows. *First, a b c d, Fig.* X, represents the Plan, *Fig.* Y and V, the two intersecting Arches. Draw the Bases of the Groins *a g d,* and *c g b,* make the Length T equal to the Girt of *Fig.* V, including the two Piers *a l,* and *m b,* make the Length of the Parallelogram *Fig.* R, equal to the Girt of the Semi-ellipsis *l m n,* also make its Breadth equal to the Girt of the Semi-circle *i c k*; draw Ordinates at pleasure from the Ellipsis, *Fig.* V, to divide the Semi-transverse Diameter of the Plan 1 *g,* in the Points 1 2 3 4 5 6 7 8. Draw *c k,* in *Fig.* R, through the Center *g,* divide *g f,* in *Fig.* R, in the same Proportion as half the Semi-ellipsis *l n,* and through the several Divisions draw Ordinates, equal to the circular Curves that stand over the dotted Lines included between the Lines *a g,* and *g c,* in *Fig.* X; and then Lines being traced through the Extremes of those Ordinates, the *Figure* included by them and the Line *d f,* will be the Covering to the Part *a g c.* But if the Lines *g f* and *g k,* in *Fig.* R, be each divided in the same Proportion as the Semi-transverse Diameter 1 *g,* in *Fig.* X, and right Lines be drawn through them, as Mr. *Price* in his Treatise of Carpentry directs, their Intersections will not form the Covering for *a g c* in *Fig.* X, nor will the Parallelogram *a e l b, Fig.* R, be the Covering to the two intersecting Arches of *Fig.* X, as he mistakenly has asserted.

To *describe curved Groins,* Fig. K I F, Plate LXV.

LET *a b c d* be the given Plan.

CONTINUE *a c* and *b d,* until they meet in the Point 1 in the Line *e f.* Bisect *a c,* and *b d,* and describe the two Semi-circles, *a g c,* and *b k d.* Divide the Diameter of either Semi-circle, as *b d,* into any Number of equal Parts, suppose ten, and draw the Ordinates 5, 4, 3, 2, 1, &c. on the Point 1 in the Line *e f*; from the several Parts in the Diameter *b d,* describe concentrick Arches to the Line *a c,* divide the Arch *a 5 b* into the same Number of equal Parts as the Diameter *b d* is divided into, and from the Point 1 in the Line *e f* draw right Lines, which will intersect the aforesaid concentrick Arches, in the Points through which the Curves *c 1 b,* and *a 1 d,* the Bases of the Groins, must be traced.

To *describe inner and outer Ribs.*

DRAW *a b, Fig.* F, equal to the Girt of the outer Curve *a 5 b,* also *e f* equal to the inner Curve *c e d,* and divide each into ten equal Parts, from which erect Ordinates equal to the respective Ordinates in the Semi-circle *b k d,* and through their Extremes trace Curves, which will complete both Ribs, being so bent or worked, as to stand on the Curves *a 5 b,* and *c e d.*

To find the *Curvatures of the Groins.*

MAKE the Base Line of *Fig.* H, equal to the Curve Line *a i,* also make the Base Line of *Fig.* W, equal to the Curve Line *i d.* Divide each into five equal Parts, and thereon raise Ordinates, equal to those in the Quadrant *b b k,* and through their Extremes trace Curves; and which being bent or worked so as to stand on the Curves *a i,* and *i d,* they together will form the circular Groin *a i d,* and the other being found in the same Manner, will be the Groins as required.

Fig. C exhibits the Manner of framing trussed Ribs for the Centers of large Arches, Stone or Brick, whose Parts are to be put together, as the Arch is raised on the Sides. The Struts 3 *n o* are supposed to be placed on upright Timbers at *a* and *i,* which at the taking down of the Center are to be taken away. As in the springing of the Arch there is very little Weight that bears on the Center, therefore the first horizontal Beam *b b* must be placed at some considerable Height above the springing of the Arch; and the Struts, 3 *n o,* are sufficient to carry its Weight. When the Arch is raised up to *b* and *b,* then the second horizontal Beam *c g* must be raised with its several Bases, Struts and Discharges *y z e x w v n,* which together will strongly resist the Weight on the Sides,

for

for as the Braces, &c. on the one Side have their Dependance on the other Side, nothing can injure them; when the Arch is brought up to c g, then the upper Part may be completed: The Mortises in the several Parts of this Truss must be all Pully-Mortises; that when the Arch is keyed in, each Tenon may be driven out of its Mortise; and every Part taken down gradually at pleasure.

LECTURE XXIX.

Of Stair-Cases.

WITH regard to the great Varieties of Buildings, I have in *Plate* LXVI. given 12 different Designs for Stair-Cases, from which the ingenious Workman may form such others as his Occasions may require. *Fig.* A is a Triangular; D C, and D E, are Circular; D I, and D K, are Elliptical; D L, Octangular; D M, Semi-circular; D F, a Trapezia; D, a geometrical Square; D A, and D B, are Parallelograms, which in general may be made fit for any Nobleman's Palace.

BEFORE a Stair-Case is made, we should consider, *first*, the Height of the Floor, to which we are to ascend. *Secondly*, the Rise, and Number of Steps that are necessary for the Height. *Thirdly*, To divide the Number of Steps by such half Spaces (or breathing Places) that are necessary for reposing on the Way. *Fourthly*, that the Space above the Head, commonly called Head Way, be spacious. And, *lastly*, that the Breadth of the Ascent be proportionable to the whole Building, and sufficient for the Purpose intended; so as to avoid Encounters by Persons ascending and descending at the same Time. The Height of Steps should not be less than 5 Inches, nor more than 7 Inches, except in such Cases where Necessity obliges a higher Rise. The Breadth of Steps should not be less than 10 Inches, nor more than 15 or 16, although some allow 18 Inches, which I think is too much. The Light to a Stair-case should always be liberal, to avoid Slips, Falls, &c. and which may proceed from the Sides, from a Cupola or Sky-Light at the Top; as the Situation will best admit. Before this Kind of Work is begun, 'tis best to make a Plan, and to lay out the whole in Ledgement, as follows.

LET *t, o, 9, 11, Fig.* D G, *Plate* LXVI. be a given Plan.

MAKE *d s* equal to the Breadth of the Ascent, which may be made from 3 Feet and ½, to 10 Feet. Draw *d b, b a,* and *a m,* parallel to the Outlines of the Plan. Divide *d b, b a,* and *a m,* each into such a Number of Steps, whose several Heights are equal to the whole Height to be ascended; within the Parallelogram *a b m d,* draw the Thickness of the Hand Rail. Add into one Sum the Heights of the several Steps, between *b* and *d,* and at that Distance, draw *q r,* parallel to *o s;* draw the Hypothenusal Line *r s,* and continue out the Plan of each Step to meet the Line *r s* at *s;* set up the Height of the first Step, and draw it parallel to *o s,* until it meet the Base Line of the 2d Step; then set up the Height of the 2d Step, and draw it parallel to *o s;* proceed in like Manner to set up the Heights of all the remaining Steps unto *r:* make *o p* equal to *o q,* and draw 2 *p* parallel to *t o;* at the Point 2, begin to set up the Steps unto the Point 1, and draw *v* 1 parallel to *t o:* make *t w* equal to *t v,* and draw *w* 8 parallel to *t 9;* at *g* begin to set the Steps as aforesaid unto *i,* then will *i e* be equal to the Height of the Story, and the several Figures *o q r s, o p 2 1 v t, t w g i 7 9,* will be the Sides of the Stair-Case laid out in Ledgement, as required.

THE Plan *Fig.* B, is in like Manner represented by *Fig.* C, which may be considered as its Section, wherein *l m* is the Height to be ascended; *g h* the first Flight, *h o* the ½ Space; *h i,* the second Flight, *i n,* the ¼ Space; *i k* the last Flight, whose Landing, as Workmen term it, is *l k.*

Note, The Parallel dotted Lines between *g h,* and *i k,* represent Strings of Wood which are cased underneath, to represent solid Steps.

THE *Fig.* Q represents the half Space of one Flight of Stairs; *Fig.* P represents *Fig.* Q with its Banisters; and *Fig.* O represents *Fig.* P completed with the Moldings of its Hand-rail, Base, &c.

THE next Thing to be considered is the Manner of placing the Newels to Stairs
Y and

and half Spaces. In *Fig.* E, *Plate* LXVI. the half Spaces are made square to the Angles of the Newels which causes the Hand-rail of the first Flight to drop the Height of 2 Steps below the Rail of the 2d Flight. In *Fig.* F, the Stairs are set to the Middle of the Newel, which causes its Rail to drop two Steps, and in *Fig.* G they are placed to the Outside of the Newel, and drop but one Step. Lastly, in *Fig.* H the Stairs are set half their Breadth clear without the Newel, which causes the Rails to meet as in *Fig.* O.

To preserve a Regularity in *Fig.* I and K, which have large Moldings, set the Stairs the Breadth of half a Stair clear on the Outside of the Moldings. It is also to be observed, that as 'tis usual to place half Ballusters against Newels, therefore when it happens that the Interval or Space is too great, then the Newel should be augmented as in *Fig.* K.

Fig. L exhibits the regular Method, and *Fig.* M a shameful Method of joining Rails and Balusters, which last is to be seen in the Stair-cases at the West-end of the Parish Church of *St. Martin's in the Fields, London,* and which was executed under the Direction of Mr JAMES GIBBS, Architect.

Fig. N exhibits the Manner of dividing the Heights of raking Balusters by continuing the Members of the straight Balusters; and *Fig.* X and Y, *Plate* LXVIII. exhibits the Manner of placing straight and raking Balusters over each other.

THE Figures I K L M N O P Q are divers Examples of Balusters as were used by the Antients; as also are *Fig.* T V W and R divers Guilochis and Ornaments, which were often used instead of Balusters, and which, when well executed, are very grand.

IT was the Custom of the Antients to begin the Balustrade of a grand Staircase with a Pedestal, as *Fig.* S, *Plate* LXVIII. which to a large Stair-case is yet the most grand Manner; but many modern Architects, who think themselves wiser, place a twisted Rail at the lowermost Stair instead of a Pedestal.

IN small Buildings a twisted Rail is very proper, but in magnificent Buildings I think them vastly inferior to a noble Pedestal.

To describe a twisted Rail is the next Work in Order, which may be performed as following:

LET the Lines B D E, *Fig.* IV. *Plate* LXVII. represent the Edges of the two lower Stairs of a Stair-case.

DIVIDE *b* 9, the Tread of the second Stair, into 9 equal Parts, continue the Line D towards the left at pleasure. Draw N F, parallel to 9 *b*, at the Distance of 7 Parts, also draw the Line 14 *d* at the Distance of 3 Parts, then *d b* is the Breadth of the Hand-rail. Draw A *n* parallel to 9 *b*, at the Distance of *b* 9, then the Point *n* is the Center of the Eye of the Scroll. On the Point *a* describe the Quadrants *b c* and *d e*, which is the Length of the twisted Part of the Rail, the remaining Part to *n*, the Eye, being level. On *n* describe the Circle *x x p*, whose Diameter *w p* must be equal to *d b*, the Breadth of the Hand-rail. Divide the Radius *n p* into four equal Parts, and through the first Part at *o*, draw the Line *r l*, cutting the Line N F in *x*; on *x* describe the Quadrants *c f*, and *e g*, make *o t* equal unto 2 Parts of *n p*, and draw the Line *t s* parallel to A *n*. On the Point *t* describe the Quadrants *f h*, and *g x*, make *n w* equal to 3 Parts of *n p*, and through the Point *w* draw the Line *x k*, parallel to *r x*; on *x* describe the Quadrant *b v*, and on *w* the Quadrant *v p*, and then is the Plan completed.

To describe the Mold for the Twist.

CONTINUE *b* 9 towards M, and F N towards *b*, in *Fig.* I, also draw L I parallel to *b* N, at the Distance of N K, in any Part of N *b*, as at *c*, draw the Line *a f* at right Angles to *b* N, and on *c* describe the Semi-circle *a b f*, make *a d*, and *f t*, each equal to the Rise of one Stair, and draw the Line *d e t*. Make *c* N equal to *c t*, divide *b c* into any Number of equal Parts, and draw the Ordinates 15, 1; 16, 2; *k* 3, &c. divide *c* N into the same Number of equal Parts as in *b c*, and make the Ordinates thereon equal to the Ordinates on *b c*, and through their Extremes trace the Curve N *f*, which is the Curve of the Outside of the Mold. Make *b k* equal to the Breadth of the Hand-rail, and on *c*,

with

with the Radius *c k*, defcribe the inner Semi-circle. Make *c b* equal to *r t*.
On *k c*, the Semi-diameter of the inner Semi-circle, make Ordinates, which
transfer on *c h*, as before, and through their Extremes trace the Curve of the
Mold, which will complete the whole, as required. For as the Outlines of the
Plan of the twifted Part of the Rail *b c* and *d e* are Quadrants, therefore the
outer and inner Curves of the Mold will be both a quarter Part of two
Ellipfes; becaufe the twifted Rail, ftrictly confidered, is no other than the
Section of a Cylinder, as L M I K, whofe Diameter *a f* is equal to twice *a b*,
in *Fig.* IV. and its tranfverfe Diameter equal to *d t*, and conjugate Diameter
to *a f*.

The Twift of a Rail over a circular Bafe at a half Space, as *a b*, *Fig.* II. is the
very fame Thing as the preceding, as being the fourth Part of an Ellipfis, made
by the Section of a Cylinder, whofe Diameter is equal to twice *a c*.

The Manner of making the Knees and Ramps of Rails, is the next that is to
be confidered, which are thus defcribed

Let *m r*, *q t*, *s v*, and *w*, be four given Stairs. From *p*, the Middle of the
lower Stair, draw the raking Line *p f*, fo as to be parallel to *q s w*, the Nofes
of the Stairs: alfo draw *k b* parallel to *p f*, at the Diftance of the Rail's Thicknefs. Continue *t x* to *g*, and make *f b* equal to *f g*, and draw *a d* parallel to *m x*.
From the Point *p* draw the under Part of the Knee, parallel to *m r*; as alfo *l k*,
at the Diftance of the Rail's Thicknefs, and then the Knee will be completed.
Divide the Angle *n f b* into two equal Parts, by the Line *f a*, cutting the Line
a b in *a*. On *a*, with the Radius *a b*, defcribe the Arches *g b*, and *i e*, which is
the Ramp required. Now this Rail being fet up on the Ballufters to its affigned
Height, fo for the Points *l* and *b*, to ftand over the Points *m* and *x*, it will be completed, as required.

Fig. IX. is the Bafe of a Newel-poft, whofe Sides are fluted in various Manners,
as exprefsed at *a b c d*, &c. and *Fig.* VI. is a View of the Molding of a Hand-rail
for a common Stair-cafe.

To find the Mold of a twifted Rail, to a circular or elliptical Stair-cafe,
Fig. VII. *and* VIII. *Plate* LXVII.

Let A B C D, *Fig.* VII. be the Plan of a cylindrical Stair-cafe, whofe Bafe
is a Circle, and whofe Stairs wind about the Cylinder *a b d*, &c. The Plan
of the Stairs being divided, continue out the Diameter *d a*, towards the Left-
hand, as to *f*, of Length at pleafure. Make *a f* equal to the Girt of the Semi-
circle *a b d*, which divide into the fame Number of equal Parts as there are
Stairs in the Plan of the Semi-circle *a b d*, as at the Points 1 2 3 4, &c.
from which erect Perpendiculars, as 1 *a*, 2 *a*, 3 *a*, &c. of Length at pleafure.
Confider the Rife of a Stair, and make the Perpendicular *f g*, equal to the Rife
of all the 12 Stairs that go round the Semi-circle *a b d*; and divide the Perpendicular *f g* into 12 equal Parts, as at the Points 1 2 3 4, &c. from which
draw Lines parallel to *f d*, continued out towards the Right-hand, at pleafure,
which will intersect the Perpendiculars on the Line *f a d*, in the Points *a c*,
a c, *a c*, &c. and which are the Breadths and Heights of the Treads and Rifes
of the 12 Stairs, at the Side of the Semi-cylinder *a b d*; for was the whole
Figure *g f a* applied about the Semi-cylinder, then the Parts *a c*, *a-c*, &c.
would be in the refpective Place of each Stair. Let *a e* reprefent the Breadth
of the Hand-rail, and the Semi-circle *e* 10 *c* its Bafe, over which its Infide
is to ftand. Divide its Diameter *e c* into any Number of equal Parts, as at
1 2 3 4, &c. and draw the Ordinates 1, 6; 2, 7; 3, 8; 4, 9, &c. which continue upwards, fo as to meet the horizontal Lines drawn from the Perpendicular
g f, in the Points 28, 27, 26, 25, &c. through which trace the Ogee Curve
28, 14, *a*, which is the Sectional Line of the Cylinder, over which it ftands.
Make the Diftances 15, 21; 19, 14; 18, 13; 17, 12; and 16, 11, equal to
the Ordinates 10, 5; 9, 4; 8, 3; 7, 2; and 6, 1; and through the Points
20, 19, 18, 17, 16, to *a*, on the Line *f d*, trace the Curve, 20, 16, *a*, which
is the infide Curve of the Mold, and whofe Out-curve 21 *a*, being made con-

centric

centric thereto, will be the Mold required, whose End 21, 20, when set up in its Place, will stand perpendicular over its Base *b* 10.

Note, This Mold, though made but for one 4th Part of the Cylinder, will serve for the whole, by repeating the same, or adding three or more others of the same Kind, to the Ends of each other as often as there are Revolutions in the Cylinder.

Fig. VIII. is the Plan of an Elliptical Stair-case, whose Mold *i k* is described in the same Manner, and therefore needs no other Description.

LECTURE XXX.

Of Compartments for Monumental Inscriptions and Shields ; also divers Ornaments for Buildings and Gardens.

AS in the preceding Lectures I have explained the principal Parts of Buildings, I shall now conclude this Part with some particular Ornaments, which are in common Use, and which are as necessary for the Enrichment of Drawings, as of Buildings themselves.

IN Plates LXIX. and LXX. are contained fourteen Designs of Compartments, for Monumental Inscriptions, Coats of Arms, to be placed in open Pediments, &c. In Plate LXXI. are contained, first, eleven Kinds of Vases, as A B C D E F G H I K L, for the Enrichment of Piers to Gates, Parapet Walls, &c. as also are the Balls P Q, and Pine-apple R. The Figures M O S are Designs for Flower-pots, which are to be employed as Ornaments, in such Places where Vases will be too large. As the principal Parts of these Ornaments are proportioned by equal Parts, as expressed in divers Places between them, the young Student will see how easy it is to make them to any given Height.

THE *Fig.* W Y, A B, A C, have their principal Parts determined by equal Parts also. Figures W and Y are Designs for Christening Fonts ; and A B, A C, for Pedestals to horizontal Dials ; and indeed, when horizontal Dials are very large, the Figures W and Y may be employed to their Pedestals,

Fig. X is a Kind of Pedestal, called a *Terme,* from *Terminus,* the God of Bounds or Land-marks, who being anciently made standing in a Sheath, these Kinds of Pedestals were taken for the Support of Bustos, and are thus proportioned to any given Height. Divide the given Height into 10 equal Parts ; give the upper 1 to the Height of the upper Astragal, Fillet, and Cavetto ; and the lower 1 to the Height of the Plinth, Fillet and inverted Cima. The Projection of the great Astragal is two Parts on each Side the central Line, and of the small Astragal in the Base, one Part on each Side, from which the other Moldings take their Projections, as common in Columns.

To flute these Pedestals.

DIVIDE the Breadth into twenty-one equal Parts, give one to each Fillet, and three to each Flute.

THE *Fig.* N represents a *Harpy,* a fictitious Monster, said to have the Head of a Maiden, and Body of a Bird ; and if such are made in Stone or Metal, having the Bodies of Turtle-doves, Owls, and Magpies, they will be pretty Emblems of the Innocency, Wisdom, and babbling Nonsense of Women.

THE Figures Z, A D, A E, and A F, represent the Monster called *Sphinx,* whose Head and Breast are like those of a Woman, its Voice like a Man's, its Body like a Lion's, and Wings as a Bird ; but sometimes their Wings are omitted, as *Fig.* A D and A E. The Figures T and Y are two Kinds of Obelisks, for Lamp-posts, &c. the one square, the other octangular ; and *Fig.* A G is the Design of a Shell, for to enrich the Head of a Niche, &c.

PART IV.

Of the MENSURATION of *Superficies* and *Solids.*

AS the Foot is the Standard Meafure of moft Nations, I fhall therefore pre-fix to the following Rules a Table of Foreign Feet, carefully compared with the Englifh Foot, wherein 'tis fuppofed, that the *Englifh* Foot is divided into 1000 equal Parts, as alfo into 12 Inches, and each Inch into 10 equal Parts.

	Engl. Feet. Decim.	F.Inc.10ths.	
English *Foot,*	1,000	0 12	0
Paris, *the Royal Foot.*	1,068	1 00	8
Paris *Foot,* by *Dr.* Bernard.	1,066		
Amfterdam *Foot.*	,942	0 11	3
Antwerp *Foot.*	,946	0 11	3
Leyden *Foot.*	1,033	1 00	3
Strafburg *Foot.*	,920	0 11	0
Frankfort ad Mænam *Foot.*	,948	0 11	6
Spanifh *Foot.*	1,001	1 00	0
Venice *Foot.*	1,162	1 01	9
Dantzick *Foot.*	,944	0 11	3
Copenhagen *Foot,*	,965	0 11	6
Prague *Foot.*	1,026	1 00	3
Roman *Foot.*	,967	0 11	6
Old Roman *Foot.*	,970		
Greek *Foot.*	1,007	1 00	1
China *Cubit.*	1,016	1 00	2
Cairo *Cubit.*	1,824	1 09	9
Old { Babylonian *Cubit.*	,	1 06 $\frac{24}{100}$	
Greek *Cubit.*	,	1 06 $\frac{11}{100}$	
Roman *Cubit.*	,	1 05 $\frac{456}{1000}$	
Turkifh *Pike.*	2,200	2 02	4
Perfian *Arafh.*	3,197	3 02	3

LECTURE I.

Of Rules for meafuring the Superficies of geometrical Figures, **Plate LXXII.**

RULE I. *To meafure any plain Triangle,* Fig. A B C D.

AS 1 : half the Bafe *c d* or *h i,* Fig. A or B : : *b d* or *g i,* the Perpendicular, : the Area; or as 1 : the whole Bafe *m s,* or *z y, Fig.* C or D : : ½ the Perpendicular : Area.

To find the Area of any plain Triangle, having the Sides only given.

ADD the three Sides together; from the half Sum fubtraĉt each Side feverally, and note their Differences. Multiply any two of the Differences together, and their Product by the other Difference. Multiply the laft Product by the half Sum of 3 Sides, and the fquare Root of their Product is the Area required.

RULE II. *To meafure a geometrical Square, or Parallelogram, as the Figures* E F.

AS 1 : *c d* the Length : : *a c* the Breadth : Area.

RULE III. *To meafure a Rhombus or Rhomboides, as the Figures* G *and* H.

AS 1 : *a d,* equal to *c e* the Length : : *b c* the Perpendicular Height : Area.

RULE IV. *To meafure a Trapezoid, as* Fig. I.

AS 1 : ½ the Bafe *f e,* : : the perpendicular Height *b f :* Area.

RULE V. *To meafure a Trapezia, as* Fig. K.

AS 1 : a Diagonal, as *b g :* : half the Sum of the 2 Perpendiculars *a d* and *c e :* Area.

RULE

RULE VI. *To meafure any Polygon, as the Hexagon* L.

As 1 : ¼ the Circumference *a k*, : : ½ the Diameter *e g*, equal to *b a* : Area.

RULE VII. *To meafure any irregular right-lined Figure, as* Fig. M.

DIVIDE the Figure into Trapeziums, as *d e, e f, c d, b e*, and the Triangle *b a e*, whofe Areas find by RULES I. and V. and their Areas added together is the Area required.

RULE VIII. *To find the Length of an Arch of any Circle, as* a c d, *Fig.* S.

DIVIDE the Chord Line into 4 equal Parts, make the Chord Line of *a b* equal to 1 Part, then *b d* is nearly equal to half the Arch Line required : *Or thus Arithmetically :* Multiply *a c*, the Chord of half the Arch, by 8 ; from the Product fubtract *a d.* Divide the Remains by 3, and the Quotient will be equal to the Length of the Arch Line *a c d* required. *Or thus :* From the Chords *a c* and *c d*, fubtract the Chord *a d.* Divide the Remains by 3, and then the Quotient added to the Chord Lines *a c* and *c d*, the Sum will be nearly equal to the Arch Line *a c d*, required.

RULE IX. *To meafure a Quadrant, as* b c e, *Fig.* O.

As 1 : ¼ the Arch *c e*, : : a Side, as *b e* : Area.

RULE X. *To meafure a Semi-circle, as* a d c, *Fig.* O.

As 1 : ¼ the Arch *a d c*, : : the Diameter *a c* : Area.

RULE XI. *The Diameter of a Circle being given, to find its Circumference.*

As 7 : 22, : : the given Diameter : Circumference required. Or, as 113 : 355, : : the given Diameter : Circumference required. Or, as 1 : 3,141593, : : the given Diameter to the Circumference required. Or, as 1,00000,00000,00000,00000,00000,00000,00000 : is to 3,14159,26535,89793, 23846,26433,83279,50288, fo is the Diameter given, to the Circumference required.

RULE XII. *The Circumference of a Circle being given, to find its Diameter.*

As 22 : 7, : : the Circumference given : Diameter required. Or, as 355 : 113, : : the Circumference : Diameter. Or, as 3,141593 : 1 : : the Circumference to the Diameter.

RULE XIII. *The Diameter of a Circle being given, as* a c, *Fig.* N, *to find its Area.*

I. *By* VAN CULEN's *Analogy.*

As 1 : ,7854, : : the Square of the Diameter : Area.

II. *By* METIUS's *Analogy.*

As 452 : 355, : : the Square of the Diameter : Area.

III. *By* ARCHIMEDES's *Analogy.*

As 14 : 11, : : the Square of the Diameter : Area.

RULE XIV. *The Circumference of a Circle being given, to find its Area.*

As 1 : ,07958 : : the Square of the Circumference : Area.

RULE XV. *The Area of a Circle being given, to find its Diameter.*

As 1 : 1,2732, : : the Area : Diameter required.

RULE XVI. *The Area of a Circle being given, to find its Circumference.*

As 1 : 12,56637, : : the Area : Circumference required.

RULE XVII. *The Diameter of a Circle being given, to find the Side of a Square nearly equal to the given Circle.*

As 1 : ,8862, : : the Diameter : Side required.

RULE XVIII. *The Circumference of a Circle being given, to find the Side of a Square nearly equal to the given Circle.*

As 1 : ,2821, : : the Circumference : Side required.

RULE XIX. *The Diameter of a Circle being given, to find the Side of a Square infcribed.*

As 1 : ,7071, : : the Diameter : Side required.

RULE XX. *The Circumference of a Circle being given, to find the Side of a Square infcribed.*

As 1 : ,2251, : : the Circumference : Side required.

RULE

RULE XXI. *The Area of a Circle being given, to find the Side of a Square inscribed.*

As 1 : ,6366, : : Area : Side required.

RULE XXII. *The Side of a Square being given, to find the Diameter of its circumscribing Circle.*

As 1 : 1,4142 : : the Side of the Square : Diameter required.

RULE XXIII. *The Side of a Square being given, to find the Circumference of its circumscribing Circle.*

As 1 : 4,443, : : the Side of the Square : Circumference required.

RULE XXIV. *The Side of a Square being given, to find the Diameter of a Circle, nearly equal to the Square.*

As 1 : 1,128, : : the Side of the Square : Diameter required.

RULE XXV. *The Side of a Square being given, to find the Circumference of a Circle, nearly equal to the Square.*

As : 3,545, : : the Side of the Square : Circumference required.

RULE XXVI. *To find the Diameter of a Circle, as* c e, *Fig.* T, *having the Chord Line* a b, *and Height* c d, *of the Segment* a c b, *given.*

SQUARE *a d,* and divide the Product by *c d,* the Quotient will be equal to *d e,* then *c d,* more *d e,* is the Diameter required.

RULE XXVII. *To measure the Sector of a Circle, as* c b a, *or* d a e f, *Fig.* R.

As 1 : ½ the Arch Line, : : the Radius *d a,* or *c a* : Area.

RULE XXVIII. *To measure the Segment of a Circle, as* a b c, *Fig.* P.

IMAGINE Lines to be drawn from *a* and *c,* to the Center P; and *a b c* P, will be a Sector; which being measured by RULE XXVII. and the supposed Triangle *a c* P, being deducted from it, the Remains will be the Content of the Segment required.

To measure the great Segment of a Circle, as d e f.

IMAGINE Lines drawn from *d* and *e,* to the Center P, as *d a* and *a e,* in *Fig.* R. Then to the Area of the Sector *d a e f,* found by RULE XXVII. add the Area of the Triangle *d a e,* by RULE I. and their Sum is the Area of the greater Segment required. Hence 'tis plain, that the Center of a given Segment of a Circle must be known, before its Area can be found.

RULE XXIX. *To measure the Zone of a Circle, as* a d e f b c, *Fig.* Q.

To the Parallelogram *d f a b,* add the Segments *d e f,* and *a b c,* and their Sum is the Area of the Zone required.

RULE XXX. *To measure the Superficies of any irregular curvilineal Figure, as the Figure* V.

DIVIDE the curved Bounds into Segments, as n p a, a b c, c d e, e f g, g h i, i k l, l m n. To the Area of the right-lined Figure *n a c e g i l n,* add the Area of the Segments *n p a, c d e, g h i, i k l,* and from the Sum subtract the Areas of the Segments *a b c, e f g,* and *n m l,* and the Remains will be the Area of the irregular Figure required.

RULE XXXI. *To measure an Ox Eye, as Fig.* W.

DRAW the Line *a d,* then add the Area of the Segment *a c d,* to the Segment *a b d.*

RULE XXXII. *To measure any spherical Triangle, as* X Y Z, *and* A, *Fig.* II.

FIRST, *Figure* X, to the plain Triangle *a c e,* add the Segments *a b e, c d e,* and *a e m,* their Sum is the Area required. Secondly, *Fig.* Y, to the Area of the plain Triangle *a b f,* add the Segments *a c b,* and *b d f,* and from the Sum subtract the Segment *e a f,* and the Remains is the Area required. Thirdly, *Fig.* Z, from the plain Triangle *a e c,* subtract the Segments *e a d,* and *b a c,* and to the Remains add the Segment *e c n,* the Sum is the Area required. Fourthly, *Fig.* A, from the plain Triangle, *a d f,* subtract the Segments *c b e,* the Remains is the Area required.

RULE XXXIII. *To measure any mixtilineal Triangle, as* B C D E, *Fig.* II.

FIRST, the Triangle C, from the plain Triangle, *c a d,* subtract the Segments *a c b,* and *e c d,* the Remains is the Area required. Secondly, the Triangle

D, to the Triangle *c a e*, add the Segments *b c a*, and *c e d*, the Sum is the Area required. Thirdly, to the plain Triangle E, add the Segment *b a c*, the Sum is the Area required.

RULE XXXIV. *To measure compound regular Figures, as* F G H, *Fig.* II.

FIRST, the *Fig.* F, to the geometrical Square *a b c d*, add the Semi-circles *e* and *f*, the Sum is the Area required. Secondly, the *Fig.* G, from the geometrical Square 1 2 3 4, subtract the Quadrants 1 *a b*, 2 *c d*, *b* 3 *g*, *e f* 4, the Remains is the Area required. Thirdly, the *Fig.* H, from the Parallelogram 1 2 3 4, subtract the Triangles 1 *b e*, *d* 2 *e*, *a* 3 *h*, and *f g* 4, the Remains is the Area required.

RULE XXXV. *To measure Egg and Heart Ovals, as Fig.* O P Q.

FIRST, the Egg Oval, *Fig.* O. To the Trapezoid *a d f h*, add the Semi-circle *a c d*, and the Segments *a f*, *f h g*, and *d h*, the Sum is the Area required. Secondly, *Fig.* P. To the plain Triangle *a c d*, add the Semi-circle *a b c*, and the two Segments *a d*, and *c d*, the Sum is the Area required. Thirdly, the Heart Oval Q. To the plain Triangle *a b g*, add the two Semi-circles *a d c*, *c e b*, and two Segments *a f g*, and *b g f*, the Sum is the Area required.

RULE XXXVI. *To measure an Ellipsis, as the* Fig. I K.

As 1 : ,7854 : : the Square of two Diameters : Area. The Area of every Ellipsis is a mean proportional between the Areas of its circumscribing and inscribing Circles, as in *Fig.* N.

FOR as the Area of the circumscribing Circle *a b f m* : the Area of the Ellipsis *a g p x* : : the Area of the Ellipsis *a g p x* : Area of the inscribed Circle *b g o x*.

RULE XXXVII. *To measure the Segment of an Ellipsis, as* e f i, *Fig.* M, *or* d g n, *Fig.* N.

FIRST, The Segment of an Ellipsis whose Base is parallel to the conjugate Diameter, as *e f i*, *Fig.* M, is in proportion to the Segment *d f n*, of the same Height of the circumscribing Circle; as *b m*, the Diameter of the circumscribing Circle : *c k* the conjugated Diameter of the Ellipsis : : the Area of *d f n*, the Circle's Segment : *e f i*, the Area of the Segment of the Ellipsis. Secondly, the Segment of an Ellipsis whose Base is parallel to the transverse Diameter as *d n*, *Fig.* N, is in proportion, as the Area of the inscribed Circle *b g o x* : the Area of the Ellipsis *a g p x* : : the Area of the Segment of the inscribed Circle : *d g n* the Area of the Ellipsis required. Or as *g x* the Diameter of the inscribed Circle : *a p* the transverse Diameter : : the Area of the Segment of the inscribed Circle : Area of the Segment of the Ellipsis. The *Fig.* K and L, are each a Semi-Ellipsis, the first on the transverse, and the last on the conjugate Diameter, whose Areas are to be found by considering each of them as a whole Ellipsis, and take ¼ the Area so found, for their Areas required.

The Fig. I K, *shews how to describe any Ellipsis by the Help of three straight Laths,* &c. *as following:*

DRAW the 2 Diameters *a f* and *b n* at right Angles, to their given Lengths. Make *n d*, and *n e*, each equal to half the transverse Diameter, then *a* and *e* are the two focus Points, whereon fix two Laths, as on Centers, as *d g* and *e h*, each equal to the transverse Diameter. To their Ends *h* and *g* fix a third Lath, equal to the Distance of *d e*, so that the Ends at *h* and *g* may be moveable as the Joint of a two-foot Rule. Then the three Laths being moved about the two focus Points, their several Points of Intersection will trace out the Ellipsis required.

RULE XXXVIII. *To measure the Area of a Parabola, as Figures* R *or* S.

EVERY Parabola is equal to two thirds of its inscribing Parallelogram. Therefore as 1 : *d f*, *Fig.* R, or *a f*, *Fig.* S : : *a d*, *Fig.* R, or *b a*, *Fig.* S : a 4th Number, two thirds of which is the Area required.

LECTURE I.

Of Rules for measuring the Solidity of all Kinds of Bodies, and their Superficies.

RULE I. *To measure the Solidity of the Cube* R, *or the Parallelopipedon* W.

A S 1 : the Area of any End or Side : : the Depth or Length from that End or Side : the Solidity required.

THE

THE Superficies of the Cube R, is the geometrical Squares 1 2 3 4 5 6, *Fig.* S, and of the Parallelopipedon W, the Parallelograms 1 X, 4 5 and geometrical Squares 2 3, *Fig.* X.

RULE II. *To measure the Solidity of any Prism as the Figures* V, A B, *and* A D.

As 1 : the Area of one End : : the Length : Solidity required; the Superficies of the triangular Prism V, is the Parallelogram 1 2 5, and Triangles 3, 4, *Fig.* Z. Of the hexangular Prism A B, the Parallelograms 1 2 3 4 5 6, and Hexagons 7 8. And of the Trapezia Prism A B, the Parallelograms 2, 3, 4, 5, and Trapezias 1, 6.

RULE III. *To measure the Solidity of a Cylinder, whose Base is a Circle, as* Fig. A, Plate LXXIV. *or an Ellipsis, as* Fig. I, Plate LXXIII.

As 1 : the Area of one End : : the Length the Solidity required. The Superficies of the elliptical Cylinder I, is the Parallelogram *l n m o*, (whose Length is equal to the Circumference of the Cylinder) and the 2 Ellipses *c k d a*, and *e i g f*. And the Superficies of the circular Cylinder A is the Parallelogram *a*, and two Circles D C.

RULE IV. *To measure the Solidity of a Tetrahedron, as* Fig. T, Plate LXXII. *the Pyramis* A G *and* A F, *and Cone*, Fig. R. Plate LXXIV.

IN every of these Bodies, as 1 : the Area of its Base : : ⅓ of its Altitude : the Solidity required. The Reason hereof is, that every Cone is equal to ¼ of its circumscribing Cylinder; that is, to a Cylinder of the same Base and Altitude. So likewise every Tetrahedron and Pyramis is equal to ⅓ of its circumscribing Prism, whose Base and Altitude is the same as those of the Tetrahedron and Pyramis, and therefore it follows, that as 1 : the Area of the Base of a Cylinder or Prism : : the Length of its Axis : a 4th Number, one 3d of which is equal to the Solidity of the Cone or Pyramis inscribed therein.

THE Superficies of the Tetrahedron is the equilateral Triangles 1, 2, 3, 4.

THE Superficies of the square Pyramis A F is the geometrical Square A E, and the Isosceles Triangle *a e b*, *b g d*, *d h e*, and *a c f*. The Superficies of the octangular Pyramis A G is the Octagon A F, and Isosceles Triangles *a b c d e f g h*; and the Superficies of the Cone is the Sector *b h i f*, and Circle *k l*.

Note, The Length of the Arch *k i f* is equal to the Circumference of the Base of the Cone. And the Radius *b h*, to *b f*, the Side of the Cone.

RULE V. *To measure the Solidity of a Sphere, as* Fig. T, Plate LXXIV.

As 21 : 11 : : the Cube of the Sphere's Axis : Solidity required, or as 1 : ,5236 : : the Cube of the Sphere's Axis : Solidity required; for if the Axis of a Sphere be 11, its Solidity is ,5236.

EVERY Sphere is equal to a Cone, whose Axis is equal to the Radius of the Sphere, and its Base to the Area of the Sphere. Or every Sphere is equal to two Thirds of its circumscribing Cylinder. Therefore, as 1 : the Area of a great Circle of the Sphere : : the Diameter : 4th Number, two Thirds of which is the Solidity of the Sphere.

As a Cone is equal to ⅓ of a Cylinder of equal Base and Altitude, and as a Sphere is equal to ⅔ of a Cylinder of equal Diameter and Altitude, 'tis therefore evident that a Cone whose Base is equal to a great Circle of a Sphere, and its Axis equal to the Axis of the Sphere, its Solidity is equal to ⅓ the Solidity of the Sphere.

AND a Cone, whose Axis is equal to the Semi-axis of the Sphere, and the Diameter of its Base to twice the Diameter of the Sphere, will be equal to the Sphere; as also is a Cone whose Axis is equal to twice the Diameter of the Sphere, and the Diameter of its Base equal to the Diameter of the Sphere.

RULE VI. *To measure the Superficies of a Sphere.*

THE Area of every Sphere is equal to four great Circles thereof, so the Area of the Sphere, *Fig.* T, *Plate* LXXIV. is equal to the Circles V W X Y. Or as 1 : the Diameter : : the Circumference to the Area required.

Note, THE Area of a circumscribing Cylinder is to the Area of the inscribed Sphere, as 3 is to 2; and, which is the same Proportion that the Solidity of the Cylinder has to the Solidity of the Sphere.　　　　Z　　　　*Note*,

Note, IF the Covering or Area of a Semi-sphere be laid out, as taught in the Covering of the Heads of Semi-circular Niches, in LECT. XXV. hereof, as is exhibited in *Fig.* M, by *t v w x, &c.* and the Area of a Part, as of Z, be multiplied by twice the Number of Parts laid out, the Product will be the Superficies of the Sphere required. *Note also,* The several occult Arches in this *Fig.* are no more than a Repetition of those in *Fig.* K, *Plate* LVI. which I have inserted here again, for the easier understanding the Manner of describing the several Parts, *t v w x, &c.* which are the Superficies of the Semi-sphere laid open.

RULE VII. *To measure the Solidity of any Segment of a Sphere, as* f 1, 7; Fig. M, Plate LXXIII.

I. *The Diameter and Altitude of the Frustum being given.*

To 3 times the Square of *f* 3, the Semi-diameter of its Base, add the Square of 3,1, its Altitude. Multiply the Sum by the Height, and that Product again by ,5236, the Product, cutting off 4 Decimals to the Right-hand, is the Solidity required.

II. *The Axis of the Sphere* k g, *and* 1 3, *the Height of the Segment given.*

FROM 3 Times the Axis, subtract twice the Height of the Segment. Multiply the Remainder by the Square of the Segment's Height, and that Product by 5236, the Product, cutting off 4 Decimals to the Right-hand, is the Solidity required.

RULE VIII. *To measure the Solidity of any Frustum of a Sphere, as* h k b, Fig. A L, Plate LXXIV

FROM the Solidity of the whole Sphere, deduct the Segment *h m k,* and the Remains is the Solidity of the Frustum required.

RULE IX. *To measure the Zone of a Sphere, as* h k d e, Fig. A, L, Plate LXXIV.

FROM the Solidity of the whole Sphere, deduct the two Segments *h m k* and *d e b,* the Remains is the Solidity of the Zone required.

RULE X. *To measure the Zone of a Spheroid, as* Fig. L, Plate LXXIII.

MULTIPLY the Square of *h k,* the conjugate Diameter, by *a n,* the transverse Diameter, and that Product by ,5236, the Product, cutting off the 4 Decimals, is the Solidity required.

Note, EVERY Spheroid, as *a c e g, Fig.* Q, *Plate* LXXIII. is equal to two Thirds of a Cylinder, as *a d n f,* whose Diameter is equal to the conjugate Diameter, and Height to the transverse Diameter.

RULE XI. *To measure the Solidity of the Segment, or Frustum of any Spheroid.*

INSCRIBE the Spheroid in a Sphere; then as the Solidity of the Sphere is to the Solidity of the Spheroid, so is any Part of the Sphere to the like Part of the Spheroid.

RULE XII. *To measure the Solidity of a parabolick Conoid, as* Fig. N, Plate LXXIII.

THIS Solid is generated by the Revolution of a Semi-parabola, on its Axis, and is thus measured, *viz.* Multiply the Square of its Diameter, by ,7854, and its Product by Half the perpendicular Altitude, the Product (cutting off the 4 Decimals) is the Solidity required.

RULE XIII. *To measure the Solidity of the Frustum of a Parabolick Conoid, as* f a c g, Fig. N, Plate LXXIII.

MULTIPLY the Sum of the Squares of *a c* and *f g,* the lesser and greater Diameters, by ,3927, and that Product by the perpendicular Height of the Frustum, the last Product is the Solidity required.

RULE XIV. *To measure the Solidity of a parabolick Spindle, as* Fig. W, Plate LXXIII.

MULTIPLY the Square of *g l* its greatest Diameter, by ,41888, (being ⅗ of ,7854) and that Product by *h q* its Length, the last Product, cutting off the Decimals, is the Solidity required.

RULE

RULE XV. *To measure the Solidity of a Frustum of a Parabolick Spindle, as* d f g l, *or of a Zone, as* d f m o.

MULTIPLY the Square of *g l*, the greatest Diameter, by 1,5708; also multiply the Square of *d f* the lesser Diameter, by ,7854 , also multiply the Square of the Difference of the Diameters, by ,31416; then from the Sum of the two former Products subtract the last Product, and multiplying the Remainder by one Third of the perpendicular Length, that Product is equal to the Solidity of the Zone *d f m o*, whose half Part is equal to the Frustum *d f g l*,

RULE XVI. *To measure the Solidities of the five regular Bodies, viz. The Tetra-hedron,* Fig. T, Plate LXXII. *The Octahedron,* Fig. O, Plate LXXIII. *The Hexahedron or Cube,* Fig. R, Plate LXXII. *The Icosahedron,* Fig. T, *and Dode-cahedron,* Fig. R, Plate LXXIII.

IF the Side of each Body be considered as 1 or unity, their Solidities are as follows, viz.

	Solidities.	Superficies.
Tetrahedron	0,1178511 —	1,732051
Octahedron	0,4714045 —	3,464102
Hexahedron	1,0000000 —	6,000000
Icosahedron	2,181695 —	8,660254
Dodecahedron	7,663119 —	20,645729

To find the Solidities of either of these Bodies.

As 1 : the solid Content in the Table, : : the Cube of the Side of the like Body to be measured : Solidity required; or if each Face be considered as the Base of a Pyramis, whose Vertex is in the Center of the Body, then one such Pyramis being measured singly, and its Solidity multiplied by the Number of Faces contained in the Body, the Product will be the Solidity of the Body required.

To find the Superficies of either of these Bodies.

As 1 : the superficial Content in the Table, : : the square Side of the like Body to be measured superficial Content thereof; or if the Area of one Face be first found, and multiplied by the Number of Faces contained in the Body, the Product will be the superficial Content of the whole, as required.

Note, The superficies of the Tetrahedron is the *Fig.* V. of the Cube, the *Fig.* S, *Plate* LXXII. as has been already observed. Of the Octahedron, the 8 equi-lateral Triangles 1 2 4 3 5 8 6 7, *Fig.* P; of the Dodecahedron, the 12 Penta-gons 1 2 3 4 5 6 7 8 9 10 11 12, *Fig.* S; and of the Icosahedron, the 20 equi-lateral Triangles 1 2 3 4, *&c. Fig.* V. *Plate* LXXIII; and which being de-lineated on Paper or Pasteboard, as exhibited in the several Figures, and then cut out and folded up together, will form the several Bodies in just Propor-tion.

RULE XVII. *To measure the Solidity of any Frustum of a Pyramis or Cone, whose Base is right-angled to its Axis, as the Frustums of Pyramis's Figures* A C *and* E, Plate LXXIII. *and the Frustum of a Cone,* Fig. S, *Plate* LXXIV.

MULTIPLY the Area of the greater End, by the Area of the lesser End, and extract the square Root of the Product. Add the square Root to the Areas of both Ends, and the Sum multiplied by one Third of the Frustum's Length, the Product is the Solidity required.

THE Superficies of the Frustum of the triangular Pyramis A, *Plate* LXXIII. is the three Trapezoids, *a b c d, d h b f, c f* 1 3, and two equilateral Triangles 1 2 3, and *c d f,* in *Fig.* B. The Superficies of the Frustum of the Pyramid C is the four Trapezoids *a b 5 8, 8 2 d 7, 6 7 e f,* 2 5 4 6; and the two geometrical Squares 1 2 3 4, and 5 8 6 7, *Fig.* D. The Superficies of the Frustum of the octangular Pyramis, *Fig.* E, are the four Trapezoids on each Side, and the two Octagons *w*, and *a 5 g f, &c.* The *Fig.* F, is also the Superficies of the octan-gular Frustum E, where the Trapezoids 1 2 3 4 5 6 7 8 9 are its Sides. The Octagon F its Base, and the Octagon 4 its Top.

Z 2

The Superficies of the Fruſtum of a Cone, *Fig.* S, *Plate* LXXIV. is the imperfect Superficies *d e q f c r,* and the Circles *n n,* and *h k l.*

Rule XVIII. *To meaſure the Solidity of a Priſmoid, or Fruſtum of an irregular Pyramid, whoſe Ends are diſproportionable,* Fig. G, Plate LXXIII.

To *f h* add half *b d,* which multiply by *h g,* the greater Breadth, and reſerve the Product. To *b d,* add half *f h,* which multiply by *c d* the leſſer Breadth, to which add the former Product reſerved, and the Sum being multiplied by one Third of the perpendicular Height, the Product is the Solidity required.

The Superficies of this Fruſtum is the 4 Trapezoids 1 2 4 5, and the 2 Parallelograms 3 and 6, *Fig.* H.

Rule XIX. *To meaſure the Solidity of an oblique Fragment of a Cylinder, as* a c, Fig. P, *Plate* LXXIV.

As 1 : the Area of its Baſe *a,* : : half its Length : the Solidity required. The Superficies of this Fragment is the Iſoſceles Triangle *f g e,* the Ellipſis *b,* and the Circle *d.*

Note, Fig. Z is a double Fragment, whoſe Superficies is the two Ellipſes *e* and *f,* and geometrical Square 1 *g m n ;* and *Fig.* O is the Outſide of *d e a b,* which is a Fragment of a Fragment of the Cylinder *h d g b.*

Rule XX. *To meaſure the Solidity of a Cylinder, whoſe Ends are oblique to its Axis, as* Fig. L, *Plate* LXXIV.

By Rule XIX. meaſure the Fragments *a* and *b* ſeparately, and add their Solidities to the Solidity of the Cylinder *p q,* the Sum is the Solidity required. The Superficies of this Cylinder is the double Trapezoid *e f h g, b g k i,* and the two Ellipſes *e* and *d.* The Figures E I K are other Examples of this Kind, whoſe Superficies produce different Figures, according to the various Sections of their Ends, which I have added for further Examples of this Kind.

Rule XXI. *To meaſure the Fragment of a Cone, as* b d c, Fig. A B, *Plate* LXXIV.

As 1 : the Area of its Baſe, : : $\frac{1}{5\cdot 5}$ of its Altitude : its Solidity required. The Superficies of this Fragment is the curved Figure *c* 8 *e i,* the Circle *q o r,* and the Ellipſis *a b d e, Fig.* A X.

Rule XXII. *To meaſure the Fruſtum of a Cone, whoſe Ends are oblique to the Axis, as* Fig. A C, *and* A D, *Plate* LXXIV.

First, meaſure the Fruſtum, as a Fruſtum whoſe Baſe is right-angled to the Axis, and from that Solidity deduct the Fragments that are deficient at the Ends, and the Remains will be the Solidity required.

The Superficies of theſe Fruſtums are laid out as following, *Fig.* A B. On *a* deſcribe the Arch *c m l, &c. e,* equal to the Circumference of the Baſe of the Cone, which divide into 8 equal Parts, at the Points *m l k i, &c,* and draw the Lines *a m, a l, a k, &c.* Draw *b* 1 parallel to *d c,* and divide 1 *c* into four equal Parts. Make *a* 5, *a* 11, each equal to *a* 4 ; make *a* 6, *a* 10, each equal to *a* 3 ; make *a* 7, *a* 9, each equal to *a* 2 ; make *a* 8 equal to *a* 1. Through the Points 11, 10, 9, 8, and 7, 6, 5, trace the Curves *e* 8, and 8 *e ;* then the Figure *c* 8 *e i c* is the Superficies of the Side. The Superficies A C, and A D are deſcribed in the ſame Manner.

PART V.

Of Plain TRIGONOMETRY, Geometrically performed.

LECTURE I.

Of the Solution of plain Triangles.

I. DEFINITIONS.

FIRST, plain Triangles are right-angled or oblique-angled. Secondly, a right-angled Triangle is such a Triangle as hath one right Angle and two acute Angles, as the Triangle A, *Plate* LXXV. whose Angle *b c a* is a right Angle, and the Angles *c b a*, and *b a c*, are both acute Angles. Thirdly, an oblique Triangle is such a Triangle as hath one obtuse Angle, and two acute Angles, as the Triangle B, whose Angle *b c a* is obtuse, and the Angles *c b a*, and *c a b*, are both acute Angles. Fourthly, in every right-angled plain Triangle, that Side which subtendeth (or is opposite to) the right Angle, as *b a*, in Figure A, is called the *Hypothenuse*; and of the other two Sides, the one, as *c a*, is called the *Base;* and the other, as *c b*, is called the *Perpendicular*. Fifthly, in every oblique plain Triangle, as *Fig.* C, the longest Side is generally called the *Base*, as *c a;* but sometimes one of the other two Sides is made the *Base*. Sixthly, in every right-lined Triangle, the Sum of the Degrees contained in the three Angles, are equal to 180 Degrees; therefore if you have any two Angles given, you have also the third given, it being the Complement to 180 Degrees. Seventhly, and as in a right-angled plain Triangle, the right Angle contains 90 Degrees, therefore if any one of the two acute Angles be given, the other acute is also given, because it is the Complement of the other acute Angle to 90 Degrees; or of the other acute Angle and right Angle to 180 Degrees. Eighthly, in all plain Triangles whatsoever the Sides are proportional to the Sines of their opposite Angles.

THE Solution of plain Triangles has always consisted of 12 Cases, but herein I have reduced them unto 8 Cases, of which 4 are of Triangles right-angled, and 4 of Triangles oblique; and which answer every particular exactly the same as those of other Authors divided into 12 Cases.

I. Of right-angled plain Triangles.

IN the Solution of right-angled plain Triangles, there are always two Parts given, as two Sides; or an Angle and one Side; to find a Side or an Angle required.

CASE I. Fig. A, Plate LXXV.

The Base, c a 80 *Feet, and Perpendicular* c b 60 *Feet, being given, to find the acute Angles* c b a *and* b a c, *and the Hypothenuse.*

MAKE *c a* (by a Scale of Feet) equal to 80 Feet, and *c b* equal to 60 Feet, and draw *b a*, which is the Hypothenuse required. With 60 Degrees of Chords, on the angular Points *b* and *a*, describe the Arches *e d* and *g f*, which being measured on the Scale of Chords, *e d* will contain 52 Deg. 30 Min. and *g f* 37 Deg. 30 Min. which are the Angles required.

CASE II. Fig. A, Plate LXXV.

The Hypothenuse b a 100 *Feet, and the Base* c a 80 *Feet, being given, to find the acute Angles, and Perpendicular* b c.

MAKE

Make *c a* equal to 80 Feet; erect the Perpendicular *c b* of Length at pleasure; on *a*, with the Length of 100 Feet, intersect the Perpendicular at *b*, and draw the Line *b a*; then measure the Degrees in each Angle, as in Case I. and *b c* will be the Perpendicular required.

Case III. *Fig.* A. *Plate* LXXV.

The Base c a 80 *Feet, and the Angle* c a b, *opposite to the Perpendicular* 37 *Degrees* 30 *Min. being given, to find the Perpendicular* c b, *and Hypothenuse* b a.

Make *c a* equal to 80 Foot; erect the Perpendicular *c b* of Length at pleasure; make the Angle *b a c* equal to 37 Deg. 30 Min. and draw the Line *a b*, which will cut the Perpendicular in *b*, then *b c* is the Perpendicular, and *b a* is the Hypothenuse required.

Case IV. *Fig.* A, *Plate* LXXV.

The Hypothenuse b a 100 *Feet, and the Angle* c b a 52 *Deg.* 30 *Min. opposite to the Base, being given, to find the Length of the Base* c a, *and of the Perpendicular* c b.

Draw *b a* equal to 100 Feet; make the Angle *b a c* equal to 52 Deg. 30 Min. and draw *b c* of Length at pleasure; make the Angle *b a c* equal to the Complement of the Angle *c b a*, and draw the Line *a c*, which will cut *b c* in *c*; then *c a* is the Base, and *b c* the Perpendicular required.

II. *Of oblique-angled plain Triangles.*

In the Solution of oblique-angled plain Triangles, there are always three Parts given, as two Sides and an Angle, or two Angles and a Side, to find a Side or an Angle required.

Case I. *Fig.* B. *Plate* LXXV.

Two Sides and an Angle opposite to one of the Sides, being given, to find the third Side.

This admits of three Varieties, as,

First, *The Base* b a 100 *Feet, and Side* b c 50 *Feet, with the Angle* b a c 28 *Deg. opposite to the Side* b c, *being given, to find the Side* c a 60 *Feet.*

Make *b a* equal to 100 Feet; on *b*, with the Length of 50 Feet, describe the Arch *d c* at pleasure; in any Part of *b a*, as at *b*, make an Angle, as *b b c*, equal to the given Angle 28 Degrees; from *a*, draw the Line *a c* parallel to *b c*, which will cut the Arch *d c* in *c*, then the Line *c a* is the Length of the Side required.

Secondly, *The Base* c a Fig. C, 100 *Feet, and Side* b a 50 *Feet, with the Angle* c b a 110 *Degrees, opposite to the Base* c a, *being given, to find the Side* c b 60 *Feet.*

Make *b a* equal to 50 Feet; make the Angle *c b a* equal to 110 Degrees, and draw *b c* of Length at pleasure; on *c*, with the Length of the Base 100 Feet, intersect the Line *b c* in *c*, then *c b* is the Length of the Side required.

Thirdly, *The two Sides* c b 60 *Feet, and* b a 50 *Feet, with the Angle* b c a 28 *Degrees, opposite to the Side* b a, *being given, to find the Length of the Base* 100 *Feet.*

Draw *c a* at pleasure; on *c* make the Angle *a c b*, equal to the given Angle 28 Degrees, and make *c b* equal to 60 Feet; on *b*, with the Length of 50 Feet, intersect the Line *c a* in *a*, then *c a* is the Length of the Base required.

Case II. *Fig.* C, *Plate* LXXV.

The Base c a 100 *Feet, and the Side* c b 60 *Feet, with the Angle* b c a 28 *Deg. contained between them, to find the third Side* b a, *and the Angles* c b a *and* b a c.

Make *c a* equal to 100 Feet; make the Angle *b c a* equal to 28 Deg. and the Side *c b* equal to 60 Feet; draw the Line *b a*, which is the third Side required; then measure the Angles *c b a* and *b a c*, as in Case I. of right-angled plain Triangles.

Case III. *Fig.* C, *Plate* LXXV.

The three Sides c a 100 *Feet,* c b 60 *Feet, and* b a 50 *Feet, being given, to find all the Angles.*

By Prob. I. Lect. IV. Part II. complete the Triangle *b c a*, and by Case I. of right-angled plain Triangles, find the Quantity of each Angle.

Case

CASE IV. *Fig.* C, *Plate* LXXV.

Two Angles, as b c a 28 *Deg.* b a c 42 *Deg. and one Side, as* c b 60 *Feet, being given, to find the other two Sides* b a 50 *Feet, and* c a 100 *Feet.*

MAKE c b equal to 60 Feet; make the Angle b c a equal to 28 Deg. and the Angle b a c equal to 42 Deg. continue out the Lines b a and c a, and they will interfect each other in the Point a; then c a and b a are the two Sides required.

Note, The Doctrine of plain Triangles, performed by the Tables of Logarithms, Sines, Tangents and Secants, being more difficult to be underſtood by Learners, than the preceding, and as to have added thoſe Tables would have ſwelled the whole beyond its intended Bulk and Price, I therefore omitted the Analogies and Tables, which, if this Work be favourably accepted, I will publiſh hereafter in a ſeparate Volume.

LECTURE II.

Of Menſuration of Heights and Diſtances.

THE proper Inſtruments for theſe Purpoſes are a Quadrant, as *Fig.* D, and a ten Feet Rod, Chain, &c.

PROB. I. *Fig.* F, *Plate* LXXV.

To take the Altitude of an Object, as the Obeliſk b n, *by the Help of a Quadrant.*

MOVE from the Object, until, looking through the Sights of the Quadrant to the Top of the Object, the Plumb-line cut 63 Deg. 26 Min. on the Limb, as at b; then the Height of your Eye being added to your Diſtance from the central Line of the Object, is equal to half the Height of the Object: Or move backward, until the Plumb-line cut 45 Deg. as at i, and the Height of your Eye added to your Diſtance as before, the Sum is the Height required. And ſo in like Manner moving backwards, until the Plumb-line cut 33 Deg. 20 Min. as at k, then ⅔ of the Diſtance is the Altitude. And at l, where the Plumb-line cuts 26 Deg. 34 Min. the Diſtance is double the Altitude.

If any Obſtruction is between you and the Object, ſo that you cannot meaſure to its Baſe, then go nearer, or farther, until the Plumb-line cut 26 Deg. 34 Min. as at l, and there make a Mark on the Ground; move backward in a right Line with your firſt Station and the Object, until the Plumb-line cut 18 Deg. 26 Min. as at m, then the Diſtance between your two Stations l and m, is equal to the Altitude required.

PROB. II. *Fig.* G, *Plate* LXXV.

To find the Altitude of an Object, by knowing the Length of its Shadow.

SET up a Stick of any known Length, ſuppoſe 3 Feet, as d e: let the Length of the Shadow of the Object be b e, and of the Stick e g; then as the Length of the Shadow of the Stick is to the Height of the Stick; ſo is the Length of the Shadow of the Object to the Height of the Object.

PROB. III. *Fig.* H, *Plate* LXXV.

To take the Altitude of an Object that is acceſſible, by the Help of a ten Feet Rod and a Stick only.

Let the Obeliſk a b *be an acceſſible Object, whoſe Altitude is required.*

ERECT a ten Feet Rod in any Place, as at m, and a Stick, as n f, equal to the Height of your Eye, at any Diſtance in a right Line with the Building; look from the Top of the Stick, level to the Building, and againſt your Ray of Sight, at the ten Feet Rod, make a Mark, as at e; cauſe a ſecond Perſon to ſlide a Piece of Paper up the ten Feet Rod; ſo that, looking from the Top of the Stick f, to b the Top of the Object, you ſee the Top of the Paper, as at d, at which Place make a Mark: This done, meaſure the Diſtance of the two Marks on the ten Feet Rod e and d, alſo the Diſtance e f; then as e f is to e d, ſo is c f, the Diſtance of the Stick from the Object, to c a the Height of the Object above the Level-line c f, to which add the Height of the Stick n f, and the Sum is the Altitude required.

PROB.

PROB. IV. *Fig.* G, *Plate* LXXV.

To take the Altitude of an Object that is inaccessible, by its Shadow.

SUPPOSE the Shadow of the Object reach from *b* to *e*, and, at the same Time, the Shadow of a Staff reach from *e* to *g*; at about two or three Hours after, when the Sun is risen considerably higher, place down a Mark at the End of the Object's Shadow, which suppose to be at *c*; also, at the same Time, make a Mark at the End of the Shadow of the Stick, suppose at *f*; now, as the Triangle *d f g* is similar to the Triangle *a c e*, and as the Triangle *d e f* is similar to the Triangle *a c b*, therefore, as *f g* is to the Height of the Staff *d e*, so is *c e* to the Height of the Object required.

PROB. V. *Fig.* I, K, *Plate* LXXV.

To measure the Altitude of a Hill or Mountain, by the Help of a Spirit-Level and Station-Staffs.

(1.) ERECT your Level truly horizontal on the Top, as at 5, and directly against the Instrument, let a second Person hold up a sliding Station-staff, with a Vane fixed thereon, which he is to move up, until, looking through the Sights of your Level, you see its upper Edge, as at *n*: This done, let the second Person write down the Number of Inches and Parts of Inches that his Vane is above the Ground at *m*, let a third Person write down the Number of Inches and Parts of Inches that your Instrument is above the Surface of the Ground at 5. (2.) Remove your Level down the Hill, as to 4, and your 2d Assistant to *k*, and let your 3d Assistant erect his Station-staff at *m*, the Place where your 2d Assistant first stood: This done, fix your Instrument truly horizontal, and looking to your 3d Assistant at *m*, let him slide up his Vane until you see its upper Edge, at which Time he is to set down, under the Height of the Instrument observed at 5, the Inches and Parts of Inches that his Vane is then above the Ground; also look to the Station-staff of your 2d Assistant, and cause him to slide up his Vane, until you see its upper Edge, as at *l*, and let him place down the Inches and Parts that his Vane is above the Ground, under his first Height observed at *m*. Proceed in like Manner at every other Observation, as may be required to descend unto the Bottom at *b*. (3.) Let each Assistant add into one Sum the Heights of his several Observations, and then that of your 3d Assistant's being subtracted from that of your 2d Assistant's, the Difference is the Altitude of the Hill required.

PROB. VI. *Fig.* P, O, M, *Plate* LXXV.

To measure an inaccessible Distance.

INACCESSIBLE Distances may be measured by many Methods, as,

First, *To find the Distance of the two Trees* 7 *and* 8, Fig. P, *which are rendered inaccessible by the River* b b.

ASSIGN any Point on the Ground, from which you can measure directly unto the two Objects 7 and 8, as the Point 9; continue 7, 9 unto 11, and 8, 9 unto 10, making the Distance of 9, 11 equal to 7, 9, and the Distance of 9, 10 equal to 8, 9, then the Distance from 10 to 11 is equal to the Distance of 7, 8 required.

Secondly, *To find the Distance of the Tree at* r, *in* Fig. M, *from the Point* v, *which is rendered inaccessible by the River* b b.

IMAGINE a Line to be drawn from *v* to *r*, and thereon erect the Perpendicular *v w*, of any Length, and let *r v* be continued at pleasure towards *y*, which may be done by straining a Pack-thread Line from *v* towards *y*, in a right Line with *v r*. In any Part of the Perpendicular *v w*, assign a Point as *w*, and at any Distance from you, place a Stake in a right Line between *w* and *r*, as at *s*; also another on the Perpendicular, at any Distance from *w*, as at *t*. Make the Triangle *w t x*, equal to the Triangle *w s t*; and continue *w x*, until it meet the Line *v y* in *y*; then the Distance *v y* is equal to the Distance *v r*, required.

Thirdly,

Thirdly, *To find the Diſtance of the two Trees,* 12 *and* 13, Fig. O, *which is rendered inacceſſible by the River* d.

Aſſign a Point as 16, from which you can meaſure to both the Objects. Place two Stakes at any Diſtance in right Lines, from the Point 16, to the two Objects, as at the Points 14 and 15, and meaſure the Sides of the Triangle 14, 15, 16, alſo the Diſtances from the Point 16, to the Objects 12 and 13. On Paper, with a Scale of Feet, make a Triangle, whoſe reſpective Sides are equal to the Meaſures of the Sides of the Triangle 14, 15, 16, and continue out the Sides, reſpecting the Sides 16, 14, and 16, 15, each equal to the Meaſures of 16, 12, and 16, 13. Then the Diſtance between the Extremes of thoſe Lines, being meaſured on your Scale of Feet, will be the Diſtance required.

P R O B. VII. *Fig.* N K L. Plate LXXV.

To meaſure an inacceſſible Diſtance, by Help of a geometrical Square, right-angled or equilateral Triangle.

Firſt, *To meaſure the Diſtance* 5 b, Fig. N, *which is rendered inacceſſible by the River* c, *by Help of a geometrical Square.*

IMAGINE a right Line to be drawn from 5, to the Object *b*, which continues towards 4. On the Point 5 erect the Perpendicular 5 z of Length at pleaſure, and therein aſſign a Point, as z, where with a Piece of Board make a geometrical Square, apply its Angle over the Point z, and direct its Side z 1, to the Object; alſo at the ſame Time cauſe an Aſſiſtant to move along the Line 5, 4, until by the Side of the geometrical Square z 3, you ſee his Station-ſtaff erect, at 4. This done, meaſure the Sides of the Triangle 5 z 4; and then as the Side 5, 4, is to the Perpendicular z 5, ſo is the Perpendicular z 5, to 5 b, the Diſtance required.

Secondly, *To meaſure the Diſtance* l k, Fig. L, *which is rendered inacceſſible by the River* b.

BEING furniſhed with a Piece of Board that is an equilateral Triangle, as *l m n*, apply one of its Angles over the Point *l*, and direct a Side, as *l m* to *k*, and at the ſame Time direct an Aſſiſtant to fix up a Station-ſtaff in a direct Line with the other Side *l n*, at any Diſtance from you, as at *p*, and then ſet up a Mark in the Point *l*. This being done, move along the Line *l p*, until by the Sides of the equilateral Triangle you can ſee both the Mark ſet up at *l*, and the Object at *k*, which you will do at the Point *p*; then the Diſtance of *l p* is equal to the Diſtance *l k*, required.

Note, In the ſame Manner, an inacceſſible Diſtance, as *f a*, Fig. K, may be found by a right-angled plain Triangle, as *e f g*, whoſe Sides *e f*, and *f g*, are equal, as is evident to Inſpection.

P R O B. VIII. *Fig.* Q. Plate LXXV.

To meaſure the Diſtances of divers Objects, that are inacceſſible at two Stations, by the Help of a common ſmall Table, or Joint-ſtool, and a ſtraight Rule, with perpendicular Sights fixed at each End thereof.

LET the ſeveral Objects be *a b c d,* and the two Stations *i k,* at 100 Feet, Yards, &c. Diſtance.

BEING furniſhed with a ſtraight Rule, about two Feet, or two Feet and a half, in Length, with perpendicular Sights ſo fixed at each End, that the Slits of the Sights ſtand perpendicular over the thin Edge of the Rule (which is generally called an Index), and a ſmall Table or Stool, that hath a ſmooth and even Surface, proceed as follows, *viz.* With a Scale of Feet, &c. draw a Line in the Middle of the Table, as *i k,* equal to 100 Feet, the Diſtance between the two Stations; and then being at one of the Stations, as at *i,* lay the Edge of the Index to the Line *i k,* and move the Table, until through the Sights of the Index you ſee the other Station *k,* and there fix your Table faſt. On the Point *i* on your Table fix a Pin, and applying the Edge of your Index to the Pin, look through the Sights, to the firſt Object at *a;* and draw a Line from the Pin, by the Edge of the Index at pleaſure, as *i a.* Move your Index in like Manner to every of the remaining Objects, drawing Lines from the Pin, towards each Object, as at firſt.

A a   This

This done, remove your Table unto *k*, your second Station, and placing the Point *i* on your Table, towards the first Station, lay your Index to the Line *k i* on your Table, and move the Table, until through the Sights you see your first Station, and there fix your Table fast. Fix a Pin in the Point *k* on your Table, and then applying the Side of the Index to the Pin, direct the Sights unto every of the Objects, and draw Lines, as before, at the first Station, which will intersect the former in the Points *a b e d*, and whose Distances (or the Distances from the two Stations *i* and *k*) being measured on the same Scale by which the Line *i k* was drawn on the Table, will be the true Distances of each Object required.

Note, By the same Method of working, the Plan of any open Field may be taken, if the Angles are considered as so many different Objects, and can be all seen at each Station.

P A R T   VI.

Of Surveying L A N D S, *&c.*

THE usual Instruments for this Purpose are generally the Plain Table, Theo-dolite, Circumferentor, and Chain : but as the three first are Instruments of great Expence, beyond the Reach of common Workmen, for whose sake I have published this Work, I shall therefore give some few Examples, to shew how, by the Help of a ten Feet Rod, or Chain, and a Joint-stool or Table, they may make the Plan of any Piece of Land, that is not of very great Dimensions, with the utmost Exactness.

N. B. The Chain is that which is called *Gunter's* Chain, whose Length is equal to 4 Statute Poles, or 66 Feet, divided into 100 Links, each 7 Inches $\frac{92}{100}$ in Length.

P R O B. I. *Fig.* S. *Plate* LXXV.
To make the Plan of an irregular Side of a Field, as i h g f e d c a b.

Make an Eye-draught on Paper, expressing the several Angles, and therein draw the occult Line *b a* ; as also the several perpendicular Off-sets 12 *h*, 42 *g*, 56 *f*, *&c.* This done, in the Field, measure in a right Line from *i*, towards *a* ; and when you come against the Angle *h*, as at the Point 12, write down on your Eye-draught the Distance measured from *i*, as also the Length of the Off-set 12 *h*, which place on the Off-set. Proceed in like Manner to measure the remaining Distances to every Off-set, and the Length of each Off-set. This done, draw a Line on Paper, and with a Scale of Feet set off from *i* all the several Distances, as *i* 12, *i* 42, *i* 56, *&c.* and from those Points erect Perpendiculars, making each equal to their respec-tive Measures in the Eye-draught, and then right Lines, as *i b*, *b g*, *g f*, *&c.* being drawn from *i* to *h*, from *h* to *g*, from *g* to *f*, *&c.* they will be the Plan of the irre-gular Side of the Field, as required.

Note, If the Side of the Field be curved, as *Fig.* R, then take Off-sets at every remarkable Bending, as at *h g e i k*, *&c.* which measure and plan as before, and through their Extremes trace the Curve, as required.

P R O B. II. *Fig.* V. *Plate* LXXV.
To make the Plan of a Field, by the Help of a Chain only, as Fig. a c d g f e.

MAKE an Eye-draught of the Field, and divide it into Triangles. Measure the Sides of the Field, and of every imaginary Triangle, which place on each respec-tive Side, with a diagonal Scale of Chains and Links, as expressed by *Fig.* IV.

Plate

Plate IX. By **P R O B.** I. **L E C T.** IV. **P A R T** II. delineate all the several Triangles, as represented in your Eye-draught, and they will complete the Plan of the Field, as required.

P R O B. III. *Fig.* Y. *Plate* LXXV.

To make the Plan of an irregular curved Field, by Help of the Chain only, as
b c d e f g h i k.

F I R S T fix up Marks, such as Pieces of Paper fixed into the slit Ends of Sticks, at proper Places, as at *b c d e f g h i k,* and imagine Lines to be drawn from one to the other, as *b c, c d, d e, e f, &c.* Assign a Station towards the Middle of the Field, as at *a,* and imagine right Lines to be drawn from thence, unto the several Marks at *b c d e f, &c.* which will divide the whole into imaginary Triangles. Make an Eye-draught as before directed, expressing every Triangle, *&c.*

By **P R O B.** II. hereof measure and delineate the several Triangles; and by **P R O B.** I. measure and delineate the Off-sets on the Out-lines of the several Triangles, necessary for describing the curved Boundaries, which will complete the whole, as required.

Note, Chains and Links are thus written, *viz.* 3 **Chains,** 75 **Links,** as from *b* to *a,* thus, 3 : 75, and two Chains, and 10 Links, as from *c* to *a,* thus, 2 : 10, *&c.*

P R O B. IV. *Fig.* A C. *Plate* LXXV.

To make the Plan of a Field, whose Angles cannot be all seen under three Stations, as at a d c, *by Help of a Table and Chain.*

A S S I G N 3 Stations in the Field, as *a d c,* at any Distances, suppose *a d,* at 3 Chains Distance, and *d c,* at 3 Chains, and 35 Links. Draw a Line on your Table, by your Scale of Chains and Links, to represent 3 Chains, the Distance between the Stations *a* and *d.* Place your Table in the Field, over the stationary Point *a,* and laying your Index on the Line *a d,* move the Table about, until you see the Station *d,* and there make your Table fast. Fix a Pin in your Table, at the Point *a,* and laying your Index thereto, direct the Sights to the several Angles *m n o v w x* 3, and draw right Lines from the Pin, towards each Angle. Measure the Distances from your Station *a,* unto every of the Angles, and from your Scale of Chains and Links set from the Pin, on each Line, as *a m, a n, a o, a v, &c.* their respective Lengths, as 2 : 75; 3 : 75; 3 : 65; *&c.* and draw the Lines *m n, n o, o v, v w, w x,* and *x* 3. Move your Table to the second Station *d,* and laying your Index on the Line *a d,* move the Table about, until through the Sights you see your first Station at *a,* and there make it fast. Fix a Pin in your Table at the Point *d,* and laying your Index to the Pin, turn it about, until through the Sights you see your third Station at *c;* and by the Side of the Index draw the Line *d c,* which make equal to 3 Chains, 25 Links, the Distance of the third Station *c* from *d.* Also, from the Pin on the Table, direct the Index to the Angle *y,* and draw the Line *d y,* equal to its measured Length, and join the Side 3 *y.* Remove your Table to *c,* the third Station; lay the Index on the Line *d c,* and move the Table about, until through the Sights you see the Station *d,* and there make it fast. Fix a Pin in your Table, at the Point *c,* and laying your Index thereto, direct the Sights to the Angles *z h i l,* and draw Lines towards each Angle, equal to their respective Measures, from the Station *c.* Then the right Lines *y z, z h, h i, i l,* and *l m,* being drawn, they will complete the Plan, as required.

P R O B. V. *Fig.* A C. *Plate* LXXV.

To make the Plan of a Field, by going about it without-side, by Help of a Table and Chain.

F I R S T, go about the Field, and at proper Distances make choice of Stations, as at *a, p, q, r, s, g,* whereat fix up Sticks with Paper as aforesaid. Then beginning at any one Station, as at *a,* measure the Distance from *a* to *g,* and from *a* to *p.* Draw a Line on one Side of your Table, on which set from your Scale of Chains

and

and Links, the Length from *a* to *g*, place your Table over the Point *a*. Lay your Index on the Line reprefenting the Line *a g*, and move the Table about until through the Sights you fee the Mark at *g*, and there make it faft. Fix a Pin in your Table at the Point *a*, and laying your Index to the Pin, direct the Sights to the Mark at *p*, and by its Side draw the Line *a p*, equal to its Length before meafured. By Prob. I. hereof, on the Line *a g*, meafure and delineate the Off-fets *b o*, *c n*, *d m*, alfo the Off-fet *k l*, from the Off-fet *d m*; then *e i*, and *f h*, alfo the Off-fets *t v* and *i w*, on the Line *a p*. Through the Extremes of the aforefaid Off-fets draw the Lines *w v*, *v o*, *o n*, *n m*, *m l*, *l i*, and *i h*.

PLACE your Table over *p*, and laying the Index on the Line *p a*, move your Table about until through the Sights you fee the Mark at *a*, and there make it faft. Fix a Pin in your Table at the Point *p*, and laying your Index to the Pin, direct the Sights to the Mark *q*, and by its Side draw the Line *p q*, which make equal to the Diftance that the Mark at *q* is from the Station at *p*. Meafure and delineate the Off-fet *q x*, and draw the Line *w x*. Repeat thefe Operations at the Stations *q r s*, and you will complete the whole, as required.

Note, By the fame Rule, the Plan of a Field may be made, by going about it within-fide, as fignified in *Fig*. Y, by the ftationary Diftances, *s l m n o q r t s*.

PROB. VI. *Fig*. T. *Plate* LXXV.
To make the Plan of an enclofed Road, Street, &c.

Firft, Make choice of proper Stations as at *s t* and *v*, at which Places fix up Marks as aforefaid; meafure the Diftances *t s*, and *t v*, draw a Line on your Table, to reprefent the Line *t v*, on which from your Scale of Chains and Links fet its meafured Length. Place your Table over the ftationary Point *t*, and laying the Index to the Line *t v*, move the Table about until through the Sights you fee the Mark at *v*, and there make it faft. Fix a Pin in your Table at the Point *t*, and laying the Index to the Pin, direct the Sights to the Mark at *s*, and by its Side draw the Line *t s*, equal to its meafured Length.

By Prob. I. hereof, meafure and delineate an Off-fet againft every Angle, contained in the two Sides of the Road or Street, and right Lines being drawn to their Extremes will be the Plan of the Road or Street, as required.

PROB. VIII. *Fig*. XX. *Plate* LXXV.
To make the Plan of an irregular Wall, by the Help of a ten Foot Rod only.

Firft, Make an Eye-draught as W W, and thereon fet down the Length of every refpective Side, contained in X, X; and then proceed to meafure the Angles as following, *viz*.

(1.) *To meafure the Angle* x a e, imagine the Side X *a*, to be continued 10 Feet, as from *a* to *b*, alfo fet 10 Feet from *a* to *c*, and meafure the Diftance *b c*, which fuppofe to be 5 Feet. Place the Meafures of this Angle on your Eye-draught as at *a b c*. (2.) *To meafure the Angle* a e i, fet 10 Feet on each Side the angular Point *e*, as to *d* and *f*, and meafure the Line *f d*, which fuppofe to be 20 Feet, place thefe Meafures on the Eye-draught, as at *d e f*. Proceed in like Manner to take the Meafures of all the remaining Angles, at *i m p r w*, &c.

To delineate this Plan from the Eye-draught.

MAKE W *a*, equal to 21 Feet, the Length of X *a*, on *a* in *Fig*. W, with a Radius equal to 10 Feet of your Scale, by which you delineate the Plan. Defcribe an Arch, as *b e*, make *b c* equal to 5 Feet, and through the Point *c* draw *b c* equal to 5 Feet, and through the Point *c* draw *a e* equal to 32 Feet, the Length of the Side *a e*. On the Point *e* with a Radius of 10 Feet defcribe the Arch *d f*, and therein fet 20 Feet from *d* to *f*. Through the Point *f* draw the Line *e i*, equal to 23 Feet, the Length of the Side *e i*. Proceed to defcribe the remaining Angles and Sides, in the fame Manner, which will complete the Plan, as required.

PROB. IX. *Fig*. A B. *Plate* LXXV.
To make the Plan of a Serpentine River.

Firft, Affign ftationary Diftances, as *f c d a c b*, and fix up Marks as aforefaid. Make an Eye-draught of the whole, meafure the ftationary Diftances, and fet
their

their Measures on their respective Places in the Eye-draught. Draw a Line on your Table, to represent the Line *a b*, which by your Scale of equal Parts make equal to 3 Chains 20 Min. its measured Length; place your Table over the stationary Point *a*. Lay your Index to the Line *a b* on your Table, and move the Table about until through the Sights you see the Mark at *b*, and there fix your Table fast. Fix a Pin in your Table on the Point *a*, apply your Index to the Pin, and direct the Sights, first to *c*, and then to *d*, drawing Lines on the Table towards the stationary Marks *c* and *d*, which by your Scale of Chains and Links make equal to their respective measured Lengths, *viz. c a*, 6 Chains 20 Links, and *a d*, 4 Chains 75 Links. By Prob. I. hereof measure and delineate proper Off-sets, and through their Extremes trace the Curvature of the River. Remove your Table to the Station *d*, setting up a Mark again at *a*. Lay the Index on the Line, representing the Line *a d;* move the Table about until through the Sights you see the Mark at *a*, and make the Table fast: fix a Pin in the Table at the Point *d*, apply the Index to the Pin, and directing the Sights to the Station *e*, draw the Line *d e*, which make equal to 8 Chains 36 Links, its measured Length. Then by Prob. I. hereof, measure and delineate the Off-sets to the Side of the River, which are here described by dotted Lines, and through their Extremes trace on the Curvature of the River. Remove your Table to the Station *e*, and repeating the same Kind of Operation as at *d*, you will complete the whole, as required.

Note, When the Weather is dry, you may seal down a Sheet of Paper smooth on the Table, and make your Plans thereon; but if the Weather be moist or wet, the Paper will not do, and indeed not so well as the Table in dry Weather; because Paper is always shrinking or swelling very sensibly, as the Temperature of the Air is more or less dry, which the Table does not in so great a Degree.

P R O B L E M X.

To find the Quantities of Lands in Acres, Roods, and Poles, whose Dimensions are taken by Gunter's *Chain.*

RULE, Place your Dimensions, and multiply them together as in Decimal Multiplication, as in the Margin. From the Product cut off 5 Figures to the Right-hand; the Remains to the Left, when any, are Acres. Multiply the 5 Figures cut off by 4, the Roods in an Acre, and from its Product cut off five Figures to the Right as before; the Remains to the Left, when any, are Roods. Multiply the last 5 Figures cut off, by 40, the Rods in a Rood, and from the Product cut off 5 Figures to the Right; the Remains, if any, to the Left are Poles. So in this Example the Product is 110 Acres, 1 Rood, and 36 Poles, which is thus written, A. R. P.

110   1   36

27	92
39	57
195	44
1396	0
25128	
8376	
Acres 110)47944	
	4
Roods 1)91776	
	40
Poles 36)71040	

PART VII. Of MECHANICKS.

LECTURE I.

Definitions of Matter, Gravity, and Motion.

1. BY Mechanicks is meant, Geometrical Rules for demonstrating Motion, and the Effect of Powers or Forces in removing the Matter of Bodies.

2. MATTER

2. MATTER is an impenetrable, divisible, and paffive Subftance, and therefore has Extenfion and Refiftance, which are the Properties of all Kinds of Bodies, and whofe univerfal Principle is *Gravity*.

3. GRAVITY is that Force by which Bodies are carried, or tend, towards the Center of the Earth, and which is in Proportion to the Quantity of Matter they contain. Gravity is abfolute, accelerate or relative ; *Gravity Abfolute*, is the whole Force by which Bodies tend towards the Center of the Earth. *Gravity Accelerate*, is Force of Gravity confidered as growing greater as it approaches the attracting Point, as in Bodies falling. *Gravity Relative*, is the Excefs of the Gravity in any Body above the fpecifick Gravity of a Fluid, as of Air or Water in which it moves.

4. SPECIFICK Gravity is the appropriate and peculiar Gravity or real Weight which any Species of natural Bodies have, and which arifes from the more or lefs Compactnefs of the Matter of which Bodies are compofed.

5. MOTION is that Force by which a Body continually changes its Place, and therefore is a continual and fucceffive Mutation of Place. Motion is either Abfolute or Relative. *Abfolute Motion*, is the Change of the *Locus Abfolutus* of any moving Body ; and its Celerity will be meafured by the Quantity of the abfolute Space which the moveable Body hath paffed through.

6. RELATIVE *Motion* is a Mutation of the vulgar or common Place of the moving Body ; and fo hath its Celerity accounted or meafured by the Quantity of relative Space which the moveable Body moves over.

7. CELERITY is the Swiftnefs of any Body in Motion ; and that Force which is in Bodies moving, and whereby they continually move, is called their *Momentum*, which arifes from their Weight or Quantity of Matter, and the Velocity of their Motion wherewith they move.

8. THE Motion of all Bodies is naturally Recti-linear, and therefore the Velocity of a Body will be conftantly the fame, if no external Caufe obftruct the Motion, or make any Alteration in its Line of Direction.

9. THE Line of Direction is that Line wherein any Body or Power endeavours to move, that is to fay, it is the Line of Motion that any Body goes in, according to the Force impreffed upon it. And the Change of Places, or continual Paffage of a Body along fuch a Line, is called its *Local Motion*.

10. VELOCITY is that Affection of Motion which is meafured by comparing together the Quantity of Space which a Body hath paffed through, and the Time in which it was paffing that Space. Thus equal Velocity is that, whereby equal Space is paffed over in equal Time. So if two Bodies are put in Motion at the fame Inftant of Time, and both pafs the Length of one Mile in an Hour, &c. their Velocities are then faid to be equal. Greater Velocity is that whereby either a greater Length is paffed over in the fame Time (as when either of the aforefaid Bodies travels two Miles in an Hour), or an equal Length in lefs Time (as when the aforefaid Body travelled one Mile in half an Hour), &c.

HENCE it follows, that if two Bodies are put in Motion at the fame Time, and one travel a hundred Miles, whilft the other travel but fifty Miles, that Body which travels one hundred Miles, moves with double the Velocity of the other ; the like is to be underftood of Velocities trebled, quadrupled, &c.

11. As the natural Motion of falling Bodies arifes from the Principle of their Gravity or Weight, and is found by Experience to be a Motion uniformly accelerated ; and being attended with the fame Gravity or Weight, at every Degree of Velocity, it therefore comes to pafs, that the Spaces through which Bodies fall perpendicularly are, as the Squares of the Times wherein they fall, accounting from the Beginning of the Fall.

As for Example, Fig. I. *Plate* LXXVI.

THE perpendicular Defcent of Bodies is at the Rate of 15 Feet in the firft Second of Time, and in every fucceeding Second the Spaces are as the Squares of the Seconds, *viz*. If a Body be 5 Seconds of Time in falling from *a* to *f*, and

and in the firſt Second it falls 15 Feet as from *a* to *b*, at the End of the ſecond Second of its falling, it will have fell 4 times *a b* equal to 60 Feet, as to 4 which is equal to 2 multiplied in 2, the Square of the Seconds or Times in falling. So in like Manner at the End of the third Second it will have fell 9 times 15 Feet, equal to 135 Feet, which is equal to 3 multiplied into 3, the Square of the Seconds or Times in falling ; and in the fourth Second, 16 times 15 Feet, equal to 204 Feet, as to 16. Hence 'tis plain that the Increaſe of Motion in every Minute, &c. is according to the Series of the uneven Numbers, *viz.* 1, 3, 5, 7, 9, 11, &c. which are the Differences of the Squares, 1, 4, 9, 16, 25, &c.

12. As the Motions of Bodies are accelerated in falling, their Forces are thereby increaſed in the ſame Proportion. And therefore if the Body *a*, in falling from *a* to *b*, has a Force at *b* equal to 1 Pound Weight, it will have a Force at 4, equal to 4 Pounds Weight ; for as its Velocity from *a* to 4 is three Times as great as from *a* to *b*, it will therefore have a Force three Times greater at 4 than when at *b*, and ſo in like Manner in its falling to 16 its Force will be equal to 16 Pounds, and at 25 to 25 Pounds, &c.

13. And it is alſo to be obſerved, that equal Bodies falling on inclined Planes whoſe loweſt Parts are in the ſame Level, have the ſame Force and Velocity at the End of their Falls, as when let fall perpendicular, but employ a longer Time in their Deſcents. So if the Body *b*, *Plate* LXXVI. deſcend in the perpendicular Line *b g*, or in either of the oblique Lines *b f* or *b h*, it will have the ſame Force at *f* or *h*, as at *g*, but it will be longer in falling from *b* to *f*, than from *b* to *g*, and longer from *b* to *h*, than from *b* to *f*, &c.

14. If a Body deſcend on an inclined Plane, as *d b*, *Fig.* C, it will by its acquired Velocity aſcend another Plane of equal Inclination, as *b c*, unto the ſame Height, allowing for the Reſiſtance of the Air, and Friction of the Plane.

15. If Bodies fall in the Lines *c f*, *d f*, *e f*, *b f*, *a f*, &c. deſcribed in the Circle, *Fig.* B, they will from the Points in the Circumference *a b c d e*, come to the Baſe *f* at the ſame Time. For as the Lengths of their Lines of Deſcent are to one another, ſo are their Velocities to each other.

16. If a Body, as *b Fig.* E, be thrown perpendicularly upward with any Force, the Velocity wherewith the Body aſcends, will continually diminiſh, till at length it be wholly taken away ; and from that Inſtant of Time, the Body will deſcend in the ſame Line with ſuch an increaſing Velocity, as to fall from *a* to *c*, with the ſame Force and in the ſame Time as it was thrown up from *c* to *a*. The like is alſo in Bodies thrown up on inclined Planes ; for if in *Fig.* C. the Body *a* be thrown from *b* to *d*, with a certain Force, and in a certain Time, it will by its own Weight return again to *b*, with the ſame Force and in the ſame Time as it aſcended.

17. If a Body deſcend in the Arch of a Circle, as *c Fig.* D, in the Arch *d e*, the Velocity will always be anſwerable to the perpendicular Height *b e*, from which the Body fell ; but the Time of the Body's Deſcent will be greater from *c* to *e*, than from *b* to *e*.

18. Now from hence it follows that the Body *a Fig.* F. to deſcend the Arch Line *a c*, or the Chord Line *a c*, will require more Time than were it to fall in the Perpendicular *b c*, but will in all the Deſcents have an equal Force at *c*.

LECTURE I.

Of the Laws of Nature.

IT is to be obſerved, that all the Varieties of Motion of Bodies in general are conformable to the following three Laws.

Law I.

All Bodies continue in their State of Reſt, or Motion, uniformly in a right Line, excepting they are obliged to change that State, by Forces impreſſed ; and therefore it follows,

First, If a Body be abfolutely at Reft, and unfurnifhed with any Principle, whereby it could put itſelf into Motion, it will for ever continue in the ſame Place, till acted upon by an external Body.

Secondly, When a Body is put into Motion, it has no Power within itſelf, to make any Change in the Direction of that Motion, and therefore muſt move forward in a right Line, as I have before obſerved, without declining any Way whatever.

Thirdly, All Bodies endeavour to remain in their State of Reft or Motion, and therefore ſome actual Force is required to put Bodies out of a State of Reft, into Motion, or to change the Motion which they before received. This Quality in Bodies, whereby they ſo preſerve their preſent State of Motion or Reft, till ſome active Force diſturb them, is called the *Vis Inertiæ* of Matter. It is by this Property, that *Matter* unactive of itſelf retains all the Power impreſſed upon it, and will not ceaſe to act, until oppoſed by as great a Power as that which firſt moved it.

Law II.

All Change of Motion is proportional to the Power of the moving Force impreſſed, and is always made according to the right Line in which that Force is impreſſed.

That is to ſay, firſt, If in one Minute of Time, two Bodies, as *a c*, *Fig.* G, move from *a* and B, towards *f* and *d*, with equal Velocities, ſo that when the Body *a* is arrived at *b*, the Body *c*, which moved from B, may act its full Force againſt the Body at *b ;* then will the Line of Direction of the Body *a*, which was in the Line *a d*, be changed into the diagonal Line *b e*, of the geometrical Square *f b e d ;* and by the Action of the Body *c*, on the Body *b*, the Velocity of the Body *b* will be ſo accelerated, as to paſs, in the ſecond Minute, through the Diagonal *b e*, the Side of whoſe Square is equal to *a b*, the Space which the Body *b* travelled through in the firſt Minute. Again, if at the End of the ſecond Minute, when the Body *b* is arrived at *e*, another Body ſtrike againſt it at *g*, with the ſame Velocity as *b* then has, then will the Line of Direction of the Body *b*, in the ſecond Minute, which is *b k*, the Diagonal continued, be changed into the Diagonal *e n*, of the Square *n i k e ;* and by the Force of this ſecond Body, the Velocity of the Body at *e* will be ſo accelerated, as to paſs, in the third Minute, through the Diagonal *n e*, the Sides of whoſe Square is equal to the Space which the Body *b* travelled through in the ſecond Minute. If at the End of the third Minute, when the Body *b* is arrived at the Point *n*, it be again acted upon by a third Body at *m*, with the ſame Velocity as the Body at *n* then has, then will the Line of Direction of the Body at *n*, in the third Minute, which is the Diagonal *e n*, continued to *p*, be changed into the diagonal Line *n r*, of the Square *r o p n ;* and by the Force received from this third Body, the Velocity of the Body at *n* will be ſo accelerated, as to paſs, in the fourth Minute, through the Diagonal *n r*, the Sides of whoſe Square is equal to the Space which the Body travelled through in the third Minute. And if at the End of the fourth Minute, when the Body is arrived at *r*, it be again acted upon by a fourth Body, as *s*, whoſe Velocity is equal to that which the Body *b* then hath, the Line of Direction of the Body at *r*, which then is the Diagonal *n r* continued to *x*, will be changed into the diagonal Line *r v*, which is directly retrograde, or contrary to its firſt Line of Direction from *a* to *b ;* and by this laſt additional Force, the Velocity of the Body at *r* will be ſo accelerated, as to paſs through the Diagonal *r v*, of the Square *x v r t*, in the fifth Minute. In this Manner, by the continual Actions of Bodies, whoſe Velocities are alike increaſed, at the End of every Minute, the Velocity of a Body may be ſo increaſed, as to travel ten thouſand Millions of Millions of Millions of Miles in a Minute.

Secondly, That the Change of Direction is always proportional to the Force impreſſed, is evident by all the preceding Lines of Direction of the Body *b*, for the diagonal Line *b e* is the ſame to the Line *b d*, as it is to the Line *f b*. That is, the Angles *f b e*, and *e b d*, are equal, and conſequently the Diagonal *b e*,

which

which is the second Line of Direction of the Body *b*, is perpendicular to the Angle *f b d*, and therefore is proportional to the Force impressed at *b*.

THE like is to be understood of the Diagonal *u e*, which is perpendicular to the Angle *i e k* ; also of the Diagonal *r n*, which is perpendicular to the Angle *o n p* ; and of the Diagonal *r v*, which is a Perpendicular to the Angle *t r x*, &c.

THAT the Increase or Diminution of Motion, or the Velocity with which any Body is moved by the Action of a Power upon it, is proportional to that Power, is evident ; for if I apply a certain Power to a Body, that will make it move with such Velocity, as to pass in one Minute 500 Yards ; to make two such Bodies pass 500 Yards in one Minute, will require a Power double to the former, because there is double the Quantity of Matter to be removed in the same Time. And, on the other Hand, if this double Force be applied to either one of the aforesaid Bodies, which are supposed to be equal, its Velocity will be doubled, and consequently it will travel a thousand Yards in one Minute. Hence 'tis plain, that the Degree of Motion, into which any Body is put out of a State of Rest by any Force or Power, will be proportional to that Power ; that is, a double Power will give twice the Velocity, a treble Power three times the Velocity, a quadruple Power four times the Velocity, &c.

LAW III.

Repulse, or Re-action, is always equal, and in contrary Direction to Impulse or Action ; i. e. The Actions of two Bodies upon each other are always equal, and in contrary Directions.

WHEN any Body acts upon another, the Action of that Body upon the other is equalled by the contrary Re-action of that other Body upon the first, and are both contrary in their Directions. The Re-action of Bodies is caused by their Elasticity, which all Bodies in Nature have in some Degree or other, though none are perfectly elastic. If the Body *a*, *Fig.* C, *Plate* LXXVI. descend obliquely to *b*, and strike the horizontal Line at *b*, it will by its Elasticity rebound up towards *e* ; and the Angle *f b c*, which is called the Angle of Reflection, will be equal to the Angle *d b e*, the Angle of Incidents. The Elasticity of a Body is a Springiness of its Parts, in the Recovery of its Form, immediately after its Form has been altered by another Body acting against it ; as in Wool, when its Figure, after being pressed down, is changed, it will, when the Pressure is taken away, spring up to its natural State as before ; so likewise a Bladder, blown full of Air, by being pressed on any Part, its Form is changed, but the very Instant of Time that the Pressure is removed, it will, by the Spring of Air within, recover its former Figure ; and every Force so applied has at the same Time an equal springing Force acting against it, which is the Re-action of the Body. So an Hoop of Iron or Wood, truly circular, as *b g*, *Fig.* I, by being struck on, or let fall on the Ground, will at the Instant of the Stroke, or Fall, be changed into an Ellipsis, as *c f e g* ; but by its Elasticity, or springiness of Parts, it will recover itself into a Circle again. The Action and Re-action of Bodies on Water is very easily understood ; for if *b* and *c*, *Fig.* H, represent two Boats of equal Magnitude and Weight, floating on a stagnant Water, and a Man standing in *b*, by Means of a Rope, pull the Boat *c* unto him, the Vessel *c* will react, and at the same Time pull the Vessel *b* towards it, with the same Force, so that both Vessels will meet at *a*, which is the Middle between both. Now 'tis very plain, that if the Vessel *c* did not re-act the same Force on the Person in the Vessel *b* as the Force of the Person in *b* acts on *c*, they would not meet at *a*.

Now, since by this 'tis plain that Action and Re-action are equal, therefore a Body at Rest cannot be removed by any Force that is less than its Weight ; and as I have, in the falling of Bodies, demonstrated the Increase of Force, it is therefore to be understood, that all Manner of Force, given by Pressure, Blows, Liftings, Pullings, Drawings, &c. is equal to some certain Weight. For if I put a Pound Weight into a Scale, and with my Hand press down the other, so as juft to balance the Weight, the Force of my Preffure is then equal to a Pound ; and fo in the like Manner I may continue to increafe that Force on the one Side, againft Weight in the other, until I prefs the whole Weight of my Body on the Scale : and which being the greateft Force of this Kind that I can make, therefore no Man, with a fingle Pulley, can raife any Weight greater than that of his own Body, unlefs his Body is confined to the Ground.

Again, If with a Hammer I ftrike a blow in an empty Scale, fo as juft to raife a Pound Weight in the other Scale, the Force of that Blow may be faid to be equal to one Pound ; although in reality 'tis fomething more, otherwife it could not juft raife the Weight above the Level of the Scales.

In this Manner, the Force of Blows may be made equal to any given Weights ; and by this Method of ftriking into an empty Scale, againft Weight increafed or diminithed, as Occafion may require, the Force of any Blow may be nearly and eafily difcovered ; and fince that Bodies at reft cannot be removed, or put into Action, but by Means of Forces or Powers fuperior to their Weights, therefore to remove heavy Bodies there has been an abfolute Neceffity of inventing divers Kinds of Powers, which with the Strength of a few Men will raife and remove Bodies of very great Weights at Pleafure.

LECT. III.

Of the Mechanical Powers in general.

THE Powers ufed for thefe Purpofes are ufually reckoned in Number fix, *viz.* Firft, *Libra*, the Balance. Secondly, *Vectis*, the Lever, or Leaver. Thirdly, *Trochlea*, the Pulley. Fourthly, *Axis in Peritrochio*, or the Axis in the Wheel, and in the Wind-lace. Fifthly, *Cuneus*, the Wedge. And, fixthly, *Cochlea*, the Screw. But, as I proceed, I fhall prove the Balance, the Pulley, and the Axis in Peritrochio, to be no other than Leavers, and the Screw to be no more than a Wedge, fixed about the Body of a Cylinder : therefore the fix Powers are reducible unto three.

All the Effects of thefe Powers may be judged of by this

RULE.

When two Weights are applied to any of thefe Powers, the Weights will equiponderate, if when put into Motion their Velocities be reciprocally proportional to their refpective Weights.

First, Reciprocal Proportion is, when in four Numbers the fourth is leffer than the fecond, by fo much as the third is greater than the firft, and *vice verfa*.

The whole Effect of thefe Powers, to raife or fuftain great Weights with a fmall Power, is produced by a Diminution of the Velocity of the Weight to be raifed, and increafing that of the Power, in a reciprocal Proportion of the two Weights and their Velocities ; that is, by giving as much more Velocity to the Power, as it weighs lefs than the Weight, that the Quantity of Matter fixed at each End of a Leaver or other Power, being multiplied by its Velocity, may fhew that there is an equal Quantity of Motion at each End ; and therefore it will follow, that, when equal Motions act with contrary Directions, they caufe an Equilibrium.

Secondly, An Equilibrium is, when the two Ends of a Balance hang fo exactly level, that neither doth afcend or defcend, but both keep in a Pofition parallel to the Horizon ; which is caufed by their being both charged with equal Weight, as the Bodies *d e*, hanging at the Ends of the Balance *a b*, in *Fig.* M.

In every Body there are properly three Kinds of Centers, *viz.* its Center of Magnitude, its Center of Motion, and its Center of Gravity.

First, The Center of Magnitude of any Body is that Point which is equally diftant from its extreme Parts, as the central Point *a* of the Sphere, *Fig.* L, *&c.* Secondly, the Center of Motion of any Body is a Point about which any Body moves, when faftened any ways to it, or made to revolve or turn about it. So the Body *e*, in *Fig.* N, being faftened with a String to the Point *a*, and made to turn about it in the Circle *c b d*, the Point *a* is the Center of Motion to the Body *e*.

In the following Lectures on the Balance, Leaver, and Axis in Peritrochio, the Center of their Motion is called *Fulcrum*. Thirdly, the Center of Gravity of any Body is that Point on which, if the Body be supported or suspended from it, the Body will rest in any given Situation.

In all regular Bodies, whose Matter is equally the same throughout, the Centers of Magnitude and Gravity are in the same Points, but in irregular Bodies not so ; and therefore in irregular Bodies the Center of Gravity will descend, till it gets under the Center of Motion, unless it be perpendicularly over it ; and from hence we are taught a Method of finding the Center of Gravity of any irregular Body, as follows, *viz.* Suspend or hang up such a Body successively by different Sides, and with a Plumb-Line, let fall from the Center of Suspension, so as to touch the Body in each Case. Observe where those Plumb-Lines would intersect each other, being continued through the Body, and their Point of Intersection is the center of Gravity required.

To find the Center of Gravity common to two or more Bodies, connected together by an inflexible Rod, or Rods, Fig. V *and* Z, Plate LXXVI.

First, Let the Bodies *a e, Fig.* V, connected together by the inflexible Rod *a c* of any known Length, be given. Divide *a e* in *b ;* so that *a b* is to *b c*, as the Body *e* is to the Body *a ;* then the Point *b* is the Center of Gravity required.

Secondly, Let *b d g, Fig.* Z, be three Bodies, whose respective Centers of Gravity are joined by the Lines *b d, b g*, and *d g*. The Line *b d*, being so divided in *c*, that *b c* bears the same Proportion to *c d*, as the Body *d* bears to the Body *b, c* is the Center of Gravity common to those Bodies, as before in *Fig.* V. Draw the Line *c g*, which divide in *f ;* so that *c f* shall be to *f g*, as the Weight of the two Bodies *b* and *d* are to the Body *g ;* then the Point *f* will be the Center of Gravity common to the three Bodies *b, d, g ;* and they being suspended at that Point, will hang in a horizontal Position.

To find the Center of Gravity of a Hemisphere, Fig. Y.

Make *b c* equal to ⅜ of its Radius ; then the Point *c* is the Center of Gravity required.

The Center of Gravity in Geometrical Squares, Parallelograms, Rhombus's, and Rhomboides, is the Point in each Figure where the two Diagonals intersect each other.

All the Parts of *Homogeneous* Bodies have an equal Pressure about their Centers of Gravity ; and therefore when the Center of Gravity of any Body cannot descend, the Body will remain fixed. This is manifest by the Geometrical Square *a b d f, Fig.* A B, whose Center of Gravity is the Point *c*, and which cannot descend, until the Diagonal *a f*, raised on the Angle *f*, has passed the Perpendicular *i f*, which will carry *c*, the Center of Gravity, with it beyond *g*, the Perpendicular of its Base, when it will consequently descend. The same is also to be observed of the Rhombus *r t l n*, whose Center of Gravity is *q*, and which must be removed in the Arch *q p*, beyond *o*, the perpendicular Limit of its Base *l n*, before it can descend ; but the Rhomboides *x y 1 w*, whose Center of Gravity *z*, being without *v w*, the perpendicular Limit of its Base *1 v* ; its Center *z* will descend in the Arch *z 2*, and consequently the *Fig. z y 1 w* cannot stand on the Base *1 w*. From hence 'tis plain, first, That all Bodies, whose Centers of Gravity are within the perpendicular Limits of their Base, cannot fall. Secondly, That all Bodies, whose Centers of Gravity are beyond the perpendicular Limits of their Base, cannot stand. Thirdly, That the lesser the Base of any Body is, the easier it will be moved out of its Position ; because the least Change is capable of removing the Line of Direction beyond its Base. This is the Cause why a Ball, whose Base is a Point, and a Cylinder, whose Base is a Line, are rolled easily by a small Force on a horizontal Plane.

- In the following Lectures it is to be obferved,

FIRST, That when a Power applied can fuftain a Weight by the Means of a Balance, Leaver, Pulley, &c. if an Addition of Power, though it be as little as can be imagined, be made, it will overpoife or raife the Weight.

SECONDLY, That the Weight of Leavers, Pulleys, &c. and their Friction, are not fuppofed to be any Thing, although Rules will be given to find both.

THIRDLY, that a Leaver is confidered as a right Line ; and the Pin on which a Pulley moves, the fame.

FOURTHLY, By Power applied is meant a Force, as that of Weight, Water, Wind, &c.

FIFTHLY, That whatever any of thefe Powers gain in Strength, they lofe in Time.

L E C T U R E   IV.

Of the Balance.

THERE are three Kinds of Balance, *viz.* The common Balance, as ufed to common Scales ; the *Statera Romana*, *Roman* Balance, or Steel-yard ; and the Falfe Balance.

FIRST, The common Balance is no other than a Beam divided into two equal Parts, as *b f*, at *c*, *Fig.* O (and by the enfuing Lecture will appear to be a Leaver of the firft Kind), which inftead of refting on its Fulcrum at *c*, the Center of its Motion, is there fufpended. The two half Parts *b c*, and *c f*, are called *Brachias*:

To have the Balance horizontal, the Center of Motion muft be fomething above the Center of its Gravity ; for were they to be both in one Point, which they would be, was the Beam to be a right Line, as *a c*, then thofe Weights which equiponderated when the Beam hung horizontally, would alfo equiponderate in any other Pofition ; whereas, when the Center of Motion is placed a little above that of Gravity, as aforefaid, if the Beam be inclined either way, the Weight moft elevated will furmount the other, and defcend, caufing the Beam to fwing, until by Degrees it recovers its horizontal Pofition.

THE Reafon is very plain. Suppofe *a i*, *Fig.* P, be the Beam of a Balance put into an oblique Pofition, and the Perpendiculars *a c*, and *i g*, be drawn from its Extremes *a* and *i*, to the horizontal Line *c h*, 'tis evident that *c e*, the Diftance of the Perpendicular *a c*, is greater than *e g*, the Diftance of the Perpendicular *g i* ; and as the Weight *m* is equal to the Weight *o*, the Weight *m* will therefore raife up the Weight *o*. But was the Balance a right Line, as *b k*, having its Center of Motion and of Gravity both in the Point *c*, then the Diftances *d c*, and *c h*, of the Perpendiculars *b d* and *h k*, would be equal, and the equal Weights *l* and *n* would equiponderate in that oblique Pofition ; which the Beam *a c i* cannot do, becaufe the Center of its Motion is above the Center of its Gravity, which caufes the upper Point *a* to be the Diftance of *c d*, without the Perpendicular *b d* ; and the lower Point *i* to be the Diftance of *g h*, within the Perpendicular *h k*, and therefore *c e* is longer than *c g*, by twice *c d*.

THE Proportion that the Power has to the Weight in the common Balance, is as 1, the Length of one Brachia, is to 1, the Length of the other Brachia ; fo is the Power applied, to the Weight required to equipoife it.

II. THE *Statera Romana*, or *Roman Bulance*, commonly called the Steel-yard, *Fig.* R and Q, *Plate* LXXVI.

THIS Sort of Balance is called the *Roman Balance*, from its being ufed in common at *Rome* ; and it being originally made about 3 Feet in Length, and of Steel, 'twas therefore called a *Steel-yard*, and is thus made : Prepare a fmall fquare Bar of Iron or Steel, as 12 *a*, *Fig.* R, of any Length, and of equal Thicknefs, and let the Point *a* be the Center of Motion. Make the flat End *b z* of fuch Solidity, as to balance the Part 12 *a*. At any Diftance from *a* fix a Point, as *c*, on which the feveral Things to be weighed are to be fufpended.

Note,

Note, *The Point* c *is here fixed below the straight Line* 12 b, *for the same Reason at in the common Balance.*

Draw c b perpendicular to the Line 12 b; make the Divisions, a 1; 1, 2; a, 3; 3. 4; &c. each equal to a b. Then 1 Pound Weight, applied at 1, will equipoise 1 Pound at c; also 1 Pound Weight at 2, will equipoise 2 Pounds at c; also 1 Pound Weight at 3, will equipoise 3 Pounds at c; and 1 Pound at 12, will equipoise 12 Pounds at c, &c. For as a b, equal to one Part, is to a 12, 12 Parts; so is 1 Pound Weight at 12, to 12 Pounds (as the Body f), at c; and therefore the Point a is the common Center of Gravity of the two Weights, because 13, the Sum of the two Weights, is to 1, the least Weight, as the Length of the Balance is to one Part, the Distance of the great Weight from the Center of Gravity.

To find the common Center of Gravity of two Bodies applied to a Beam of a known Weight and Length, which is not balanced, as Fig. R *was supposed to be, by the more solid Part* b c.

Let d b, *Fig.* Q, be divided into 13 Parts; let the Body x be 1 Pound, and the Body k 12 Pounds; and let the Point a be their common Center of Gravity, and the Weight of the Beam equal to 3 Pounds. On a, the common Center of Gravity, hang the Weight l, equal to the Weights x and k; and at b, the Center of Gravity of the Beam, hang the Weight g, equal to 3 Pounds, the Weight of the Beam. Then as the Sum of the Weights g and l, 16 Pounds, is to 3, the lesser Weight g; so is the Distance b a, of those two new Weights, 5 $\frac{1}{2}$, to 1 $\frac{1}{12}$, the Distance of a from the true Center of Gravity required.

III. A false Balance, as *Fig.* S, has its Beam unequally divided, as c e, and e d, which are to one another as 9 is to 10, &c. and its Scales being also in the same Proportion, they will therefore equiponderate as the just Balance; and whatever is weighed in the Scale hanging on e, will be $\frac{1}{10}$ less Weight than it really ought to be; but this Cheat is immediately discovered by changing the Scales.

LECTURE V.

Of the Lever, commonly called the Leaver.

THERE are three Sorts of Leavers, which are distinguished by the different Manners of applying the Power and Weight.

A Leaver of the first Kind is that, whose Fulcrum is between the Power applied, and the Weight that is to be raised, as *Fig.* A Q, *Plate* LXXVI. where the Power is applied at d, the Weight at c, and the Fulcrum at a. Hence 'tis plain, that the common Balance *Fig.* O, the false Balance *Fig.* S, and the *Roman* Balance *Fig.* R, are all Leavers of the first Kind, because their Centers of Motion, as Fulcrums, are between their Powers and Weights.

To know what Weight can be raised by a Leaver of the first Kind, this is the Analogy:

As the lesser Brachia a c *is to the greater Brachia* d a, *so is the Power applied at* d *to the Weight it will equipoise at* c. Therefore a little more being added to the Power at b, will raise the Weight required.

The Length of a Brachia is the Distance of a Power, or of a Weight, from a Fulcrum, and is always equal to a Perpendicular let fall from the Fulcrum, upon the Line of Direction of the Power or Weight. So b i, *Fig.* A N, is the Distance of the Power at d, because 'tis perpendicular to the Line of Direction d b, of the Power at d; in like Manner the Line i e, which is perpendicular to e b, the Line of Direction of the Power e, is the Distance of the Power at e; as also is a i the Distance of the Power at c. Hence 'tis plain, that the greatest Power is that at d, whose Line of Direction is right-angled with the Leaver b k; and which is yet more evidently so by the Power applied at g, whose Distance from the Fulcrum is no more than b i, equal to the Perpendicular i f. The like is also to be understood of bended Leavers, as *Fig.* A F, A E, A G, and A L.

I t

It matters not whether the Brachias of a Leaver be ftraight or curved, as *Fig.* A M, and A I; for in both thefe Cafes the Diftances of the Powers and of the Weights from their Fulcrums are the Chord Lines of the Arches, and not the Arches themfelves. The nearer the Weight is to, and the farther the Power is from, the Fulcrum, the lefs will be the Power, and the lefs will be the Height that the Weight can be raifed; for if the Body *k*, in *Fig.* W, be removed nearer to the Fulcrum from *o p* unto *n m*, it will not require fo great a Power at *s* to raife it, as when at *o p*, nor can it be raifed fo high as when at *o p*; for if two equal Bodies be placed at *n m* and *o p*, and *s*, the End of the Leaver *s p*, be forced down to *t*, the Body *o p* will be raifed to *a q*, and the Body *n m* but to *c b*.

When a Body is on the End of a Leaver, as the Body *n o l c*, *Fig.* A K, fo as to have its Center of Gravity above the Leaver, and is equipoifed by a Power at *v*, whofe Line of Direction is perpendicular to the Leaver *l v*; that Power will be increafed as the Body is raifed, as to *p a*, and decreafed as the faid Body is let lower to *f g*; for, in the firft, the Center of Gravity of the Body at *p* is brought nearer to the Fulcrum; and in the laft, at *k*, it is farther. When a Body, fixed to the End of a Leaver, has its Center of Gravity below the Leaver, as the Body 8, 11, 10, 12, *Fig.* A H, to raife the Body as to 7, 5, the Power muft be increafed; but to let the Body down as to 16, 14, the Power muft be decreafed; for 'tis evident that 13, 14, the central Line of the Body at 16 14, is nearer to the Fulcrum than 3, 1, the central Line of the Body at 7, 5, and confequently will be equipoifed at *b* by a leffer Power, as *c*, than that of *g*, required at *f*.

These being underftood, the Nature of Leavers in general will be made eafy, as in the following Problems doth appear.

Problem I.

The Length and Weight of a Beam, which has a Body of known Weight fixed to one End, being given, to find the Center of Gravity on the Beam, on which one Part of the Beam fhall equipoife the other Part, and the given Body alfo.

Rule, As the Sum of the Weights of the Balance and of the Body is to the Length of the Balance, fo is the Weight of the Body to the leffer Brachia; or fo is the Weight of the Balance only, to the greater Brachia.

Prob. II. *Fig.* T. *Plate* LXXV.

Two Bodies, as e g, of known Weights, of which g is hung at b, to the End of a Beam of known Weight and Length, wherein the Fulcrum is fixed at a, to find a Point as c, to hang the Weight e, fo that the Weight e, and the Weight of the Balance, fhall equipoife the Weight g.

Let the Length of the Beam be 14 Inches, its Weight 2 Ounces, and the Fulcrum *a* one Inch from *b*; let the Body *g* be 15 Ounces, and the Body *e* 1 Ounce; divide the Beam in the Middle at *d*, and there hang the Body *f*, equal to 2 Ounces, the Weight of the Beam. Then as *a b*, one Inch, the leffer Brachia, is to *a d*, fix Inches, the greater Brachia; fo is the leffer Body *f*, 2 Ounces, to 12 Ounces, which is a Part of the Body *g*, whofe Weight is 15 Ounces, which is 3 Ounces more than the 12 aforefaid. To find the Point *c* where the Body *e*, equal to 1 Ounce, will equipoife the aforefaid 3 Ounces: Say, as the Body *e*, 1 Ounce, is to 3, the remaining Ounces in the Body *g*; fo is 1, the leffer Brachia *b a*, to 3, the Diftance of the Point: from the Fulcrum *a*. Then the Body *f*, equal to 2 Ounces, is to 12 Ounces in the Body *g*, as the Body *e*, equal to 1 Ounce, is to the 3 Ounces in *g*; and therefore the Bodies *f* and *e*, being fixed at *d* and *c*, will equipoife the Body *g* on the Fulcrum *a*.

A Leaver of the fecond Kind is that, whofe Fulcrum is at one End, the Power at the other, and hath the Weight between them, as *Fig.* X, *Plate* LXXVI. where *a r* is the Leaver, *a* its Fulcrum, *r* the Place where the Power is to be applied, and *m n* and *o p*, Weights placed between them to be raifed.

To know what Weight can be raifed by a Leaver of the fecond Kind, this is the Analogy:

As the Diftance of the Weight from the Fulcrum is to the Diftance of the Power from the Fulcrum, fo is the Power to the Weight that will equipoife it.

Hence

Hence 'tis plain, that if a Leaver, as *d l*, *Fig.* A O, be divided into four equal Parts at *e f i*, if the Body *c* be applied as a Power equal to 1 Pound, it will require 2 Pounds to equipoife it in the Middle at *f*, becaufe 1 Pound will be fuftained by the Fulcrum at *l*. And for the fame Reafon the Body at *s* muft be 1 Pound, and ½, and that at *i* muft be 4 Pounds.

A Leaver of the third Kind hath its Fulcrum at one of its Ends, the Weight at the other, and the Power applied in fome Part between them, as in *Fig.* A P, where *n e* is a Leaver whofe Fulcrum is at *e*, its Weight at *n*, and Power applied between them as at *k h g*, the equal divided Parts, as in *Fig.* A O.

To know what Weight can be raifed by a Leaver of the third Kind, this is the Analogy:

As the Length of the Leaver is to the Diftance of the Power from the Fulcrum, fo is the Power applied to the Weight it will equipoife.

Now as the Power is applied between the Fulcrum and the Weight, therefore the Power muft always be fuperior to the Weight; for if the Body *m* be equal to 1 Pound, it will require a Power equal to 2 Pounds at *h*; of 1 Pound and ⅓ at *k*, and of 4 Pounds at *g*, to equipoife it.

To thefe three Kinds of Leavers fome add what they call a Leaver of the fourth Kind, as *Fig.* A L, which in Fact is no more than a Leaver of the firft Kind, as having its Fulcrum *e* between the two Brachias *b e* and *e d*.

LECTURE VI,
Of the Pulley.

AN upper Pulley adds nothing to the Power; for in *Fig.* A, *Plate* LXXVII. to fuftain the Body *f* at *c*, there muft be a Power applied by *e* at *a*, which is equal to the Weight of the Body *f*; becaufe *a d*, the Diftance of the Power from *d*, the Center of the Pulley, is equal to *d e*, the Diftance of the Body from the Centre; and from hence 'tis plain, that an upper Pulley is a Leaver of the firft Kind; becaufe, confidering its Diameter as the Length of the Leaver, its Center is the Fulcrum and as both the Brachias *a d* and *d e* are equal, therefore an upper Pulley is of no other Ufe, than to communicate the Motion of the Rope to an under Pulley.

An under Pulley, as *Fig.* I, doubles its Force; for if the Body *f* weighs 2 Pounds, 'tis plain that the Power applied at *d* can fuftain but half the Weight, becaufe the Line on the Hook *a* fuftains the like Quantity. Now if the Diameter *b d* be truly confidered, it will appear to be a Leaver of the fecond Kind; for as the Pulley is always rifing on the Line at *b*, therefore the Point *b* is the Fulcrum; and as the Line is always lifting at *d*, therefore that End of the Diameter is to be confidered as the Power; and as the Center of the Pulley is in the midft between thefe Points on which the Weight hangs, therefore a Power equal to 1 Pound, will equipoife a Weight of 2 Pounds at *c*. For as *b e* 1, the Diftance of the Weight from *b* the Fulcrum, is to *b d* 2, the Diftance of the Power; fo is 1, the Power applied, to 2, the Weight it will equipoife. And in all Tackles of under Pulleys, the Power will be to the Weight it fuftains, as 1 is to the Number of Ropes applied to the lower Pulleys; fo in *Fig.* B, the Power at *k* is to the Weight, as 1 is to 2; in *Fig.* C, as 1 is to 3; in *Fig.* D, as 1 is to 4; in *Fig.* E, as 1 is to 5; and in *Fig.* F, as 1 is to 6.

Weights may be fuftained by Pulleys, with a fmall Power, the Pulleys being applied as in *Fig.* G, where the Body *l*, equal to 1 Pound, will equipoife the Body *s*, equal to 8 Pounds. For as 1 Pound applied at *m*, by Means of the upper Pully *i k*, will equipoife 2 Pounds at *e*, fo 2 Pounds applied at *p* will equipoife 4 Pounds at *c*, and 4 Pounds applied at *r* will equipoife 8 Pounds at *a*, &c. For as 1 at *m* is to 2 at *e*, fo is 2 at *p* to 4 at *c*, and 4 at *r* to 8 at *a*.

A Weight may be alfo fuftained by Pulleys with a fmall Power, the Pulleys being applied as in *Fig.* M; for if the Power at *m* be equal to 1 Pound, and againſt it be hung the Body *l*, equal to 1 Pound, they will together equipoiſe the Body *g*, equal to 2 Pounds; and the Body *g*, with the Power 1, and Body *l* equal to 1, which together are equal to 4 Pounds, will equipoiſe the Body *k*, equal to 4 Pounds, &c. In *Fig.* H, the Power at *i*, equal to 1 Pound, equipoiſes 1 Pound of the Body *k*, which together, by Means of the Pulley *e f*, equipoiſes 2 Pounds more of the Body *k*; and theſe together being equal to 4 Pounds, by Means of the upper Pulley *b d*, equipoiſe 4 Pounds more in the Body *k*; ſo that, in this Example, the Power at *i* equipoiſes ſeven Times its own Weight.

LECTURE VII.

Of the Axis in Peritrochio, commonly called the Wheel and Axis.

THIS Inſtrument is no other than a Wheel fixed on a Cylinder, as *d i* on *a b*, *Fig.* W, *Plate* LXXVII. The central Line *a b* of the Cylinder is called the Axis, and the Wheel *d k i* is called the Peritrochio.

IF *b d*, and *e f*, be fixed on an Axis as *a b*, directly oppoſite and parallel, and conſidered as the two Brachias of a Leaver, then the Axis *a b*, on which they are fixed, will be the Fulcrum; and if *b d* be conſidered as the Radius of a Wheel, as *d c*, *Fig.* W; and *e f*, *Fig.* T, the Radius of a Cylinder, on which the Wheel is fixed, as *e f*, *Fig.* W; 'tis plain that this Machine is a Leaver of the firſt Kind: and therefore, *as* e f, *the Radius of the Cylinder*, Fig. W, *is to* d c, *the Radius of the Wheel; ſo is the Power to the Weight: and when Spakes or Teeth are fixed in Wheels*, then, *as the Diſtance of the Extremes of thoſe on the Pinion, or ſmaller Wheel, from the Axis, is to the Diſtance of the Extremes of thoſe on the greater Wheel, ſo is the Power to the Weight.*

By the Multiplication of Wheels, very great Weights may be raiſed; an Example of which I have given in *Fig.* K, where the Body *q*, equal to one Pound, equipoiſes the Body r, equal to 105 Pounds. By Means of the four Wheels *n f o c*, on whoſe Cylinders are fixed the ſmall Wheels *g e b*, whoſe Teeth work in the Circumference of the large Wheels, the Radius of every ſmall Wheel on the Cylinders is 1 Foot. The Radius of the great Wheels are as follows, viz. The Radius of the Wheel *c* is 2 Feet and half; of the Wheel *o*, 3 Feet; of the Wheel *m*, 3 Feet and half; and of the Wheel *n*, 4 Feet. Now the Power *q* to the Weight *r* is thus calculated: Firſt, *As* 1, *the Radius of the ſmall Wheel* b, *is to* 2 *and half, the Radius of the great Wheel* c; *ſo is* 1, *the Power* q, *to* 2 *and half, the Weight that it will equipoiſe at* o. Secondly, *As* 1, *the Radius of the ſmall Wheel* c, *is to* 3, *the Radius of the great Wheel* o; *ſo is* 2 ½, *the Power applied at* o *by the ſmall Wheel* b, *to* 7 ½, *the Weight that will equipoiſe at* g. Thirdly, *As* 1, *the Radius of the ſmall Wheel* g, *is to* 3 *and* ½, *the Radius of the great Wheel* m; *ſo is* 7 *and* ½, *the Power applied at* g *by the ſmall Wheel* c, *to* 26 *and* ¼, *the Weight that will equipoiſe at* n. Fourthly, *As* 1, *the Radius of the Cylinder* p, *is to* 4, *the Radius of the great Wheel* n, *ſo is* 26 *and* ¼, *the Power applied at* n *by the ſmall Wheel* g, *to* 105, *the Weight* r, *that will but equipoiſe the Body* q *equal to* 1 *Pound*.

THE Application of a Power to a Wheel is always the greateſt when applied at right Angles to its Radius, as the Power *g f*, *Fig.* L, *Plate* LXXVII. which is perpendicular to the Radius *c f*, and at the Diſtance of *c f* from the Fulcrum *c*; therefore when a Power is applied obliquely, as *b d* to the Radius *c d*, the Power is leſſened in Proportion, as *f e* is to *e c*.

LECTURE VIII.

Of the Wedge or inclined Plane.

A WEDGE is the moſt plain and ſimple Inſtrument of all the mechanical Powers, and is put into Action by the acting or ſtriking of another Body upon it, which is called *Percuſſion*.

The Center of Percuſſion is a Point on the top Surface of a Wedge, which is directly againſt the Center of the Body ſtruck thereon ; ſo the Point *c*, *Fig.* A C is the Center of Percuſſion, as being directly againſt *a*, the Center of the Body or Mallet *b c*, whoſe Line of Direction is *b d.*

It is to be obſerved here, as in the preceding Powers, that the greateſt Force is made, when the ſtriking Body falls perpendicular upon the upper Surface of the Wedge, as the Mallet *b c*, on the Wedge *f*, in the Body *d*, *Fig.* A D, whoſe Line of Direction is *c d.*

To underſtand the Power of the Wedge, which is ſuppoſed to be right-angled, as *a b c*, *Fig.* X, the Length of its Baſe *b c*, and of its perpendicular Height *b a*, muſt be known ; for as the perpendicular Height *b a*, equal to 2, is to the Baſe *b c*, equal to 4, ſo is a Force equal to 10 Pounds, to 20, the Weight it will raiſe ; and therefore the longer the Baſe is, with reſpect to the Height, the leſſer is the Power required ; and the ſhorter the Baſe is, the greater the Power muſt be. For ſuppoſing the Triangle *c e g* to be a Wedge of equal Weight with *a b c*, whoſe Baſe *c g* is equal to 3 ; then as 2 is to 3, ſo is 10, the aforeſaid Power, applied to 15, which is 5 leſs than 20, the Weight raiſed with the ſame Power by the Wedge *a b c*; and therefore to raiſe a Weight of 20 Pounds with the Wedge *c g e*, the Power muſt be increaſed to 13 Pounds $\frac{1}{3}$: for as 2 is to 3, ſo is 13 $\frac{1}{3}$ to 20. But *note*, That in all theſe Calculations, it is ſuppoſed, that there is no Obſtruction by Friction, but that the Surfaces of Planes, Wedges, &c. are perfectly ſmooth. Bodies may be raiſed by the Means of one Wedge, as the Body *d* unto *c*, by the Wedge *a b c*, *Fig.* Z, if there be a reſiſting Body, as *f g*, that will admit the Wedge *a b c*, to paſs along the Line *b g* to *k*; or when two Wedges mutually reſiſt the Weight of the Body to be raiſed, as *a b c*, and *c e f*, *Fig.* O ; which being equally driven by each other's Sides, will raiſe the Body O unto the Line *a e*.

To raiſe a Body from the Ground, as *a h b g*, *Fig.* N, by Means of the Wedge *c f e*, is the ſame Thing as to ſplit a Body aſunder, as Y, by the Wedge *h d*; for if the adhering of the Parts of the Body together, which are to be diſunited by the Wedge, be conſidered as Weight, the Power in both Caſes muſt be equal ; and the Force with which a Wedge will ſo lift a Weight, or diſunite the Parts of a Body, by a Blow upon its End, will bear the ſame Proportion to the Force wherewith the Blow would act on the Weight, if directly applied to it, as the Velocity which the Wedge receives from the Blow bears to the Velocity wherewith the Weight is lifted, or the Parts of the Body diſunited by the Wedge.

Bodies may be equipoiſed on an inclined Plane, as the Body *e*, *Fig.* P, Plate LXXVII. by a Weight of leſs Force, as the Body *a*, provided that the Body *a* be to the Body *e*, as the perpendicular Height of the inclined Plane is to its Hypothenuſe.

LECTURE IX;

Of the Screw.

THIS Power is nothing more than a Wedge, or an inclined Plane, fixed about the Body of a Cylinder, as *Fig.* A B, Plate LXXVII; or it may be conſidered as a Cylinder cut into continued inclined concave Surfaces, as *s t*, *w v*, *y x*, bounded by divers circumvolving Helixes or Threads, as *e d*, *k h*, *o l*, *z q*, &c.

The Screw is applied in two different Manners ; as, firſt, to work in a hollow Screw, which is called the Female Screw or Nut, fixed in ſome particular Manner, as the Nature of the Occaſion requires ; and ſometimes to the Teeth of a Wheel, as to the Spindle of the Flyers of a Kitchen Jack, &c.

The Force of a Screw is according to the Angle that the Helix or Thread makes with the Baſe of the Cylinder ; for, as it is really a Wedge, therefore the more acute the Aſcent of the Thread is, the leſs Power is required to raiſe a Body. For, as the Height of the Thread on one half Revolution, is to the Semi-circum-

ference

ference of the Cylinder's Base, so is the Power to the Weight; because the Height of the Thread is considered as the Height of a Wedge; and the Semi-circumference of the Cylinder's Base, as the Base of a Wedge: and as this Power is worked by Leaver of the second Kind, it may be made of prodigious Force. Suppose a Screw of 7 Inches Diameter, whose Circumference is 22 Inches, have its Thread to rise 1 Inch in half a Revolution, then the Power of such a Screw will be as 1, the Height of the half Revolution of the Thread, is to 11, the half Circumference of the Cylinder; so will the Power be to the Weight it will equipoise. And if a Lever of 10 Feet in Length have its End put into the Cylinder of the Screw, so as to be just at the Axis of the Screw, which is done by putting 3 Inches and a half of the Lever into the Cylinder, then the Axis of the Screw will be the Fulcrum of the Lever, and the Outside of the Cylinder will be the Weight to be removed. Now as the remaining Length of the Lever, *viz.* 9 Feet, 8 Inches, and a half, equal to 116 Inches, contains 3 Inches and a half, the Distance of the Weight from the Fulcrum, 33 times and $\frac{1}{7}$; therefore the Power of the Lever only is as 1 is to 33 and $\frac{1}{7}$. Now suppose a Man's Strength to be equal to 100 Pounds, then as 1 is to 33 and $\frac{1}{7}$, so is 100 to 3300$\frac{5}{7}$; and as the Force of the Screw is s 61 is to 11, so is 3300$\frac{5}{7}$, the Power applied on the Screw by the Lever, to 23,201 Pounds $\frac{9}{11}$, its Equipoise; which, by a small additional Power continued, may be raised to the Height of the Screw.

LECTURE X.

Of the Velocities with which Bodies are raised, and the Spaces through which they and their Powers move.

WHAT any Engine gains in Power, it loses in Space: In the Lever, *Fig.* W, *Plate* LXXVI. if *s r* be double to *r p*, the End *s* being moved down to *t*, must move with twice the Velocity that the End *p* will do, in moving to *q*, and the Arch *p q* will be but half the Arch *s t*.

THE same is also to be observed in the Lever *a r*, of the second Kind, *Fig.* X; for in raising its End *r* to *g*, the Body at *m n*, removed to *c b*, the End *r* will move with double the Velocity of the Body *m n*, for the Arch *r g* is double the Arch *n b*. In the raising of a Weight by one or more under Pulleys, the Space through which the Power must pass, is to the Space through which the Weight must rise, as the Power is to the Weight; so in *Fig.* F, *Plate* LXXVII. as 1, the Power at *x*, is to 6, the Weight at W, so is 1 to 6, the Space through which the Power must pass; and therefore to raise the Body W, 1 Foot in Height, the Power *x* must descend 6 Feet, and consequently must move with 6 times the Velocity of that of the Weight.

THE like is also in the Wheel and its Axis; for to cause 1 Revolution of the greatest Wheel *n*, on which the Body *r* is fixed, the little Wheel *c* must make 42 Revolutions; and if the Diameter of the Cylinder *p* be 2 Feet, the Weight will be raised 6 Feet $\frac{2}{7}$. But as the Diameter of the small Wheel *c* is 5 Feet, the Power *q*, equal to 1 Pound, must pass through a Space equal to 42 times 15 Feet $\frac{5}{7}$, its own circumference, equal to 660 Feet; or so much Rope must be drawn at *q* from off the Wheel *c*.

As I have already noted, that the more acute the Angle of a Wedge is made, the less Force is required; therefore whatever is gained in Force by the Acuteness of the Wedge, so much is lost in Space or Time; because the more acute a Wedge be made, the greater Length the Wedge must be, to rise equal in Height with another Wedge, whose Angle is less acute; and, in the aforesaid Example of the Wedge and Lever, the Power must revolve 30 times in a Circle of 20 Feet Diameter, whose Circumference is 62 Feet $\frac{6}{7}$, to raise the Weight 5 Feet in Height, which Space is equal to 1885 Feet, $\frac{5}{7}$.

PART

PART VIII:

Of HYDROSTATICKS.

THE Word *Hydrostaticks* is derived from ὕδωρ *Water*, and ϛατικὴ the Science of *Weight*, from ϛατέω *to weigh*. As to fully illustrate this Science in every of its Particulars, would not only swell this Volume much beyond its intended Bulk, but would contain many Particulars which are not immediately useful to Workmen, for whom this Work is designed, I shall therefore only speak of such Parts as are absolutely necessary to be understood by Workmen in general.

BEFORE we proceed to this Subject, I must first explain the Nature and Properties of Air.

AIR is an invisible fluid Substance, which not only environs the whole Globe of Earth and Water, but is also contained in the Interstices or Pores of all Bodies. Its principal Properties are *Fluidity*, *Transparency*, *Rarefication*, *Condensation*, *Elasticity*, and *Weight* or *Gravity*.

THAT Air is a Fluid, is evident by its yielding to every Force; that 'tis transparent, is evident to every Eye; that it may be rarefied, is evident by the Experiment of an empty Bladder tied close at its Neck, and laid before a Fire, which will so rarefy the little inclosed Air as to make it extend the Bladder to its utmost Stretch, and at last break through it, with a Report equal to a Gun. And by Computation it is proved, that the Air at 7 Miles Altitude from the Earth is 4 times rarer or thinner than at the Surface; at 14 Miles Altitude 16 times rarer; at 21 Miles 64 times; at 28 Miles 256; at 35 Miles 1024 times; at 70 Miles about 1,000,000; and so on in a geometrical Proportion of Rarity, compared with the arithmetical Proportion of its Altitude. *Vide* Sir *Isaac Newton*'s Opticks, page 342.

BY various Experiments it hath been proved, that Air may be so condensed as to take up but $\frac{1}{13}$ Part of the Space it possessed before; and Mr. *Boyle* found its Spring or Elasticity so great, as to dilate or expand itself so as to take up 13,769 times a greater Space than before. This Power of Elasticity is according to its Density, and its Density is found by Experiments to be equal to its Compression.

THE Weight or Gravity of the Air has been proved by divers Experiments of the Air-pump, and Barometer; and 'tis found that a cubical Foot of Air at the Earth's Surface is 830 times lighter than a Cube Foot of River Water, and therefore its Weight is something more than 1 Ounce and $\frac{6166}{10000}$; but the Weight of a Column of the Atmosphere, on a square Foot of the Earth's Surface when the Air is the heaviest, is found to be equal to 2259 Pounds *Avoirdupoise* (at which Time the Mercury will rise to 31 Inches), which is 15 Pounds and 11 Ounces on every square Inch. But when the Air is lightest, so that the Mercury is raised but to 28 Inches, then the Weight of the Atmosphere on every square Foot is but 2025 Pounds, and on every square Inch 14 Pounds and 1 Ounce.

THE greatest Extent of that Part of the Air which is called *Atmosphere*, from the Surface of the Earth and Seas, is about 45 Miles in Height. The Weight of the Air is greater, the nearer it is to the Earth's Surface, which is caused by the great Weight of the Air next above it.

To

To find the Weight of a Pillar of the Atmosphere.

TAKE a glafs Tube, of about 3 Feet in Length, and about $\frac{1}{20}$ or $\frac{1}{10}$ of an Inch in Diameter, hermetically fealed at one End: fill it full of Quickfilver; immerfe the open End in a fmall Bafon of Quickfilver; and then, holding the Tube perpendicular, the Quickfilver within the Tube will fubfide or run out into the Bafon, until it be fufpended at fome Height above 28 Inches perpendicular Height.

THE Reafon why the Quickfilver will be fo fufpended, is, that the Top of the Tube being fealed, the Preffure of the Pillar of the Atmofphere, perpendicularly over the Top of the Tube, is made on the Top of the Tube only, and not on any Part of the Quickfilver within it; and if it be confidered, that every Part of the Quickfilver's Surface, in the Bafon about the Tube, equal to the Bafe of the Tube, is preffed by the fame Weight of Air as that on the Top of the Tube, 'tis evident that the Preffure of any one of thofe Parts is equal to the Weight of the Quickfilver preffing on its own Bafe; therefore the Quickfilver cannot defcend lower; and therefore the Weight of the Quickfilver in the Tube is equal to the Weight of a Pillar of the Atmofphere of its own Diameter.

On this Principle depends the raifing of Water out of Wells, by the Help of a common Pump.

IN Page 24 may be feen, that a Cube Foot of Quickfilver weighs 874 Pounds $\frac{7}{10}$, and a Cube Foot of River Water 62 Pounds $\frac{5}{10}$; therefore Quickfilver is fomething more than 14 times heavier than River Water; and therefore, in a re-curved Tube placed with the Ends upwards and open, 1 Inch of Quickfilver will keep in Equilibrio 14 Inches of Water.

Now to find how high Well Water can be raifed by a Pump in any Place, obferve how many Inches the Quickfilver will rife in the Tube as aforefaid; and fo many times 14 Inches Water may be raifed by a Pump, becaufe every 14 Inches Height of Water is but the Equipoife of an Inch of Quickfilver. Therefore when a Pillar of the Atmofphere is equipoifed by a Pillar of Quickfilver, whofe Height is 30 Inches, to equipoife a like Pillar of the Atmofphere with a Pillar of Water of the fame Bafe, its Altitude muft be 35 Feet, which is 30 times 14 Inches, and which is generally the greateft Height that Water can be made to rife by the Help of a Pump.

THE *Antlia*, or common Pump, *Fig.* Q, *Plate* LXXVII. is a Machine of a very long Date, which is faid to be the Invention of *Ctefebes*, a Mathematician of *Alexandria*, about 120 Years before *Chrift*. This Machine made of Lead confifts of a fucking Pipe, as *o p*, foldered to the Bottom of a larger Pipe or Barrel, as at *n m*, but, being made of Wood, is no more than a common Pipe, open at both Ends; but, be it made either of Lead or Wood, at a proper Diftance below its Top, as at *l m*, is placed a Valve as *l*, which opens upwards; within the upper Part of the Barrel is fitted a *Pifton* or Bucket, as *g*, juft as big as the Bore of the Barrel, in which alfo is a Valve, that opens upwards. To this Pifton or Bucket is fixed an Iron Rod, as *c h*, which by a Pin is fixed to the End of the Handle *e f*; but as thereby the Rod is drawn out of a Perpendicular, tho' there may be a Joint in the Rod near the Pifton, the Power muft be greater than was the Rod to rife up and down perpendicularly, which may be eafily effected by the Arch *b d*, fixed to the upper Part of the Handle, and by two Chains fixed from *a* to *d*, and from *c* to *b*, which will rife up and force down the Pifton truly perpendicular, and with the leaft Friction.

Now the Manner of the Pump's Performance is eafily underftood; for when the Pifton is forced down towards *n*, and a Quantity of Water poured in at the Top, the 2 Valves being then fhut, and the external Air being feparated from that within the fucking Pipe *o p*, whofe End *p* is before immerfed in Water, therefore as foon as the Pifton with the Water poured on it is raifed, the Air within the fucking Pipe by the Force of the Atmofphere on the Surface of the Water in the Well is pufhed up through the Valve at *l*, and fills that Part of

the

the Barrel, in which the Piston afcended, at which Inftant the Valve at *l* is fhut. Now as much Air as is contained between the Valve at *n m*, and the Bottom of the Piston, fo much Water at the fame Inftant afcended at the lower Part of the fucking Pipe. The Piston being again forced down the Barrel towards *n m*, the confined Air under it is compelled to force open the Valve at *g*, as the Piston defcends; and it being lighter than the Water, is by the Water pufhed up into the external Air, and the Valve of the Piston is inftantly fhut. Then the Piston being raifed, the Air fucceeds, and the Water below afcends after the Air, by the Preffure of the Atmofphere aforefaid; and fo by a few Repetitions the whole Air is pumped out, and the fucking Pipe and Barrel filled with Water.

Now to raife the Water as the Piston is forced down the Barrel, the Valve at *n m* being then fhut, the Water under the Piston, as before was faid of the Air, in that Part is compelled to open the Valve of the Piston, and admit the Piston to defcend into it, which Valve is fhut the very Inftant that the Piston is down; and then the Piston being raifed as its Valve is then fhut, that Water cannot return back, and is therefore lifted up by the Piston, in the upper Part of the Barrel, fo as to be received at the Spout *i*, and at the fame Time the Valve at *n m* is forced open by the afcending Water in the Pipe *o p*; and the lower Part of the Barrel being again filled, the Valve at *n m* fhuts, and retains it for the next Defcent of the Piston; and thus the Action of the Pump may be continued in raifing Water at pleafure.

THE *Syphon* or *Crane,* b, *Fig.* R, *Plate* LXXVII. is nothing more than a recurved or bended Pipe, having one Side longer than the other. And as the afcending Liquid is forced up into the fhorter Side (the Air being firft exhaufted), by the Preffure of the Atmofphere as before in the Pump, therefore Mercury will run from one Veffel to another by the Means of this Inftrument, provided that the Bend of the Syphon is not more than 30 or 31 Inches above the Surface of the Mercury, and Water, or Wine, if the Height of the Bend doth not exceed 35 Feet; but in both thefe Cafes the Mouth of the defcending Tube muft be fomething lower than the Surface of the Mercury, or Water, into which the fhort Tube is immerfed; for if the defcending Tube be equal to the afcending Tube, the Fluid will remain in the Syphon, unlefs fome external Caufe more than the Air force it out; becaufe the Weight of the Fluid on both Sides is equal. By this Method, Water may be carried over Hills, as expreffed in *Fig.* V, *Plate* LXXVII. if their perpendicular Height above the Surface of the Water, as *q r*, be lefs than 35 Feet.

By the Preffure of the Atmofphere it is, that Mercury will afcend to the fame Altitude in all Kinds of Veffels, and in any Situation, as is fhewn in *Fig.* S, *Plate* LXXVII. provided that their upper Parts be perfectly clofe, fo as not to admit any Air to enter in; and by the Preffure of the Atmofphere it is, that Water in Refervoirs is forced to enter the Conduit-Pipes for conveying of Water to any Fountain, *&c.* that is below the Horizon or Level of the Refervoir, be the Diftance ever fo great.

F I N I S.